THE
GODS OF
VICE

I nodded and rose to leave, needing fresh air that wasn't full of Hana's smell and her hands and her body, but before I had taken more than a step, Katashi gripped my hand—hard and sure to show he knew what would happen. And it did, as easily as on every other occasion our souls had connected, but in the bright glare of his very being, it was not my sister I saw. Not the throne nor the empire nor the crown. It was Kin. Kin choking. Kin bleeding. Kin screaming. Kin dying. Katashi's anger and obsession choked everything it touched, while the mantra of his inner thoughts echoed through his soul.

I will have my vengeance.

THE GODS OF VICE

THE VENGEANCE TRILOGY:
BOOK TWO

DEVIN MADSON

www.orbitbooks.net

ORBIT

First published in 2013
First published in Great Britain in 2020 by Orbit

1 3 5 7 9 10 8 6 4 2

Copyright © 2013 by Devin Madson

Map by Charis Loke

Excerpt from *The Grave at Storm's End* by Devin Madson
Copyright © 2016 by Devin Madson

The moral right of the author has been asserted.

A CIP catalogue record for this book is available from the British Library.

ISBN 978-0-356-51531-1

Orbit
An imprint of
Little, Brown Book Group
Carmelite House
50 Victoria Embankment
London EC4Y 0DZ

An Hachette UK Company
www.hachette.co.uk

www.orbitbooks.net

For my loving husband.
You are my best friend. You are my rock.
Thank you for being there every step of the way along
this mad journey.

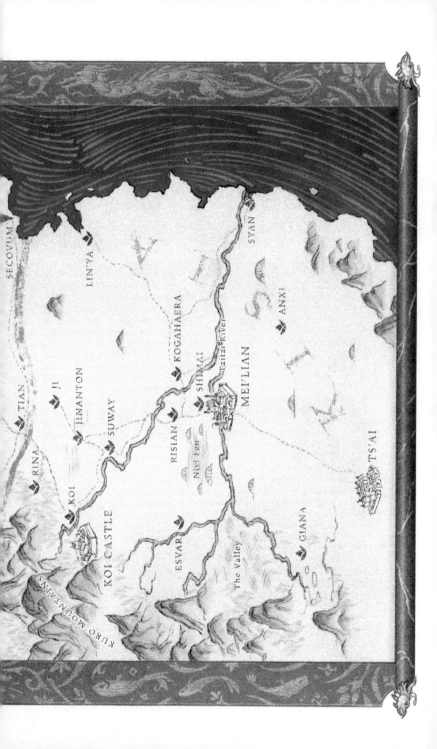

Character List

Ts'ai

Honour Is Wealth.

Emperor Kin Ts'ai—Emperor of Kisia
General Hade Ryoji—Master of the Imperial Guard
General Rini—General of the Rising Army
General Jikuko—General of the Rising Army
Father Kokoro—Court priest
Master Kenji—Imperial physician
Raijin—Kin's brindle horse

Otako

We Conquer. You Bleed.

Emperor Lan Otako—Deceased. Eldest son
Emperor Tianto Otako—Deceased. Youngest son
Empress Li—Deceased. Mother to Hana and Takehiko
Emperor Katashi Otako, *"Monarch"*—Only son of Emperor Tianto
Hacho—Katashi's bow
Lady Hana Otako, *"Regent"*—Only living daughter of Emperor Lan
Tili—Lady Hana's maid
Shin Metai—A Pike and Lady Hana's protector
Wen—A Pike and healer

Pike Captains—Captain Tan, Captain Chalpo, Captain Roni
The Traitor Generals—General Manshin, General Roi, General
 Tikita

Laroth

Sight Without Seeing

Lord Nyraek Laroth—Deceased. Fifth Count of Esvar
"Malice" "Whoreson" Laroth—Illegitimate son of Nyraek Laroth
Lord Darius Laroth—Legitimate heir of Nyraek Laroth. Sixth
 Count of Esvar
Lord Takehiko Otako, *"Endymion"*—Illegitimate son of Nyraek
 Laroth
Kaze—Endymion's horse

Vices

Vice Without Virtue

Lady Kimiko Otako, *"Adversity"*—Katashi's twin sister
Avarice—Once employed on the Laroth estate
Hope—Once Lord Arata Toi, heir to the Duke of Syan, now a Vice
Vices—Spite, Conceit, Ire, Folly, Apostasy, Parsimony, Pride, and
 Rancour

The greatest fight is the fight within
Against the nature of man
Against self
Against the god that lives inside us all

1. HANA

I had woken disoriented from many bad dreams before, but never to a stomach intent on spilling my horror onto the matting floor. Tili sang and shushed my cries, patting my back as I purged darkness from my stomach. And it felt like darkness, like a horror and a disgust so deep I might never smile again.

Slowly, the warmth of the sun began to touch my skin, and I didn't just hear her song; I felt it. It was like waking from another layer of dream, trembling and ill.

"It's going to be all right, my lady," Tili said as she rubbed my back. She had draped blankets over me at some point, the weight of them on my shoulders comforting. "Everything is going to be all right."

Outside, birds went on singing. A bee buzzed onto the late-blooming jasmine coiled around the balcony railing. I could not recall my room at Koi having had a balcony, but the smell sent a wistful blade deep into my soul. Tears came next, and Tili held me to her, her weight and her warmth even more comforting than the blankets, and when at last I could cry no more, I finally felt alive. Exhausted, broken, but alive.

"No one seems to know what happened," Tili said, fussing around while I picked at some thinly sliced fruit. "But everyone who was in the room has suffered like this, and some..."

She stopped. Her fussing got fussier.

"Dead?" I said, my first word, but it felt appropriate. For a while there, death would have been a relief.

"Yes, my lady, but let's not think about that. You are safe and you are well and that is all that matters."

Her words owned a brittle cheeriness, her smile as fragile as glass. "Tili, tell me what happened. Please," I added when she pursed her lips and would not speak. "I need to know."

"Lord Otako—Emperor Katashi, I mean, holds the city now. He's taken the oath and everyone has to kneel before him and swear loyalty to their new emperor and"—Having begun to speak, she seemed unable to stop, words spilling from her like bile had spilled from me—"if they refuse, they are being... being executed, and anyone who had a position with Emperor Kin is being executed, and the imperial guards who didn't escape are all dead, and most of the servants who came from Mei'lian, and... and..." Grief overtook her, tears choking her words. She rubbed her eyes with the sleeve of her robe. "I'm sorry, my lady, I did not mean to tell you until you were feeling better, I—"

"Kin?"

I could remember the fury and the blade and the flash of hurt in his dark eyes but not much else. Had he been in that room with me? Had Katashi caught him?

Tili looked down and shook her head, sending fear thundering through my numb veins. "I'm sorry, my lady, but I don't know. He seems to have just..." She lowered her voice to a whisper. "...disappeared."

"Disappeared?"

"Hush, we should not talk so in case someone is listening, my lady. I do not want to... be thought a traitor and..." She pressed her sleeve to her eyes and stayed there silently shaking.

Disappeared. Perhaps I had something to thank Malice for after all.

I gripped Tili's arm. "It's going to be all right," I said, repeating her words back to her. "I will not let him hurt you." I let her cry as she had let me cry. Most of the servants who had travelled with us from Mei'lian had been known to her, some of the guards too. She might have exaggerated the number of deaths in her distress, but there were still many lives to fear for.

"What of Minister Laroth?" I said. "What happened to him?"

I had been in his room. Shin had been there. A strange young man too, tied to the divan. All I had wanted to do was get out of the castle, and then he had given me Malice's blood.

"I . . . I hear he hasn't woken, my lady." Tili sniffed. "But there are some men in black robes who are caring for him. Everyone says they are Vices." She whispered the last word with the horror and awe that seemed to follow the Vices everywhere, but to me they were familiar faces.

Almost I told Tili not to worry about them either, but while my ability to protect her from Katashi needed no explanation, I had not the energy to explain Malice.

I nibbled a few individual pomegranate arils and stared at the table while Tili went back to fussing. I appeared to have a lot more robes than before, and she seemed intent on refolding them all.

Kin had disappeared. Katashi had taken the oath. Darius was asleep, while Malice and his Vices were stalking about. And tucked away in this pretty room, I was as inconsequential as the breeze. I crunched a few more arils and tapped the table. I needed to see Katashi.

"I will wash and dress," I said. My body ached at the very thought, but I had to see the new world for myself. I had fallen asleep and everything had changed.

"Are you sure, my lady? You still look very pale and you've hardly eaten anything. Emperor Katashi said I was to look after you and make sure no one troubled you and—"

"I'm fine, Tili, I promise. Just tired, but... not the sort of tired sleep can fix. Will you choose something for me to wear?"

With a nod, she walked away along the line of chests while I finished what I could stomach of my meal. "Blue, my lady?" She held up a lovely light-blue and white robe, edged in dark blue waves. It was pretty but cut low at the back of the neck and not one of mine.

"No, one of the ones you altered for me."

Tili hadn't a smile to lose, but her gaze slid toward the door. "As they were gifts from the Usurper, they have been taken away and replaced with... and unfortunately, my lady, I haven't been able... there just hasn't been time to—"

She sucked a panicked breath, and I leapt up from my mat to take her hands, leaving the pretty robe to fall unheeded on the floor. "Tili, Tili, it's all right; you cannot think I would be mad at you for that. I understand, you're afraid, and if my cousin is making a nuisance of himself, then I can't but—"

"A nuisance? My lady, poor Ilo got executed just for having been born in Ts'ai, he is—"

Again, she looked at the door. Her hands shook.

"Surely there must have been more to it than that," I said.

"No! Ilo would never hurt a fly. I... I was born in Ts'ai, my lady. I lived there all my life until I moved to Mei'lian and took work at the palace. The only reason my head is not out there with theirs is because I am your maid."

Beneath the sound of her shuddering breath, there was nothing but the patter of footsteps, some chatter, and even a distant laugh—the sounds of a castle in which nothing had changed. And yet Tili trembled all over like an aspen leaf in a storm.

"Tili," I said. "How long have I been asleep?"

"Three days, my lady."

"Three days? I—" I bent and grabbed the robe off the floor. "I have to see Katashi. Here, I don't suppose there is a robe with less of a come-fuck-me neckline, is there?"

Her eyes widened, and cheeks turning pink, she gasped. "My lady!"

I laughed at her look of mingled horror and awe. "I'm sorry, but you shouldn't be surprised anymore that I'm hardly a lady. A less... attention-seeking neckline then, is that better?"

"Yes, but... no. I'm afraid they all have... come-fuck-me necklines." She squeaked at her own daring and covered her mouth with both hands as though she could push the words back in.

For a blissful moment, there was nothing but companionable giggles, but it did not last. All too soon, the knowledge of where we were and what had happened dropped its shroud over us, and she helped me dress in silence. Having grown up on a farm, I was only used to wearing full robes on special occasions. The tunic and breeches style Tili had sewn had been as much for my own comfort as to annoy Emperor Kin. This court robe, however stunning it might look, was both too tight and too loose in all the wrong places, and its neckline that dropped below my fifth vertebra made me squirm.

By the time Tili was finished, I might have walked right out of a court portrait.

I hated the very sight of myself.

"It'll have to do," I said as she tried and failed to make a comb stick in my short hair.

"Shall I come with you, my lady?"

"No, you stay." I walked to the door and slid it open. "I'm sure someone will be able to tell me where—"

"Lady Hana!"

I spun around. A man in an imperial uniform had been standing outside my room, his black sash all that marked him as one of Katashi's men, not one of Kin's. Though I would have known him from one glance at his face. "Wen," I said before I could think better of it and immediately thought better of it as he frowned. Captain Regent of the Vices had known Wen, not Lady Hana Otako.

"I want to see Katashi," I said, drawing myself up to maximum pride in an attempt to cover the mistake.

"Cap—His Majesty is busy with his council, my lady," he said, struggling with his own confusion in a way that might have given us something to laugh over had the situation not been so fraught and unsure. "But I can inform him that you're feeling better and—"

"No. I will see him now." I walked on past Wen, sure that while he might grab my arm if he was very bold, he would not harm me.

He was not very bold, but he did hurry to walk ahead of me as I made my way along the passage. "Lady Hana, His Majesty is meeting with his generals and would not appreciate—"

"You know what else he would not appreciate? His cousin being forced to shout for him in the passage, making a scene. However, if you'd prefer I got his attention that way, by all means stand in my way."

Wen's eyes widened and he fell back. I had shaken him off balance, but he followed as I got my bearings and made for the emperor's apartments.

At the sound of Katashi's voice, my steps faltered. My heart seemed to drop right through the floor as I realised the enormity of what I was about to do. Like Wen, Katashi had only known Captain Regent, never Lady Hana.

I rapped on the door before fear got the better of me.

Inside, the voices halted, and letting out a gust of breath, Wen slid open the door. "Excuse me, Your Majesty," he said, the polished words not coming easily to his tongue. "It's Lady Hana. She is very intent on seeing you."

"Tell her I will see her when I am finished here. We have important business—"

"Then I will join you," I said, stepping in and drawing the gaze of half a dozen men I didn't recognise—and Katashi. He knelt at the end of a long table in the same crimson robes Kin wore, but in all other ways, he was the Captain Monarch I had first met at Nivi Fen, right down to his beautifully lopsided smile. "My dear cousin," he said, emphasising the word as though in reproof for the secret I had kept. "I am so glad to see you are finally up and about. We have all been very concerned for your well-being."

In a flurry of silk and awkward coughs, the other men at the table rose and bowed, murmuring my name.

"My thanks, Your Majesty," I said, acknowledging them with a nod. "I am, as you see, quite well now." I settled myself at an empty place at the table. "Do continue the meeting."

All eyes turned to Katashi, and with a nod to the gathered men, he said, "Family will not wait, it seems. Let us adjourn until General Manshin arrives this afternoon."

With many a nod and bow and murmuring of "Your Majesty," the men once more rose from the table and headed for the door. Annoyed that he would rather send them away than let me take part, I might have protested, but Katashi's smile had vanished beneath a thundercloud. I kept my peace and waited until the last one departed, leaving Wen to slide the door closed behind them.

From the other end of the table, Katashi sighed. "Are you so intent on embarrassing me?" he said. "First you don't tell me who you are so I must suffer the humiliation of having my cousin captured by the Usurper, and now you force your way into an important meeting with generals newly come to my cause. Any who believed you to be in Kin's confidence, or his bed, have only more reason to think so now!"

He could not have shocked me more with a slap. I leant back, fingers gripping the edge of the table. "Excuse me?"

"Why else the desperate need to listen in on our plans?"

Katashi gave a satisfied huff as my jaw dropped. All too well could I see why his allies might make such an assumption. "I am no spy."

"No? Well, Cousin, I feel proper introductions are in order then, since this is the first time we've met. I am Emperor—"

"Oh no, don't do that. I'm sorry, all right? Malice is... very good at... persuasion. He had a hundred reasons why it was important you didn't know who I was, and they all sounded sensible. And some of them were. If you had known who I was, you would never have allowed me to do any of the things I wanted to be a part of, would you?"

"Allow you to parade around as a soldier and risk your life for nothing but the fun of it? No."

"See? I had no interest in exchanging one pair of shackles for another."

He frowned at me across the table, that expression the brooding look I'd often stared at across a crowded camp, wanting him to look my way. "You could have died," he said at last. "And what then?"

"Since you didn't know I was alive, you would never have known let alone cared."

"But I knew *you*. And I would have cared."

The words sent my heart racing, but I shook my head. "Now *that* is nonsense."

His lips curved into an amused smile and my heart beat all the faster. "Is it? You're very sure of yourself. I wondered how different you would be as yourself, how much of Captain Regent had been an act. I'm glad to see not much, since I had begun to like him all too well."

How impossible to respond to such words with my heart in my

throat. This was not the conversation I had expected, and I swallowed hard, trying to recall what I'd come to say.

When nothing came out, Katashi nodded at the cushion next to him. "Come, sit closer. I feel like I have to shout with you all the way down there."

Almost I refused, the memory of the kiss that might have been a sudden specter. I had wanted it more than anything in that moment and did not trust myself. Did not trust a body that yearned so fiercely to be near him.

I rose and shifted closer, not to the cushion beside him but to the one a spot farther away. "You think I'm going to bite, sweet Regent?" he mocked.

"No, but you probably shouldn't call me that in case someone hears you."

"There is no one else to hear me. Now why don't you tell me what was so important it couldn't wait until I had finished meeting with my council?"

Could I demand to know how many people he had executed in the last few days? It ought not to have been a question that needed asking. "Did so many people have to die, Katashi?" I said, a softer plea than I had meant to charge him with. "Tili tells me you have not only had Kin's courtiers and councillors executed if they did not swear to you, but servants too."

"I have done no more or less than Kin himself did after he took the throne," he said, brows lifting in surprise. "The number of people who were labelled traitors and executed with my father was in the hundreds, many who had done nothing but be employed by our family. Whatever your maid has told you, I have not gone that far, but neither can I give *anyone* the opportunity to betray me. If I do, this will all have been for nothing. This may look like a big win, Hana, but my power is fragile until I can consolidate my hold on the north. Or find Kin." Eyes that had been looking at the table pinned me then. "It would be good to know where he is."

"You say that like you think I know. I have been asleep for three days."

"And living with him for three weeks."

I attempted haughty disdain. "If you think he told me anything of his plans in that time, then you are very mistaken. He trusted me no more than you seem to."

"You haven't given me any reason to yet."

"How can you say so? I may not have told you who I was, but I fought for you." I reached for his hand only to pull back and rest mine upon the table. "I wanted to fight for the throne and for our family so much that Malice brought his Vices into play. Where would you have been without them? Without us?"

Katashi pulled back his silk sleeve and gently set his hand on mine. His was larger, his skin darker, but both were hands used to work, with calluses and scars and short fingernails—nothing like the hands a lord and lady ought to have. I stared at them. It was just a hand, just a touch, yet again, I was back beneath the Kissing Tree with my whole body aflame.

"I don't like your Malice," Katashi said as though he were not holding my hand. "I don't trust him."

"Neither do I anymore."

He'd sent me a message in that blood. A message full of hate.

Katashi threaded his fingers around mine. "The Usurper told me he asked you to marry him."

"He did."

"There has been a lot of talk that you were . . . on his side."

He looked at our hands, joined in a tangle upon the smooth tabletop. I hoped he could not feel just how hard my heart was pounding. "I did not accept him."

"People still talk."

"And they will say I am here now."

A smile flittered about his lips, and he leant in, closing the space between us that had already been too small. His fingers tightened around mine. "You're right. It doesn't matter. Once we're married, I'll have more claim than—"

"Married?" I slipped my hand from his, leaving the room much colder. "Katashi, I never said I would marry you. I never said I wanted to marry at all."

"No, you didn't." He grimaced. "I had not meant to say it so ... presumptuously, but my advisors speak much of your political value." His admission brought Kin to mind, pacing before me as he spoke of responsibilities and duty. "I didn't tell them you were already more valuable to me than that. I have regretted not kissing you that night, you know, Captain, every day fearing I might never have the opportunity again."

When I did not speak, he leant still closer until I could feel the touch of his breath. A delighted shiver rippled through my skin. "Did you think of me too? Or not? My heart is yours to break."

I had thought of him, had often imagined that kiss, had even imagined his smile made sleepy on a pillow beside me. "Every day," I said, stupidly truthful, for whatever my mind said, my body yearned for his, intoxicated by his confidence and his smile, his strength and those bright eyes rimmed in long, dark lashes. Always so expressive, always laughing or frowning or mocking or owning a hunger that sent my heart racing.

He traced a line down my cheek. "But you don't want to marry me?"

"It's not ... you. I don't want to marry anyone."

"Why not?" he whispered in my ear, his cheek against mine. "Don't you want to experience the joys of being a woman? I can assure you they are ... quite considerable."

There was a lot of fabric in my robe and under-robe, and yet his hand seemed to slip through with ease, knowing its way. His lips brushed mine, and with that teasing graze of skin on skin, I could think of nothing but how much I wanted to feel everything his hands and his lips promised.

But it was not why I had come, not what I had wanted, and I fought the haze of desire that made every thought fuzzy. "I'm sure they are," I said, gripping his arm to halt his hand upon my knee. "But..."

An uncertain little half smile hovered about his lips while his gaze hunted my face. "If you're worried I only want you for your political value, then I am even more sorry I didn't say something sooner. I kept telling myself you had to be a Vice. It seemed foolish to hope you were your own master." I thought of all the times I could have spoken and how different things might have been. "You look surprised," he added when I did not speak. "Did I need to know who you really were to want you?"

He made to slide his hand free of my robe, but I kept hold of his arm. "I knew who you were," I said.

"That doesn't mean my name was the only reason you stared at me." Once again, he leant in close but did not touch his lips to mine. Heat seared through my every vein. "May I make up for my mistakes now, Captain?"

I leant the rest of the way, thinking of nothing but the kiss that had already once been denied me. "They aren't only your mistakes. *Captain.*"

He laughed, a delicious sound cut off abruptly as he finally pressed a full kiss to my lips, a fierce kiss that pushed me to the floor and left me breathless. The hand he'd wormed inside my robe slid up my leg, and losing all sense, I pressed myself against him. He groaned, and while I wasn't sure what I wanted him to do, I wanted him to do it now.

What had started as a slow caress of my leg became a frenzied gathering of my robe. He ran a hungry line of kisses down my neck and onto the silk, tracking on down my body until his lips found my stomach and his broad shoulders were between my legs.

I wanted to ask what he was doing but did not want him to stop. I wanted to ask why he was kissing me there but dared not interrupt. And then when his tongue slid inside me, I had no thought of questions except how this feeling could be made to last forever.

A tap sounded on the door, shocking me back to a meeting room where only thin paper screens stood between us and the rest of the world. "Your Majesty, you wanted to know when General—"

The door slid. Pinned beneath Katashi, I could only yelp, but propped on his elbows he reared up with a snarl. "Damn it, Wen, not now!"

As hastily as the door had been opened, the door closed, leaving Katashi and I in an awkward tangle. Lifting my rucked-up robe, he kissed my stomach, but all desire had fled, leaving behind nothing but cold reality.

"No. No! Katashi, please, stop," I said, gripping a handful of his hair as his lips once more caressed my skin. "I...I think I know why you are doing this, and I still don't want to marry you." I wriggled away from him, and as he lifted his head, a flash of anger lit his eyes.

"You want someone else?"

"No! I just...don't want to be a wife, even of an emperor."

"Then what do you want?"

I laid my head upon the floor and stared at the heavy beams of the ceiling rather than at him. "I want...I want my own position," I said, my chest rapidly rising and falling. "I want to make a difference, Katashi. I want to be someone, not just someone's wife."

"Reduced to a mere someone," he said, seeming to mock himself with a breathless laugh. "How utterly set down I am."

For the briefest of moments, he rested his forehead upon my leg, before he sat up, the fragile sense of companionship broken. "You had better go," he said, rising to his feet and straightening his robe and his topknot, all hint of a smile vanishing as he turned away. "I have a lot a work to do."

I got to my feet and tried to tidy my robe and my sash, but fixing one seemed only to make the other sit more askew.

"Wen," Katashi called, and the red-faced Pike slid open the door. "Ensure Lady Hana makes it safely back to her room."

"Yes, Your Majesty."

Katashi would not look at me, and unable to think of something to say, I let Wen usher me out. It wasn't until I reached my room that I realised I had asked only one of my questions, and I felt even more lost than I had before.

2. ENDYMION

Darius lay upon the divan, unmoving, unspeaking, his expression frozen in an infinitesimal frown. The rise and fall of his silk-clad chest was the only sign he lived at all. Sometimes even his breath seemed to abandon him, so I stayed and I watched, afraid his death would go unnoticed.

Malice had come to see him only once since Katashi's avowal. He had brought Hope with him, and for a long time, the young Vice had sat with a hand upon Darius's cheek.

"He won't let me in, Master," he'd said at last. "Or maybe it's that there's just... nothing to hold on to, I can't say."

With his fists and jaw clenched, Malice had departed. The role of nurse didn't suit him.

Avarice slid open the door, a bowl of warm water in one hand and a bunch of fresh incense caught between two fingers of the other. I had come to rely on his ugly scowl, he and I alone in our anxiety. Beyond this room, the world was changing, but here, there was just Darius. Avarice had given up ordering me out, the loyalty I showed his precious charge helping to temper his dislike.

He put the bowl down, slopping water over the edge. "Anything?"

"Nothing," I said.

It had become our little ritual.

Avarice wrung out a cloth, and with an old carer's practicality, he opened Darius's robe, exposing his pale skin to the sunlight. A scar marred his chest, a raised line, shiny and puckered. There, the knife had been thrust into his body, the pain such that I would not soon forget. Darius hadn't meant to share it with me, or the memory that had come with it.

The linen cloth sailed across Darius's chest before being returned to the bowl. Avarice squeezed it out, water dripping from his sturdy fingers.

"You looked after him, didn't you?" I said. "When Malice did that."

The cloth paused in its passage across the scar. "Malice wouldn't have done that. He loves Master Darius."

"But not as much as you do?"

He didn't even look up. The cloth sailed on while outside, a woman laughed. People chattered. Bars of hot sunlight cut across the matting, bringing in the endless summer.

Avarice dropped the cloth into the water. "Yes, I looked after him. I worked for his father, and when the late lord passed, I stayed with Master Darius."

"And now you serve Malice."

He grunted and said no more. Once he had finished with the cloth, he rose and strode across the room to change the incense. He lit fresh sticks before returning to flip the cushions beneath Darius's head, fussing about him as though he were a little boy laid up ill. Avarice—friend, carer, father. Nyraek had not been there. He had been in Mei'lian fathering me.

The smell of sandalwood freshened the air, and still that porcelain face did not move.

"Malice needs me," Avarice said. "Send a message if anything changes."

I nodded and the man went out, leaving me with the half-brother I had never known I had. Many silent hours spent alone had given me the opportunity to stare at him from every angle, trying to divine some similarity between us. I could find none. But I could see Malice in the way his brows arched and in the fine line of his nose, yet while Malice might be the spider Katashi called him, Darius was a broken bird, his wings clipped to keep him from flying.

Darius's chest rose and fell, and satisfied that he still lived, I went to the window. Avarice would never open it, but I had been sitting too long in the close air waiting for a groan or a flutter or anything that might herald my brother's return. I needed to taste life.

With a grunt of effort, I forced it open. Humid air brushed my face, thick with the scent of dying flowers, and I breathed deeply. A storm was brewing to the east. Heavy clouds hung in the sky, flickering with summer lightning.

The castle had changed—its mood, its smell. Now it was Emperor Katashi's men who patrolled the wall, their black sashes flying proudly.

But out there, another emperor lived.

"Endymion."

I turned, heart jolting. The door was closed and the room empty but for Darius, blinking at me from the divan.

"Darius." Three quick steps took me to his side, and I sank to my knees. "You're awake."

"Obviously." His voice crackled from disuse, the syllables running together. "Kin? Hana?"

"Alive. Hana is here."

"And Kin?" he asked, his fear no longer hidden.

"The Vices got him out before Katashi could have his head, but I don't know where they took him or why."

He closed his eyes, a sigh brushing dry lips. "It is enough for now."

A long silence followed, and I thought him asleep until he

gathered enough strength to open his eyes again. "He's here, isn't he?" he said. "I can smell him."

"Why didn't you tell me you were my brother?"

His gaze did not waver. "When would you have liked me to tell you? When I found you locked up in Shimai? Or when you came here to kill me?"

"I didn't come to kill you."

"You were angry enough to try."

He didn't have to tell me I'd been foolish to listen to Malice, or that Hana hadn't needed my help, or even how disastrous it had been to give her the blood—they were thoughts that had been with me constantly since, filling the silent days with shame. "I'm sorry."

"Are you?" His lip curled. "Sorry for me or for you?"

"For getting you into this. It's my fault you're stuck here." I swallowed hard. "You're afraid of him, aren't you? Of Malice?"

Darius struggled to sit, his brows caught close. "Do you know what happens to Empaths who lose themselves?"

"No. Who would have told me? I never met an Empath before Malice."

A horse whinnied down in the courtyard, and turning my head, I caught shouts and marching steps. One hundred and thirty-four soldiers in the yard, and forty-one on the walls; a scout party of six at the gate; two peasant boys collecting wood in the forest. And stretching the miles through Koi City, one hundred and fifty-two thousand nine hundred and twenty-one souls living through a new day. The numbers were in my head just as if the light of each stood like a flame before my eyes.

"Endymion?"

I shook away the haze. "What?"

"Where did you just go?"

"I was thinking," I said. "Did you even know I existed?"

Darius took a moment to reply, his shrewd gaze peering through half-closed eyes. "I knew Takehiko existed, but I neither knew for sure you were alive or that you were my half-brother. I assume you realise that makes you Hana's half-brother too. What fools our parents were to make such a mess."

"Malice knows," I said, seized by a sudden desire to spill all my fears and worries. "He thinks I should take the throne, that it ought to be mine, that—"

Darius lay back against the cushions. "Of course he knows. I told him. The rest is not surprising; he is skilled at putting people to good use."

"You told him?"

"Don't worry, I didn't want to. I'm not that much your enemy."

"Why are you different? I can feel you now."

He didn't answer, nor did his expression change—his mastery over it as strong as his mastery over his Empathy had been. With a strength of mind I could not even begin to fathom, he had buried it so deep it seemed not to exist at all.

"You said…" I fiddled with the hem of my robe. "You asked if I knew what happens to Empaths who lose themselves. What did you mean?"

Darius pressed a hand to his forehead, his fingers trembling. "Did you plan to finish me off by asking me endless questions and spilling yourself all over me? If so, it is working admirably."

He looked paler than he had while sleeping, and I could imagine Avarice's scold should he come back to find Darius worse than he had left him. "I'm sorry."

"You say that a lot."

"I have a lot to be sorry about."

A laugh became a cough, and he lapsed into silence with his eyes closed and his hands shaking. One he set upon his brow, the movement drawing his sleeve back just enough to show the tip of the birthmark on his inner wrist. I stared at it, at this mark I had kept hidden all my life, upon the skin of the brother I had never known I had.

I shuffled a little closer. "I really am sorry. What can I do to help?"

"You can't help me," he said, still with his eyes closed. "You can't even help yourself."

"What do you mean?"

"Oh, go away. Go make yourself useful. I'm parched and starving."

"You think I'm stupid, but I'm—"

"You are stupid. And you're going to tear this empire apart more completely than Kin and Katashi ever could, now go away!"

"Then what were you made to do?" Kokoro had asked. *"You were made to steal and to hurt. You were made to break and destroy and kill."*

I sat back, my heartbeat a thundering storm in my chest. Until I had been branded, I had never harmed anyone, and hadn't since without being pushed to it, and yet everyone looked at me and saw the greatest monster there could ever be.

"I don't want the—"

"Go away!" he howled. Lines of pain marred Darius's brow as though merely existing caused him agony. "Bring me food. Bring me water. Do anything but sit there and consume me with your needs."

The sudden flare of his anguish hollowed my stomach and stole my voice, leaving me scrambling to the door, but even with it closed between us, I could still feel the rapid hammer of the heart he had wished would stop beating.

I leant my head back against the wall while the tumultuous emotions faded slowly away, leaving silence in their wake. Peace. I could breathe again.

Despite the number of people who lived within its walls, Koi

Castle was quiet today, fear throwing a blanket over its blackened posts and narrow halls. It was a symbol of old power, of Otako power, every sign of Ts'ai occupation already being scrubbed from its innards. On the first day, a pile of Ts'ai banners had burned slowly, sending billows of black smoke into the air. Papers and books were going the same way, saddlecloths, tea sets and bone-handled knives—anything bearing the dragon Katashi had come to hate so much.

"What happened?" Avarice came along the passage hunched like a bear, his hooded tunic fraying around the edges.

"He's awake," I said. "He wants food and drink." *And death.* But I couldn't say that, not to him.

Avarice's relief refilled the pool of emotion that always lapped around me. His grin only lasted a moment, yet his joy seemed endless.

"Go to the kitchens," he said. "Tea, green pear, plain rice, and mild fish, very thinly sliced."

It ought to have been a servant's job, or at least someone who knew where the kitchens were, but desperate to do something, anything, to undo the harm I had caused, I nodded.

It took me ten minutes to find the stairs, but I did not ask for help because having a mission meant not having to think about what Darius had said. Occupation also kept me grounded in the world where my feet walked. If I let my Empathy wander, it would pull me out onto the walls for a sullen guard change, or into the upper chambers where fear hung heavy amid whispering men.

When I descended into the lower keep, I found the ghost of Katashi walking at my side, black-clad, his hair dripping moat water and his soul a glorious light in which I had bathed. I had wanted him to succeed at his mission and reunite our family. Foolish not to have considered the consequences, not to have realised there would also be a platform in the courtyard that dripped blood.

As though summoned by my thoughts, a pair of Katashi's Pikes found me on my return from the kitchen. They were no longer unkempt rebels camping in forest clearings and travelling only by night. Now they had legitimacy, purpose, and these two wore the uniforms of imperial guards as proudly as Kin's men ever had.

"Endymion?" one said, slowing as he approached.

"Yes?"

He jerked his thumb in the direction of the throne room. "Emperor Katashi wants to talk to you."

"Can I take this to Lord Laroth first?"

"Awake, is he? Well, the captain will be glad to hear that."

I noted the *captain* and also that he made no effort to correct himself. There were some who had been with Katashi long enough it would take time to adjust, even when he was perched on the throne with a crown on his head.

"Here." The other guard reached for the tray. "I'll take the dead man his last meal. His Majesty was in no mood to be kept waiting."

"Dead man?"

"Just our little joke." A smile passed between them, but I let the Pike take the tray from my hands. Better to ask Katashi what had been meant. I had managed to avoid him since he had taken the castle, burying all yearning for his presence beneath the need to help Darius, but of course it could not last. Whether to demand my allegiance or to execute me, this summons had always been coming.

I fell in behind the Pike who led the way, our steps out of time as we clacked along the passage.

Stinking Vices. The captain ought to be rid of the lot of them.

The whisper came like a hiss in my ear.

They're all freaks. Even Kimiko. Damn, but I liked her, she was good, that skin, that fire—

The Pike turned a scowl on me, such confusion and anger in

his face that I could not meet his gaze. Skin hadn't been necessary, curiosity enough to carry me into his head.

He walked on, and as we approached the end of the passage, sorrow sheared into me, a scream on its heels. A woman wailed, no words, just a mess of broken curses caught between sobs.

"Keep coming," the Pike said, glancing back. "That will be Lady Talamir. She asked to see her husband."

We turned into the main hall to find a woman kneeling before the throne room doors, her fine robe dishevelled and her silken hair slipping from its bun. Two guards were trying to pull her to her feet, but she wrenched from their grip. "Don't you dare touch me, you filthy traitors!" she spat at them. "Kin will gut you for what you've done. He will hang you by your hair until your scalp rips from your skull!"

One of them slapped her, knocking her back. "Watch what you say, or you'll be the next to guard this hallway. Right up there beside your husband." He pointed to a row of severed heads, watching on with glassy gazes. The sight of them seemed to sap all her strength, and she collapsed in a sobbing heap, allowing the guard to lead her away.

My Pike guide shot me an expressive grimace, signalling sympathy at having to suffer through such a noise, but the woman's pain was no mere irritation, it was a cut to the soul that would never heal. Almost I reached out to make him feel it, but he'd already set his hands on the doors.

The hinges groaned as he pushed them open, spilling crimson light through the widening aperture. At the far end of the room, Katashi sat upon the Crimson Throne, the broad skirt of his robe reaching to the floor. His new chancellor hovered, awaiting orders, but Katashi waved him away and got to his feet, Hacho adding to his already impressive height.

"Endymion, welcome," he said, smiling and holding his arms

wide. His aura filled the room as completely as the stained light. "Come. Sit by me."

You would not smile if you knew my name, I thought. *You would not ask me to sit at your side if you knew the truth.*

Katashi beckoned as the doors closed behind me. I had feared an audience, but only a few Pikes were present to watch my progress up the room to the dais. An insistent finger indicated the divan at his side, and I perched upon its edge.

"Is the seat hot?" he said, settling back upon a throne that might have been made for him, so well did he look upon it. "Or perhaps you think I am going to bite you? I haven't forgotten what help you were the night I took Koi."

I said nothing. In the vast space, the sucking silence was oppressive. Each blade of crimson light that cut through the room was speckled with dust.

"Nor what help you were at the meeting," he added when still I did not speak.

Any other courtier would have been overjoyed at so friendly a reception, but they could not feel the trouble and confusion his smile hid, the lust and the hurt and the fear.

"You were kind to me," I said, at last finding words that might satisfy. "It was the least I could do to repay you."

Katashi barked a sudden laugh. "Because I gave you a bow and let you kill one of my Pikes?" I winced but he went on. "If you base your choices on who is kind to you, you'll only ever get used."

Brother Jian had always been kind, expecting nothing in return—a thought accompanied by the shameful realisation I had forgotten him of late.

"Whatever your reasons, you have been of help to me," he said, perhaps reading some of my misery in my face. "But I have something more I must ask of you and your... particular skills."

Fear yawned its bottomless maw in my stomach at the mere

thought of making use of my skills for anyone, but they were words I could not say. "Why not ask Malice?" I said, playing for time.

"Malice has already had more from me than bears thinking about," Katashi said. "I would not ask him for water were I dying in a desert."

Curiosity almost bade me ask what more the Vice Master could demand, but before I could speak, he went on. "This is about Hana." And I had my answer.

"Lady Hana?" I said, hoping he could not hear the speeding beat of my heart as I could hear the growing whisper of his thoughts. "Has she woken?"

"Oh yes."

And when she pressed against me—by the gods, I should have Wen whipped.

I clenched my teeth as though it might slam shut my Sight, but Katashi had always been so open I could almost feel the warmth of her body and the tingles her moans had sent through his skin. I clenched my teeth harder.

"She's awake, yes, and seems to have recovered from—" He stopped rather than make the observation that the very man he was asking for help had been responsible for that scene in the audience chamber. So many men had never woken again. "—She seems well," he amended, "but I'm concerned that she..."

Kin had said he would have no unwilling wife, but if he was expecting to make an announcement soon, then... did she consider it? Had she agreed?

"You told me the night we took this castle that you can feel everything," Katashi said, his calm exterior somehow managing to hide his inner turmoil. "You said you could feel anger and glee and lust. Can you feel loyalty? Trust?"

"Nothing... nothing comes to me in neat little boxes." I hesitated on whether I ought to call him Majesty, to give him the respect his new position demanded. But whatever had changed, he was still the man I had loosed arrows with in the forest while talking of fletchings and techniques, he was still, as complicated as it was, my cousin. "I can't sit next to someone and feel the . . . individual pieces," I went on, though with him it was almost untrue. "I only get an impression of the whole, and even then it comes to me without reason, without intent. I don't feel the why or the how, only the is."

"Could you"—*That grip in my hair*—"tell me how Hana feels about Kin?"

I need to be sure. I have to be sure. She could ruin everything if she chose.

It was a stark demand after all the tiptoed meandering, but I had seen it coming. Heard it in the thoughts I could not mute. "I don't know—maybe," I amended when his scowl darkened everything. "If I was standing beside her and only her when his name was mentioned, or the possibility of . . . marrying him came up, but even then, without touching her, I couldn't be sure of the emotions, let alone her thoughts."

"But you could if you touched her? You could read her mind like you read Tori's?"

Moments before he died.

"Not without her knowing I was doing it. She would have to agree, would have to . . . I don't know, stand still and let me poke around without minding that I was seeing her every thought."

He snorted. *Not likely. She'd probably burn his hand if he tried. Gods but she's intense. Too wild for Kin, but she's good for his empire and he loved her mother. And if she's shown him even half the fire she's shown me, he'd want her. Just for the joy of having an Otako at his feet, he'd want her. Even just to harm me.*

His thoughts tumbled over the same ideas while he gnawed on his lower lip and stared at nothing.

"You were at the meeting," he said abruptly. "Kin said she would marry him and it seemed ridiculous at the time, ridiculous even now, but...I cannot be easy in my mind." He stood and began to pace along the dais. "I *need* to know, because if I give her a position of her own and she leaves, marries Kin, then everything I have fought for, everything I have sacrificed will be for nothing! If he is in her mind..." Katashi's hands clenched to fists, closing upon an ache even his thoughts had no words for.

Desperate to escape the rising wash of his emotions, I said, "Just marry her yourself!"

"She won't have me!"

His words rang through the empty throne room. "She refuses," he added quietly when the echoes had died away. "Which, I can assure you, is quite a painful enough blow to my ego without the fear she might choose him instead. Or that he might work his lies on her or force her to the altar. I cannot let her legitimise him. I can't."

"If you believe he would force her into marriage, then it doesn't matter how she feels about him, there is still a risk."

As though my words had contained the sharp prick of a pin, Katashi slumped onto the throne with a sigh. "You're right. And whatever his proclaimed honour, a man does what he must in desperate times. She can't leave. I have to keep her close, that's the only option."

I could find no words to answer, could only bend beneath the weight of his determination and try not to see the teasing light in her eyes or the mulish set of her chin, try not to hear her laugh or her breathless moans as they passed across his memory.

"Don't tell her I asked," he said at last, straightening his back. "Don't tell Malice I asked. Don't tell anyone that I asked."

I nodded and rose to leave, needing fresh air that wasn't full of Hana's smell and her hands and her body, but before I had taken more than a step, Katashi gripped my hand—hard and sure to show he knew what would happen. And it did, as easily as on every other occasion our souls had connected, but in the bright glare of his very being, it was not my sister I saw. Not the throne nor the empire nor the crown. It was Kin. Kin choking. Kin bleeding. Kin screaming. Kin dying. Katashi's anger and obsession choked everything it touched, while the mantra of his inner thoughts echoed through his soul.

I will have my vengeance.

"I mean it, Endymion," he said, letting go. "Don't betray me on this or anything, because I know who to go after to make you hurt." Katashi tapped the hand that had just gripped mine, and I walked to the doors, shaking, afraid of who he had seen in return.

3. DARIUS

Malice stood in the doorway like a ghost from my past, wearing the same blue robe he had dressed Endymion in because he liked his little jokes.

"He wakes," he said, entering on light feet. It had been dark at our last meeting, but now I could see how much five years had changed him. His silken hair had the same glossy sheen, yet the bone ribbon was a new touch, a new nod to the name he had taken on and couldn't shed. His face too was so much the man I remembered, and yet there were the tracings of lines beginning to show if one knew where to look. He was five years older yet not five years different.

"Nothing to say? No glorious reminiscence or pleasure at being properly reunited?" He sat on the edge of the divan and it sank beneath him, drawing me closer to the silk of that robe. "I missed you, yes?"

Malice ran his long fingers through my hair.

"My little Darius," he went on, breathing deep of some scent only he could recognise. "I missed you more than words can say. You felt the same, yes?"

I had. In those early years, I had often found myself talking to him, imagining what I would tell him about the stupidity of a councillor or the sexual intrigues of the court that Kin alone took no interest in. It had been Malice's company I longed for and Malice I spoke to in the darkness of my mind. He had been brother, friend, ally, and protector for many years, a staple of every day. The contours of his hand were so deeply etched upon my palm that to hold any other felt wrong.

"Darius," he said, fingers halting their progress through my tangled hair. "You can't tell me you've lost your voice."

"No, you're right. If I had, I couldn't tell you that."

Malice grinned. "And you haven't lost your pedantic wit either, I see." His smile faded and he sighed. "You look so different, yes? I thought so that night at the Gilded Cherry, but now I can see you better, you look so much older."

No surprise we had seen the same in each other. Empathy had never been kind to the bodies that wielded it.

"What are you going to do with Endymion?"

"Again you leap, Darius. Such important matters should come after the pleasantries, yes? I say you have changed and you should comment on whether I have. We could perhaps reminisce upon the night we met in the back field. I think of it often."

"Is that why you wore that robe?"

The smile returned, giving him the appearance of volatility, but unlike truly mercurial men, Malice's smiles were as likely to fade because he grew tired of holding them there. He had never been naturally expressive. "You remember," he said. "I hoped you would."

"It's a night that's hard to forget."

"I wish I could take that to mean meeting me was hard to forget, Darius, but I will not presume upon the territory of our beloved father. Now would be a good time to mention Endymion, yes? I think perhaps the old man had a sense of humour. A Laroth-Otako bastard?" He laughed. "What better way to get back at the family he detested?"

"He cared about Hana."

"Perhaps out of guilt. You know as well as I that he hated all Otakos save one."

It was so tempting to fall into conversation as though we were brothers united once again, but that would be to pretend there was no hurt, no anger. That nothing had changed.

Malice slipped his hand into mine. It filled the mould of my palm, the feeling of relief palpable. The curse wanted to be used. For five years, my Empathy had scratched at the doors I shut upon it, its nails bleeding. It wanted to feel, to own, to control, every moment a fight to suppress it, to swallow it like a lump in my throat. To choose to be better. To do better. To serve.

I had made those choices, but I couldn't pull my hand away.

"Five years is too long, my brother," Malice said. "Think of everything we might have achieved. In that time, the empire might already have bowed to us. But no matter, no matter, we have time, yes? And this way it is so very neat, so very clever, and I know how much you love clever. Can you see it, Darius? Can you see how easy it is when they are all such fools?"

"You helped Katashi rise to an even footing so he and Kin could rip the empire apart between them. Then you could rise like a saviour from the ashes."

"So poetic. How very much I missed you, Darius. No one else sees, no one else understands."

"No, nor would they see that you don't really mean to do that at all."

Malice's hand tensed in mine. "You see something more?"

"I see you have kept Endymion despite the threat he poses to everything. Why? If we didn't need him before, then we don't need him now."

"We?"

"A slip of the tongue," I said.

Malice looked down at our still-joined hands, and I pulled mine out of his grip. "Oh, Darius," he laughed. "You can't lie to me, yes? I know you far too well."

"And I know you," I said. "You're going to use Endymion. You'll throw him between Kin and Katashi and see how fast they tear him apart."

His expression did not change. I couldn't read him, couldn't see if I was right without the Empathy I longed to use.

"He's getting stronger," Malice said. "You haven't been with him enough to see it, but he is getting stronger. He can tell you how many souls are in this castle and where they are. He can hear thoughts without touch. I have seen him read from another man's mind and then kill him without a blink. Do you really think Kin or Katashi could destroy him? Even he doesn't know how powerful he is, how powerful he could be if he keeps…consuming the world."

Endymion had sat beside me, all unwitting as his soul ate at mine, his desperation making it all the more voracious.

"There will be a limit of course," Malice added. "A breaking point."

There would be. We had studied the old accounts of Laroths long past in an attempt to learn what our father had been unable or unwilling to teach. A Whisperer had once been a name for any Empath with access to thoughts, not just feelings, until one scholarly Laroth had attempted to gather and categorise the information in the family library. He had discovered the few true Whisperers our family had produced over the years, men capable of hearing, feeling, controlling, and destroying, all without touch. What created one was a mystery, but what they all seemed to have in common was a rapid escalation in strength after Maturation and an early death.

"He will soon grow beyond my power alone, yes?"

I heard the words he did not speak, that it would take both of us to control Endymion if he lost himself to the Sight.

Malice was smiling again. "I think you understand me, yes? If we do this together, Kisia will have an Otako god. Can you doubt he will go that path, even without my influence?"

"I should have left him to burn." Fear crept up my skin like a thousand hurrying ants. "Father Kokoro was right."

"Burn your own brother?"

"I ordered General Ryoji to kill you."

"Only because you knew I would not die, yes?" he said.

Malice put his hand on my forehead and I stiffened, expecting the burn of his Empathy. Instead, my headache eased from splitting to merely an ache. I wanted to hate the compassion he used like a weapon and might have been able to had I not known the depths of his heart.

"You're still fighting me," he said.

"Yes."

He lifted his hand, and in the shock of the returning headache, I did not see him move, only heard the shift of cushions and the rock of the divan. Straddling my hips, Malice filled my world, nothing existing beyond his weight, his warmth, and the smell of opium lingering on his breath. The tip of his ponytail trailed across my cheek.

"Don't fight it!" he said. "You are a god, Darius, yes? Just let go."

The temptation to let go, to give in, to take his hand in mine and let the whole world of fools burn was right there at my fingertips. I could take it. I could walk away. Except the moment I did, I would fail. I would prove it was impossible to escape the curse. Prove I had been born a monster and could never change.

"No. Kin rules Kisia. Now get off me."

"That's it? That's all you have to say? I will fight for you, Darius. I don't want to have to kill you, but I will if you make me."

"You won't."

"Won't I? I won't let you leave me again. You have my word on that, yes?"

"Get off."

He bent down, lips brushing my cheek. "Make me," he said.

My stomach was eating itself with hunger and every limb felt weak. To shove him away would achieve nothing beyond his amusement, so I gripped the earring dangling from his ear, pulling hard enough to stretch the flesh of his lobe. "Get off," I repeated. "I will rip it out. You have my word on that too, yes?"

He chuckled. "I like it when you play rough."

I tried to buck him off, but he caught my wrists and drove them into the cushions above my head, pinning me there as he kissed me. Utterly trapped, an intense spike of fear jolted through me and Malice gasped. He pulled back and in his moment of shock, I rolled, throwing him to the floor in a tangle of limbs and silk.

A knock sounded on the door, and with my heart still thrumming, I pulled myself upright though every muscle ached.

"Come in," I said, leaving Malice in an ungraceful scramble to appear poised. Licking my dry lips, I could still taste him.

The door slid a few inches, just enough for Hana to peer in, seeming to consider a moment and scan the pair of us before sliding it the rest of the way. "Both here." She stepped inside. "That makes this quicker."

"Ah, Hana, my love," Malice said, having gotten to his feet and straightened his robe, regaining his usual dignity. "How lovely to see you up and about again."

"Malice," she said as she slid the door closed, her whole body stiffened to a statue of fury.

"Oh dear," he said, shaking loose hair from his eyes. "I think she's angry with me too, my love, yes?"

"You lied to me."

"Only a very little, and look how well it has turned out." Malice's gaze ran her up and down and his lips turned into a knowing smile. "When am I to wish you joy, little lamb?"

Her cheeks reddened, his jibe doing nothing to stem her anger. "Never. I do not even wish you to speak to me. How dare you treat me like nothing but a piece of meat, nothing but a coin to be spent at the earliest opportunity?"

"I preferred to think of you as a weapon, yes? Something to be employed in the task of bringing my dear Darius back to his senses."

"You would have let me die."

"Yes, but I didn't think you would. I know Darius rather too well for that." He reached a loving finger to my cheek, and as I leant away, there was no mistaking the flicker of hurt and anger that crossed his usually impassive countenance. My head hurt too much to decide whether it was good or bad that he had felt my fear of him.

Hana's fingers curled to fists at her sides. "Some guardian you are," she spat. "I hope you care more for your Vices. Even Conceit deserves better than you."

"Careful what you say, little lamb, there are some words that cannot be taken back."

"I'm not afraid of you."

"No? But you should be."

She gave him a disgusted look. "You have no more power over me, Malice. We are done." Her gaze slid to me. "I pity you, Darius, having to deal with him for so long. Allow me to lighten your burden somewhat, in gratitude for what you have done for me but in the hope I never see you again." She bowed, managing more stiff grace in that moment than she had during all my attempts to teach her decorum. "I am releasing you from your oath. I thank you for your service, Lord Laroth, but I no longer require your assistance or your presence. Now we need not pretend to like one another, and your loyalties need no longer be divided."

"There was another way to achieve the unification of my loyalties." I was too tired to hide my bitterness, too broken to care. "A way that would have seen fewer people die, but by all means, my dear, stand there like an outraged paragon and look down on me for having sacrificed everything for the good of someone other than myself."

Hana's cheeks reddened, but she set her teeth firmly. "Fine gratitude when I am giving you what you wanted. Freedom."

"If that is what you think I wanted, then you are both mistaken and selfish."

"Selfish? I—"

Another knock fell upon the door, and a serving girl slid it open enough to bow upon the threshold. "Your meal, Lord Laroth. And His Majesty requires your presence in the throne room in an hour to take your oath."

She made a second little bow to Hana as, still seething, Hana opened the door the rest of the way to let the girl in. "Your chance now, I think, to choose whether you value your life or your loyalty more, Darius," she said. "I will leave you to your meal. But I suggest you do not keep Katashi waiting."

"Spoken from experience perhaps?" Malice crooned.

Hana spun on him. "I don't want to see your face ever again. If I could order your execution, I would do it, comfortable in the knowledge that no one, *no one*, would miss you." She spat on the floor at his feet, such rage in her eyes that it held even Malice frozen long enough for her to stride out, leaving the serving maid staring intently at the wall.

Sightless eyes stared from crusted sockets, each head along the row a face I knew. They stared at the wall opposite, bloody handprints on their cheeks. Councillor Rhim, Lord Lastern, and Lord Talamir, their necks shrivelling as they dried. Even Master Hallan was there, the imperial secretary, his youthful face having something of disdain about its expression.

"Friends?"

There was a sneer in the guard's voice, but misgiving outweighed anger. Sixteen years of relative peace had come to an end, and here in this hallway, where lords and councillors were allowed no dignity, was the proof.

"Acquaintances, certainly," I said. "Tell me, did these men refuse to take the oath?"

"They did. And now it's your turn. His Majesty is waiting."

Behind me, the throne room doors creaked open and the cumulative gaze of dozens fell upon my back. A new court had gathered, not so different in appearance to the one that had clustered about Kin—some the northern lords and ladies who had long been absent from Mei'lian, others members of Kin's court who had chosen to keep their lives and their lands rather than their honour.

With unhurried steps, I made my way to where Malice stood waiting before the throne, apparently oblivious to all the interest he was causing. I was surprised to see him, having assumed he had a prior understanding with Katashi, but as I joined him, he flashed me an amused smile.

Upon the throne, Katashi Otako looked every bit an emperor, tall and regal and proud, despite the black sash he had chosen to wear like a slash of darkness across his stomach. He leant forward as I halted at the Humble Stone, and pulled back the broad sleeves of his robe to display powerful forearms.

For a time, he didn't speak. Tension strangled breath from the air. At Katashi's side, a guard shifted his weight.

"Whoreson Laroth," Katashi intoned at last, wiping the smile from Malice's face. "You are called here to take the Imperial Oath of Allegiance before these witnesses. Not having had a *noble* upbringing, I do not expect you to know the words, but I have no doubt your brother can prompt you."

Malice was unarmed, but every guard knew what he was and edged their hands toward their swords.

"I know the oath very well, Your Majesty," Malice said. "I do not require prompting."

"Then kneel and take it."

I was sure he would refuse as he had refused to kneel before anyone, but after the shortest of hesitations, he knelt, gracefully lowering his head toward the floor. "I swear on the bones of my mad father," he said, his words resonating off the wooden boards. "On my name and my honour, that I will be loyal to one of our two emperors, the great Emperor Katashi, the however-manyeth of his name. I will not stick a knife in him, nor lie to his face. I will give every last ounce of my strength and my not inconsiderable intellect and will die in his service if the gods are so very cruel." He glanced sideways then, looking up toward me. "I will be as nothing and no one in service to you."

Malice could not rise until his oath had been accepted, but he sat back, smiling as shocked whispers sped around the room. Scowling, Katashi held up his hand for silence. There was no precedent to execute a man for speaking the wrong words, and gripping the arms of the throne, he left Malice kneeling and turned his attention to me. "Lord Darius Kirei Laroth," he said. "Sixth count of Esvar and former minister of the left in the court of the Usurper Kin Ts'ai."

"That would be me," I said flatly.

"Your father, Lord Nyraek Laroth," he went on, "the fifth count of Esvar, was once sworn to the service of my uncle, Emperor Lan."

"He was," I said.

"Do you intend to follow his example?"

"I do."

"Then you may kneel and take the oath."

There was a moment of strained silence, and glancing sidelong at Malice, I could see the unspoken words on his lips: *Behave*, he urged. But a good man was not something you were, rather something you chose to be every moment of every day. I had already chosen my emperor and already taken my oath. I would not kneel before this man, would not bow, would not even acknowledge the position he claimed with a stolen crown and an oath he would never live up to, because if my word meant nothing, I would soon be nothing.

Remaining on my feet, I said, "I intend to follow my father's example in choosing to give my allegiance to Emperor Kin, as my father did before he died."

Katashi narrowed his eyes. "From insanity, I believe."

"Yes. In a pool of his own filth."

Nervous laughter added to the constriction in the room. I recognised a few of those tittering behind their hands, but one had to have been living in a hole for the last twenty years to miss the rumours about my father.

"Perhaps you too are insane," Katashi said. "You seem to have very little care for your own life. Do you imagine I will grant you freedom if you refuse?"

"Not if the heads of my fellow councillors are anything to go by. I never knew it was standard practice to execute people who fail to agree with you."

"We are at war."

"Yes, having stolen the emperor's crown and his castle, I am sure you are."

Low whispers ran rife. I caught sight of Hana shifting to the front of the crowd. Her expression was unreadable.

"Will you or will you not take the oath?" Katashi demanded.

Malice's gaze seemed to burn its warning into me, and I knew then why he had bowed. He had known I would refuse, and it was easier to save me from my own stupidity if he could still walk freely around the castle. I could have laughed, as much from his foresight as from the bitter knowledge that my choice meant nothing. There would be no consequence to standing up for what was right if Malice and his Vices would save me anyway.

"I thought I had made myself clear," I said, unable to keep the anger from my voice. "But if you wish further clarification, you may have it. I have already taken an oath, already bowed at the feet of the True Emperor of Kisia. I am loyal to His Imperial Majesty, the great Emperor Kin, first of his name, Lord Protector of the Kisian Empire. I am his until death. If it is your decree that I should be executed, then I go to the headsman with my honour intact. Long live Emperor Kin."

Shocked whispers held the room until Katashi got to his feet. Taller, broader, and fiercer than Kin, yet I did not fear him because Katashi Otako had never given me any respect that he could take away.

"Lord Darius Laroth, you are hereby sentenced to a traitor's death. You will be branded and executed in the morning, and all your property returned to imperial hands." He turned his attention to Malice. "Whoreson Laroth, you are no longer welcome in my castle or in any lands belonging to the Imperial Expanse of Kisia. You are hereby exiled on pain of death, by I, Emperor Katashi Otako, *third* of my name, True Emperor of Kisia. You will be escorted immediately from these walls, along with every member of your little troupe. May you never set foot within my empire again."

I let go a held breath, fighting the urge to laugh. Malice's anger pulsed through him, but the struggle did not show on his face as he rose, baring his teeth in smile. Guards approached through the milling court. "Escort him out," Katashi ordered. "And make sure he takes all his Vices with him."

Malice did not threaten or rage, just lifted his hand to the guards making their approach. "There is no need to drag me away. I am quite capable of walking, yes? But before I go, I would request permission to remain until the morning. I would see my brother executed with my own eyes."

The court shifted as one, their hissed words washing over me, but so detached did I feel from the scene that my head might already have been severed from my neck. Malice filled my world. *Send him away*, I begged. *Send him away.*

"No." The word a sharp snap. "I do not trust you, Spider. Consider yourself fortunate that you are leaving with your life. Get them both out of here."

4. HANA

I left the uproar behind, the baying of Katashi's court slowly drowning beneath my thundering pulse. Frustration had sent me from the throne room, but as I stormed up the stairs, I realised I had no idea where I was going. Tili would listen but would not understand, and I had no other friend, no other confidant who would care for Darius's fate. I stopped. No, there was one, and annoyed I had not thought of him before, I turned back the way I had come.

The infirmary had likely been full in the days after the coup, but now its occupants had thinned to the sick and the few injured who still had a chance of survival. Mats lay in lines on the floor, and a pair of physicians bustled. One caught sight of me and hurried over, bowing as he walked. "My lady, what an honour for you to grace us with your presence. Is there something you require? Do allow me to wait on you in your apartments rather than have you endure such sights and smells as this poor infirmary."

He bowed again when he had finished speaking, and though he seemed only to want to help, his deference was unnerving. All Kin's servants had been polite, but none had treated me with such self-demeaning reverence.

"I am not in need of any help." The weight of so many curious eyes upon me made me wish Tili would soon alter one of these robes to something more modest. "I am here to see a friend."

The physician's fuzzy brows shot into his hairline and he looked around. "Here?"

"Yes, here." I pointed at the recumbent figure sitting propped against the window seat, his impassive gaze already upon us. "He is well, I hope?"

"Ah, Lord Metai," he said as I began walking, and it was all I could do not to stop in shock at the sound of both the title and family name I had never known. "He is much better, my lady, but still a bit...slow. Tired. He took quite a beating, and it may be a few more days before he is steady on his feet again. I did ask if he wished to be moved to his own room, as befits his rank, but I'm afraid he refused, and His Majesty—"

I held up my hand to stop him. "Thank you," I said and went the rest of the way on my own.

Shin acknowledged my arrival with a nod. To have done more looked like it would have been painful. Bruises covered his already scarred face, and a split lip gave him the look of a permanently amused smile.

I sat down on the other end of the window seat as a languid breeze blew in from the small garden. It did nothing to shift the stink of blood and shit that pervaded the room.

"Are you sure you wouldn't like your own room, Lord Metai?" I said. "It smells pretty bad in here."

The look he gave me could have rusted freshly forged steel. "I know where I belong, *my lady*," he said, his voice croaky, though whether from injury or disuse I couldn't tell.

"You never told me you were a lord."

"And you never told me you were a lady."

"I didn't have to, you figured that out for yourself."

Another of his meaningful looks. "At least one of us is observant."

"I'm observant. You don't look like any Kisian lord I've ever seen."

"Because I'm not a Kisian lord."

"Oh? Where are you—"

He snorted a little breath as he shifted his weight, even so small a movement seeming to cause pain. "Did you come here for a reason beyond interrogating me about my family history?"

"You started it!" I said, stung. "If you didn't want to talk about it, you shouldn't have needled me for not realising you were a lord. And speaking of lords, yes, I did come for a reason, but some of that reason was to see how you were. I heard...I heard that you fought for me that night."

Shin made no answer.

"Katashi has named Darius a traitor," I said when the silence dragged. "He's to be executed tomorrow."

"What?"

"He refused to take the oath, and unless he changes his mind, he will go to the executioner in the morning. I know Katashi only wants loyal people around him, but Darius doesn't deserve this. Without him, I would be dead by now, perhaps a few times over."

"As true as that is, he was given a choice. That's more than most men get."

He scowled down into the small band of garden wedged between an inner and outer wall, its clumps of gaily coloured flowers seeming out of place. Birds sang as they fluttered from branch to branch, blossom to blossom, and I envied them their wings.

Shin was right, yet it still felt wrong, but I couldn't give voice to the confusion of feelings that writhed inside me.

"Lord Laroth made his mistake in choosing to serve the Usurper," he said when I made no answer. "That's two choices he's fucked up. If he was so clever, he'd not have—"

"That is too severe, Shin."

"No. Smart men should know better."

His tone chilled me, but before I could challenge his words, a flurry of activity drew my gaze to the door. The two physicians were bustling forward, bowing deeply with reverent "Your Majesty"s.

"Hana," Katashi said, striding down the room. "I've been looking everywhere for you."

Such simple words to set my heart racing, and I was desperate not to show it. "I came to see Shin."

He nodded to his Pike, and Shin nodded back. "Lucky Shin. Shall I leave you?"

"Not at all necessary, Captain," Shin said, and the way he avoided Katashi's gaze made me wonder if he was out of favour. Perhaps he had admitted he'd known who I was before the ill-advised mission into the palace.

"I merely wished to thank Shin for risking his life to stay with me. But for him, I might have been dead many times over," I added, consciously echoing what I had said of Darius. If Shin noticed, he made no sign.

"Then if you are done, will you walk with me?" Katashi asked, the words a cold snap.

I was sure then that he was angry with his most loyal advisor and could only wish I had not been the cause. Donning my own chilliness, I bowed. "As you wish, Your Majesty."

"Such formality." Katashi scowled. "Once again, I am foolish to have wished for something more. Shall we?"

With a fleeting smile at Shin, I let Katashi lead the way out of the infirmary and along the passage. I lagged a step behind, pressing cool hands to my hot cheeks.

"We need to talk." He halted and turned toward me.

"We do," I agreed. "About Darius."

"That was not what I meant."

"You can't execute him."

A flicker of fire glinted in his eyes. "Can't?"

I touched his arm. "You don't understand. Before I lived with

Malice and his Vices, Darius was my guardian. It was his father who saved me from the assassin that killed my family, and I have been in his care ever since. Yes, I know you will say he ought not to have served Kin—"

"Yes, that's exactly what I'm going to say."

"But . . . I don't think he left me because he wanted to serve Kin. I think he served Kin to escape Malice." There had been real fear in Darius's face when I had gone to see him that morning, his whole being seeming to flinch away from Malice's possessive smile. "I mean, when you're running from the most powerful man in Kisia, where is there to go but to the second most powerful?"

Seeing Katashi's frown, I wished I had not spoken and let my hand fall. "I don't know what I'm trying to say. I just . . . don't want you to kill him."

"He gave me no choice, Hana. What else could I have done after what he said? Lord Laroth was the leader of Kin's armies. He is too important, too dangerous, and has made too great a scene to just be imprisoned."

It was true. There was no going back, and yet I had loved him once, the grand, awe-inspiring guardian I had followed everywhere. He could have told me I was no one, he could have chosen not to educate me, not to encourage me, not to ensure I had everything I needed to become the person I wanted to be, but he hadn't. And in the end, he hadn't walked away from his oath.

"Maybe if I talk to him."

Katashi shrugged. "You may do so if you wish, but you won't change his mind or mine. Neither about him nor Malice."

"Oh, you could have executed Malice with my blessing."

He flicked my cheek. "Bloodthirsty, my dear? Sadly I've seen too much of what he and his Vices can do to risk it. His Vices would come for him."

My thoughts crept around the idea that if Malice didn't want Darius to die, the Vices would come for him too. Not something to share with Katashi in case he tried to stop them, though whether Darius would be glad or sorry to be beholden to Malice was a whole other question.

I stared at the floor, trying to unravel the puzzle that was my guardians and the complicated feelings they had left tangled in my heart. How could love and gratitude be so caught up with disgust and dislike, as though I were two different people sharing the same skin? Perhaps that explained how I could be glad Kin lived despite the anger I could not let go.

When I finally looked up again, it was to find Katashi with his arms folded, frowning down at me with the same haughty annoyance he had once shown Captain Regent, and I had to laugh. "Oh dear, was I ignoring you, Your Majesty? Do accept my humble apologies, my thoughts were elsewhere."

"And that isn't even the cruellest thing you've said to me today."

At his words, I was back in the council chamber with his head between my legs, and I couldn't meet his gaze. "I'm…I'm sorry, cruelty was not my intention. I think perhaps it would be best for me to leave Koi as soon as I can to spare—"

"And where would you go?"

"I'm not sure yet, but I know I can be of better use to Kisia elsewhere rather than sitting around in pretty robes with nothing to do but be stared at and whispered over by everyone who comes to pledge you their allegiance. You of course, not me." I hated the stark bitterness in my voice. I had dreamed so long of sitting on my father's throne and ruling his empire, but Katashi's success had only made mine more difficult. What lord or soldier loyal to the Otako name would ever choose to fight for me when they could fight for him? "Perhaps I will…" I fluttered a restless hand. "Hand out rice sacks to the poor and treat the injured."

Katashi's frown was back. "Would you really prefer to do that than marry me?"

"Katashi, it's not... you, I—"

He winced and held up a hand. "You don't want to be subjugated to a man, yes, I remember. But you haven't actually allowed me to say why I came looking for you in the first place."

"Oh?"

"Now that I am the emperor, I cannot by law also be the duke of Koi. I could grant the right to someone else, but as far as I can tell from a brief look in the records, it has never truly been held by any but an Otako."

I stared at him, and he shrugged almost apologetically. "It is your choice of course, but you could stay. You could have a title and a position that didn't rely on anything quite as heinous as a man."

"Are you mocking me?"

"Not intentionally."

"Duke of Koi?"

His lips quirked into one of his half smiles. "Duchess, really, but... yes. If it is what you want. There are a lot of details that would have to be considered and... understandings we would have to come to, but those are conversations I would rather not have in a hallway, however deserted it might appear to be." He lowered his voice and stepped close. "I learnt that lesson the hard way this morning."

His words heated my cheeks, but I said, "When would it be convenient for you to discuss the details, Your Majesty?"

With a self-mocking little laugh, he stepped back. "Set down again. I am dining with my generals and some of the lords who have been so generous with their funds, but I will come to see you after if you are not too busy handing out sacks of rice and tending the injured."

"Shall I organise for a scribe to join us?"

"As you wish," he said, retreating behind his chilly imperial façade. "Until later then, Lady Hana." And he made a mock little bow before striding away, his ill temper, like his robe, trailing behind him.

I spent the rest of the day consulting with Master Woti, an imperial scribe who had travelled with the court from Mei'lian and chosen to give Katashi his oath. Once he got over the shock of my request, he entered into the discussions with gusto, took down all of my requests, and promised to bring draft papers up to the castle that night.

With nothing else left to do, I spent the evening in a state of restless anxiety, flitting between plans of what to do with my own position and fears that Katashi hadn't meant it at all. Tili drew me a bath and sat chatting about how far away everything was, and how shocked a local seamstress had been when she had requested black silk for my tunics, and a dozen other things that seemed to have the purpose of diverting her mind as well as my own.

She left me alone with my thoughts when a serving girl brought my evening meal, and I sat picking at it, wondering how long I would have to wait for Katashi. If he was dining with lords, it could be a long night, but I was just wondering whether to reschedule with Master Woti when a knock sounded on the door and Katashi walked in.

"No scribe yet?" he said, dismissing his two Pike guards with a nod and sliding the door closed behind him.

"No, but I'm sure he will be here soon. You're rather earlier than I expected."

"A messenger arrived that turned our dinner into a terse strategy meeting, not the sort of thing one lingers at to enjoy." Possessing a restless energy, Katashi strode around the room—stirring coals in the brazier, checking the latch on the shutter, then plucking a chestnut from the remains of my dinner. Crunching it between strong teeth, he finally stopped long enough to look at me. "Kin is at Risian."

I was as startled by the unexpected news as by the flash of relief I had not thought to feel. "What? How?"

"I don't know, but however he got out of this castle, he has now made it safely back to his own territory." Katashi ground the remains of the chestnut, his fierce gaze raking over me. "I had hoped to avoid as much bloodshed as possible, but this changes everything. I march out the day after tomorrow with half of my army."

"You were always going to have to fight," I said. "Whether it was against him or his family or his generals, you were going to have to fight for this."

"Yes, I was." Some of his frustration drained out in a sigh and he pointed to the table. "You have thoughtfully supplied wine for the upcoming discussions. I hope you know I am quite capable of drinking a substantial amount without making rash decisions."

"That," I said, bristling, "is not at all why we have wine."

"No? You must prove it by drinking with me. I will only drink a bowl if you do too."

"Then I will be the one making rash decisions because I am not as used to it."

He laughed. "One bowl will not impair your bargaining skills I am sure. Come."

I joined him at the table and accepted a bowl he poured himself, the act one of special respect, though he did it seemingly without thinking. While I nursed mine, he lifted his to his lips and savoured the taste. "That," he said, letting out another sigh. "Is much better. Now, as the border of your land will remain unchanged, I feel the most important things to discuss are the size of your tithe and the number of soldiers that have to be supported as part of my standing army." He took another sip, looking over the bowl at me. "Well?"

"You're really going to do this?"

"I said I was, didn't I?"

"Yes, but... I am well used to being humoured. Malice and Darius never opened their mouths but to mock."

He set his bowl down and leant on the table, bringing his bright eyes close enough that I had to fight the urge to look away. "Do I look like I'm mocking you?"

"No," I admitted, escaping the intensity of his gaze for an instant by glancing down at my wine bowl. I drank a mouthful, as much to cover my sudden breathlessness as for something to do.

Ceramic scraped on the table as he picked up his wine again. "Good," he said and, still watching me over the rim of the bowl, took another sip. I did so too, my skin prickling with heat. He hadn't done anything to make me think back to the morning on the floor of the council chamber, but there I was, wanting him to touch every inch of my skin.

No, don't think about that, I told myself. The papers were more important. If he was not mocking me, then I was so close to holding a position of wealth and power in my own right, a position only a step away from the throne I had always wanted.

"You're staring at me," he said. "Must I further convince you that I am serious? I could write up the papers with my own hand if you wish."

"No," I said. "That won't be necessary; I'm sure the scribe will be here soon."

Yet part of me was beginning to wish he wouldn't come at all.

Focus, Hana!

Katashi took another sip from his wine bowl. "Very well, but you're still staring at me like I've done something wrong."

"I was thinking about this morning," I blurted.

Not charming words, but they made him lower his bowl. "What about this morning?"

If I had thought it hard to breathe before, it was impossible now. "I was thinking that Wen has the worst timing of anyone I've ever met."

Another sip. Slow. Cautious. "Do you want—?"

"Yes."

Katashi threw back the last of his wine and was rising from the table, when a knock fell upon the door. "My lady?" Wen again, and I knew not whether to laugh or cry as he went on. "There's a scribe here to see you. Master Woti, says he has all the papers you asked to have drafted."

Half-risen from the table, Katashi stared at me. I stared back, twin desires warring in my breast. He turned to the door. "He can come back—"

"Tell him to come in."

Katashi's glare could have burned the skin from my bones, but he knelt back at the table as the door slid, and for a brief moment, Wen was visible in the passage, his face so waxen I could almost pity him.

Whatever the Pike might have suspected, the scribe who entered with a bundle of scrolls under one arm showed no sign of awkwardness, not even in having to bow before a new emperor he had never served before—an emperor who looked ready to spit fire.

I had spent the afternoon going over the standard papers and marking out which passages we needed to discuss, but as Master Woti finished bowing for the third time and joined us at the table, I could remember none of it. He spoke and I must have answered, Katashi too, for the papers were handed back and forth in a sluggish blur. My eyes were on his hands, on his lips, on the proud tilt of his chin and the tracing of his tongue along his teeth while he was thinking. He did not look at me at all, and while Master Woti was mixing ink for the final signing, I found myself thinking back through all the times that we'd almost touched, almost kissed, almost allowed ourselves to speak and wondered if this was just going to be another to look back on with an ache so deep I wanted to curl upon it.

I wanted him, but I wanted the position more and forced myself to focus on the moment of triumph when at last it was time to sign the papers. My hand was steady as I took up the brush to make my mark—a mark that would forever change the amount of power I possessed.

Once I had signed, Katashi took the brush and made his mark, and it was done. I was Her Grace of Koi, subject to no one barring my emperor—an emperor who looked cold and grim as Master Woti witnessed the papers and bowed himself out. Almost I wished he would stay, because then I would not have to face Katashi's chill imperiousness.

As the scribe's footsteps faded away along the passage, Katashi let out a long breath. "Well, Your Grace," he said, rising to his feet. "How humbling your company is. Now you have what you want, I hope you will do something wise with it."

"Like fight for you?"

His eyes narrowed. "Had I known that part was in question, I wouldn't have signed the papers."

"I don't just mean ensuring the Koi estate continues to supply your cause with money and soldiers, Your Majesty. I've been thinking for most of the day about what I want to do now I have this position, and the answer is that I want to fight. When you leave here with your army, I am coming with you. Given the historical weight of this position, it would be wrong to do anything else."

"Hana, this isn't a game."

"No, it's not. We're at war. This is the future of our family and our empire and our people we are fighting for. As both an Otako and the duke of Koi, it is not only my right but my duty to be a part of it."

Katashi ran his hand through his hair, loosening his topknot in agitation. "You cannot go back to masquerading as a man so—"

"I was never going to! Why be a mere Captain Regent when I can be myself? I told you I did not want to sit around and do nothing and I meant it. I have more to give than that."

I knew his mercurial temper too well to be surprised by his sudden laugh, the appearance of his smile loosening the knot of anger that had begun to tighten in my stomach. "Will you ever just be what people expect?"

"I hope not."

"Well, Your Grace, if you are insistent, then by all means ride out with my army. The presence of Lady Hana Otako at my side can only draw more people to our cause. I will not let you risk your life, however, so don't think for even a moment you will be allowed to fight in battle."

I lifted my chin, mulish at his attitude more than his words. "You think I cannot?"

"I know you cannot. No—" He lifted his hand to halt my argument. "There is nothing you can say that will change my mind. You know how to kill and you are used to small skirmishes, but this is war, Hana, and you have no Vices with you anymore. Be satisfied that you are allowed to come and leave it at that."

"Allowed? Because a woman needs the permission of a man to—"

"No, because everyone, regardless of their name or their position or what hangs between their legs, needs their emperor's permission to ride with his army. Now I will bid you goodnight, Your Grace, before that damned tongue of yours says something we both might regret."

With a swish of crimson silk, he departed, leaving my triumph tasting bitter on my tongue.

5. DARIUS

Of all the people I had least expected to find at the bars of my cell, Shin had been high on the list. Yet there he stood, arms folded, his shoulder leaning against the bars and his face mottled with bruises. Unlike the rest of Katashi's loyal Pikes, he still wore the light uniform of a military messenger I had procured for him. Between that and his scowl, I drew my own conclusions.

"Out of favour enough to think me the better choice, Shin," I said. "Oh how I pity you." I turned my head upon my makeshift pillow. No matter how tired one is, stone is not comfortable bedding. "Let me guess, you were foolish enough to admit to Katashi that you knew who Hana was."

His lack of response was answer enough.

"And now what? Hoping to earn back some favour by making me change my mind?"

"Not for that reason," he said eventually, still leaning against the bars. "He's a good man, you know, owning no faults that good advisors can't temper."

"Such as a ruthless and inhumane disregard for life."

Shin glared through the bars. "That wasn't deemed a fault when it was Kin giving the orders."

"He spared Katashi's life."

"Is that what he told you?"

"It is what historical accounts of the day tell me." I pulled myself up off the floor to sit leaning against the wall, unable to suppress a groan of pain as all my joints twinged. "I have already given my answer, Shin, but I am so very humbled that you care about my fate enough to come all the way down here to talk me out of dying."

Again, he just eyed me through the bars, something of a cynical gleam in his lidless eye.

"Ah, I am wrong," I said. "Hana asked you to come. You are very devoted to her."

"And you are very devoted to Kin."

I shrugged, though it produced the unpleasant sound of silk scratching on rough stone, no doubt ripping threads. "I have debts. What's your reason?"

Shin mirrored my shrug. "I have debts."

"I thought you might. Hana is unaware of course, but does Katashi know it was you who killed Emperor Lan? You who murdered his whole family?"

His eyes narrowed. It was always so nice to be right.

"Ah, he does," I said, happy to take some of my anger out on an easy and willing target. "What a loyal servant you are. It would be a shame if Hana found out Katashi had known all along that his father killed hers."

Shin's fists clenched.

"Don't worry, I acquit him of having been involved himself given his age at the time, but harbouring her mother's assassin ever since? You know her too well to doubt how she'll take such news, not to mention the discovery that her selfless protector—"

"Enough." He stood very straight now, no longer leaning upon the bars though he looked more tired than ever. Almost I felt ashamed, but my head ached and fear lived in my skin. Baiting him allowed me, just for an instant, to forget Malice was coming.

Not the choice of the good man I had forced myself to be, but in that moment, I didn't care as long as someone else hurt as much as I did.

"Enough?" I repeated. "Are you going to stand there and preach about how you were just a tool? Or that they deserved to die? Are you going to—?"

Shin gripped the bars, teeth bared in a snarl. "You think you're so clever. You think you know everything. You think you're better than everyone else. Well fuck you." He spat on the stone floor of my cell. "I'll enjoy watching you die."

"Did you enjoy watching them die too? Even Empress Li?"

His desire to rip me to pieces might have powered him through the bars themselves had he not gathered his rage into a tight ball and turned to stalk away, ruining all my fun.

"Give my love to Hana!" I called after him, the words left to echo along the passage. The distant door creaked open. It creaked closed. And once again, I was alone with my fear.

I had not seen Malice escorted from the castle, but he would have gone without complaint rather than risk Katashi increasing his security. Unless he hoped I would fight for my own life, thereby proving I could not bear to be without him after all. It was exactly the act of devotion he would most enjoy but would only risk if he was very, very sure of me.

I lay down, adjusting the bunched sash beneath my head. With nothing else to do, I closed my eyes and tried to sleep. Perhaps I dozed or perhaps I didn't, time meaning nothing until a footstep scuffed by my ear. "Good evening, Lord Laroth."

Keeping my eyes closed, I sighed. "Good evening, Lady Kimiko. I was wondering when you would show up." I opened my eyes to find a riot of dark curls hanging over me. "The Vice who can walk through walls."

"How did you...?"

It really was nice to be right.

Once more, I pulled myself up to sitting, no part of me feeling less sore from the short rest I had been afforded. "I know how Malice works," I said, finding Lady Kimiko eyeing me suspiciously. "He only takes the most important people from those who seek his help. Katashi needs a way into the castle and now Malice has a Vice who can disappear into sadness—it's not very difficult to piece together."

Her brows rose. They were thicker than usual but did her unique features no disservice. "You surprise me, Lord Laroth. Avarice speaks highly of you, but I have not yet found any Vice to have even a passing degree of intelligence."

"Don't disparage Avarice to me."

Those thick brows rose even higher. "A soft spot?"

"If we are to spar with those, you'd lose. My brother did not sell me to a madman."

"No, your brother *is* the madman." She tilted her head. "Oh, look at that, your face still knows how to make a genuine look of surprise; I had thought you as dead as Malice. And no, he didn't tell me you were brothers, but you aren't the only one with eyes and ears and a brain."

Like Hana, she had a quick tongue and a direct gaze, but she was more sure of herself than Hana had ever been—perhaps the effect of age more than temperament. Either way, it was where their resemblance ended. Lady Kimiko had very traditional Kisian features, except for her hair. There was nothing traditional about unruly curls. Nor her diminutive stature. I was reminded of an old limerick and said, "*Katashi the tall. Kimiko the small. He took all the room, in their mother's small womb, so for her there was no room at all.*"

"Why thank you for that," she said, her smile the sort that could cut glass. "I really wanted to be reminded of that wonderful little rhyme."

"Did you indeed? Then I am so pleased to have been of service in these dark times."

Her disdain was beautiful to behold, edged in contempt and owning the sort of hauteur that can only be bred in. "I see all the rumours of your—"

She broke off mid retort, her head tilting at the sound of footsteps. As they approached along the passage, she stepped back through the wall, leaving me to face my second visitor alone. The door creaked open. I did not recognise the man who entered, but I knew that expression of dead calm. Even without it, his lack of uniform and the bow he carried were all the clues I needed to know his purpose. My heart thumped uncomfortably hard in my chest.

"Good evening," I said, remaining seated on the stones.

The man drew an arrow from his quiver.

"I see His Majesty is afraid I might escape before morning and wishes to be entirely sure I'm dead."

He nocked the arrow to his string. A cold-blooded killer could have loosed two through me by now, but this man was enjoying himself, a cruel smile turning his lips as he lifted the bow. I fought the urge to get to my feet and scurry about my cell, which was no doubt exactly what he wanted.

"You're running out of time," I called out, hating the panicked edge in my voice. I hated still more how unnecessary it was, because Lady Kimiko reappeared before all the words were out of my mouth. She stepped through the wall behind the man and in one fluid movement jammed a blade into his side. Another skimmed his throat, and with a series of wet little gasps, he collapsed, bow and arrow clattering on the stones.

Showing no flicker of remorse or disgust or even interest, Lady Kimiko wiped her blades on the man's back before sliding both into her sash. Looking up to find me watching, she lifted her chin. "And you're running out of time to sit there admiring me."

"Who says I'm admiring you?"

"I have a mirror."

"How can you be sure I'm not just staring because you have some blood on your nose?"

She was good. She didn't even touch her face, just said, "Lord Laroth," and bowed in the mocking way of someone acknowledging a hit. I had tried to teach Hana to bow like that, to hold her head just so and her hands delicately cupped. She had never achieved anything like the grace that came naturally to this woman.

Lady Kimiko stepped through the bars and, for a time, stood staring at me without speaking. I wondered if it was a game of sorts, some test to see how long I could wait before demanding her purpose.

"I have more time to waste than you," I said finally, taking up the sash I had been using as a pillow and retying it with deft fingers.

"That's not true."

"Isn't it? What are your orders?"

"To get you out of here."

I folded my arms. "And what if I refuse to go with you?"

With an amused little sneer, she set her hands on her hips. "Then I'll make you."

"If you know what I am, then you must know that's impossible."

She considered me through narrowed eyes. Outside my cell, the only sound was the sputter of the torch in the passage and the distant murmur of guards beyond the door. "You're the same as he is?"

I pulled up my sleeve and turned my wrist to the light. Lady Kimiko eyed the birthmark but didn't move, didn't speak. I let the sleeve fall back into place.

"I guess that makes sense of the stories about you," she said after a while. "Do you really eat people?"

"Not raw."

"I thought you'd be fatter."

"I only eat lean people."

She regarded me with a searching look. "I've heard people taste like chicken," she said.

"So does chicken."

That made her laugh. "Nonsense then?"

"Do I look like I eat people?" I asked. "You still appear to have all your limbs despite the fact I am starving."

"If you're hungry, then why not come with me? We could stop in and raid the kitchens on the way out."

"Really? You have no idea how long it has been since someone treated me like a child. Perhaps it does not occur to you that when they chop off my head, I won't be hungry anymore either. Next, you'll be tempting me with sweets."

Kimiko's thick brows drew together. "You didn't want that man"—she nodded in the direction of the corpse in the passage—"to kill you, but you'd rather be executed than come with me?"

"It's nothing personal."

"You're afraid of Malice." It was a sad smile she gifted. "Again with the expression of surprise. I told you, I am not stupid. Would he mark you too?"

Marking. Had he called it that or had I? It had been so haphazard in the early days, but he'd had five years to perfect the art.

I shook my head. "He tried once."

"If you can fight that, then why are you afraid of him?"

I'm not afraid of him but of who I am when I'm with him. Of how much I want to be with him. How could I say such words to anyone, let alone this woman who had been sold into his service, whose brother's craving for vengeance had outweighed a lifetime of love?

Graceful steps brought her across the cell. But for her vivacious curls, she truly was a tiny creature, her shoulders narrow and her wrists thin. "Please come with me."

Time to see just how severe Malice's orders had been.

"No."

I had expected a slow build of pain, a gradual eating away at clear thought, but the moment the word was out of my mouth, Kimiko's knees buckled. They hit the stones and she fell forward onto her hands, gasping as her hair fell in a curtain around her face.

Shocked, I reached out my Empathy without thinking, the ease with which I moved it as horrifying as the agony piercing her soul and covering her flesh like a thousand hot needles. Void, we had called it, so excited to find that Empathy could work in reverse—not opening the body up, but shutting it down. The piece of Malice inside her was killing itself and taking her with it. A fitting punishment for any Vice who did not obey.

"Shit," I hissed, Malice's desperation palpable in her agony. He would send every single one of his Vices after me rather than let me die, would set the whole world aflame if that was what it took. I could let Kimiko die, but it would make no difference. He was never going to let me go.

"All right, all right, I'll come!" I hated how my heart soared at the thought of going back, of having no choice but to return to Malice. Saving her life was the right thing to do, after all. "Kimiko? Kimiko! I'll come! Get me out of here."

I seized her trembling hand, her skin like burning coals. "Kimiko?"

She didn't answer, so far gone in her agony that she could not hear me, could not understand.

I tried to pull her up, but she just whimpered, eyes rolling back into her head. I could call for the guards; I could have her taken away to be looked at by a physician—she was Katashi's twin after all—but no matter what they did, she would still die if I stayed here.

She stiffened as I lifted her off the stones, her small hands splaying into rigid stars. Straining to hold her, I set my shoulder against the wall. All abilities were triggered by emotion—pain had been Avarice's, because pain had started it all, but deep and wretched sadness had created our original Fader.

And so, you leave me lingering, a shade of wretched fear. Ere long I'll feel the sadness, it my wont to disappear.

Malice's favourite poem. "Sadness," I said and looked around the cell of cold stone, a sad sight for sure, but it had to be the soul-draining kind that made you want to be invisible. The sort that made you want to die.

I had been willing to die rather than go back to Malice, but it was not his disappointment that had withered my soul.

Kin had forgiven me for all the terrible things I had confessed to him, had trusted me, had liked me, had become the closest thing to a friend I had ever had, and yet I had let him down. I had failed at being the man I had wanted to be. The man he had thought me.

Taking Kimiko's hand, I fed that emotion into her. She grew misty around the edges, and a faint tingling like icy water crept up my arm. I had never faded before, but I had seen it done, so holding her hand tightly, I stepped into the wall. The stones seemed hardly to exist, offering no resistance beyond a prickling pain like dipping a cold foot into a hot bath. One step, two, a third, and I breathed the air of a short passage choked with dust and the stink of a gut-tering torch. The bars of an empty cell were like bared teeth in the shadows.

Kimiko slid limp from my arms. "Don't die," I said, pressing a hand to her throat, then her cheek. "Don't die because of me."

All too well could I imagine Malice laughing.

With a sharp cry, Kimiko's eyes flew open and her confused gaze hunted my face in an effort of recollection.

"Who would have thought you could look so concerned," she said at last, each breath quick and sharp. "Almost I believe you have a heart after all."

"Don't get too fond of me. I have a stipulation to going any farther in your company."

Letting go a shaky sigh, she turned her head away. "Wonderful. What is it?"

"I won't leave here without the Hian Crown."

She ran a trembling hand across her eyes. "Fuck you," she said on a laugh. "Fuck you. Did you just think of the cruellest thing you could ask me to do? Betraying my brother?"

"As he betrayed you? No. I serve Emperor Kin and this really is the kindest thing I could ask of you to help his cause."

Her laughter died upon a vista of horrifying possibilities, of which the worst wasn't even the order to slit her own twin's throat.

"I take it all back," she said. "You are a monster."

After all these years, it ought not to have hurt, but it stung to be called so when I had made the best of the choices before me.

She struggled to her feet and almost overbalanced, but when I held out a hand to steady her, she slapped it away with a snarl. "I don't need your help. Give me your word this is all you will ask of me."

"You have my word."

"And I wish I could trust it."

"If you didn't feel you could trust it, then why ask for it?"

Flinging a disgusted look my way, Lady Kimiko strode toward the door at the far end of the passage, only to spin on her heel and return.

"Forgotten something?"

"Yes." Gripping the front of my robe, she pushed me into the bars of the nearby cell. A tingle washed up my back and over my head, then I was staring at the bars from the other side as she withdrew her hand. "Sit. Stay," she said. "Good boy." And she was gone.

A little laugh ghosted past my lips as I sank onto the stone floor of a cell that was almost exactly the same as the one I had escaped from. Hopefully, she would be quick enough that the guards did not find me missing and come searching for me. Too restless to lie down, I began to pace.

How much of this had Malice guessed would happen? How much had he planned? Had he known I wanted to return to him enough that I would not let Kimiko die to prevent it? Or had he only hoped? It had always been me with the clever plans and the masterful ploys, yet here I was dancing to every step he had laid before me.

I could go back. It would be so easy. So simple. Together, Malice and I could achieve anything—everything—we wanted, could already have done so had I not run from what I had once been so sure was my destiny. But all Empaths had been deemed traitors once and with good reason.

My hands clenched and unclenched, and I could not stop them any more than I could stop pacing. Kimiko would take me back. She had to. And if I refused to go, she would die, only for another Vice to take her place. But if I went back...

Kisia would burn.

By the time Kimiko returned, I had worked myself into an agitation I could not calm. Pacing and crushing my fingers together had made no difference, leaving me struggling to swallow down every thought of the god I'd wanted to be. Only the memory of Kin's sad look, of his deep and burning disappointment, had so far managed to keep me sane.

Prove to me the empire needs no gods.

"Here." She thrust a velvet-wrapped bundle into my arms, its contents clinking. I could feel the spikes and trailing chains of the imperial crown, but I opened it just enough to peer in and be sure. If she had somehow managed to steal me a fake, it was a damn good fake.

"Happy?" she said. "Can we go now?"

Kimiko stood before the wall and held out her hand. I stared at it. I couldn't go back. Too many people would suffer if I did, and I still had enough command over myself to know it was wrong. Such control would not survive his barrage for long.

"Well?" She shook her hand at me. "You gave me your word."

I had; there was only one way out of this now. I took her hand.

A mark was nothing more than a parcel of oneself injected into the flesh—a supreme act of dominance, and I could not fight the pleasurable shiver that thrilled through me as I found the piece of Malice living inside her and bled myself into it. His marks had always been built on his thirst for companionship, but as strong as that was, it was nothing to my hunger for mastery. For control.

You are mine and you will do as I command.

Kimiko ripped her hand from mine. "What did you do?"

"I marked you."

"You—" She stared at her hand, then at me, her thick brows colliding in such fury it thundered through me, but it was nothing to the belief filling my veins like a drug. *I am better than you. I am an Empath. You must do as I command.* I could crush her heart with a single thought.

"I had to," I said, fighting for sanity, fighting to swallow the rising god. "I had to do it or you would have— This is better for both of us."

Her fist smashed into my face, and through a burst of pain and light, I staggered back into darkness.

6. ENDYMION

The night stared back at me, full of souls, but Darius was not one of them. He felt distant, his existence slippery beneath my Empathy as though he was not entirely there, and I gnawed one jagged fingernail.

We had stopped at a crossroads, Avarice halting the wagon and Malice disappearing beneath the drooping branches of a great willow tree. It shifted in the breeze, its thin, blade-like leaves shaking—otherworldly in the moonlight.

Gathered at the side of the track, the Vices were as restless as their animals. I leant back against the old signpost and watched them, each man throwing swift glances at their silent leader.

"We need to keep moving," Ire growled, holding his black stallion's reins tight as it backed, snorting. "I don't like waiting in the dark."

"Scared?" Conceit jeered.

Ire spat on the ground. "Terrified."

Parsimony sat at the side of the road with his horse's rein looped around his wrist. "Who says she's even coming back?"

"She's marked, Pars," Ire said. "She has to obey."

"Doesn't mean she has to live. I wouldn't trust such a mission to a minnow. What's so special about Lord Laroth anyway?"

Ire stared at Parsimony, but the man just stared back. With a jerk of his head, Ire indicated Avarice sitting on a rock farther along the track, his large hands stroking the velvet cheek of Conceit's horse. "Go ask if you don't know."

Silence fell again, but only in the solid world. Leaching into every head, my Empathy heard their whispers, jumbled together like the rustling leaves.

I'd like to see him ask. Avarice bites anyone who talks about the Monster.

I wonder if they're really brothers.

That Endymion is one of them too. Never thought I'd see someone that freaked me out more than the Master.

It's those eyes.

Those eyes.

And his hands are always cold.

I had considered begging Katashi to let me stay, had considered telling him the truth, had considered even making myself known to Hana or just walking away altogether, but I could not shake the memory of Darius's pain. Or the gratitude he had felt as I sucked out his life. He had survived, though right down in the depths of his soul, he hadn't wanted to. I wanted to help him, to protect him, to do all I could to atone for the foolishness that had seen me walk into Koi Castle as Malice's pawn.

I got to my feet and brushed myself down. A few wary eyes turned my way, but no one stopped me crossing the moonlit track to the enormous willow tree.

"What do you want, Endymion?" Malice asked as I parted the curtain of hanging leaves. He had constructed a makeshift Errant board out of sticks and stones, and he sat before it, two fingers pressed to his temple.

"Your Vices are worried," I said. "They don't think Kimiko is going to make it out of the castle alive."

Malice moved a piece.

"And you want to know whether I think she will, yes? How sweet of you to worry for the brother you don't even know."

"I'm not the only one who's worried."

He looked up, slashes of moonlight cutting across his face. "You can feel me, can you?"

"Yes."

"Am I tasty?"

"You're afraid."

His fear deepened, but he forced a rictus of a smile. "What do you want, Endymion?"

To protect him. To save him from you.

"Let me go back. Katashi might listen to me."

"If you go back, you'd be dead, yes? You think Katashi would spare you because you played at bows and arrows together once? Do you think he would spare you because you helped him? Or because you are his cousin? No. Katashi Otako is ruthless at his core. He wants Darius dead, but he wants you dead too. And me. And all of my Vices, because he doesn't like power he cannot control."

"So you sent Kimiko because he wouldn't kill her."

Malice laughed, a high-pitched and manic sound that shocked some birds into hurried flight overhead. On the road, a horse snorted. "For someone who can read thoughts and emotions, you are hopelessly naive, Endymion. He sold her to me already for what he wanted most; you think he would hesitate to kill her now?"

"He didn't want to do that. It broke his heart."

"And yet he still *chose to do it*. You read a man's soul and make excuses for his conduct, but it doesn't work like that. That he knows it's wrong makes his willingness to proceed far more horrifying, yes?"

He had not flinched, had not hesitated. And once it was done, he had made no attempt to get her back.

"If he wants us dead, why not execute you with Darius?" I said.

"Because for all his assurance, he is afraid of what I can do. What we can do. And, by the gods, he should be, because if he so much as touches Darius, he will be sorry."

Anger sounded in his voice, but it was a dreadful grief I felt, a life forever without Darius too terrible to contemplate.

"You love him."

Malice looked back down at his Errant game. "Yes," he said simply. "I love him."

Shadows caressed his face as he gazed at nothing, his mind no longer seeming to be present. His features relaxed into a real smile.

"I know what you did to him," I said, the words a fearful whisper.

Malice brought his gaze back. "Oh yes? And how about what he did to me?"

The night was empty but for this man. Could Darius really have done anything deserving such a look of hurt?

"Oh, you think poor Darius is a victim?" Malice said, perhaps seeing my shock. "You saw his memory, yes? Of the night he tried to leave me. Tell me, do you think I knew? Do you think I knew which side of his chest held his heart?"

"Did you?"

"I am asking you that question, yes?"

Our eyes locked. I knew him to be the mastermind behind every moment of suffering in Darius's heart. He had orchestrated his downfall, had played me false, but now he had planted a seed of doubt. Darius's soul owned places even I could not go.

"You didn't want him to leave you," I said. "You wanted to hurt him."

"Yes. And he deserved it."

"He didn't deserve it."

Malice sighed. "It's that beautiful face of his," he said. "It's so perfect, yes? No one wants to believe ill of him. He is like a shrine doll: every feature perfectly in proportion, ethereal, divine, and yet somehow never entirely present. Our father didn't understand him. No one understands him except me. He is not what you think. He is never what people think, never what they expect."

The corners of his lips trembled. As the true spider of the Laroth crest, Malice had always lived up to his name, but now he was somewhere else, someone else, his expression more rueful than angry.

For many minutes, I let him stare through me, through time itself, until I could no longer hold back my troubled thoughts. Darius's soul felt no closer. No more solid.

"He could die."

"He could. We are not immortal. Not even you are proof against sheer force of numbers nor accident nor old age. Did you know that our father died insane? He went mad not long after Emperor Lan died. Some say his heart was broken, yes? It was common knowledge he was in love with your mother, and she died along with the rest of your family. And then the great Nyraek Laroth turned on his own men. Day by day, he grew increasingly strange, until he died, friendless and alone and raving in a puddle of piss."

"Why are you telling me this?" I said, the picture he drew so unlike the man I remembered.

Malice spread his hands. "Why do I tell you these things indeed," he said. "Perhaps I just want to frighten you, yes? Or perhaps I am going soft and I want you to understand that we are strongest together. Allies. Brothers. Or perhaps I would rather think of *anything* but the chance Darius won't make it out of that castle alive."

Approaching hoofbeats emerged from the night, breaking the peace in our little hollow. A distant lantern flickered through the willow fronds, and Malice rose, stones scattering into the grass as he kicked his improvised board.

On the track, the Vices had gathered to watch the riders approach, their black horses almost indistinguishable from the night.

"Spite," someone called as the riders slowed. "What news?"

Hooves kicked up dirt as they reined in, the flanks of their horses heaving. "Nothing," Spite said, addressing Malice. "I'm sorry, Master, but there is no sign of them and no news from the castle."

"Of course there isn't," one of the others said. "You think Otako would shout about it if Lord Laroth escaped?"

"No, but he would shout about it if he was dead."

Malice's fingers shook infinitesimally against the dark silk of his robe. "Still inside the castle?"

"It seems that way, Master."

"I see. Conceit? Folly?"

"Yes, Master?" they replied in unison.

"Find a way inside. Don't let them take his head."

"Yes, Master."

Low conversation broke out as the two Vices readied their mounts, but Malice had already turned away. "Wait," I said, striding after him. "What if we went together, you and I. We could do what Darius and I did. We could—"

"No," he snapped, spinning back.

"Why not?"

Fear fluttered beneath his façade, and his smile slipped. "Because it would not work, yes?" he said, hitching the smile back in place. "Even you cannot kill a whole castle. We must move on before Katashi's scouts find us."

"His scouts? You think he's hunting for us?"

"Stop asking questions and get on the wagon, yes?"

Leaving me behind, he picked his way across the uneven ground to where his wagon waited. It stood beside a rocky ditch that might have been a stream, before the hot, interminable summer drank it dry.

"Go on, move it." Avarice pushed past, shunting me with his shoulder. "You're with us."

The others were mounting. Conceit and Folly were shrinking into the distance, and as Spite extinguished his lantern, the night consumed us too.

"Be quick," Hope said, passing me. "I don't think the Master will be forgiving tonight."

Malice had disappeared into the wagon, closing its door on the night. Lantern light seeped beneath it, stretching its fingers toward the step where Hope took up his vigil. Avarice sat on the box, the reins already gathered. "Kumre," he said, clicking his tongue the moment I climbed onto the running board. "Kumre."

The horses started forward, drawing the wagon from the ditch. It jolted over rocks and tufts of grass before finding the track, and as it swayed, I crossed my arms, resigning myself to an uncomfortable night.

Half of the Vices rode ahead, each a dark shape in the shredded moonlight. We might have been a cavalcade of shadows— black riders on black horses—but for the bright colours of Malice's wagon.

Unsure where we were heading, I watched the road and looked for moonlit landmarks, but soon we wound into a clump of trees that became a forest, its broad canopy stealing all but a few shreds of moonlight. I closed my eyes and let my Sight wander. Nearby, a village of eighty-seven souls came and went without a sound.

One wheel juddered into a pothole and Avarice swore. The back wheel followed with a jolt, but we kept moving, the oak trees pressing ever closer until I could barely see the silken tail of the horse ahead. With no light, our pace slackened to a walk.

"Ask the Master for the lanterns," Avarice growled as the wagon lurched again. "Or we're going to break a wheel."

Hope rose, holding tight to the doorframe as he lifted the latch. Light spilled out, sluggish as treacle, the smell of opium sweet on the air. Acorns cracked beneath the wheels. Another jolt almost sent me head first onto the road.

A few minutes later, Hope returned with half a dozen lit lanterns hanging from his fingers.

"What kept you?" Avarice snapped.

"The Master."

"But he gave permission?"

"In his way." Hope stretched up to hang a lantern on the wagon's spar. "He's not all there."

With the procession moving so slowly, Hope dropped onto the track and jogged ahead. Two lanterns went to the Vices in the lead, while a third he hung on the crossbar, revealing potholes in the road. The last two he gave to Vices behind us, before gripping the slow-moving running board and hauling himself back onto the wagon.

Avarice had relaxed, but the erratic lantern light threw strange shadows. It turned the young oak leaves into golden hands, their grasping branches smothering a woodcutter's shack set back from the road. There, two souls lay fast asleep.

They slid away as we continued on.

"Why are you still travelling with us?" Hope said abruptly as he settled back in front of the doorway.

Avarice hissed in warning.

"No, Av, I want to know. He isn't marked, so he must have a reason."

Because I don't know where else to go. Because Darius and Malice are the only people who understand me.

"Must I have one?" I said. "Is there anything wrong with just enjoying your company?"

One new soul emerged from the night ahead. No, four. Six.

"That's rich," Avarice said with one of his rare laughs. "Because we're such a cheery bunch."

"Oh, not your company, Avarice, but Hope is nice and Ire always makes me laugh—"

"Qualities you could never find anywhere else." He took his eyes off the road long enough to flick Hope a pitying look. "You hear that? You're *nice*."

Hope sniffed. "Better than being a cranky old mule," he said, though mortification hung in a fug around him and he did not look my way.

"Mule? At least where I'm from, our mules aren't the sorry beasts we have here. Better than these horses some of them."

Seven souls. Nine. Twelve.

"Where are you from?" I asked, but Avarice seemed to have thought better of reminiscing, for his usual glower was on the air— Avarice able to make expressions felt even if they couldn't be seen. I directed my questioning gaze at Hope, curiosity piqued. "Do you know where he's from?"

"No. Across the Eye Sea somewhere I've always thought, but it must have been a long time ago, because his Kisian is flawless."

"Why thank you," Avarice grumbled. "A bow to you both."

Still wedged into his place in the doorframe, Hope grinned. His smile was as rare as Avarice's but far more infectious. I grinned back.

Fifteen souls. Sixteen.

"Why are you even called Avarice?" I said.

"Because I stole silver."

"From who?"

"Master Darius."

"So it has nothing to do with your skill? What is it that you do?"

Twenty-four. Forty.

Avarice did not answer. In the doorway, Hope shifted position. "Some of us don't like that question," he said. "It's personal. Some of us have random abilities, others were...deliberate creations."

"You heal people."

Avarice snorted, and Hope lifted his brows, his face glistening in the light. The heat had covered us all in a sheen of sweat. "Do I?"

"Don't you?"

"I will say yes," he said with one of his sad smiles. "But only because it's a nice lie."

Fifty-two. It must have been another village, although they were coming to my Sight in dribs and drabs rather than all together like the last village had.

I wanted to ask Hope what he meant. Wanted to ask what he had been doing to Kimiko and Darius if not healing them, but when I turned to ask, tears stood in his eyes. My stomach flip-flopped and I looked away. "What was Darius like as a child?" I asked Avarice instead, desperate to change the conversation.

Avarice didn't turn around. "Master Darius was Master Darius."

"That isn't a good answer."

"It wasn't a good question."

I stared at him, though it was Hope's pain that called to me. "Did you look after him when his mother died?"

Avarice scowled at the road.

"How did she die?"

"In childbirth."

"With Darius?"

He turned the scowl on me. "No, he was easy born. Lady Laroth always said he wanted to come into the world. His sister was not so keen."

"What happened to her?"

"She died," he said, the short, sharp words of someone trying to end a conversation.

"How?"

One hundred and four souls. Yet there was no sound above the grind of the wheels and the desultory crunch of hooves upon the road. The night was growing quiet.

"You ask a lot of questions," Avarice said.

"I have a lot of ignorance."

"Knowledge won't fix that."

"What do you mean?"

Avarice shrugged one large shoulder and spoke like a man reciting from a page. " 'Knowledge is nothing but the absence of comprehension.' "

One hundred and fifty-one. The night stilled.

"Did Master Darius say that?"

An arrow pierced the golden aura of our lanterns and buried itself, juddering, in the side of the wagon. Shouts rent the night. A horse squealed. Ahead, Apostasy reached for his sickle, controlling his skittering horse with a single hand on the reins. The weapon came free from his belt, the thin hooks along its outer edge crying out for flesh. Perhaps he saw the flicker of a red fletching, for he looked up and the arrowhead pierced his eye, throwing him from the saddle.

Hope scrabbled at the door. "Master!" he cried, trying to grip the latch in a shaking hand. "We're under attack!"

Pain chipped at my body, all cuts and torn flesh and gaping throats gasping air.

An arrow clipped a wheeler's nose, and the horse backed with a squeal, almost tipping the wagon off the track. The others panicked, but Avarice held them steady even as an arrow flew for his neck. A wave of pain poured into the night, and the projectile glanced off skin turned grey and mottled like blood-soaked stone.

Avarice didn't flinch.

"Master!"

Shadowy figures moved between the trees. A man stepped into the light, dodging the swing of a sickle, but its sharp hooks ripped his flesh. Blood spattered the Vice's face and the man howled.

Bodies already covered the road. Another fell screaming from the trees, hitting the ground with a crack of bone, his neck twisted and pale ooze leaking from his head. In his hand a broken bow, and around his waist a black sash.

Katashi's men.

"How many are there?" Malice was beside me, curls of smoke caught to his hair. "Don't just stare at me," he snarled. "My men are dying. How many are there?"

"One hundred and eleven still alive." I gasped. A scream ended in a gurgle as flesh tore. "One hundred and ten."

Perched on the running board, Hope nocked an arrow to his bow as more Pikes rushed from the trees. Let loose, the arrow found its mark, slamming into the chest of an oncoming solider.

"One hundred and nine."

Malice gripped the front of my robe, pulling me so close I could taste the opium on his breath. "Kill them," he hissed and took my hand. It was easy to push through his barriers, to hear the fearful whisper of his thoughts, but it was not enough. The drug had dulled his hatred, dulled his anger.

"I can't," I said. "Your emotions aren't strong enough."

Malice stared at me, no words, no orders left upon his tongue.

Pikes swarmed the road. A curved blade swung inches from Hope's thigh, throwing him off balance. He hit the running board, bow skidding away onto the road.

A man launched himself at the wagon, his blade slicing into Avarice's arm. The old Vice hissed and his skin mottled, hardening around the metal. The Pike yanked on the hilt but it would not budge, and he fell back, slamming into the running board. Hope caught him, gripping the Pike's face between his hands. The soldier's eyes widened. From fear to horror. Desolation. It sucked flesh from his bones and hollowed his cheeks.

The man jerked out of the Hope's hands, tears streaming, and with great wracking sobs, he cried as though his heart was breaking before thrusting his knife into his own gut.

Hope retched.

"Kill them, Endymion," Malice ordered. "Now! Use Hope."

But I couldn't pull my eyes from the solider. He knelt, skewered on his own blade, a faint smile tracing bloodied lips.

"What about your Vices?"

"They have thick skins. Do it."

Two steps to Hope's side, and all it took was a touch. I cupped my hand to his cheek, the same caress with which he had destroyed everything that man had lived for.

One hundred and four enemies and without moving, I could reach them all. Letting go a slow breath, I spread the despair that filled Hope's soul, turning the air to poison. The sounds of battle slowed. Steps faltered. Men gasped. Then building from low moans, the despair grew. The Pikes on the road fell to their knees, tore at their hair, keening, crying, shredding their souls. Vices pressed hands to their ears, but the hopelessness seeped through their skin, every pore breathing the despair deep, and they too buckled.

One by one, the Pikes still in the trees began to leap. Heads smashed into the wagon roof. Others hit the stones or landed on their comrades, spilling blood and brains. Everywhere, they turned their weapons on themselves, but I could not pull my hand from Hope's cheek, could only stare at the growing carnage. Until the last Pike stood upon the blanket of broken flesh, of twisted limbs and bloody throats and, looking up at the sky, pressed his blade through his own neck.

Hope wrenched away and vomited over the edge of the wagon with a wet splatter. It stuck in his hair and he trembled, gilded tears running fast.

Not all the Pikes were dead. Some were bleeding out slowly from wounds in arms and legs and guts, but there were no cries of pain, no howls of grief. They lay still, barely twitching, the night full of gentle, warm satisfaction.

I flinched at Malice's touch on my shoulder. He spoke. Perhaps he thanked me, or shouted or told me I was a monster. I couldn't tell because Hope was still retching over the side of the wagon. That hopelessness, all of it, was what lived inside him every moment of every day.

My gaze shied back to the dead Pikes on the road, staring toward the heavens with sightless eyes.

One hundred and fifty-nine dead men. Horses spilling their guts onto the track. Down the hillside, two frightened souls huddled in a woodcutter's cabin. Eighty-seven souls in the village we had passed. And from its vast distances, Kisia spoke to me.

That's wrong. That shouldn't be possible.

Shit, this hurts.

The screaming has stopped. Should we go see what happened? What if someone needed help and we just hid here and did nothing?

The gods will judge.

They will judge.

They will.

They must.

7. HANA

It felt no different waking as Her Grace of Koi, but as I lay watching the first hints of dawn creep across the matting, I thought of all the things it changed and smiled to myself.

If I was to ride out with the army the next day there was much to organise—my own entourage and supplies, armour and tent and horse and weapons and all the many other things that would no doubt come to mind. Yet, before any of that, I needed to see Darius.

I sat up, and owning the acute hearing of a serving maid, Tili opened the door from her adjoining room and came in. She had her long hair caught back in its customary bun, and she smiled, but there were dark rings beneath her eyes.

"Good morning, my lady," she said. "I hope you were not woken last night."

"No? Should I have been?"

She set back the lid of a chest and removed a dressing robe, a single layer of thin tan linen, close around the throat. "I hoped not, but His Majesty insisted on looking in on you, in case Lord Laroth should have been here."

"Katashi came back last night?"

"I refused to let any of the guards enter, my lady," she said, shaking out the dressing robe with a snap. "I could not, however, stop

His Majesty from doing whatever he wished. He looked in not long before sunrise, my lady."

"Looking for Darius? Did he escape?"

I could not hide the hope in my tone, but Tili did not acknowledge it. "It appears so, my lady. Along with the Hian Crown."

"The—" I pressed my hand to my lips. I had thought it likely Malice would not let Darius go to the headsman, but that he would steal the crown on the way out I had not considered. Darius was loyal to Kin, but Malice was loyal to no one. He would only play such a trick for mischief, or to keep Darius happy.

"Well," I said, at last finding my voice again. "I will dress. There is a lot to do today, but I think I had better see His Majesty first."

Fear flashed across Tili's face, but she made no attempt to turn me from my purpose and accepted without question that we would be packing that day to travel with the army.

By the time I was dressed, the whole castle seemed to be awake. Servants and guards were hurrying through the passages, and from many rooms away, I could hear Katashi's rage.

As I approached his door, Shin came striding out, more alive than he had been the day before but no less bruised. It looked like he had chosen a poor day to leave the infirmary.

"I wouldn't go in there if I were you," he said in his usual low growl. "It's been a morning of bad news. We'll have to replace all the ornaments. He's always liked breaking things."

"Worse news than the crown going missing?"

"Kin's officially denounced him as a traitor to the throne and is threatening all our supporters with everything from fines to disinheritance and execution, depending on their level of involvement. Rumour says he's already marching his army north."

Something smashed in the room behind him, a hundred tiny shards raining onto the matting floor. Katashi had stopped shouting, but the silence was hardly an improvement.

"I'll take my chances," I said. A nod and a bow and Shin strode past me, leaving behind a waft of soured herbs.

Having been in earshot of our conversation, the Pike standing guard outside Katashi's rooms did not seek to discourage me from entering, merely grimaced as he slid open the door.

"Lady Hana is here to see you, Your Majesty," he said. I didn't wait for an invitation to enter, afraid to linger lest my courage fail.

Katashi was standing at one end of a grand room with Hacho in his hands. As the door closed behind me, he loosed an arrow at the wall, piercing a vase and sending its contents and its ceramic raining onto the ground.

"No sign of the crown then?"

"No," he growled and nocked a fresh arrow. With swift skill, he sent it through the painted eye of an unknown man, the paper screen breaking with a loud snap.

I clasped my hands demurely in front of me. "Do excuse me, Your Majesty," I said. "But as this is my castle now, I would prefer if you did not destroy the few pretty things it possesses."

He had nocked another arrow, and I felt sure he would ignore me and loose it, but he dropped the point and glared at me over his shoulder. Then he laughed. "How stern you look," he said, letting the arrow fall from his string as he came toward me. "Forgive me, Your Grace. I am a great beast when I'm enraged. But by the gods, I do not think I can take more bad news today."

"Shin told me about the message from Mei'lian," I said. "Was it really so unexpected? Putting pressure on your allies is the first thing I would have done had I been Kin."

"And what would be the second thing?"

I caught the grim note and looked up into a face that no longer laughed. "You still think I know something of his plans?"

"No. Not really." He began to pace, and I buried a stab of hurt at his lingering suspicion. "But I have been building to this for years,

Hana, making alliances, forming plans, chipping away at Kin's precious stability. It might have taken me another year to reach this point without the Vices, but if I had waited, they wouldn't be causing me such grief now. Never trust someone else to do a job you ought to be doing, nor someone you know deep down cannot be trusted."

Katashi set Hacho down. "On the other hand, if I had not made a deal with him, perhaps I would not have met you. Or might never have found myself able to take the throne at all." Taking my hand, he kissed the back of my fingers, but though the touch of his lips to my skin sent a little dance of joy through me, it seemed little more than a perfunctory motion to him, and he let my hand go as quickly as he had grasped it.

He went back to pacing, leaving me to wonder if it had been nothing more than a Chiltaen custom he had picked up in his years of exile.

"The crown doesn't matter for another year," I said, clasping my hands tightly together. "Kin's threats are far more troubling. What will you do about them?"

Katashi stopped pacing as he neared the window and looked back over his shoulder. "Intent on becoming one of my advisors now too? You are very ambitious."

"I have a lot to say."

"Ha! Many men have a lot to say, but is it worth hearing? What would you do to counteract Kin's threats against my supporters?"

"I have not yet had the chance to give it much thought, Your Majesty, but the one thing you cannot do is retake the land Kin gave to the Chiltaens with the last treaty, no matter how much support you would get by returning it to its rightful owners. It will already take all you have to beat Kin without having to protect Kisia against an invasion as well. At least the new treaty should mean they stay out of whatever mess we make while it benefits them to do so."

He eyed me from the other side of the room long after I had stopped speaking.

"Do we still depart tomorrow?" I asked when he made no reply.

"Yes. Generals Tikita and Roi are to keep to the Willow Road and meet the force Kin is sending north, while General Manshin and I march on the Valley. Kin cannot hang on to an empire he can't feed. If we can manage to disrupt the rice trade, a few favours may be all that's needed to make Lin'ya blockade the southern ports, then—"

"You're dealing with pirates?" Shock stiffened my every limb.

"I'll deal with anyone if it helps me achieve my end," he said, not in the least troubled. "After making a deal with Malice, you cannot think pirates any worse."

"No, I suppose not," I said, yet in some strange way it seemed far more risky. The pirate enclave at Lin'ya was long established and had been giving the empire grief for as long as I could remember. Even living in a farming compound on the other side of the empire I had heard of them.

"In fact," he said, returning across the room toward me. "They are far easier to deal with because all they want is freedom of movement and money. I'm still not quite sure what Malice wants."

"I think he got it last night." Seeing from Katashi's scowl that an unpleasant diatribe about my old guardians was forthcoming, I forced a smile. "As we are still to depart tomorrow, I will leave you now, Your Majesty. There are many preparations to make."

His scowl did not lighten. "Indeed there are," he agreed. "I have appointed both Shin and Wen to your entourage. And yes, I know you were perfectly capable of organising such things for yourself, but you would have been hesitant to take my men from me despite familiar guards being far more pleasant than unfamiliar ones. Even you cannot deny that."

"Then in turn, you cannot deny that it's useful to have someone you trust spying on me."

"I can when such was not my intent. Is it so terrible of me to want to ensure you're safe? There are many who would stigmatise me allowing you to travel with my army as barbarously callous and inconsiderate of a lady's comfort."

I snorted, and his lips twitched in an attempt to keep a straight face. "Yes, exactly my thoughts," he agreed. "But whatever my opinion of your... ladylike manners, I cannot let my cousin, whatever her position, be protected by men who have not earned my trust."

"Then of course it will be a great honour to have Shin and Wen with me, Your Majesty," I said, matching his gravity though it was hard not to smile. "I thank you for your gracious kindness."

"Oh, go on, get out, you minx," he laughed. "I have better things to do than stand around being mocked by you."

With many of my own preparations to make, I bowed and departed. There would be plenty of time to discuss his plans and strategies once we were on the road, and plenty of time to give voice to my own.

Katashi's combined army of Pikes and imperial soldiers departed Koi to a fanfare the following morning, the half under the command of Generals Tikita and Roi keeping to the Willow Road while the rest of us crossed the Nuord River and travelled south toward the Valley.

In the short time we'd had to prepare, Tili had made what alterations she could to an imperial uniform, and for the first time I rode proud in its splendour. It was exhilarating. No suffocating palanquin like I had been forced to endure on the ride north with

Kin's court, rather my own horse and my own entourage, my own place and my own power.

Even though she was my maid, I had insisted Tili ride with me, and with Shin and Wen behind us, we rode close enough to the front that I could watch Katashi and his advisors—noting the constant shift of men manoeuvring to be near him. It had been the same when Kin rode north, and watching Katashi lead the way with his crimson surcoat brushing the flanks of his horse, I couldn't but think of Kin on that journey. I had watched him out of curiosity, had challenged him on everything from the Chiltaen peace treaty to his protection of my family, and he had borne it with greater fortitude than many a man would have done. The man behind whom I rode now was the fire to Kin's sturdy stone, more impetuous and mercurial, but equally more adored. How many of his Pikes had been swept up in this merely due to his magnificence? Had I?

"I hope I am not interrupting a deep and profound thought, Your Grace," a cool voice said, drawing me from just such a deep and profound thought, though one I was happy not to consider. General Manshin was riding alongside, a slightly amused smile the only sign of disrespect.

"Not at all, General," I said.

"Perhaps you have not been marching with an army long enough to become prey to them yet. There is certainly much excitement in the beginning—I remember that myself—but once that wears off, you must reach the height of general as soon as you can so you have more mundane things to occupy your mind. While you have supply trains and terrains to worry about, you have no time to be troubled for your soul."

"That," I said, eyeing him curiously, "is quite the observation."

The general's wrinkles creased around his eyes, but the lower portion of his face managed to look solemn. "I am quite the observer. It's a useful trait in a general. I observe, for instance, that you are no stranger to either riding astride or wearing armour. In fact, you look to be quite in your element, Your Grace."

"I was not born to be a lady, general."

"I must admit to being very curious on that score."

"You were perhaps not a general yet at the time I was born and therefore still prone to fits of deep thought."

He grinned, acknowledging the hit. "Well said, Your Grace, well said. I was not a general then, as you say, merely a captain or perhaps a commander, I lose track of the years—something else you will soon grow accustomed to. What interests me, Your Grace, is the singularly unique position in which you find yourself. Not so long ago the guest of one emperor, now riding with the army of another. Are you perhaps the token that ensures success? A charm of good fortune?"

"Surely such things are in the hands of the gods."

General Manshin gestured in Katashi's direction. "Ah, but which gods, Your Grace? Which gods?"

"Is there something specific you wish to ask, General?"

"I see you lack the court penchant for dancing around one's words with hints and winking. If you wish me to be more direct, then I can be very direct. Where do you stand in all this, Your Grace? Another of the things a general must worry about is whether they are to be stabbed in the back."

Shocked by his question, I frowned at him while our horses carried us on without missing a step. "Have I done something to rouse your suspicion, General Manshin?"

"A general's suspicion should always be roused and only slowly quieted."

"If you doubt my loyalty to Katashi because I was Emperor Kin's prisoner for a few weeks, then consider how much doubt I must have about you." They were bold words, but I would not be made to feel like a snake in the grass by this smiling traitor.

I had expected him to scowl, but instead he laughed, causing Katashi to look around. "Ah, you serve back so delightfully," the general said, heedless of his emperor's interest. "But you see, Your Grace, the difference is that I risk much with my treason, while you risk nothing at all."

"Then I feel there is nothing I could say that would quieten your suspicion, General."

"Very true, Your Grace, very true."

Rather than leaving me to my reflections, he rode along at my side for at least the next hour, talking first about his estate south of Suway and then his eldest son, Captain Ryo Manshin, in whose competent hands he had left its protection. After that, my every attempt to bring the conversation around to strategy was met with descriptions of his numerous grandchildren, and I almost wished he would return to openly pricking me with his distrust.

It was late afternoon by the time we stopped to set up camp. While I had seen the Pikes and the Vices do so often, there was something doubly impressive about the military precision of General Manshin's imperial soldiers. It took mere minutes for the central tents to go up, and by the time my chests had been carried in, smoke was already rising from cooking fires. Horses were rubbed down, more tents were erected, carts unloaded, and Tili brought both washing water and wine as though we were back in Koi.

Food came about an hour later, and while I ate, Tili lingered, unrolled my sleeping mat, laying out my armour to air and tidying the small jumble of cases and chests we had brought with us. I was sure I ought to feel tired after a day in the saddle, but having washed and rested while the camp went up around us, I was wide awake and getting restless. Outside, men were talking and laughing and going about their tasks, the camp a symphony of footsteps and clatters and thuds in the last of the daylight.

Wen had said that he would take the first shift outside my tent, so when I pushed my lap table away, I called his name.

"Your Grace?" he said, peering in through the entrance.

"Can you find out when His Majesty is meeting with his advisors? I wish to attend."

The young man winced. "I'm afraid I saw the general and some others entering the meeting tent almost an hour ago, Your Grace."

"An hour?" I let out a deflating breath. I could still join them, but it was likely they were nearly finished, and I could recall how well it had gone the last time I had walked in on Katashi's council. "All right. Take a message to His Majesty. I want a word with him when he's done."

"Yes, Your Grace."

Wen disappeared, taking my good mood with him.

I picked at the last of my meal. The longer I waited, the surer I became that I ought to have joined them and that it was now too late. The indecision made me testy, and soon I sent Tili away with my half uneaten meal.

Eventually, Katashi came, attired not in his armour but in his crimson regalia.

"You sent for me, Your Grace," he said, his tone exactly matching my sour mood. "I hope you don't mean to make a habit of demanding your emperor's attendance."

"I wouldn't have had to at all if you had invited me to the meeting."

"By all means, join us next time. Would you like my robe for the occasion too? And my throne? I'd offer you my crown, but your dear Darius stole it from me."

He had folded his arms and seemed to fill the doorway, but I refused to be intimidated. "Is it so great a thing I ask for? If you had given my dukedom to a man, would he have been invited to join you at the meeting?"

"That would depend on who he was."

"If he was your cousin?"

Katashi looked down at my wine, and with a sigh, he knelt to pour himself a bowl. "Do you really expect to overturn centuries of precedent within a week?"

"I can try. But you need to help me."

"Marrying me is easier."

I leant my elbows on the table. "Oh yes, and what would you say if I did? You'd order me back to the safety of Koi to wait out the war."

"Would I?" he said, looking at me over the top of his wine bowl. "There would hardly be any fun in that."

I had tried not to think about him since we'd signed the papers, tried not to wonder what might have happened had Master Woti been half an hour late. Impossible when Katashi looked at me like that, when he could say such things with apparent calm. My breath fled my body, but he just took another sip of his wine.

Did any words exist that could bring back his former fervour? Something witty and charming like the words that seemed to fall so naturally from his lips the moment he opened his mouth. I could think of nothing.

He finished his wine and set the bowl down. "Well, my dear, if an invitation to tomorrow's meeting is all you wanted, then I shall depart."

"It's not."

"No?"

Was that the hint of a smile? Oh, if only I had Malice's ability for just an instant to be sure. "No," I said. "You... don't have to go."

"I know. I'm an emperor, I don't have to do anything."

He got up to leave, and I reached out to stop him. "I mean I don't want you to go."

A smile flickered as he looked back down at me. "Oh?"

"Is this punishment?"

Katashi approached with his long stride. There was no rush, no eagerness; he just perched on the lap table beside me, his silk robe rustling. "Perhaps," he said, leaning down, the gentle touch of his hand upon my cheek the sweetest thing I had ever felt. "Can you blame me?"

His kiss owned none of its former ferocity, but with his lips to mine, I breathed in the full heady scent of him and rose into an embrace so soft and intimate that my heart sang.

"I had begun to wonder if you didn't want me after all," he whispered as our lips parted. "Didn't want this."

"I've wanted this since I first met you," I whispered back, lips as near to his as they could be. "And then I saw you use your bow."

Katashi laughed, a husky sound that sent a delighted shiver through my skin. "Ought I have brought Hacho with me, then?"

"Oh no, that would just make me more jealous of her than I already am."

"No need for that." He plucked at the knot in my sash, skilled fingers soon sending it sliding to the floor. The ties of my under-robe came next, and once again, his hands were on my skin, sliding across my stomach and down my sides, his little groan of enjoyment as he traced my flesh making it all the more exhilarating. "I have been thinking of this for the last two days." His fingers slipped between my legs. "Wanting to feel you press against me and hear exactly that little moan you just made. I wish you would do it again."

I had spent two days trying to put him from my mind, but all too often, my thoughts had slipped back to the sight of his head between my legs.

"I'll make it again if you—" I stopped, shocked by how brazen the rest of the words sounded even in my head.

Katashi smiled and kissed my cheek and my jaw and my throat.

"Liked that, did you?" And without awaiting an answer, he slid from the edge of the table, a hand on my shoulder all the encouragement I needed to sit before him. This time, the spread of my open robe created an unbroken path of skin down which he could kiss, and he did so, each one a slow tease accompanied by a glance of bright eyes through long lashes.

I dropped onto my elbows as his broad shoulders spread my knees, drawing a groan from my throat. Without thinking, I lifted my hips into his chin. He chuckled at my silent plea, and with a last look up, he set first one of my feet and then the other onto his strong shoulders, and lowered his head between my legs.

Gripping tight to my thighs, he once more slid his tongue inside me, the sudden sensation all the more glorious for how long he had made me wait. I hardly knew what followed, unsure which parts he did with his mouth or his fingers, only that I never wanted him to stop. All strength and sense fled and my elbows gave way, but when I dropped onto my back, he just slid his hands under my hips and lifted me to an angle that sent his tongue deeper.

All too soon, pleasure tore through me, and I could not stop myself bucking into him. He must have expected it, for he stopped, gripping my hips with his strong hands as ecstasy tumbled through me. When at last I had regained my breath and the tremors had stopped shaking my legs, I managed a laugh that ended in a groan. "That was amazing. How do you even do that?"

"Same as archery," he said, shifting to lie beside me on the old carpet. "Practice. I don't like to do anything poorly."

I could not but think of all the women who had had this joy before me and hate them just a little, as foolish and unfair a thought as it was. He must have seen it in my face, for he propped himself up on an elbow and said, "I didn't ask any of them to marry me."

"And you wouldn't have asked me if you hadn't thought it politically important to do so."

"Oh, wouldn't I? Where else was I going to find a woman who knows how to slit a man's throat?" He whispered the last words against my neck, punctuated with a kiss. "Or who rides fearlessly into a fight? I've seen you with a bow too, and I can promise you my breeches did not fit anywhere near as well after that."

He had arrived still dressed in his crimson court robes, and although mine lay spread open around me, even his sash was still knotted. Yet lying as he was, it was impossible to miss the hard bulge constrained beneath the silks. Unlike him, I knew nothing about how to please a partner or even if there was some unspoken etiquette, and suddenly breathless, I said, "Ought I..." But again I could not finish, so bold and shameful the words sounded.

"Ought you what?" he said between still more kisses ranged along my collarbone. "Oh, return the favour? No, you're not even comfortable touching me yet. Kiss my neck before you kiss my cock."

"Katashi!"

He lifted his head, all lopsided smile. "What? Don't turn prudish on me now, love, you were doing so well."

"Prudish? I'm the one lying here all but naked, while you haven't even—"

Before I could finish, he was on his feet, the knot of his black sash half untied.

"I didn't mean—" I faltered. "You don't have to—"

But his sash joined mine upon the floor, and with a sigh of shifting fabric, he dropped first one robe and then the other. He was magnificent, from his powerful thighs to his broad shoulders, every muscle carved from weathered bronze. "Better?" He held his arms wide, inviting my gaze with a complete lack of modesty or shame, though his hair had come free of its topknot and his manhood stood rigid.

I wanted to answer, but air seemed to have abandoned my lungs, and all I could do was stare as heat stirred once more inside me. With shallow little breaths, my chest rose and fell, and I could not be calm, fearing what was to come as much as I desired it. He must have sensed the change, for amusement drained from his smile, leaving something far hungrier in its wake.

All lithe grace, he dropped back down at my side and, threading his hands into my hair, drew me close. I knew not whether he kissed me or I kissed him, only that it was filled with such ardour I could barely breathe. Pressing against him, our skin met along the whole length of my body, every part of him warm as though it were aflame. And against my leg, the stiff weight of his manhood—a feeling I had once before had reason to fear.

Perhaps because he didn't know that, or perhaps because he did, he gently took my hand and pressed it to the hardness between us, its length far smoother and softer than I had expected.

"I want you, Hana," he breathed against my neck. "I want this. May I?"

Surprised by the question, I drew back enough to see his face. "May you what?"

"Make love to you. I won't without your permission."

My fingers stilled their tracing of his soft skin. I owned just enough fear to consider his words, but my ache for him was too deep to be quieted. "Yes," I said, little more than a breathless gasp. "Yes. Please."

He let out a slow, steadying breath that danced across my cheek. "Don't let me hurt you, all right?"

A little shake of the head was all I could manage as he moved once more between my legs, the bunch and ripple of every muscle owning such animal grace. His hair too, loose to his shoulders, had the look of a dark mane, and I could catch no breath at all as, with his eyes not wavering from my face, he guided himself inside me. My gasp drew in all the air I had been missing and more as slowly, bit by bit, he filled me. It stung more than I had expected, but though he had told me not to let him hurt me, I didn't want him to stop. I wanted him inside me as far as he could go, and I wrapped my arms around his neck and clung to him. He pulled me closer, his palms upon my back and his chin on my shoulder, and there we stayed a long moment just breathing in and out in time, our chests pressed close.

When again he moved, he did so slowly, letting me keep clinging to him as he set up a slow rhythm, seeming to pull my breath out with him only to thrust it back in. His breath huffed hot against my skin, and as he slid all the way back inside he gave a little grunt of pleasure. Liking the sound, I pressed my hips up into him and was rewarded with a groan.

He pressed deeper and harder as if in payback, and I let out a cry equal parts pleasure and pain. Pausing, he kissed the tip of my chin and went on kissing all the way down the ridge of my throat until he could reach no farther without loosening my grip.

"I'm sorry," he whispered. "Do you want me to stop?"

I tightened my hold around his neck. "Don't you dare. Don't forget I know how to slit throats."

His body shook with laughter, and thrusting upon each word for emphasis, he said, "You. Wouldn't. Dare."

"Not if you're going to keep doing that," I said with a moan I could not contain.

"Doing. What. This?"

"Yes, yes, that! Please keep doing that."

He complied, speeding his pace, and I could not tell when pleasure had started to outweigh the pain, only that I wanted that burst of rapture again and urged him on. I didn't care how loud my cries were or how tightly I gripped his arms, his shoulders, his back, anywhere I could reach, so long as he didn't stop and kept pushing me toward the edge.

It came all of a sudden and with the same shock wave, ripping through me from head to toe. I cried out, and my body tightened around him, but he did not stop. Each thrust began to ache, but the little notches of pleasure between his brows were as glorious as his own rising series of moans, and when he did at last reach his climax, it was with so heartfelt a cry that I pressed into him with resurgent need.

Having thrust deep, he stayed there, breathing heavily as the last of his own pleasurable tremors faded away. Then letting out a groan, he dropped more of his weight onto me, our bodies entirely aligned and finally at rest. Except for my inability to take a deep breath.

"You're heavy," I said.

"It's all the muscles."

"Then can you move some of your muscles off me?"

He laughed. "Being kicked out already?" He slid back, and though he pulled out of me slowly, it hurt a lot more than I expected, and I winced. Something wet dribbled after.

"Oh shit, hold on," he said. "I didn't think of that." And with a tired groan, he reached for the linen cloth on the wine tray. "Here, you might need to clean up."

"How glamorous." I pressed the cloth between my legs as I might have done had it been a bleeding day, but if he found anything incongruous or displeasing in the sight, he didn't say so, just lay back beside me with a contented sigh. He wriggled an arm around me, and I found a comfortable spot with my head on his shoulder.

He was warm and soft, and for a time, the sound of his breathing was more delightful than the cheery songs echoing from the distant campfires.

"Is it... normal for men to ask permission like that?" I asked after a while, still holding the linen between my legs.

Beneath me, his shoulder jerked a little shrug. "I haven't been in another man's bed to know, but I doubt it. When... when my father was executed"—the word came hard from his lips, a jagged edge to its syllables—"we were left with nothing. In the beginning, there were a few lords willing to feed us and house us, but the longer Kin sat on the throne, the less trouble we were worth. We were poor, forced to move constantly, and Kimiko and I were only children. My mother did what she had to do to feed us, but the men who took joy in breaking her spirit slowly succeeded. And there was nothing I could do."

I rolled to look at him, but he kept his frowning gaze upon the tent ceiling. "I'm sorry," I said, unable to think of words that could ever bring comfort.

His arm tightened around my shoulder as though in thanks, and I pressed my lips to his cheek, lingering there as I breathed in the scent of his skin and ran my fingers through his hair.

From outside, Wen cleared his throat. "Your Majesty?"

"What is it?" Katashi called back, not moving.

"The messenger has returned from Suway with responses to your ascendance, Your Majesty. It is quite a full sack, and the messenger thought you might want to have them brought to you at once in case—"

I prepared for Katashi to leave, but keeping his arm around me, he called back, "Are the contents of those letters likely to change between now and morning?"

"Um, no, Your Majesty."

"Then they can wait until morning."

"Very good, Your Majesty."

"You don't have to stay," I said as Wen repeated this to the unseen messenger. "I know you have a lot to do."

He turned his head, mussing his hair even more. "I know I don't have to stay, but you wanted me to and I want to. Unless you wish to see the back of me."

"You do have a very nice back."

His smile flickered, though he tried to keep a straight face. "Archery will do that if you work hard. See this muscle here—" He rolled, pointing to one on the broad expanse of his back, but his shoulders shook with barely contained laughter and I slapped his arm.

"Very funny. Of course I want you to stay," I said. "Even if all you talk about is archery and Hacho, I still want you to stay."

Katashi rolled back, and kissing first my cheek and then my lips, he said, "One should never talk about their first love."

No more messages came, but although we spent the night lying upon my sleeping mat, neither of us got much sleep.

8. DARIUS

I woke with a dry mouth and the taste of horse on my tongue. When I drew a breath, there was still more horse, and I seemed to be rocking back and forth to the rhythm of clopping hooves. The sound hammered into my aching head, but the crowning agony of all was the throaty warble of someone singing.

I groaned and tried to open my eyes, but the light was too bright and I closed them again. At least the singing stopped.

"Awake, are you?" said a familiar voice. "Pity. I was enjoying the peace and quiet."

Licking my lips was like rubbing sandpaper on sandpaper. "Water," I managed.

Lady Kimiko sighed. "Fine, I guess we can stop for a bit."

The horse began to slow, and shade soon darkened the world behind my closed eyes. Grass muffled Kimiko's footfall, then as we stopped, her voice sounded behind me. "Need help getting down?"

Despite my uncomfortable position, the very idea of moving made me cringe, but without waiting for an answer, she gripped my hips. "Don't fall on your arse now, will you, my lord," she said as she pulled and I began to slide backward. My feet met the grass, but my knees buckled and I fell, hissing in pain, onto my hands and knees.

"What," I said when I had regained some breath, "did you punch me with?"

"Not sure what it is," she replied as she rustled about. "But your lovely brother gave it to me, so I figured it wouldn't kill you. I made you drink it when you came around a few seconds after I punched you, which felt really good by the way. I'm hoping to get another chance at it."

"You ... made me drink borabark?"

"I said I don't know what it was, only that he said I could use it to knock you out if I needed to. If you were being ... *recalcitrant* I think was his exact choice of word."

A waterskin was thrust into my hand and I drank, so desperate for the water that some poured down my chin and onto my robe.

"Hey, watch it." Kimiko snatched the waterskin away. "We don't know how far it is to the next water source."

I closed my eyes at the endless drumming in my head and a body that seemed more ache than flesh. "Borabark," I said. "And you call me a monster."

"Did I? Well honestly, if I'd had to listen to you say another word, I might have strangled you, so really the bark stuff saved your life."

"It's not even made from bark, it's made from sap, but when Master Yoto asked the people of the Eppachi tribe about it in 1102, they pointed at the bora tree, which has very unique and spiky—"

"Darius. Shut up or I'll make you drink the rest."

"That would only make it worse," I said. "One of its side effects is making the brain ... spin faster."

"Brains don't spin."

I sighed. "Not literally. Oh gods, I think I preferred your singing."

"Monster."

My mind went on freewheeling through lines of unconnected

thoughts, jumping around inside my head even as my body melted into the grass hopefully never to move again. We had given borabark to potential Vices in the early days, needing to keep them dopey and compliant while we worked, but it had only ever been a small dose. Consuming too much could knock someone out for days.

Kimiko had moved away and seemed to be talking to the horse. Where had she gotten it? At Koi? How had we even gotten out of the castle? Had she dragged me through the walls? Which way could she have escaped unseen carrying a dead weight? The questions piled around me as my thoughts went on dancing, but when at last I managed to open my eyes, the one I uttered was, "Where are we?"

We looked to have stopped on the side of a country track, the view nothing but fields and hills and trees and little flowers dancing in the breeze. A bird fluttered past, followed by its mate.

Kimiko stepped back from the horse's head and set a hand on her hip. "I don't know," she said, tossing her wild curls as the wind tried to push them into her face. "You're the one who's telling me where to go, aren't you?"

My confusion must have shown on my face, for she pointed at her heart where I had corrupted Malice's mark the night before. Or had it been the night before that? Time felt slippery like an eel.

"First I tried leaving you there," she said, counting this attempt on a finger. "When that was agony, I got you out of the damn castle and tried leaving you in the woods." She checked off another finger. "Then I thought, hey, I'm not marked by Malice anymore, maybe I'll go find Katashi. That one really hurt. So I tried to make it to the north road to head to Ji, but even dragging you with me, that was excruciating. So I tried doing nothing and just sitting there, which was soon almost as bad. Then I tried to kill you."

She had recycled fingers by this point, and every breath she took seemed to be swelling her fury. "But that was even more terrible than all the rest, so I guess despite your self-professed willingness to die, you didn't actually want to, so I stole a horse and have been taking you in the only direction it doesn't hurt to travel. I have no idea where we are anymore, because I turn whenever there's a tug of pain, and the rest of the time I daydream about all the ways I'd like to see you die."

Kimiko turned away, a hand to her mouth as the last of her words lashed out, and I felt their sting as they hollowed my stomach and reddened my face. She had said nothing I had not deserved.

"I'm sorry," I said, the words so weak and useless that I may as well have left them unsaid. "I didn't know that would happen. I can't even think where I've been unconsciously ordering you to take us."

"Somewhere that's '*better for both of us*,' I imagine," she said with a bitter laugh.

I set my head in my hands and wished the headache threatening to split my skull in two would just get on with it. "I said that, didn't I."

"You did. And that you had no choice and there was no other way, and you know what?" Kimiko turned back, her eyes red and her jaw pugnaciously jutting. "Had you said as much and we'd sat down and had an actual conversation about it and made a plan, I probably would have agreed and we could have avoided all of this. But no, you just had to go and do your—" She wiggled her fingers at me. "—thing without even letting me know, let alone asking for permission."

"I'm sorry," I said again. "I'm sorry, all right?"

"Not all right, no. Sorry isn't good enough."

"I panicked! All I could think about was that I didn't want to go back to Malice—couldn't—not if there was to be any chance of still being—"

I broke off. Even with the effect of the borabark, it was foolish to spill such truth to someone I had only just met and had no reason to trust.

"Of still being—?" she prompted when I shut my mouth with a snap. "Do please go on, because right now, I can't make sense of you at all."

I could refuse, could brush her off, could accept her hatred of me as the price I had to pay to safeguard my soul rather than let her in, but that was a choice I hadn't let her have when I'd marked her.

"Good," I said. "Me. Still being... this. I don't know how to explain it to someone who isn't an Empath, but..." I leant back against the trunk of the tree and closed my eyes. "There is... so much power in being able to feel every emotion and read people's hearts, being able to... inject emotion into people, to change their behaviours, to modify people to your exact specifications or simply break them by overloading their hearts."

I paused, but she said nothing, no sound remaining but the rush of the wind through the leaves.

"We revelled in it when we were younger. We discovered we could mark people. We discovered we could give people an odd assortment of abilities, and we started testing to see how it worked. We took *joy* in the manipulation we could achieve with a single glancing touch or a drop of blood, and our enthusiasm fed one another. It was..." I drew a deep breath and let it out slowly. "Wonderful."

A little crease appeared between her brows, but there was no judgement, no anger, just curiosity, and explanation went on pouring from my lips.

"I had been sick and weak and alone all my life, and now here was this brother who loved me and this strength I'd never had, and I didn't have to be the boy who cried himself to sleep beneath a rotting blanket again. I could be whatever I wanted, whoever I wanted, and no one could stop me." I sighed. "If you had taken me back to him, I'm afraid I wouldn't have had the strength to keep telling myself that it's wrong. I have been a monster too long to ever forget how much I loved it."

When still she made no answer, I smacked my hands on my thighs. "Now why don't you tell me which daydream you liked best so we can get my death over with?"

Kimiko tilted her head to the side, a curious little sparrow twitch at odds with the fierce glare of her bright eyes. Eventually, she shook her head. "No, even if you deserve it, you don't get to escape that easily."

"Why not? You tried to."

She had turned back to the horse but looked over her shoulder at that. "What do you mean?"

"The borabark. You had it the whole time, yet you didn't use it on me when I refused to go with you. You chose not to use it."

A little smile twitched on her lips. "Yes," she said. "I suppose I did."

We had both been willing to die rather than go back to Malice, just for different reasons.

"Shall we keep moving, *Master*?" she said with sunny sarcasm. "To wherever it is you were so desperate to go."

I winced but didn't rise to the bait. Instead, I looked up at the sun peeking through the branches overhead. "South?" There was no sign of a main road or a settlement and no outline of the mountains that clustered close to Koi. "How far back did we leave the Willow Road?"

"I never joined it."

"West of the road then." I closed my eyes for a pained moment. "I think I know where we were going."

"You think? They were your orders."

"While I was unconscious." I listened to her moving around as though checking the horse over. "Where would you want to go if you were broken of body and spirit?"

"I don't know, a shrine? A physician's house? The...healing waters in Giana?"

"No. Home."

Kimiko folded her arms and flashed a brittle smile. "I wouldn't know since I haven't had one for quite a long time."

"I'm sorry."

"Still not good enough." She patted the horse's rump. "Shall we keep moving? Now you're upright, we can probably both ride and cover the ground a bit faster. I didn't find a saddle, but those are a pain with two people anyway, so if you're worried for your pair, you're welcome to ride side-saddle."

Genuinely weary, I just gave her a dour look, which earned a grin. "Am I being too cheery for you? You're more than welcome to remove the mark on me and then you can go the rest of the way on your own. I'll even let you keep the horse."

"I've never removed a mark before," I said. "I don't know how or even if it's possible."

That wiped away her smile. "Not in all that time experimenting did you think to try it?"

"You're only the second person I've ever marked. And believe me, I tried to remove the first. Many times. Many. Times."

She glared at me a long moment, but whether or not she believed me, she asked no more questions. "Fine," she said at last. "We should get moving then. I'll help you up before me, then all you need to do is not fall off, all right? Assuming you still want to go home rather than somewhere more interesting, like back to Koi to hand yourself over to my brother for execution."

"It's tempting, but no. Given dear Katashi's undoubted interest in upsetting Kisia's food supply, home is exactly where I need to be right now."

I had not been home for years, so many years I couldn't even be sure how many. I had not visited in the five years I had served Emperor Kin, despite it being expected for councillors to attend to their estates. I had not returned after escaping Malice either, and for many years before that, Mei'lian had been a more fruitful source of souls, emotion, and power.

"Well," Kimiko said as the outer wall of the compound came into sight, overgrown and missing stones. The second floor of the manor that peeked above looked even worse than I remembered. "This is a shithole."

She slid from the horse's back and approached the outer gates, both chipped and with paint peeling. She lifted the rusted knocker disdainfully. "This isn't really your family estate, is it?"

"It is, I'm afraid," I said and slowly dismounted. Everything still ached despite having recovered from the borabark over the last few days.

"But... I heard you were one of the wealthiest men at court."

"I was. Witness this fine if very ruined robe I have travelled all this way in. Purple thread is so expensive, but it looks lovely with my eyes."

Kimiko looked at my eyes as though noticing their unusual colour for the first time. "Sure. But this place looks like it fell on hard times a few generations back. I've never seen bramble sop grow this big before." She poked a branch of the thorny tangle covered in white flowers. "If nothing else, you could have been selling this off to make cheap jasmine perfume. The smell is almost the same if a bit bitter."

"I don't lack for money. I just don't use it repair my house."

"But why not?"

"Ministers of the left are very busy people, you know."

She folded her arms. "Yes, like every other lord that ever danced attendance at court. But they all have land agents and stewards and...and relatives who help maintain the proper dignity of the family."

"I'm sorry you feel my dignity is maligned by a few tumbling-down buildings."

The gate lock had long since rusted into disuse, so taking the handle, I hauled the heavy door open to a chorus of tortured metal. "Welcome to Esvar," I said with a bow.

Kimiko peered in through the open gate with a grimace. "It's even worse than I thought. Also, not to alarm you, Darius, but you seem to have some guests."

"Guests? The rats?" I stepped up beside her and found two boys peeking at us from behind one of the portico's main pillars. "Oh, no doubt they've dared each other to come up here and see if the place is haunted."

"It's not haunted, but it smells bad!" one of them called out, sniggering as his companion punched his arm.

"Don't," his friend hissed. "What if that's Lord Laroth? He might eat us."

Kimiko looked up at me. "And you said you didn't eat people."

"I don't."

"Shit, it is him! Run!" The frightened boy grabbed his friend's arm and managed to drag him a few paces before the braver of the two planted his feet and would go no farther.

"Are you really the dead lord?"

"No, I'm the alive one. Here, do you want to earn some coin?"

The boy hovered, looking from me to Kimiko and then back at his friend, who hissed that they should run before I chopped them up. "Coin?"

"Yes, they are these little round discs—"

"I know what they are," the boy snapped, and I admired his

disdain in the face of a fearful apparition. "What do you want us to do?"

"Fetch Kata Monomoro up here. Tell him I'm home and I want to see him."

The boy hovered halfway between running and staying, but his friend stopped hissing at him. "You mean Agent Monomoro?"

"Yes," I said. "Do you know where to find him?"

"Of course. What'll you pay us?"

Kimiko leant close enough to whisper. "We don't have any coins."

"Monomoro will give you each a silver from my coffers."

"A silver each? Just for running to Monomoro's house?"

"Yes," I said, clenching my teeth in gathering annoyance. "Anything to have the job done and both of you out of my courtyard. Now go on!"

They ran off between the manor and the outer wall, which meant either the side gate had been left open or part of the wall had come down.

Kimiko took our horse's reins and led it into the courtyard now empty of intruders. "I don't suppose the stables even have a solid roof."

"Oh no, I imagine the stables are the only place that has one, and if all the horse boxes aren't still in one piece, I'll be amazed. Avarice was always very particular about horses."

"Avarice? Did he work here then?"

Having been drawn into saying more than I'd meant, I followed in silence, letting my gaze sweep the all too familiar courtyard. The wisteria had taken over entirely since the last time I'd been home, and moss covered all but the Errant board the boys had been using, their pebble pieces left part way through a game.

"Darius? Is that tree growing *through* the roof?"

"Oh yes, that's been there as long as I can remember."

"I should think so given how big it is. Why in the world would anyone let a tree grow *inside* their house? It's not like you couldn't have pulled it out when it was a sapling. Or chopped it down before it got so big it would crush half the house if it fell."

I pointed her in the direction of the stables. "But it's not a normal tree," I said, walking alongside. "Its wood is too hard. You can't chop off even the thinnest twig. I don't know how it was when it was small, but some of the records mention failed attempts to pull it out. It is connected to the ground by steely roots."

Kimiko grinned over her shoulder. "Now you're making fun of me."

"Not sure how."

"A tree that can't be chopped down?"

I shrugged and pushed open the stable door. "You're welcome to find an axe and try. You can't imagine I would be sad to see half—or all—this disgusting pile collapse beneath it. The tree may crush everything and good riddance."

The stables had hardly changed, and I breathed in the scent of old hay and dust and the oil Avarice had used to clean the saddles. This had been his favourite place and he'd managed to fix it up because my father had never come in here, always leaving his horse at the door on the rare occasions he came home.

"You hate it."

"Pardon?" I said, returning from my memories to find Kimiko watching me, her head tilted in that little bird way she had.

"You hate this place. That's why you haven't done anything to look after it. You've just been hoping nature will slowly swallow it."

"It wasn't a pleasant place to grow up."

Her head tilted a little farther. "Was it like this when you were a boy?"

"Worse."

Because my father had never been home, or sometimes because he was. Both had been terrible.

"Did you father hate the place too?"

I shrugged and took down one of Avarice's old brushes. "No doubt. Or perhaps the house wishes not to be salvaged and resists all attempts to fix it."

"It's not alive."

I used to think it was.

"Darius?"

"Hmm?"

"Where do you keep going in that head of yours?"

Setting the brush to the horse's coat, I forced a smile. "Nowhere pleasant, my dear. Why don't you see if there's any dry hay?"

We had just finished seeing to the horse when the gate screeched again and the slow clop of hooves entered the courtyard. "Hello? Is anyone here?"

I strode out to find a stranger with reddened cheeks mounted upon a small horse, its mane full of the same prickles we had just been picking from our horse's hair. "Are you Kata Monomoro?"

The man looked down at me, greying brows low. "Are you Lord Darius Laroth?"

"I am. I know we've never met, but I had the honour of receiving the few letters you sent me at court."

"As I had the honour of receiving your eloquent replies." He gestured to the house. "I have complied with your wishes, as you see, my lord."

"So you have. Now I have new orders I would like you to carry out on my behalf. I would invite you into the house to discuss them, but very likely one of us would fall through the floor."

Finally seeming to accept I was who I claimed to be, he dismounted and bowed. "Is my lord wishing to set his house and lands in order? The rest of your estate and your tenants have been very well tended, I assure you, it's just this—"

"I may repair it, yes, but I have some work to do first. I'm going to need a secretary and a pair of messengers and a couple of men who know the countryside between here and Hamaba very well."

"My lord?"

"It's 'Your Excellency' or 'minister,' and don't stand there goggling at me; I have a lot of work to do."

9. ENDYMION

We left the bodies on the road and continued our journey, a smaller group than had departed Koi in the afternoon heat. Malice kept me close. He did not look at me. Did not speak. He lay upon his divan, letting his body rock with the motion of the wagon while the air thickened with opium smoke. Slowly its sweetness sucked all cares from my heart while the gentle sway of the wagon lulled me into a doze. There, strange dreams roamed the edges of my mind. Colours blurred together in the lamplight, and I touched the raised scab on my cheek, caressing the smooth surface and puckered ridges of my first Traitor's Mark.

Malice exhaled a stream of smoke, his heavy-lidded eyes making him appear half asleep. Outside the shuttered windows, another village passed. One hundred and eighty-one souls, momentarily distinguished by proximity. Soon they would fade into the mass of life like all the others, leaving only a handful of Vices at the touch of my latent Empathy. Silent. Sullen. Fearful.

Having lost all concept of time, I knew not how long we travelled before the wagon stopped. Muffled voices sounded outside and the door opened, pale, hazy light drifting in. Then Avarice, his large, dark form blocking the doorway.

"We've arrived, Master," he said.

Malice let out a long sigh. "Delightful."

"There's no sign of Conceit or Folly, Master."

"Not so delightful, yes? We will wait here for news."

"And if it doesn't come?"

He clicked his tongue. "Not a thing to be suggested, yes? They will come."

He will not leave me.

The whisper came without touch, shearing through the air. The words Malice had left unspoken. *Darius would never die to escape me, could not, even if he tried.*

"Staring at me, Endymion?" Malice said.

"Yes." My tongue felt lazy and fat. "What if you're wrong? What if he dies?"

Malice froze in the act of curling his ponytail around his finger. Then, lifting the opium pipe, he tapped it against his forehead. "Stay out, yes?"

"Then don't shout."

A smile flickered on his lips. "What good advice, yes? Hope?"

The young Vice came to the door, his face pale and his eyes dark-rimmed.

"Show Endymion to his room."

"Master," he murmured but did not wait.

Trying to shake the lingering fumes, I stirred my limbs to action, each heavy with a weight I had never known. I gripped the panelling with trembling hands. Outside, there were eleven marked Vices and twenty-one unmarked men, and another sixty-two farther up the mountain. The numbers flowed through my head as easily as thoughts. A village of seventy souls sat at the edge of my Sight and the vast bulk of Kisia was at my fingertips, its precise numbers eluding my touch.

"I believe I asked you to leave, yes?"

I found I had frozen mid rise and blinked.

"Try to stay with us, yes?" Malice said. "I don't know how to bring you back." He waved a hand toward the door. "Go, clean yourself up. Eat. Rest. And Endymion? Don't let my Vices eat you, yes?"

"Yes," I said, stepping into the pale haze of a new day.

The wagon stood in a courtyard beneath the boughs of a large tree. Men in common peasant clothes were unloading supplies from beneath the running board, while the Vices rubbed down their jittery horses. Entirely in his element, Avarice was taking the time to pass his hand over each velvety nose, murmuring words of comfort under his breath.

A squat tower blocked some of the morning sky, its stones speckled. It looked like part of an old castle, its rampart tumbling. The scrubby hillside was littered with the jutting remains of old walls and a second collapsed tower adorned the next spur.

Hope stood at the edge of the courtyard, staring back the way we had come. There the road wound down the mountainside and into a dense oak forest, its canopy a green blanket that seemed to stretch over Kisia all the way to the rising sun.

Out there was a place he had once called home and a man he had once been.

"Where are we?" I asked, forcing my lips to frame words.

"One of Rina's many old outposts."

As though my question had reminded him of his orders, he turned toward the tower. Dodging moving men, he made his way across a wide courtyard to the open doors, not seeming to care whether I followed. Most of the Vices ignored him, turning their shoulders and stepping out of his way, but Spite, a long gash still bloody upon his face, stood his ground, forcing the shrinking Hope to go around him. His scowl followed us, burning into the back of my head.

The gods will judge.

I followed Hope through the large doors and into a dark hall, its stones smoke-blackened. Beams the colour of rusted iron twisted across the roof, each one hung with dozens of dark lanterns. They might once have made grand constellations, but now the old paper covers were moth-eaten and barely hung together.

"Hope," I said, as he led the way along a winding passage full of tight spaces. "I'm sorry, I—"

He lifted a shaking hand. "Don't." His pace quickened, fingers clenching into fists.

He led the way to an upper gallery where arrow slits let in shafts of light and thin partitions separated one alcove from the next, each containing a sleeping mat and nothing more. "Here is your room," Hope said, stopping at one of the openings. "In fact you could have any of these. Dead men need no beds."

He let out a strained laugh and turned to leave, but I gripped his arm, my fingers closing around fabric. Although it wasn't his skin I touched, Hope yanked his arm free. "Don't touch me."

"They attacked us, Hope."

"And that is an excuse? What man deserves to die like that? Next time you want to kill people and feel powerful, leave me out of it."

I let him go, watched him walk away out of sight along the narrow gallery. *Next time you want to kill people and feel powerful.* What had he seen in our connection? Had I really wanted to do it? I hadn't thought so. But I hadn't hesitated either.

In my alcove, the sleeping mat called to me. I couldn't remember when I had last slept. It felt like weeks.

Sleep.

And if the gods judged, I might never wake.

———————

I woke. Something wasn't right. A change in the air, a whisper in the warm afternoon. I sat up, suddenly alert. Hope was standing in the doorway. "The Master wants you to eat," he said, meeting my gaze.

"Why does he always send you?"

"Because he's a snob."

"Eh?"

"My father was a duke, and I have a pretty face. Conceit's father was a merchant. Ire's, a blacksmith."

"And you're useful."

Hope bowed ironically. "Yes. I heal the minds of new Vices, which is why the Master takes me everywhere with him."

"You are your name—Hope, to be given and taken. That's a formidable power."

"And the breath of a beetle compared to you."

He went out on the words, leaving me to follow along the upper gallery. Distant voices echoed below, but though it sounded like a meal was in progress, Hope led the way up a creaky flight of stairs instead of down. At the top, a second gallery continued around the building, at some places little more than a walkway hanging precariously over the lower hall. Hope strode fearlessly across these, but I found my steps slowing, shuffling as I tried not to look down.

"Where are we going?" I said as he mounted the first of a series of ladders.

"Up. You'll see."

Breathing deeply and forcing myself not to look down, I followed him up until the final ladder spat us out on the roof. Wind rippled my half robe as I straightened, and I gripped Hope's arm for fear it would blow me over the edge.

"There's no parapet," I said, still holding his arm.

"No, but you won't fall. Are you afraid of heights? Do you want to go back down?"

I did want to go back down, but the middle of the flat roof had been cleared of rubble and a spread of food lay waiting on a cloth. "Did you bring all that up here?"

"I like it up here," Hope said. "It's peaceful and the view reminds me of home, just with less ocean. We can go down though if you prefer. I just thought you might not want to eat with the others after . . ." He let out a huff of breath. "I wanted to apologise for what I said earlier too. I know you didn't have a choice. It was use my ability or let us all die, and despite how often I think we deserve to die, I don't really want to, so thank you. And I'm sorry. Not only for what I said but because you had to . . . feel it. The hopelessness. It's awful."

Having let out all those words, he deflated, his shoulders hunching like a dog expecting trouble. And even had I been desperately afraid of heights, I could not have climbed down. "I'm . . . I'm sorry too," I said. "For using it. For making you use it."

He nodded at the weathered stone beneath our feet, and long seconds passed in awkward silence before I realised I was still holding his arm. I let go, steadying myself as the wind went on gusting around us.

"There's nothing too exciting to eat, but you must be hungry," Hope said, walking over to sit before the spread of dishes. "The wine spilled a bit, but Rancour was already going to be mad at me for stealing it, so it doesn't matter."

I joined him, trying not to think about how close the edge of the roof was. "Do you get along with any of the Vices?"

"Only Ire. Most of the others dislike me for one reason or another. Though I suspect in Rancour's case it's because I helped him heal when he was marked."

I looked a question and Hope shrugged. "Some people hate anyone who has seen their vulnerabilities. Hate anyone who even knows they have vulnerabilities."

"Don't we all have them?"

"I've always thought so. Surely you know so." He took an egg-and-millet fritter from the spread and began tearing it into small pieces. Jian would have slapped my hand for so childish an eating habit, but I just watched Hope's deft fingers work, honoured that he was comfortable being so honestly himself in my presence. Unable to say so, I picked one up and began doing the same. When he noticed, he grinned. "What's it like being an Empath? The Master never talks about it, he just…disappears sometimes. Mentally, not physically."

I shrugged one shoulder. "I don't know what it's like not being an Empath. The world has just always been loud."

"Do you feel everyone?"

Another shrug, and able to feel him clearer than ever up here away from the other Vices, I couldn't meet his gaze. "Yes, but some more than others. Katashi, for example, is very loud. For someone who has suffered as much as he has, he doesn't hide away from his feelings."

"Is anyone quiet?"

"Avarice."

Hope had been holding a piece of fritter while he listened, but he laughed and popped it in his mouth at that. "Oh, no one understands Avarice. He's not marked, did you know that? I mean, he must have been once, I guess, because he can do the whole stone skin thing, but he could disobey the Master if he wanted. He could walk away and the Master wouldn't be able to stop him. But he doesn't."

"Really? I assumed you were all…" I grimaced rather than finish my words.

"Oh, the rest of us are. Stuck here against our will for all eternity." He put another piece of fritter in his mouth and spoke around it. "Or at least until some injury or illness puts the Master out of his misery."

Misery. Despite Malice's façade of calm, predatory confidence, no word had ever suited him more. Hope, who had no special Sight to draw upon, had seen more even than I had, and for the first time, I wondered what he saw when he looked at me. Another question

I could not ask added to the pile of words I could not say, and for a few minutes, we ate in silence, both staring out at the far horizon.

The wind had not abated and it went on blustering around us as we ate. Every now and then we would fall into short bursts of conversation only to be silent as long. It wasn't an awkward silence but a companionable one, something of the seeds of understanding having been sown in blood that night upon the road.

"How long do you think we're staying here?" I asked as Hope finished off the last slice of dried plum. "Just tonight or until there's news of Darius?"

Darius, his soul had drawn no nearer since we arrived. If anything, he felt smaller, quieter, farther away.

"I don't know." Hope began gathering the remains of the meal into the centre of the cloth. "Whatever it may appear, the Master doesn't tell me things. What I know, I guess or overhear, just like everyone else. He'll be waiting for you though."

"What, now?"

A mischievous smile lifted the corner of Hope's mouth. "He didn't tell me to make sure you ate. He told me to fetch you to him."

"Doesn't it hurt to disobey?"

"Proper orders, yes, not lazy requests with no immediacy. It might start hurting if he begins to worry though, so we probably shouldn't keep him waiting much longer."

I reluctantly agreed and helped him pack the dishes into a bundle he could sling over his shoulder. Together we climbed down, leaving the sense of companionship behind with the tumultuous wind. Away from the solitude of the rooftop, Hope tensed into his usual melancholy self, speaking not another word until we reached Malice's room. I thought of a dozen things I could say to bring him out of himself, but discarded them all, his gloom contagious.

"Thank you for eating with me," he said as he stopped outside Malice's door. "It was very kind of you."

"Kind? I—"

Hope tapped twice on the door and pushed it open. "Endymion is here, Master."

At the far end of the room, Malice stood at a narrow window looking out over the forest. With one hand resting lightly on the sill, he stroked the old stone, his thoughts far away.

"Do come in, Endymion," he said, not looking around. "Sit down, yes?"

Able to do nothing but grimace at Hope, I went in, leaving him to close the door behind me. It was a small room, airless and bright with lantern light. Outside, the sun still reigned, but here, a multitude of lanterns staved off the castle's artificial night.

I did not sit but hovered inside the doorway. Malice ran a hand through his long hair. "Do you believe in the gods, Endymion?"

"Yes." Jian would have been proud at the speed of my answer.

"Do you believe that they exist? Or that they do everything they are said to do? They are two different things, yes? Do you believe the gods watch over us? That they hear our prayers? That they receive our sacrifices?"

Beginning to wonder where his line of questioning was leading, I said, "I suppose so."

"You suppose? That is certainly not the answer of a devout man, yes?"

"Your point?"

"I have not yet made one. Do the gods judge us when we die? Do they decide whether our souls deserve the hells?"

"If they don't, they should."

Malice nodded slowly, still looking out the window rather than at me. "Do you believe that Emperor Kin is a god?"

"No."

He chuckled in his odd, humourless way. "The speed with which you answered gives me joy, yes? How about Emperor Tianto, was he a god?"

"His head was cut off."

"Does that preclude him being a deity?"

"He was a man."

"And Emperor Lan?"

I nodded.

Malice finally turned from the window, lifting one of his immaculate brows. "Not a god?"

"No."

"And did they do well by our beloved Kisia?"

"Where are all these questions leading?"

He pressed a finger to his lips and hushed me gently. "Do not ruin it now; you are doing so very well, yes? Just answer the question."

"How should I know?" I said. "I was a child when Emperor Lan died and a child when Emperor Tianto died. I have only one emperor on whom to base my opinion."

"Then do so."

"The answer is still that I don't know. It seems to function."

Another dry chuckle. "It functions, yes? How well put. Our glorious empire...functions. There was a time when Darius had a dream for this empire, to return it to glory—Kisia, the centre of the world. It was once, but time moves on and we fall away. We fight amongst ourselves, we fight for tradition, when all the time the outside world presses in upon us, and it is all due to one cause, yes? No longer are we ruled by gods."

It was hard to mistake his meaning, but I asked the question all the same. "What gods?"

"Us, Endymion. We are the gods, yes?"

"No."

"Think a little. Can you feel another's pain?"

"Yes."

"Can you feel their hatred and their love?"

I paused, wishing I could speak a different answer. "Yes."

"Can you reach inside the heart of a man and see him for what he truly is?"

Letting out a long breath, I nodded.

"What are these abilities but those of a god?"

"But gods are infallible."

"So you are infallible, more so than any court, than any jury of men. You know what is right and what is wrong and you can read it, black and white, in the hearts of men."

I could, but like I had told Katashi, it was not that simple—not without touch. And even then, could I ever really see all there was to see, understand all there was to understand?

"I'm not a god," I said aloud, trying to silence the part of me that liked the sound of the title. The part of me that revelled in my power. "I'm not."

Malice moved from the window, the worn floor scuffing beneath his step. The incense had burned itself out and, in no hurry, he took a fresh stick from a narrow wooden box and set it in the spider-shaped burner, its eight legs gathered to pinch the stick in place.

"In fact you are, in every sense of the word," he said, lighting the incense from one of his many lanterns. "Come, look at this."

Motioning for me to join him, Malice knelt at the low table. A number of scrolls sat in a jumble at one end, each with a crimson ribbon and the Otako crest, signed and dated. "I believe our father burned your papers to protect your identity, but there are other copies, yes? And this."

He held a scroll out to me, sharp eyes watching from beneath heavy lids. I took it and unrolled it upon the table. Inky pikes stared back, and below the Otako crest, the heavily formed characters of an official court document.

In the eyes of the gods, I, Emperor Lan Otako, second of my name, Lord Protector of the Imperial Expanse of Kisia, hereby lay claim to the parentage of one Prince Takehiko Otako, my fourth son and heir, by the womb of my wife, Empress Li Otako. Any who speaks otherwise errs in the face of their God and Emperor and will henceforth be treated as traitors to Emperor, truth, and Empire.

It was signed and dated with a heavy brush, the Imperial Seal unmistakable in glossy crimson.

"When Emperor Lan signed that, he sealed your future, yes? You are Takehiko Otako, god emperor of Kisia, and when the people learn of your return, few will be able to deny your right to the throne. Lord Nyraek Laroth may have been your father, but you are Emperor Lan's heir. Not Grace Tianto, not Katashi, not Kin. Not even Hana. You."

I let the scroll go and it rolled up, once again hiding its words from the world. Every breath seemed harder to draw. "And if they knew it, I'd be dead. Even more dead than I would have been without this piece of paper."

"In your delightful cousin's hands, perhaps," he said, slowly re-rolling the scroll more neatly. "But I think you underestimate Emperor Kin's desire to *appear* honourable. Honour is wealth."

"The Ts'ai motto?"

He smiled in the way Jian sometimes had when my academic aptitude surprised him. "Indeed. He wrote it himself, you know. Common families have no mottos, but an Imperial family needs one, yes? Honour is wealth. He swore an oath to Emperor Lan, to your father, and to you. And while he can claim Katashi is the son of a traitor and therefore cannot be heir to the throne, you, my dear Takehiko, are no such thing. According to this"—he tapped the scroll—"you are not even the bastard we all know you are."

I thought of the fierce Emperor Kin from the meeting with Katashi, the pair of them glaring at one another through time itself. "If I showed up at the palace demanding my throne, he would still kill me."

"If you went alone and no one knew you existed, then of course he would. He's not a fool, yes? That is why tomorrow, you will be dressed as befits your station, and once preparations are complete, we will travel to Mei'lian, the official retainers of Emperor Take-hiko, fourth of his name, Emperor of Kisia."

He made his bow while kneeling, long hair falling to brush the tabletop.

The thrill of such an image shivered through me. The position. The power. The chance to belong, to go back home, to be what I had been born to be. But whatever the piece of paper said, I was not an Otako.

Those soldiers had died in the dark, choked by the night that poured into their hearts. And worse than the pain, worse than the sound of slicing flesh had been the silence—no cries, no keening agony. Those men had wanted to die so much they welcomed the opportunity to bleed out slowly, lying face down in the dirt.

"You enjoyed it, yes?" he said as though he had read my thoughts.

I thought of Hope. "No."

He chuckled. "You can't lie to me, Brother. I know. And soon you won't even lie to yourself."

You are a monster.

The words were there, sounding in his silky whisper.

Monster.

People had said the same of Darius, but I had seen beneath his skin and knew there was more to him than the darkness at his core. He had tried to save me the only way he could.

"No," I said again, swallowing the memory of his soul at my fingertips, his emotions almost as fruitful as Hope's ability had been. "I don't want to be an emperor and I don't want to be your puppet."

"A poor choice of word, Takehiko. I see no strings. I see no hand thrust inside you to turn your head and make you speak, yes?"

"Not yet. So I'll leave now, while I can."

Eleven. Twenty-one. Sixty-two. And back down the hillside, one hundred and fifty-one Pikes lying dead in their own blood, shreds of their souls left to float on the air like so much dust.

Malice started to laugh, beginning as a snigger and rising to a belly laugh full of genuine amusement. "Oh, you think you can just walk away. Surely even you are not so naive, Endymion. You're losing yourself, yes?"

Seventy. Thirty-two. Six. One hundred and four.

"You don't need to answer," Malice said, taking my hand in his and beginning to trace the lines of the Empathic Mark born onto my skin. "I told you about our father. Empathy has driven many men mad. You think you won't go so far, yes? You think you aren't naturally so cruel, yes? No." He dropped my hand. "You will need to be chained down before the end. If you want to take Kisia to the grave with you, then by all means, walk away now."

His words were an echo of my dark thoughts, but he was enjoying my pain. I had no doubt he would chain me rather than help me, able only to see a future in which my body clad in crimson furthered his cause.

"Why me?" I said. "Why can I do things that you can't?"

"Whisperers are different."

"Whisperers?"

Malice made a face. "What boring conversations you force on me, yes? Another day, another day, when I am not so weary of your company that I can almost understand Darius's desire to send you, branded, into Chiltae."

"He did that because he had to."

"And I do what I do because I must. We are all servants of necessity. "

"He's not coming."

Malice froze in the act of rising, the loose end of his bone ribbon tapping on the table. "Say that again."

"Darius. He's not coming."

"How do you know?"

"I don't know how I know. I can just...feel him..." I pressed my fist to my heart, a gesture that sent a flash of anger across Malice's face. "You said that connections leave a piece of us inside each other. I almost took so much of him in Koi that he died, so..."

His expression darkened, his whole body stiffening, and a laugh bubbled to my lips. "You hate that. You hate that someone else could have anything of him when he should be all yours. Well console yourself that he is alive, but he's trying to put as much distance between you and him as he can."

I rose from the table. "I'm done," I said. "I'm leaving. If I'm going to be anyone's puppet, I would far rather be his than yours."

Malice grabbed my hand, the tips of his fingers digging in hard. "No. No, Brother, you are not going anywhere."

The connection was not of my making, its touch aggressive, alien, a painful pulse shooting up my arm. My lips parted in a gasp and I tried to pull away, but Malice's fingers clamped tighter. "Don't fight me, Endymion," he said. "Or I will make it hurt."

I could not fight. I had no shield as Darius had, no control over the Empathy that leached from my body. There was nothing I could do but scream as Malice's heart rammed into mine with all the violence of a beast in the night.

You're mine now, Endymion, the whisper said. *A god will rule this empire. And I will rule you.*

"No!"

I threw everything I had back at him, a tangle of memories and emotions stampeding through the Empathy with which he pierced me. His grip faltered, and I tore my hand free, backing away across the room. Malice slumped onto the table, his cheek landing upon an imperial seal, its crimson wax seeming to ooze from between his lips.

"Shit," I breathed, pressing a hand to my chest. There was something there inside me, something clenched around my heart, but it felt jagged and unfinished like unhewn stone. "Malice?"

He didn't answer and I dared not touch him.

"I am not a monster," I said, backing toward the door. "I'm not. I'm not."

Malice didn't move. Didn't so much as twitch. I had to get out of there. I had to find Darius. He was the only person who could help me now.

I hurried into the empty passage and looked around. Hope was somewhere high in the castle, the call of his soul unmistakable, but even as I started in his direction, I stopped. However he felt about Malice, however he felt about me, he was constrained to obey and I could not ask him to suffer. I needed to escape before anyone saw me.

I thought of returning to my alcove first, but nothing awaited me there except a rumpled sleeping mat. I had owned possessions once, a change of robe, a second sash, and a book of prayers with which I had learnt to read. And my bow. It had been nothing to Hacho but had cost Jian more than he could afford. Archery had come naturally to me as the other six arts had not, and everywhere we went, Jian had scoured morning markets for old arrows and half-used blocks of wax, for worn leather gloves and spools of string. But those things had belonged to a different man. The branding had changed everything.

Whisperer. Was I the only one who could hear the world? Hear its thoughts, its troubles, and its wrongs? Was that what Malice had meant? Oh no, don't think about Malice. He could be dead. Had I killed my brother?

You're losing yourself, yes?

Darius had called me a Whisperer too. He knew. But he also knew how to bury his Empathy, had hidden it for years, had *chosen* not to use it.

I went to the stairs. They creaked beneath my weight, but from the landing to the narrow passage, I knew myself alone. In the main hall, the sound of laughter wafted toward the open doors as I stood beneath the arch, the wind tugging my hair. Avarice was the only soul nearby—outside the stables, talking to the horses. He had thrown off his black cloak but wore his sickle at his side, his broad shoulders squared like a stone statue.

No horse then, but if I was quick, he might not see me leave.

I strode swiftly out into the courtyard. Malice's wagon sat beneath the oak tree, its windows staring upon me as I passed. Leaves rustled overhead. More danced across the pitted stones, but Avarice did not call to me, did not look around, too busy with the horses to care for men.

A steep slope dropped from the edge of the courtyard, long shadows cutting the rocky scree. Here and there, square boulders protruded from the ground at odd angles, every face covered in carvings. They might have been part of the castle once, but now they were just debris.

From the last buckled flagstone, I stepped onto the loose rocks and my feet slid, stones cascading around me. They scraped my palms as I tried to steady myself, snatching at tufts of grass to slow my pace. No footsteps, no shouts, nothing but the clatter of sliding rocks and the call of cicadas.

When I finally reached the bottom, I stumbled backward onto the track, my sandals full of stones. I took a moment to shake them free while my Empathy flowed. At the top of the hill, the castle looked shadowy in the half-light, owning no individuals, only a mass of souls. I could not feel Malice, nor had anyone followed me.

Dregs of sunlight clung to the trees. The road would take me back the way we had come, past the small collection of towns and villages around Koi, then on to the Willow Road, but my destination was a person not a place. Darius was south, so south I would go.

I walked quickly through the fading twilight. I had brought no lantern, but even as a child, I had not been afraid of the dark. For as long as I could remember, the constant bombardment of emotions had troubled my sleep, and although exhaustion always took me eventually, I had often preferred to roam while Jian slept. The night was benign. It was people I feared.

The breathy sound of my laugh joined the breeze. I had thought my Empathy strong then, with those little dribbles into a closed mind.

I kept walking, unseen creatures scurrying from my steps. It ought to have been peaceful with only the night birds for company, and it was until my chest began to tighten, slivers of pain edging into my awareness. I concentrated on the sound of my feet crunching on the stones and tried not to think about it.

My steps faltered, all sound dying beneath the roar of my pulse.

"No." I gritted my teeth as the forest spun around me, every tree clustering close. The mark throbbed, owning its own heartbeat. Malice filled my chest, even his smell seeming to cling to me.

I am the only one who can save you from yourself, yes?

I hit the ground, pain shooting through my knees.

You're mine now, Endymion. A god will rule this empire. And I will rule you.

I crawled forward on hands and knees, deafened by the roar. The mark tightened. And from the night came the sound of Malice laughing.

"You will not...rule me," I said, forcing the words out, rocks cutting into my skin as I dragged myself along the ground. The pain was like nothing I had ever experienced—like a thousand hands slowly smothering life. I rolled over, wheezing. Twinkling stars laughed down from a patch of velvet sky, and I laughed back, a manic gasp as I thought of Malice slumped upon the table. "Are you dead? Please be dead."

Time blurred. I owned no sense beyond the pain as I tried to push myself along the road with my feet, stones cutting into my back.

"Looks like he's come as far as he can," a voice said, barely audible over the thunder in my ears. I knew the voice. I knew its owner's scowling features, knew its wide nose and its dark skin and its square-set shoulders.

Lantern light touched the shifting branches.

"The Master must have marked him." Another voice I knew well, mild and polite, its fine features always melancholic, but he had smiled at me. A sandal crunched on the stones and Hope's face appeared above me. "Endymion?"

"He won't hear you," Avarice said. "We'd best just pick him up and take him back."

A hand touched mine, and for a blessed moment, the pain rushed out through the connection. It was snatched away, and the pain poured back.

"What did you do that for, fool?"

Hope's face disappeared. "I wanted to see if it's the same for him as it is for us."

"Of course it is."

"I'm not so sure. It feels different to how mine feels. I don't think it's as strong. He might be able to hear us."

Come on! You're not even trying. Break it! Hope's voice sounded in my head.

Hands gripped me under my arms, dragging me away from the tower. The pain was like a thousand silk strings tightening, cutting into my limbs.

"What are you doing?" Avarice growled.

"You saw him kill all those men," Hope said, breathless by my ear. "He deserves to die."

Fight, damn it! Break it! I know you can.

"That isn't your choice to make."

Hope went on dragging me, the pain shearing through my flesh. "It shouldn't have been his either."

Fill it with hate, he added in my head. *Hate is what hurts him most. Hate and abandonment.*

"The Master will kill you if you let him die, you fool."

"Let him," Hope snapped. "What is life worth if this is all that's left?"

Do it, Endymion, now!

Hate. I had plenty of that. I pressed my fist to my chest.

Yes! Do it! Break it!

A scream ripped from my lips. Someone tried to prise my hand from my heart but was forced away, the two Vices shouting at one another though I could make out no words. Agony was all I had— no body, no limbs, no heart, just the pain and the dreadful knowledge that I did not want to be alone.

"You are alone!" I shouted. "No one wants you!"

Light flashed behind my eyes. Malice's grip tightened, his long fingers curling like claws. *You're mine, Takehiko. You cannot leave.*

"I can, and I will! I hate you!"

You can't leave, yes? You're a monster.

The mark's shadowy fingers squeezed tighter still, and I poured all the hate I had into it, my heartbeat laboured. "You're the monster!" Its fingers bent back, bones cracking.

No!

"Yes!"

Don't leave me.

"Darius already did."

The mark shattered like glass, its shards slicing through my body. Squeezing my eyes shut, I curled up, clasping my knees to my chest, until slowly, the pain began to ebb. Blood trickled down my side, oozing out with every heaving breath.

When I opened my eyes, I found the canopy shifting amid lantern light. Avarice and Hope stared down at me, their jaws slack. Then Hope smiled.

Run, Endymion. Run.

I rolled, slipping on stones as I scrambled to my feet. Avarice threw out his hand, but I ducked, kicking his lantern as I started to run. It bounced across the track, lighting the edge of a sharp slope before its fragile frame snapped beneath my sandal.

In darkness, I skidded down the slope, dry leaves and acorns cascading around me. I knew there were trees and rocks and nests of saplings, but only the memory of them remained without the light to see them by. Rough bark scratched my arm as I narrowly missed a tree, and rather than run into one, I slowed, listening for pursuit over the pounding of my heart.

Avarice. The pulse of his anger gave him away more surely than the sound of his feet. I could outrun him, but Malice would send more Vices to scour the trees. On horseback, they would catch me before ever I reached Koi.

I let my Empathy hunt their hearts in the darkness. Avarice was nearby, but Hope had not followed, had remained on the track with the horses.

I doubled back, using the call of Hope's soul to lead the way. Blood was dripping from my chest and every limb ached, but desperation pushed me on. If they took me back, Malice wouldn't risk me escaping again.

You will need to be chained down before the end.

I broke into a jog, sandals sinking into the soft loam.

At the top of the slope, I slowed again, able to feel the call of

Hope's heart, as loud as the cry of a hawk owl robbed of its prey. He was close. A horse snorted and I crept forward, rolling heel to toe, straining my eyes as the outline of two animals emerged from the night. One snorted and the other backed, but lunging the last step, I touched the closest and pushed my Empathy through its thick coat.

I'd never tried to connect with a horse before, and for a long moment I stood stunned. It owned a soul like no man I had ever seen. There were no flailing strings of memory or emotion, no self-ishness or deceit; the horse was everything it was and nothing more, just a neat parcel of instincts and behaviours, easily understood and beautiful to behold. I combed through it, fascinated, and the horse nuzzled my cheek, fear set aside as we learnt to understand one another. He had a name for himself—the One Who Flies.

"Kaze then," I whispered, running my hand through his mane. "For the clear sky."

Sharp points dug into the small of my back and I froze.

"I should kill you," Hope said, his voice low. "That would hurt the Master the most and by the gods do I want him to suffer."

"I know." I did not turn or take my hand from Kaze's mane. "I'm sorry. If I could take you with me, I would."

Hope lowered the sickle and I turned. In the dark, I could just make out his face, a mirror to his emotions: half sadness, half pain. "Go. Get out of here," he said.

"But you must obey. Will you be...all right?"

He gave a mirthless laugh. "You think Malice would let me die? I'm too useful. Perhaps I deserve some pain for what I am."

My heart ached at his words and I touched his cheek, a brief graze of skin because I could risk no more. "You don't, and I'm sorry. I did not want you to have to suffer for me."

"No, but that's my choice."

He smiled his melancholy smile, and for a long moment we

stood there, two shadowy figures in the dark. Who knows how long we might have stayed so had no other soul approached, breaking upon our strange peace.

"Avarice is coming."

Hope patted Kaze's neck. "You had better go then," he said. "Take my horse. I call him Hishan."

"I like that name, but it's not what he calls himself. Deep down."

"Can you read my heart too?"

I had set my foot in the stirrup, but I looked back and held out my hand. Hope put his into it without hesitation, and for a beautiful instant, we connected, the flare of his soul touched with such longing, such painful melancholy that it twisted my heart. Yet I never wanted to let go.

"Your name is Arata," I said when he took his hand from mine. "You were born this man and you will be him again."

He did not answer, just stood back and let me climb into the saddle.

"Hope!" Avarice's shout came through the trees. "Hope? Where are you, you little shit?"

"I'm here, Avarice," the Vice returned, raising his voice. "With Endymion. He's borrowing my horse, so I'm taking yours." He pulled the reins over the horse's head as he spoke. Avarice snapped harsh words to the night, their foreign syllables failing to hide their vulgarity.

"I'll see you again," Hope said, climbing into the saddle with ease. "Keep hope, Endymion."

"You fucking little—!" Avarice snarled, momentarily blocking a bolt of moonlight as he sprinted toward us. "Vatassa matas! I will break you!"

Avarice's horse reared, loath to go with its new owner, but Hope had skilled hands and managed to wheel it around. "Go!" he called. "Get out of here."

Kaze needed no goading. He started forward, breaking into a trot as Avarice lunged for the saddle. A strap slipped through his fingers, and he tumbled onto the track in my wake.

"Get back here!"

Wind whipped past my ears as Kaze sped to a gallop.

"Malice will fucking *eat* you!"

10. HANA

For many days, Katashi's army made uneventful progress. Every morning the camp was packed, and every day we travelled until mid-afternoon before stopping to set it up again. Every evening I joined Katashi's council, and every night he came to my tent, though by sunrise he was always gone. Messages came frequently from scouts and informants and the other half of his army, as well as from towns and cities choosing sides in a war that kept growing.

By the time we met our first resistance in the Valley, a clear border had developed. Katashi held the lands north of the Nuord River—Koi, Suway, Jinanton, Ji—Kin those to the south of it, and along the Willow Road fighting had broken out as far south as Yagi.

With Kin's battalions occupied maintaining this border, it was no surprise that Katashi's first skirmish was against an outpost garrison. They had been set up to protect Kisia from the ever-restless mountain tribes and had done well under Kin, their pay and conditions the best in the empire.

We met a combined force of them in the field west of Hamaba.

We was the wrong term, however, as Katashi had been good to his word and left me behind in camp. I had considered riding out anyway, but however much I might hate it, he had been right. I was not trained for war. But I was not trained to sit idly by either. I tried not to worry, tried not to be restless, but hours without word of the battle were enough to wear down even the calmest soul. And then the wounded started to arrive.

At first there were just a few, a mix of imperial soldiers and Pikes who had dragged themselves from the field alone or with the help of comrades. Physicians brought from Koi were ready and waiting, and once more I was able to witness imperial military precision at work. The hundreds of camp labourers who travelled with us were their own little army, supplying water and medicine and clean cloths, but also carrying screaming men and lifeless bodies slung between them. They worked so quickly, I might have been wholly transfixed by their efficiency had I not been watching for Katashi.

"If anything happens to him on the field, we'll hear about it long before he shows up," Shin said, joining me at the edge of the camp as more and more wounded soldiers arrived like a trail of ants.

"You're not worried?"

Shin pulled a face, his scars making the expression harder to interpret.

"You are worried."

"I am always worried, Your Grace," he said. "I've been with him a long time."

Happy to take my mind off the battle, I looked up at him. "How long is a long time? I think you said so once, but I cannot recall."

"Since before his father died."

"He has told me…some of the difficulties they had after that. You must have been one of the few who stayed with them through the hard times."

"The only one."

He said it very simply, but my throat constricted around unexpected emotion. "That's devotion."

Shin shrugged. "I have debts."

"Then by all means, Shin, go out there and look after him. You cannot think I am in any danger here."

For a long moment, he met my stare, only to shake his head and look away without reply. Something in his silence made my stomach drop, but though I wanted to ask what he meant by it, I could not get the words to my lips. It was easier to watch the wounded arrive than to consider what debt he was referring to.

"How fares the battle?" I asked the next upright soldier to trail past us, supporting a comrade with a great gash in his side. "Here, Shin, no— Wen. Wen! Help this man to the physicians."

Wen, who had been anxiously watching each new arrival, gladly took over, leaving the heavily breathing soldier to stretch now he was free of his burden. He looked to have a few cuts himself, but nothing that needed immediate attention.

"Well?" I said when his answer was nothing but a grimace. "How fares the battle? Did any of them surrender?"

"No, Your Grace." He rubbed his forehead, smearing blood. "Well, rightly they weren't given the chance to, but, well...no. The battle ought soon be over, I'd say. We had them well pushed back."

"No chance to?" I could not recall any mention at the evening meetings that surrender would not be offered. These weren't mountain folk or Chiltaens; they were Kisian soldiers. But for the luck of the draw, many of them could have been fighting on our side of the battlefield.

When the soldier vouchsafed no answer, I said, "Well, I am glad to hear it should be over soon; these are some heavy casualties."

"The others have fared much worse, I can assure you."

He seemed to think I was maligning our army's skill, and surrounded by so many dead and dying men, I had not the heart to allay his wounded pride. Instead, I forced a smile. "Then I guess it will be a busy night for their healers."

"Oh yes, Your Grace. The garrison sawbone will be a busy bee."

Seeming to want to escape as much as I wanted him to go, the soldier bowed and thanked me and fell in with a group of camp labourers jogging out to pick up more wounded.

As soon as they were out of earshot, I turned on Shin. "Did he say, 'sawbone,' as in one physician?"

"Sometimes an outpost has two if a local boy wants to apprentice," he rumbled in reply. "My old friend—"

He stopped himself. At any other time, I would have demanded he finish his anecdote in the hope of understanding him better, but all I could do was stare. "One? And maybe an apprentice if they're lucky?"

"No garrison needs more in peacetime, Your Grace."

"And when it's very suddenly not peacetime?"

"If there's no town nearby, then men die."

"Kisian men."

Shin scowled at me, yet I was sure he must see the problem. "Yes."

"Kisian soldiers who have given their lives to their empire."

"Yes."

I drew myself up. "I need you to find out where they are taking their wounded, Shin. And get Wen. And the horses. We are going for a ride."

We arrived at Hamaba in the late afternoon to find the town square packed with injured soldiers. The town was full, yet more were being carried in from the battle, and many would not even have made it this far.

Priests and physicians were making their way through the masses laid out beneath the searing sun, but there were not enough and men were suffering.

"Find somewhere to tie up our horses," I commanded as I dismounted at the edge of the disarray.

"These aren't our soldiers," Shin said, eyeing the square from the saddle.

"I don't care who they fight for, they're Kisian. We ought to help where we can. Wen, come with me, let's see what they need most."

Leaving Shin with the horses, Wen and I skirted the edge of the town square, past soldiers propped against the outer walls of inns and teahouses, or just laid upon the stones. Some were still, others writhed and moaned and screamed, the scent of blood and spilled guts hanging over it all like a haze.

"Excuse me," I said, approaching the first healer I saw. "In what way can we be of assistance?"

"I... I don't know, I'm just... trying to do what I can."

"Is no one organising the efforts here? No guard commander or mayor?"

"No, my lady, I'm afraid they were both out in the field and... we weren't expecting so many. I... I'm sorry, I'm still a bit...." He passed a hand over his eyes.

"I understand," I said. "And thank you for answering my questions. I have only one more. Is there a reason these men are being left to lie out in the sun rather than taken inside?"

The man gave a bitter laugh. "The townspeople fear the wrath of Emperor Katashi's army if they harbour his enemies. I fear it myself, but it is my sworn duty to—"

"There is no need to fear that. My name is Lady Hana Otako, Her Grace of Koi, and I—"

"My lady," Wen hissed behind me. "The captain said we ought not to say—"

"—I will take command of the relief organisation and assure you that no one, *no one*, will suffer such consequences for following my orders."

The man bowed and muttered disjointed thanks, but when I

turned to give Wen instructions, I found Shin had caught up to us. His glare could have cut flesh.

"We're doing this, Shin," I said. "Kisians are Kisians, whoever they fight for."

He met me glare for glare, then finally bowed. "Your Grace," he said, but the weight of his gaze followed me as I turned away, and I couldn't repress the shiver it sent tingling through my skin.

Night was falling by the time we returned to camp, having done what little we could to organise more physicians and supplies for the wounded soldiers at Hamaba.

Our army's first victory filled the camp with celebration, despite the number of wounded men spilling from the healing tents. Soldiers and labourers alike were drinking and singing in groups gathered around the fires, but no matter how infectious their joy, I didn't feel like celebrating. I was tired and hungry and low in spirits, and had I not wanted to address Katashi's council that night, I would have washed and rested rather than changing to join them in the meeting tent.

I'd had no reason to fear Katashi dead or injured, but it was still a relief to see him kneeling at the head of the table when I entered, his welcoming smile owning a tinge of question I could not yet answer. He did not have to rise for anyone, but every other member of his council got to their feet to greet me, some more resentfully than others.

Since our first day riding south from Koi, General Manshin had accepted my presence at meetings with nothing but a complacent smile and a watchful eye. The two commanders under him were civil enough, as was the quartermaster, but the three Pike captains, Tan, Roni, and Chalpo, barely hid their contempt. No doubt word had gotten around that I was Captain Regent, and they disliked me as much for the charade as for the Vices I had once led.

"Now that we are all present, I feel a toast is in order," General Manshin said, sitting back down and lifting his wine bowl. "To our emperor and his great victory. Long live Emperor Katashi!"

"Long live Emperor Katashi!" they chorused, lifting their bowls.

It had been my habit to listen more than speak at these meetings, partly for fear Katashi's advisors would ask him to stop me coming, and partly because I knew a lot less about military movements than I had hoped. But tonight, I could not keep my peace.

"Today was a victory for our army," I said, lifting my wine bowl in salute but not drinking. "But it was a loss for the empire."

Had I shouted it could not have grown more suddenly silent, every eye around the table turning on me with some variant between shock and fear. Only Katashi was unaffected, doing nothing more than setting his hands upon the table, a half smile hovering about his lips. "Bold words, Your Grace," he said, maintaining the formality he always used when we were in company. "Do tell us in what way Kisia has suffered this day."

"Those men you fought against were Kisian soldiers, they—"

The Pike captain Chalpo leant forward. "Who did you think we were going to fight against in this war, Your Grace?"

"I would thank you not to interrupt before I can finish," I said as little nods made their way around the table. "I did not intend to suggest we ought not to fight Kisians but rather that we ought to take care of Kisians."

The men shared looks over their wine bowls. Katashi kept his gaze on me, but his smile was less sure. "Do elaborate," he said.

"Well, Your Majesty, it was brought to my attention today that while we are well provisioned with physicians and supplies, it was not so for the outpost garrison. They lost many men today, but how many could have been saved if we had given aid to the wounded?"

"Are you suggesting," General Manshin said with perfect gravity, though someone at the table had snorted, "that we ought to assist our enemies to get back into the field faster, Your Grace?"

"I feel that is hardly the outcome we would get, General, especially given how long recovery can take. What I am suggesting is that allowing Kisian men to die when we could help them harms our cause. People don't only fight for those who are strong but also for those who give them succour and aid. Assuming I am fighting the same war you are, the aim is for Kisia to be one united empire when this is done, and that empire will be poorer for the loss of soldiers we could have saved."

Captain Chalpo looked around the table, his brows lifted in disbelief. "These are our enemies you are talking about. Men who, out on the field of battle, have killed and injured many of ours—commanders, comrades, friends. You would have us take resources from the caring of our own and give them to the care of their murderers?"

"They need not have fought for the enemy," said one of General Manshin's usually so quiet commanders.

"Were they given a chance to surrender?" I asked, recalling what the soldier had said earlier. My heart was pounding and I dared not look at Katashi seated at the other end of the table, sure his anger would lock up my tongue.

General Manshin smiled like a kindly grandfather. "Your Grace, there are times for such things and times when such things must be avoided. Today was this army's first engagement, and as such, the decisions made during it have important ramifications, not only for our soldiers and our enemy but in the eyes of the gods. These are considerations every leader must take into account. If you wish to have them all explained in greater detail, I will be only too happy to instruct you in the finer points at another time."

"But—" I met Katashi's gaze along the table. I had expected a scowl, but the infinitesimal shake of his head deflated me more surely than anything else could have. Fatigue washed over my anger and frustration, and with a stiff attempt at pride, I thanked the general and sat back.

I said nothing more for the rest of the meeting, but when the others filed out through the tent entrance, I lingered long enough to find myself facing Katashi alone. He had not risen from the table and, resting his chin on his hand, regarded me steadily. I mimicked him, sitting my own elbow on the table. "You are looking very grave, Your Majesty," I said. "Perhaps you regret allowing me to join these meetings."

"No. Your opinions reflect only upon you, not me."

My cheeks reddened in a flush of anger. "Are you saying you genuinely see no merit in my arguments? That all Kisians who are not with us are to be considered wholly as enemies?"

"How can I allow things to be otherwise? If it became common knowledge I was taking care of Kin's injured soldiers, they will be less likely to give in without a fight."

"Perhaps. But imagine how people would laugh at an emperor whose soldiers needed to be cared for by his enemy."

Katashi's temper gave way to a sudden laugh. "How very cruel you are to hatch such a plan, my dear. I feel Kin is to be congratulated for his escape. Had he married you, he would have found his ego shrivelled within a week. Come here."

I had meant to remain angry, to keep arguing, but the invitation in that smile was impossible to resist. Rising, I went to him, and no sooner had I drawn close than he took my hand and kissed my palm. "I will send some of our physicians to the town tonight. Does that satisfy you, love?"

I wasn't sure what sent the greater thrill through me, the press of his lips to my hand or to be called love. Even better to have won my point. "It does this time, yes, though perhaps if this happens again, we could send help sooner."

"A discussion for another time, I feel," he said, kissing each of my fingertips in turn now. "It has been a long day and I still have a letter to write before I can join you. Will you wait up for me, Your Grace?"

He let my hand go and kissed my stomach, sliding his hands around my thighs. I wriggled in pleasure and when he looked up, he was no longer the emperor I had faced down the length of the table. He was Katashi again, all messy hair and lopsided smile.

"Of course, Your Majesty. But don't keep me waiting too long or I might fall asleep."

"Minx. I'll be there as soon as I can."

The next morning, I woke within the circle of Katashi's arm and enjoyed the slow recollection of all that had passed in the night, glad he had stayed this once though the faint glow of predawn light was already creeping in across the carpet.

For a time, I lay watching him sleep as the growing light etched his handsome features from the gloom, before I kissed his cheek and then his lips. Keeping his eyes closed, he said in a sleepy murmur, "Good morning, Your Grace."

"Good morning, Your Majesty."

I ran my hand over his bare chest and down his stomach, eliciting a sleepy groan as I kept going all the way down. "You may have to wait for me to wake up for that."

"You seem quite awake to me."

"That would happen whether you were here or not, I'm afraid. Always happens in the mornings."

"Why?"

He shrugged, his shoulder shifting beneath me. "Honestly no idea."

"And men think women are strange creatures."

Katashi rolled a little and cracked open an eye. "Aren't you?"

"No more than you are!"

Footsteps sounded outside, and Tili backed in through the tent flap, jug in hand. "Good morning, my lady, I have your—Oh! Oh, I am so sorry, my lady, I...I...Your Majesty, I—I beg your pardon—"

"It's all right, Tili," I said, caught between annoyance and amusement. "Is that my washing water? Do set it down."

"Pretend I'm not here," Katashi said, having closed his eyes again. "If I lie perfectly still, you'll soon forget my presence and be comfortable again."

Tili, still frozen on the threshold, gaped at him. I imagined it was not the sort of thing an emperor usually said, but then Katashi had spent more time as a common outlaw than he ever had as a lord.

I beckoned Tili in, but as she recovered from the shock, the reproof in her gaze melted the smile from my face. Did she want me to be ashamed and embarrassed to be discovered so with a man who was not my husband? Convention said I ought to be, but I had refused to comply with every other piece of conduct expected of a lady and I would refuse this one too.

"Thank you," I said as she set down the water jug. "As I'm not alone, please have His Majesty's breakfast brought in with mine."

Tili's look of reproof deepened. "Yes, my lady. But I believe His Majesty's was served early, some half an hour ago."

Katashi propped himself up on an elbow, a hint of one of his scowls beginning to darken his expression. "Why?"

"I do not know the particulars, Your Majesty," Tili said, bowing twice in quick succession, her silent rebuke vanishing in fear. "I . . . I only heard it was so from the cooks at the—"

"Why?" he repeated, and I could not blame her for quailing beneath his gathering annoyance.

"They said you had a guest," she blurted. "From Lin'ya."

Throwing the covers aside, Katashi stood, snatching his under-robe from where he had discarded it the night before. Tili looked away, her cheeks reddening, and dared not turn back even once he had shrugged himself into it. He could have demanded her help with his voluminous imperial robe, but despite the awkwardness of dressing in so narrow a space, he did it himself and was picking up his sash before my tongue unfroze. "Are you still planning to ally yourself with the pirate enclave?"

He let out a breath as he tugged tight a simple knot in his sash. "You will have to excuse me, my love," he said as though I had not asked. "Duty calls."

Dressed once more in full imperial garb, he bent and pressed a kiss to my lips before he was gone, gathering his loose hair into a topknot as he stalked from the tent.

Silence reigned in his wake. I gathered the covers tightly around me, and Tili did not look up from the floor.

"I'm . . . I'm sorry, my lady," she said at last, still not looking at me. "I must apologise for anything I might have said in disparagement of—"

"Tili, you are my friend, you can say whatever you like about him without incurring my wrath. I know he can be imperious and overbearing and he has a shocking temper, but—" I longed to share with her some tiny piece of the joy his mere existence gave me, to explain how gentle he could be, how considerate and honest and charming, but every word died unspoken. I could not speak, could not explain after all he had done, and as some inklings of shame eked in, it hardened into anger. No man would have felt so for spending the night with a woman, no matter who she was.

Still looking at the floor, Tili cleared her throat. "I'm sorry, Your Grace. There is more fighting expected today, I understand. Would you like me to ready your armour?"

"No." I shook off my annoyance, intent not to let it get in the way of my plans. "Find my plainest robe. If there is to be more bloodshed, then there is no time to waste in finding more physicians. I will need all the messengers and scouts who aren't out and both Shin and Wen. There is much work to do."

11. DARIUS

While I sat shuffling papers, I could almost believe I was back in my ministerial rooms. Monomoro had sent up a fine table, and I'd found a portion of the side portico that wasn't about to collapse. There were no footsteps, no chatter, no potential for an imperial summons, but while I had problems to occupy my mind, I could bear with the differences.

A section of wall on this side of the house had collapsed, allowing an uninterrupted view of the western approach—a less overgrown track that cut steeply up the side of the hill—and the mountainous countryside beyond.

"Have you finished that letter?" I asked of the gangly youth who had been the only scribe Monomoro could find at such short notice.

"Yes, my—Your Excellency, just finishing the last word now. Your Excellency."

"Good. When you're done, run down to the library and see if you can find the most up-to-date land classification map we have."

"Yes, Your Excellency."

He dropped the finished letter on my desk, bowed as though I were the emperor himself, and hurried away so fast I could almost believe he preferred the rotting house to my company. The calligraphy on the letter was only fair, but it would have to do. I checked its contents, signed the bottom of the scroll, and rolled it up just as a head appeared over the brow of the hill. It was soon followed by shoulders, a torso, and a horse, none of them grandly clad.

"Excellency," the messenger called in the slow way peculiar to people from the Valley. "A good morning to you."

The man dismounted at the broken wall rather than risk his horse breaking a leg, and having thumped its rear and abjured it to stay as if it had been a dog, he clambered over the tumbledown stones with a saddlebag slung over his shoulder. "I've quite the heavy load o' letters for you," he said, jumping onto the portico and bowing in a way that more than made up for the boy's excessive deference. "And quite the heavy load to go back, I see." He pointed to the pile of letters all signed and sealed. "Where would you be wanting these ones?"

"In a pile on the other side," I said, deciding there was no point explaining the court system of messages coming in on the left of the desk and going out on the right. "Then by all means, you may take these and ensure they are properly delivered."

"Oh, as if I would ever think of dropping them in a ditch, my lord," he said, giving a hearty wink that made me yearn for the fearful deference at court, even if it wasn't always accompanied by competence.

He spilled the saddlebag's contents by the simple expedient of turning the bag upside down and shaking, sending scrolls tumbling. Kimiko almost stepped on one as she emerged from the house. "We're out of food again, Your Excellency," she said, picking it up and dropping it back on the pile. "Although since the kitchen roof is still as collapsed as it was before, I guess it makes no difference."

"Have food sent up," I said to the messenger as he gathered the outgoing missives. "Food that doesn't need a kitchen."

"Or we could just stay at an inn in town," Kimiko said. "Or have a carpenter come and fix the kitchens and hire a cook. If you want to stay here, you should at least make it comfortable."

"Food it is," said the messenger in his cheerful voice, once more slinging the saddlebag onto his shoulder. Another bow to me and a deeper one to Kimiko, and he jumped back off the portico and made his way toward the wall.

"That man is enraging," I said once he was out of earshot. "He seems to think highly of you though."

I picked up the closest scroll and broke its seal. "Ah, there was fighting at Hamaba and Yagi two days back." I drew a map out from beneath the other papers and made a mark with my brush, adding the date as small as I could. Beside me, Kimiko knelt to tidy the scattered scrolls, though the pale blue robe she had donned that morning made her look every bit the grand lady she had been born.

When I set the scroll aside, she handed me another from the pile. "You don't have to do that," I said, taking it. "I don't need an assistant."

"But I need something to do. Your house is boring, and with your mark on me, it's not like I can even go for a walk without you ordering me to go."

"I gave you my word I wouldn't order you to do anything, but you have my permission to go for a walk if that helps."

She sighed and leant her head back, exposing the line of her throat. "I don't even want to go for a walk. Nor do I want to get your permission for things. I don't want to be here at all, it's lonely."

Having no answer, I broke the scroll's seal and unrolled it. Another account of the clash at Hamaba, this time with estimated numbers. I tapped my chin with the tip of my brush.

Wax cracked as Kimiko opened a scroll. "Lord Laroth, as I have been apprised of your removal from the position of minister of the left, I must in good faith and service to His Majesty the great Emperor Kin Ts'ai of Kisia refuse to—"

I clenched my fists rather than snatch the scroll out of her hand.

"If you could refrain from reading my correspondence, that would be best."

"For you and very much more boring for me. This man doesn't seem to want to come visit us, Darius. How rude of him when the hospitality of this house is second to none." She looked to the bottom of the scroll. "Who is he? It's signed 'DC forty-six.'"

"District Commander Yao of the forty-sixth."

"I don't think he likes you."

"It's not my job to be likable."

"Convenient."

I held out my hand for the scroll. "Thank you for that assessment."

She smiled as she put it in my hand. "Any time."

The message said little more than had already been read out, but I read it over again before letting it curl up. "I'll have to ride over to see him." I indicated my left eye. "How is my bruise today?"

"Turning a sickly yellow colour that makes it look like a bear peed on you."

"You know, no one listening to you would ever think you were a lady."

"Phew!"

Annoyed by how easily she could goad me into unwise retorts, I took up another scroll and cracked its seal. "Ah, from Monomoro's associate about that shepherd. He knows of at least three locations that fit my description, and one even has a blind cliff. What a useful thing to know with Katashi on his way."

I had been speaking merely to focus my own thoughts, and Kimiko tensed at the sound of her twin's name. "You think he is planning to attack the valley?" she said, and someone else might have taken it for bored curiosity, but I could feel the anxiety that lay behind it. Foolish to have voiced such a belief, but the situation was not so far beyond recall.

"It is one of many possibilities," I said lightly. "This job has never just been about payrolls and red tape but about anticipating threats before they come and protecting against them."

"Except that it's not your job anymore."

"I was to be relieved of my position once I had safely seen Emperor Kin take his oath at Koi. Did that happen?"

"No, but—"

"Then it's still my job and I will keep doing it."

Kimiko tilted her head to the side in a way that was uniquely her, endearingly birdlike and yet all too searching. One corner of her lips tended to twitch up while she did so, an expression I found far too attractive for my own safety. "Why do you serve Emperor Kin?"

"Is there a reason I should not?" I asked, dragging my thoughts from her lips with an effort.

"Because you were the sworn guardian of Lady Hana Otako and the son of an Imperial Protector."

I leant back and stared out at the gardens. "My father hated your family by the end," I said. "He hated all of the Otakos except Hana. I looked after her because I was honour-bound to do so. And I chose to serve Kin because he was the one ruling Kisia." Not the whole truth, but we didn't need Malice kneeling between us right now. "Five years ago, I didn't even know whether you or your brother were alive."

"Would you have come to serve us if you had?"

"No. You scowl, but I would have been a monster indeed to seek to plunge Kisia into civil war for nothing but my own ideology. As a servant of the people, I fight for stability and prosperity. For the man who already has the throne so no one has to die."

"You know, it would be easier to hate you if you weren't such a decent person, Darius."

That her words stung surprised me, and I said, "I could tell you plenty of things that could make you hate me if that is your goal."

"It would certainly make this easier."

"Easier than liking me?"

Her bright, assessing gaze met mine for a moment, before we both looked away and the sting dug deeper into my skin. "You want to hate me because I'm an Empath," I said. "I can't say I blame you."

I pushed back from the table and stood to stretch, but Kimiko didn't move. Her restless fingers tugged gently at the frayed end of her sash. "Why did you leave Malice?"

An empty answer rose to my tongue but remained unsaid. She might hate me for the truth, but she would as surely hate me for the lie.

"Because guilt and remorse are heavy things to carry," I said. "And I wanted to prove I wasn't what he told me I was."

The honesty left my soul raw, and before she could answer, I added, "Now I'm going to see the district commander who doesn't like me. Don't pine away without me, will you?"

Her expression was unreadable, and as she shook her head, I prided myself on not reaching out to see what lay beneath. It didn't matter, after all, whether I had made her hate me more or less. It didn't matter what she thought of me at all.

District Commander Yao had an office in the local guard barracks a few miles distant, a squat old building desperately in need of expansion to accommodate the ever-increasing military presence in the Valley. It had never been small, but mountain tribes had massacred four full battalions twenty-four years earlier, and the fear had never fully subsided. It had been before my time as minister of the left, but I'd held the position long enough to wince at the poorly outfitted guardhouse.

A boy ran out to take my horse, followed by an old man with the look of a retired soldier. "Greetings, my lord. If you're wishful to report a crime—"

"No, my name is Lord Darius Laroth, minister of the left to Emperor Kin Ts'ai, and I would like to speak to District Commander Yao."

I dismounted, but even once I had turned around and smoothed the skirt of my robe, the man was still staring at me open-mouthed. The boy holding the reins did the same, and a few guards loitering in the yard had stopped mid conversation. Unseen through an overhead window, someone hissed, "It's the Monstrous Minister!" and I smiled upon them all.

"Ah, my reputation precedes me," I said. "That does make things easier."

"Excusing me, my lord," said the man, finally finding his voice. "But I did hear you were no longer minister of the left."

"An untruth, but I will not discuss it here in the road nor with you. I will see District Commander Yao now."

Even were it true, he could hardly have refused entrance to the lord upon whose land the guardhouse stood, so with a gesture half shrug, half bow, he led the way inside.

Beyond the door, a narrow corridor carved its way from the entrance to the stairs, one side owning a number of small rooms for taking complaints and asking questions of prisoners, while the other side opened onto a large but poorly lit common area. This was full of whispers and wine fumes and staring men, and I made a mental list of all the upkeep regulations the commander had broken in case they proved useful.

At the top of the stairs, my guide stopped outside a sliding door with faded watercolour panes. "Commander," he said as he knocked on the frame. "It's uh...Lord Laroth to see you. Minister of the left."

"Gods curse the man," came the voice from inside. "Did you tell him we know he's been removed from his position? Why must he insist on parading around as—?"

"Your good man did tell me that, yes, Commander," I said.

Silence. I could imagine the man biting his fist at his desk. Paper shuffled. Then a throat was cleared. "Do invite His Lordship in, Chit."

"Yes, Commander."

The man grimaced something of an apology at me, his expression owning as much regret that he had gotten himself into this situation.

"His Exce—His Lordship, Commander," he said and slid open the door with a bow.

Commander Yao had managed to compose himself and sat scowling behind his desk. "Lord Laroth," he said as I entered, though the politeness seemed to cause him some pain. "Do pray excuse my...rudeness. Perhaps you are unaware that we have a civil war brewing."

Not having been invited to sit, I stood and gave him my iciest stare until, flustered, he looked away. "I am quite aware of that, Commander," I said. "And that it is not only brewing but has already broken out and is coming this way. I have reason to believe Katashi Otako has not only taken Hamaba but is marching a second army this way to disrupt the transport of food to Mei'lian and cut the Valley off from the rest of the empire."

He stared at me a long, horrified moment, and knowing I had won, I sat down and slung the scroll canister off my shoulder. "I have estimated numbers on the size and disposition of his army, at least half of it being made up from forces that were, until recently, under my command. I have my maps too and a number of locations a smart man would seek to pull us into battle, and if you would send for some tea, I hope, between the pair of us, that we will soon have a plan for counteracting him."

Commander Yao swallowed hard and, lifting his chin, shouted toward the door. "I know you're still out there listening, Chit, so make yourself useful and go get the minister some tea."

———————

It was almost dark when I returned, and after rubbing down the horse and seeing it fed, I had to cross the courtyard by moonlight. Summer was starting to lose its grip on the world, leaving a chill in the air, but it wasn't the cold that made me shiver as I stepped into the house. I had hoped to get used to the feeling of coming home, to shed my hatred of it, but despite the sense of victory still pumping through my veins, it took all the strength I possessed to make myself walk on.

I found Kimiko in the back room where we had rolled out sleeping mats the first night. She lay curled upon the divan and didn't look up from the book in her hands. She did, however, point at a big sack of rice slumped against the wall. "You need to be more specific in your orders next time," she said, eyes still on the book. "That's all that arrived that apparently needs no kitchen."

"It doesn't need a kitchen, but I get your point," I said, setting my scroll canister upon the table. "I guess we'll have to cook some on the hot stone."

It sat in the corner, half covered in moth-eaten cushions. "Do you know how?" Kimiko gave the stone a disdainful look.

"Given the amount of time I once spent living in this room, yes. Do not bestir yourself from your book, my lady, allow me to prepare you dinner."

"Excellent." She went back to reading.

"May I ask what is so engrossing?"

Kimiko held up the book, and I recognised the cover at once. In a half dozen strides, I crossed the room and ripped it from her hand. "Hey!"

"Where did you find this?"

"The library. There's a whole bookcase of them and they're really interesting."

Had there been a fire, I would have thrown the book into it no matter how valuable the knowledge it contained. Without one I stood crushing its cover in my hands and glaring at her. She stared back, wholly unafraid.

"Actively searching for reasons to hate me now?" I said, tucking the book under my arm, though with so many in the library, any attempt to keep her from reading them might soon turn into a farce. Whichever Laroth had started keeping records about the Sight ought to have considered the consequences of someone else reading them. Or perhaps he had and I was merely the first Laroth to care.

Kimiko sat up. "Reasons to hate you? For being born different? I would rather choose to hate you for your choices than for what you cannot help. Your Empathy need not define you, Darius."

I had been afraid she would hate me for what I was, but worse had been the fear she wouldn't. The acceptance in her sad smile was truly frightening, and I turned away rather than face it. "How nice that sounds," I jeered. "And how very naive."

"Do you push everyone away?"

The book made a satisfyingly heavy thump as I dropped it on the table. "I try." I swept the cushions off the hot stone, knocking over the rice pot that had been hidden beneath them. Lunging, I caught it just before it hit the floor, but as I straightened, Kimiko's hands slid around my waist, locking together at my sternum.

"Isn't that lonely?" she said, resting her head between my shoulder blades.

There was nothing amorous in her embrace, but the gentle companionship was far worse than any amount of lust would have been. It seemed to slice me open, exposing my very bones.

"Better alone than—"

"Understood? Accepted?"

I turned, taking a step back against the hot stone to escape the circle of her arms. "Better alone than weak."

"Is that what you think love is? What friendship is?"

"I know so."

That sad smile again. "Then I'm sorry to inform you of this, Your Excellency, but you're wrong. In fact, you could not be more wrong. Would you fight so hard for Kin if he was not your friend? Would you hate this house so much if you did not love what you lost here?"

"You know nothing about what I have lost," I growled. "Read the damn book if you must, but leave me alone."

"I really did want to hate you, Darius, but I can only pity you."

"I don't want your pity!" I shouldered past her, rice pot in hand. "I don't want your compassion. I don't even want to be having this conversation."

"What are you so afraid of?" She followed me to the rice sack. "That someone might care about you?"

"The last time that happened, I got a knife between my ribs." I dropped the pot into the sack and yanked open the left side of my robe, exposing my infamous scar to the meagre light.

Expression grim, she traced the silvery line with the tip of her finger. "That should have killed you."

It was the work of a moment to take her hand and slide it beneath the right side of my robe. There, with her palm against my skin, my heart beat more strongly.

"Lucky. Did they know?"

"I've never known for sure."

I let her go, but Kimiko took no step back. She stayed staring at the silk as though she could still see the scar through it. "I know what lonely feels like," she said, stepping closer. "All my life, people have used me to get near my brother, liking and fearing me only for my name. After a while, it's easier to just stop letting people in."

"Easier still to let them think you're the reawakened dead," I said and laughed at the extreme lengths I'd gone to push people away.

Kimiko tilted her head in the way she often did, and taking my arm, she drew back my sleeve to expose skin. By the ease with which the blade came to her hand, it must have been tucked into her sash, and before I understood what she was doing, she nicked the inside of my arm. It stung and blood bloomed.

"Not only does he have a heart, he bleeds," she said, and when blood trickled down my arm, she traced its trail with her tongue, licking me clean. Her curls danced under my nose as she sucked blood out of me, and I closed my eyes as the tip of her tongue ran back down my arm.

I hardened against her. She had to be able to feel it, but she neither blushed nor pulled away, just ended her tease with a soft, lingering kiss upon my lips.

This is too dangerous, I told myself. *Walk away now. You like her too much.*

But I stayed where I was, defying the fear that tormented me as I had defied the path set before me by my blood.

Your Empathy need not define you, Darius.

"We could keep each other company for the night," she breathed against my cheek. "Better than being alone."

I had grown up alone, unloved, untouched, a weed growing in barren soil, until Malice had found me and set my soul on fire. That had been dangerous then and this was dangerous now, but I could not push her away.

"Alone is safer," I said though I stood my ground.

"No, alone is just easier."

The truth of her words pierced me deeper than I had thought possible. But here she was, offering physical companionship like a balm, not seeking to own or possess or consume, only to be, and the compassion, the humanity, the true *empathy* of it was intoxicating. When she lifted her lips it was not just my loneliness she sought to allay, but her own, and on those terms I had no weapons left to fight my soul-deep yearning for intimacy.

She kissed me again, and this time I ran my hands up her back and into the glorious mass of her hair. She leant into me, seeming to revel in this moment of letting go as much I did, and all lingering fear fled as she slid her hands up my thighs. One pressed between my legs and I moaned against her lips. It had been so long since I'd last lain with anyone that even through the layers of silk, her touch was exhilarating. I dropped onto the cushions and lay back, her dark curls spreading like a crown. My whole body seemed to pound in time to my rapid heartbeat as she opened her robes, exposing smooth skin and small breasts, her nipples pinched taut in the cool air. They rose and fell with every breath, and as much in challenge as invitation, Kimiko parted her legs.

I shed both outer and under-robes onto the floor with a shrug and grasped her hips, dragging her toward me. She weighed nothing, but the ferocity with which she gripped my hair belonged to a larger, stronger woman.

The philosopher Misi had once said anticipation was the greatest enjoyment, that instant before fulfilment that sent the senses tingling, but looking down at her—inviting me, desiring me—was torture. I could not wait another moment and, closing my eyes, I guided myself inside her. I had forgotten what it felt like, the initial sensation so overwhelming that I gasped, digging my fingers into her skin. Kimiko gave a throaty chuckle and drew me deeper, a challenge in her mocking smile.

Accepting it, I thrust hard, only for her to grip my hair and bite the taut skin of my throat. But she did not stop there. With every movement I made, she cut my skin with her nails and tore at my lip with her teeth, and refusing to let her have it all her own way, I gripped a handful of her hair and pulled hard. Crying out, she dragged her fingernails down my back.

All sense of time vanished as we fought for mastery. The night might have given way to a new day and I would not have cared. There was nothing but her, nothing but her strength and her pride, nothing but the way she purred and bit, burying her soul deeper beneath my skin with every touch. She courted the animal inside me, unafraid, and I never wanted it to end. But my body yearned toward the finish, our flesh moving in unison, panting in time in the close air.

I had thought the end far off, but suddenly her grip tightened. She tensed, a pained cry breaking through her lips. I felt her pleasure, felt it fuel my own until our joint rapture shuddered through us, shared through our skin.

As my joy fed back into her, Kimiko screamed, and afraid someone would hear her, I pressed my hand over her mouth and she gripped my wrist, holding it there, each breath hot against my palm. Together our hearts beat a tattoo of fading pleasure, and when there was nothing left but a lingering glow, I lifted my hand.

Eyes still wide, she scoured my face. "That was the strangest and most amazing thing I think I've ever felt," she said, an unusually self-conscious laugh chasing her words. "And you think being an Empath is all monstrous." She lifted her hips into me, eliciting a moan from both our lips. "Where have you been all my life, Darius?"

12. ENDYMION

Kaze rode like the wind he'd been named for, speeding over the landscape. From the thick forests around Koi, we climbed into the foothills of the Kuro Mountains where streams trickled down the hillside. There I could look out over the vast expanse of the empire as though I sat at the feet of the gods, but it was Hope I thought of, sitting atop a tumbledown roof and daydreaming of another world. Another life.

Afraid of being followed, we stopped only to eat and rest, although my mind was often too noisy to find sleep. On the rare occasions it claimed me, I dreamed of dead men. Lines of them stretching into the darkness, the number of souls awaiting judgement as numerous as the trees growing in the shadow of the hills. And even beneath the noontime sun, I would wake cold and shivering.

South. Darius is south.

The days passed unnumbered, disappearing beneath Kaze's feet.

In all our travels, Jian had avoided the Valley, and as we entered its northern reaches, I finally understood why. The Laroth estate at Esvar was no place to take Lord Nyraek Laroth's bastard son when such pains had been taken to prove him dead. I knew it was my destination as soon as I saw the untamed hills and the steep mountainsides cut with terraces.

Darius had gone home. Now I was going home too.

The town of Esvar sat nestled between two hills, its watercolour houses and rambling streets cut by a sparkling stream. This was wild country, full of sharp black crags and dense thickets of bamboo, of steep rocky slopes and twisted trees. The people of the Valley had long ago given up trying to tame it, instead growing their crops upon the mountainside, each slope a glittering tower in green and brown and gold.

One thousand seven hundred and four souls inhabited these fields and groves, basking beneath a beneficent blue sky. And then there was Darius.

Kaze started down the hill. Whispers came to me on the air with the smells of civilisation, of stagnant paddies and refuse-filled ditches, of shrine incense and smoke.

Baan hasn't come in yet. What can be keeping him?

If we don't fix the roof soon, the storms will wash it into our beds.

Someone needs to take a whip to those boys.

By the grace of the gods.

Kaze walked on, following a worn track in the dry grass. It brought us to the town's outskirts where a boy was foraging. He had a load of sticks caught beneath one arm and was bent double in the grass at the base of a pear tree. He must have heard me approach, for he looked up, eyeing me askance. Then his gaze found Kaze. Awe lit his face.

"Good evening," I said.

"E'en, m'lord," the boy replied, not glancing up from Kaze. "That's a fine trampler you have there. He must have cost you a fortune."

"Not a fortune," I answered. "Just a friend. I was hoping you could tell me how to find the Laroth estate."

This drew his interest away from Kaze. "What you want it for?" His gaze fixed on the traitor's brand marring my cheek. "You here to kill the lord?"

"No, I'm visiting. He's a ... friend."

By his expression, I might have just announced my intention to light the town on fire. "You a ghost?"

"A ghost? No, why? Do I look like a ghost?"

"Not so much, but Mama says only ghosts live there. People say it's haunted. I've heard the lord is back and putting things in order though, so maybe he's turfed them all out."

He seemed enamoured of the idea and might have elaborated had I not asked him where I would find the haunted house.

The boy jerked his head in the direction of a hill to the west, above which the sun was slowly setting. "Up there. Not far. Can't miss it. Just look f'the tree."

With a nod of thanks, I left him to his work, touching Kaze's neck to set him walking again. He was tired and so was I, but we had come too far to stop now.

The track that led up the side of the hill was overgrown, grass sprouting between old stones. Woody shrubs blocked the way, and more than once I had to dismount, leaving Kaze to push his way through reaching branches, thorns and leaves catching on his mane. There were clumps of wild imperial roses and stands of willoweed, feathergrass, and jagged fern. No doubt they had been planted for decoration, but now nests of runners choked the ground like spiderwebs. Sprawling flowers had smothered more than one tree, filling the evening with a scent like jasmine.

By the time we reached the crest of the hill, the sun sat low on the horizon. Clouds cut the stained sky, and there amid overgrown gardens stood the home of my ancestors. Low and sprawling, it covered a plateau between steeply sloping hills, an enormous complex encircled by a crumbling wall. A welcome garden sat before the open gates, and like the path, it had been left to the decay of time. Questing tree roots had buckled the carriageway, and tall weeds all but hid the garden beds from view. The boy had told me to look for the tree, and it was hard to miss. It seemed to rise from the house itself, growing through the roof of some long-neglected room.

Kaze tossed his head. "I know," I said. "But there must be a stable. You might even have company."

Though it was crumbling in places, the wall was easily twice my height, built of dark stone and chunks of black glass. Terracotta tiles ran around the top, each engraved with the eight limbs of a reaching spider.

Kaze stopped before the open gate, backing with a snort. "Don't worry, nothing's going to hurt you," I said. "It's just a house." I dismounted, patting his nose, and he let me lead him through the gate and down into a paved central courtyard. It was large and open to the sky but for a portico that ran around its outer edge. Fine fretwork might once have made patterns from the sun, but now it was barely visible beneath the rampant spread of wisteria, its flowers blooming in white and pink and purple. The smell was strong enough to make me wish I did not need to breathe.

A channel cut through the courtyard and Kaze stopped to drink, dipping his nose into its sluggish water. "Stay here," I said, patting his neck. "I'll be back soon."

He made no sound, but I heard his thoughts.

"Of course I'll feed you," I said. "Have I failed to do so yet?"

Making no further complaint, he went on drinking, and I let his reins fall, knowing he would not wander.

From behind the house, the setting sun glowed like an aura, igniting the terracotta roof to blood red. The manor had been built in the traditional style and had surely been a masterpiece before rot had claimed it. Paint flaked, the roof was missing tiles, and ornamental window frames stood empty. Only one large circular window remained unbroken, glaring like a dark eye upon my intrusion. From the courtyard, other doors led to other buildings, cookhouses and shrines, but each was as dark and lifeless as the large house in front of me.

I stood hesitant upon the threshold.

"Hello?" I said. "Darius?"

I stepped in, dry air prickling my throat. Darius was here somewhere, I knew, but I wasn't sure my Empathy could guide me through a maze.

With tentative steps, I made my way along a passage, peering into every room. They all looked the same, owning no sign of life beyond the spreading moss and the scattering of clawed feet. Even my breath seemed to echo, and when I stopped, my footsteps carried on as though the house wished to lure me deeper.

At the next turning, I stopped in a pool of faint light. Whispers filled the air, barely audible like the rustling of dry leaves. Formless. Voiceless.

I pushed out my Empathy, but I could feel nothing. Perhaps Darius wasn't here at all and I had just been sensing the house, a house desperate for company, for another Laroth to trap forever inside its string of empty rooms and winding passages. It sounded mad, but turning on the spot in the smothering shadows, I could believe it.

"Darius!"

No reply. No echo, the sound eaten by rotting wood. I walked on with quickened steps, trying to shake my fearful thoughts. It was just a house.

Taking a turn at random, I found light spilling through an open doorway and sped forward in search of life, but it was just the last of the sunset gilding a dozen broken windows in a long gallery. No sign of Darius, but the light shone upon a wall of portraits. The first had begun to fade, but it had been painted in the old style, its minuscule brushstrokes still holding a wealth of detail. The artist had depicted a grand magnolia just opening its petals, and beneath it, a fine-looking man sat astride a pale horse. His name ought to have been at the bottom of the scroll, but it had been torn away, leaving a crooked edge. Instead, words had been painted straight onto the wall beneath.

Ma'Li Laroth, the First Count of Esvar.
The son of a wild mountain man and a merchant's daughter.
He blackmailed the Emperor into bestowing a noble title upon him,
all because he caught His Imperial Majesty kissing his own niece.

I stared at the rough calligraphy and read it again. It said the same thing the second time. A glance along the gallery was enough to see ink stained the wall beneath each scroll, like the house had spawned its owner's dark secrets in retribution.

The next was a portrait of a woman, her bearing proud though her stare was vacuous. She held an overfed dog in her arms, while two children sat at her feet.

Lady Seraphine Laroth, Countess of Esvar.
Her dog Lion and her two children: Yuko and Raef Laroth.
While all sources claim her to have been a loving wife and devoted mother, this was also said about Lady Barin, who murdered her husband in his sleep.
Lady Laroth committed the more heinous crime of mothering the child of another man.
Yuko lacked the Mark and the Sight.
Seraphine Laroth was nothing but a wanton whore dressed as a lady.

I walked on. Unknown Laroths passed before my gaze, each a proud boy grown into a proud man flanked by numerous wives. All had secrets, no one safe from the damning strokes of the writer's brush.

Eventually, I came to the fourth count of Esvar—my grandfather. There was something about the set of his features that reminded me strongly of Malice, but by this time, I was more interested in reading the flourishing characters than looking at the portraits.

Ellar Laroth, the Fourth Count of Esvar.
Notable only for his lack of wit, charm, intelligence, and bravery.
This snivelling wreck, who could not call himself a man,
was the reason for the continuation of the Sight.
May justice never allow him to rest in his grave.

Hypnotised, I could not stop. I had to read them, as though by doing so I might solve some great riddle, unlocking the secrets Malice and Darius kept close.

The next portrait was our grandmother, a beautiful woman full of quiet grace. Her name was missing from the erratic scrawl, only one word painted in its place.

Bitch.

My heart leapt into my throat as I stepped to the next portrait. There, looking down at me from the canvas, was the man who had taken me to Brother Jian all those years ago. Nyraek Laroth. He needed no explanation. The Imperial Protector. Lover of Empress Li and father of Darius, Malice, and myself, each to a different woman.

Lord Nyraek Laroth.
The Sight is strong with him.
It grows stronger every day.
May there be an end soon.
May the darkness come.

I stared at the wall for a long time, thinking of how much Darius had wanted to die at Koi, how happy he had been as I drew him out of his skin. His father had wished for death too.

Only two portraits remained. Beside Nyraek was a beautiful woman, her features so fine and flawless one could easily see where Darius had inherited his perfect face.

Lady Melia Laroth, mother to Esvar's last heir.
She had not the Mark, but it took her from this world.
It saw her bleed to death upon the cursed birth of a child that never wanted to live.

Avarice had said she died in childbirth. He said Darius had wanted to live, but his unnamed sister had not. Esvar's last heir. Had the writer believed Darius would never provide the house with another Laroth?

At last, I turned to the final portrait. A boy, no more than ten years old. He looked younger, thinner, and altogether less potent than the Darius I knew, but there was no mistaking those fine features, or the cold look in his violet eyes.

Darius Kirei Laroth, the last heir of Esvar.
Lost his life in the storm of 1359.
May the Sight die and never rise again.

From his portrait, the young Darius watched as I read through the words again, sure they had to be wrong.

"Well, Endymion," spoke a voice beside me. "I see you have met the family."

I turned, choking on a cry that leapt up my throat. Darius stood at the end of the hall, half in the shadows, the silver threads of his fine robe glittering like stars.

"Darius," I managed, my heart pounding. "You're here."

"Yes, I am," he said. "I'm not a ghost. But I did not think to be found so soon. Malice?"

"I left him in some outpost on the road to Rina. Kimiko?"

"Here."

I looked back at the portrait. The young Darius met my gaze, unflinching. "I hope you enjoyed the family history," he said at last. "Shall I leave you with our glorious ancestors?"

"No."

His lips split into a smile so fast had I answered.

"No," I repeated more slowly. "But who wrote the words?"

"I think you already know the answer to that."

"You. Or our father."

"I will pretend you didn't say that. If you hadn't noticed, I have not yet gone mad." He turned away on the words and strode out into the dark passage. I followed, glad to leave the old faces behind.

"He hated his Empathy," I said, keeping up with Darius's quick step lest he vanish into the shadows.

"Yes. Or at least he tried to. As you can see, it drove him quite insane."

"I remember him."

"You do not remember him."

He spat the words and quickened his pace. I jogged to keep up, following in the wake of emotions so thick I could not believe they were his. Darius had once been so closed I had thought him dead.

"This is my head. Keep out or get out," he snapped, stopping abruptly and turning on me. "How did you find me?"

"I followed you."

"Followed me? We stopped at no inns, and where we did stop, I gave no name. How can you have followed me all the way from Koi?"

I could not meet his eyes. It had been so easy to do, so natural, and yet under his furious gaze, nothing was more monstrous. "Since the night at Koi," I began, fidgeting. "Since the night at Koi, I have been more . . . attuned to you."

Darius stared. Then with slow deliberation, he said, "You can sense me? You can smell me all the way from Koi because I left a piece of myself under your skin?" His gaze flicked down to my chest. "Like Malice did. He marked you?"

"Yes. At least, he tried, I don't know, I didn't let him finish, I—"

I faltered beneath the intensity of his stare. "You broke a mark?"

"I . . ." I thought of the emotion I had poured into it and how desperately Malice had tried to hold on, how desperately he had wanted to keep me from leaving him. "Yes."

"You and I are going to have to talk about that, but in the meantime, don't tell Kimiko."

He did not wait for a reply but continued along the empty passage, eventually bringing us to a wing of the house owning signs of recent habitation. Here, furniture filled the rooms, but still the decorative scrolls were curled and discoloured, and the floorboards were stained with the criss-cross pattern of damp reed matting. There was a musty smell to the air too, and I wondered how long it had been since anyone had opened these doors.

Light greeted us at the end of a passage, shining through the intact paper panes of a sliding door. It felt like the last bastion of warmth and life in the whole world, so long had the house held me in its decaying grip. After the dusty stink of decline, the smell of jasmine tea was uplifting.

"We have a guest, Kimiko," Darius said, sliding the door. "I found him wandering like a lost sheep."

Kimiko lay curled upon a divan, snuggled into a pile of thick furs. It was a small, cosy room owning little beyond a cooking stone, the divan, and a low table. A servant's room, not a lord's. I could imagine a young Darius lying there, curled as Kimiko was, while Avarice became both friend and carer, entertaining a little boy with stories of the outside world.

"Endymion?" Kimiko said, drawing my attention back.

"Takehiko," Darius corrected, shooting a challenging look my way.

"Takehiko?" She lurched up onto her elbow and glared at me across the room. "Takehiko Otako? Are you seriously telling me he's Takehiko, my cousin Takehiko?"

He sat upon the edge of the divan beside her. "Sorry, but yes. Shall I throw him out?"

She didn't answer, just stared at me long and hard. "You're my cousin? I thought you were another Laroth bastard like Malice. Oh, that makes sense of…" Kimiko sat up, pushing the furs aside. "I remember when you were born," she said. "No one celebrated, not like they did for Tanaka and Rikk. For them, there were parties in the streets. But for you, there was nothing."

"Kimiko," Darius said, his tone a warning.

"I didn't understand at the time why everyone was so angry," she went on, ignoring him. "But now I know. Why celebrate the birth of a bastard?"

I winced and looked away, her words stinging as though she had wielded a whip. I had been unwanted by every family I might have claimed.

Darius moved away. Kimiko's eyes followed him, her cheeks pale, her fingers clenched amid the fur. "What a mess parents make of the world," she said, her emotions betraying her smile. "The Otakos are meant to be dead, but now it seems I cannot turn around without walking into someone who is related to me."

"I'm not," Darius said, scowling through a narrow window at the thickening night. "And technically, Endymion is not either. His mother was only an Otako by marriage, just another lady who was charmed by my father's apparent wit."

"Like Malice's mother?"

"Malice's mother was a whore," Darius said, still not turning around. "Not an empress whore."

Kimiko laughed. "How charming. Don't listen to him, Endymion, he's just cranky because all the tea is stale."

He looked over his shoulder, laughing back at her, and I felt as little part of the scene as the walls themselves. I thought to leave, but the moment did not last. Kimiko pointed to the cooking stone. "There is rice if you're hungry," she said. "Darius keeps forgetting to send for more varied food."

"It's not like I've had reason to leave the house for the last few days."

The look they shared made me redden, and I stared at the rice pot. Rice clumped in the bottom of it and its cedar lid sat askew. I hadn't eaten for days, but I did not feel hungry.

"I must see Kaze stabled and fed first," I said. "Is there a stable yard?"

"Yes, and even some fresh grain," Darius said, moving from the window. "Come, I'll show you the way."

An old rein hung from the ceiling, holding a trio of lanterns. Each was lit, and Darius retrieved one, the candle flame flickering through a rip in the paper.

Kimiko said nothing, and Darius did not look back as he led the way into the dark passages once again. This time the lantern drew colour from the old house—yellowing parchment scrolls, the red tinge of the wooden floor, and a brilliant green moss gradually stealing the house back to nature.

Still walking, Darius said, "Why did you come?"

"To find you."

"Afraid for my life?"

"No."

He stopped, lifting the lantern into my face. "What do you want from me, Endymion?"

In the bright light, his expression was more mask-like than ever. "I want your help," I said.

"I thought we had agreed we were both beyond help."

"You controlled your Empathy."

His lips lilted into a sneer. "Controlled, yes. Past tense, as you can see. Do you want to know how?"

"Yes."

"You don't want to be a slave to it? Don't want to live as the monster that is beneath your skin?"

"Yes."

"It's much easier to just be what you were born than to fight against it, you know."

"But can you teach me how?"

His smile held no humour. "Perhaps. It isn't easy."

"I don't care about easy."

"And you have to want it. You have to want it more than you've ever wanted anything else." He glanced over my shoulder, back along the passage. "As soon as you want something else more, you will lose control of it. Do you understand?"

"Yes."

Darius laughed and shook his head. "You really don't, but maybe you will. I'll teach you so long as you promise that when we're done, you will leave. And I don't just mean leave this house, I mean leave Kisia. Leave Chiltae. Go somewhere far away where your name need cause no trouble."

"You were the one who told her."

He shrugged. "She'd have figured it out, and I'd rather not have her angry with me for keeping secrets. I swore *you* no oath."

"If you can grant me peace from this, then I will go wherever you want me to go."

"Peace?" Darius laughed, the long, sustained laugh of one truly amused. "There is never such a thing as peace for us. Either you choose to fight the monster every moment of every day or you struggle with the guilt and the shame and the endless noise. There isn't an in-between. We are destined to suffer, one way or another."

He turned away on the words and, with the lantern lighting his path, walked on into the darkness.

13. HANA

The soldier's grip tightened on my hand, crushing bone, but I just gritted my teeth and made no sound, my pain nothing to his.

"Almost done," Wen said. "Almost done." And I wondered whether his chanted words were for the soldier or himself as he sawed through flesh and bone. Tili stood on the soldier's other side, and we looked at one another over the man's tense and twitching body, neither of us wanting to watch Wen work. The soldier's breath huffed out hard, and he was biting deep marks into a leather strap, but even once the worst was over, the pain would not cease.

"Almost done."

I grimaced at Tili and she grimaced back.

"Almost. Almost."

A meaty thump hit the ground, but it did nothing to loosen the soldier's grip on my hand. I tried to give it a reassuring squeeze as though that would make any difference, but the man seemed hardly present at all.

"Have you seen Shin since this morning?" I said to Tili as my gaze wandered the small village hall we'd found ourselves in that day. Anything rather than watch Wen work on the man's bloody stump of a leg.

"No, Your Grace," Tili said, also hunting the dim space for any sign of him. "He may just be outside. I notice he does not like to be around such things." She gestured to the injured soldier, and almost I laughed at the thought that Shin, who could kill a man without a flash of remorse, could be uneasy about blood. But now she mentioned it, he had avoided helping the first time we aided the enemy soldiers and always stayed away from the healing tents back at camp.

"What an odd man he is," I said and left it there, the soldier lying on a pallet behind Tili having turned to watch us keenly.

Injured men were packed into the room, still more into houses around the village and in the market square. The men hereabouts ought to have been out in the fields bringing in the harvest before the rains, but instead they lay dying on pallets.

Surely there had to be another way, a way that didn't get so many people killed, but as with every time I cycled through such thoughts, I came up with nothing. Kin and Katashi would never compromise, could not, and even if they had been able to, the fervour of their followers would not allow it. The men of Katashi's council were as uncompromising as he was himself.

"I wanted to be a soldier when I was young," Tili said, filling the silence Shin's name had left. "My father was one, you see, and my oldest brother. They always looked so grand in their uniforms. And their crimson sashes. I do not think I am brave enough though, even had I been born a boy."

"It isn't bravery you need, it's conviction. And if you don't want to die, then it's a lot of luck you need rather than a lot of skill."

"Really? I had always thought skill and bravery were all a soldier needed."

" 'Disabuse no mind already turned toward its purpose,' " I said, a grimace following the quotation as I recalled its origin. "An observation from General Kin's war diaries," I added when Tili gave me a curious look. "He wrote a lot while campaigning along the border in 1346. And during the uprising of the tribes in 1349. Darius said they were required reading for every young man of rank and ambition, so I read them."

Tili opened her mouth to speak only to close it again and look down at the blood-spattered floor. "It must have been interesting to meet His Majesty after that."

"I didn't think about it, honestly, but I recall there was always something missing from the diaries, some...level of honesty. Darius said it would have been lost in the transcribing, that whatever he wrote in his original diaries would have been edited to present a particular view of him to the nobility when the works were published. But he is a little bit like that in person too. Occasional flashes of vulnerability and humanity hidden deep inside the thick shell of Emperor Kin."

Tili screwed up her face. "I'm not sure I understand."

"I don't think I do either. But I do wonder where the imperial façade ends and the man begins."

With a last tear of fabric, Wen finished binding the amputated leg. A swig of water from his waterskin and he moved on, Tili and me in his wake.

A few pallets away, one of the old healers we had lured to our cause with the promise of payment was tending a pair of severed fingers and nodded to Wen, causing the Pike to redden a little at such an acknowledgement.

"You did well," the man said, nodding in the direction of the soldier whose leg had been amputated. "Where did you train?"

"I didn't, I...I just, picked things up," Wen said. "I mean, I always wanted to, just..."

He trailed off, but the old man went on smiling, then leaning closer, he said, "Me too."

"Really? But you have—" Wen pointed at the special loop of coloured cloth most physicians wore tied to their sashes.

"War teaches much that you need to know about healing," the man said. "Whether it is the wounds of soldiers or the ailments of the poor left undernourished with dirty water. I learnt through the last civil war because there weren't enough healers to help all those who needed it and every hand was welcome, and by the time it was over, I knew more than enough to earn the title. And had seen more than I ever wanted to of suffering. War profits none but our rulers."

The healer's gaze flittered to me, and I wondered if I had stiffened or twitched or made any show of discomfort to have drawn his attention. Either way, he bowed to me in respect for my title, but his smile had gone.

"Not all rulers care so little," Wen said, perhaps sensing the awkwardness. "Lady Hana seeks always to do what is right for the people."

"How can any ruler who lives so high above the rest of us know what that is?"

"'Those who seek to do right will ever have a beacon to guide them through the murk,'" Wen quoted from the Book of Qi, and seeing the man showed every sign of wanting to argue the point, I left them to it and moved on, intent on working all the harder for the rest of the day.

When a new batch of wounded were carried in, Shin appeared with news that the battle fared well for us. The Pike gave no explanation for his absence, nor in the sudden flurry of activity could I demand one. I was too busy running for water, tearing new bandages, and performing every little task Wen apologetically asked of me.

But with every bloodied face and severed limb, with every pierced gut and head wound, and every man who did not make it, more and more doubts wormed their way into my thoughts. I had grown up believing the empire belonged to the Otakos, that we were its rightful rulers, that Kin was nothing but a Usurper, a placeholder, and when I had heard Katashi was fighting for his throne, I had left everything behind to be a part of it.

It is conviction, not bravery, that leads men to war. Another quotation from Kin's war diaries that had stuck with me over the years, and whether it was the sight of so much suffering, or the weeks I had spent in his court, my conviction was weakening. I still believed we ought to have the throne, that it had been our family's legacy for so many generations that one clever man ought not be able to supersede it, but how much death and suffering was the outcome worth?

I had no answer, no alternative, and while I hurried mindlessly through the ranks of enemy soldiers and farmers and common folk who lay dying, I felt like I was drowning in a dark sea. All I could do was run Wen's errands and gulp down bowls of the nasty wine he plied his patients with—anything to keep myself from thinking. From doubting.

By the time I gave in to Shin's insistence that we return to our camp, my head was buzzing and my vision wobbled. The ride back in the gathering gloom did nothing to help. Perhaps by claiming a headache, I could forgo the council meeting that night, avoiding at least until the following day the inevitable rebukes I would receive from Katashi's advisors. And worse, from Katashi himself. He had dismissed all my attempts to organise proper care for the wounded enemy soldiers, would not listen to my suggestions for political wins when he could crush Kin in battle, and I was beginning to fear his need for revenge drove him more surely than any desire for the throne.

With such thoughts throbbing through my head, I returned to my tent only to find him already waiting for me. I almost tripped over my feet so comically did I flinch, but he just smiled. And between that smile and the sight of him eating my dinner in his under-robe, I had to grip the tent pole and catch my breath. For whatever fears I harboured, he was a different man when he was here with me alone.

"Good evening, my dear," he said. "I am still alive, as you see, or is it too much to hope you worried for me today?"

"I always worry for you. That's why I keep myself busy." I had too fuzzy a head to attempt to spar with him and resorted to honesty. "You're angry with me because I organised aid for your injured enemies."

He tilted his head to the side with a little half smile, and for a moment, fear and frustration warred with the desire his very presence demanded of my body. "Not angry," he said at last. "Not while your actions make Kin look the fool rather than me. I do wonder, though, whether you will ever listen to what I say or believe someone else might understand the ways of war better than you do."

"I do listen."

"And then go and do exactly the opposite of what I say, yes. That, you must admit, my dear, makes it look as if it is you who rules me, not the other way around."

There was a hint of challenge in his look that sent heat coursing through me, and happy to avoid serious discussion while tired and tipsy, I strode toward him. "Well," I said, sitting on his lap, my chest pressed to his. "Perhaps I do."

Seemingly as happy as I to avoid the conversation, he wrapped his arms around me and grunted a little moan into my hair. "Do you indeed?" he said, kissing my neck. "I should like to see you try."

He pressed his next kiss to my lips only to pull a face. "Have you been drinking nettle wine?"

"Is that what it was? It was very foul and has made me feel quite wobbly."

"I'll bet it has." He grinned and kissed my neck again. "Too wobbly for this? If you eat some dinner, you may soon feel better."

I had drunk the wine to escape my doubts and had no desire to go back to them just yet. "I'd rather eat you." I snapped at his nose and he laughed, and I was sure it wasn't just my inebriated state that made me certain no sound more wonderful had ever existed. Except perhaps for the little groan he made when I kissed his ear. With another glorious laugh, he tumbled me onto the floor, and we soon lay together, breathless and sated.

While he held me to him in the fading afterglow, I thought of what I had said about Emperor Kin earlier, about wondering where the emperor ended and the man began. It was hard to see with Kin, but it had not taken long to realise Katashi was two separate men. This gentle, caring Katashi who kissed my forehead and murmured in my ear, who tightened his grip around my shoulders and traced patterns on my back was a man only I knew, only I saw. The moment he donned his robes or his armour and stepped out of my tent, he was gone.

Worries began to creep back in as the haze of wine and sex faded away. If he was a completely different man outside this space, how could I trust him? Which Katashi was the real Katashi? Would the kind man or the ruthless man be the one to sit upon the throne?

"Katashi?" I said, breaking the companionable silence. "What sort of deal are you making with the pirate enclave?"

"That," he said somewhat sleepily, "is not a very romantic question."

"Need all my questions be romantic?"

He turned his head to regard me, no smile in his eyes. "No, but you have already expressed concern that I am dealing with them. There seems little point in returning to that conversation now unless you're seeking an argument."

"No argument, just trying to understand. Do they not often raid the coast? Even attack Syan?"

"Yes, but that's not what I am asking them to do."

"But surely dealing with them at all can only anger those who suffer from such raids. Won't the duke of Syan—?"

Katashi withdrew his arm from around me and propped himself up on one elbow. "How would he know I have any dealings with them at all?"

"Is it not common knowledge?"

"No. Beyond my advisors, no one knows. You may be sure your maid was informed of just how much trouble she would be in if she spoke of their presence in my camp to anyone."

I drew back, both the afterglow and the lingering buzz from the wine entirely gone now. "You threatened Tili?"

"No one can know, Hana. No one. I told you before this all looks like a great victory, but it means nothing until I can take Mei'lian, until I can secure what I have. I cannot let it all come tumbling down because a maid talked when she ought not."

"If I trust her, I don't see why that isn't enough assurance for you."

"That must surely rank as the most naive thing you've ever said." He got to his feet on the words and started pulling on the under-robe he had so hastily discarded. "I am an emperor. I cannot trust people. I cannot leave things to chance. I cannot hope. I cannot even allow myself the luxury of considering what is good and right and honourable because any weakness, any failure could end with my head on the block like my father's before me. I have come too far to go back now, come too far to escape that end should it all go wrong, and I will do whatever it takes to ensure that doesn't happen. I will not let that man finish the job of destroying our family, and if that means I deal with pirates, then I will deal with pirates."

"I understand that, Katashi, I do, but there are some lengths that are too far. There must be better ways."

He tugged the knot of his sash tight. "It's almost time for the meeting, so you will have to excuse me, Your Grace."

"Do your other advisors know exactly what deal you are making with them?" I said, drawing my own robe around me as his chilliness touched my very skin. "Because conversation about it has been lacking at the meetings. Unless, of course, you have other meetings to which I am not invited."

"Conversations occur in many places, Your Grace," he said with the slightest of sneers, though it was enough to make me hug my robe tight. "And just as you are capable of organising an entire group of physicians to give aid to my enemies without consulting me, so am I able to make decisions without consulting you. You have no greater claim on me than that of long-lost cousin, after all, having refused to be my wife."

He strode to the tent flap through which a sliver of night peeped, only to turn back and bow. "Good evening, Your Grace," he said and was gone, leaving me to stare after him and wish my words unsaid.

We travelled the next day and I kept my distance, unsure what to do. For the first time, he had transformed so completely into his imperial self in our sacred space, but I could no more promise to keep from discussing his plans and his movements than I could stop myself from wanting him. Instead, I watched his various advisors come and go from his side as he led his army ever south, and wondered what plans they were allowed knowledge of that I was not. And worse, why.

It was an uneventful day, and the scouts brought back no news of enemy movement. The camp went up with the same ease it always did, but when the usual time for our meeting arrived, Tili brought a message that there would be no meeting that night. I was about to send her back with one civilly asking for an explanation, when Katashi arrived. As usual, he had changed his armour for his imperial robes and stood in the tent aperture as though unsure of his welcome. Equally unsure whether I wanted to welcome him, I lifted my chin. "Good evening, Your Majesty."

"Good evening, Your Grace," he said, but there was a hint of his dimple peeping despite his gravity.

"Have you come to tell me about the alliance with the pirate enclave?"

The dawning smile faded. "No." He strode in, restlessness in the way he moved about the small space from one silken wall to the other. "Hana, I know you want to be part of this. I know you want to fight and you want to have your opinions heard, but I can't let you talk me out of things that have to be done. I have lived the broken life of an exile long enough to know how to make hard choices. I have already made more hard choices than you know. I want you here, I want you at my side, but either you have to let go of the idea that you can always do the right thing, that duty and honour are more important than success, or you have to let me keep plans from you."

"Are they really so terrible?" I said.

"Yes."

"Why?"

"Because they have to be."

The hard note in his voice scared me. As Captain Monarch, he had done plenty of things a truly good man would never have done, and he had executed more members of Kin's court at Koi than I could count. Those were the harsh actions of a man who knew what needed to be done, but he hadn't shied away from me knowing of them.

"I can have a few dozen of my soldiers escort you back to Koi in the morning," he said, finally stopping his restless pacing to look down at me.

"No," I said. "I want to stay, but I want to know. Whatever your plans are, I want to know them."

"No."

I had thought I could cajole him, could argue my point until at last he let me in. But no matter what I said Katashi was stubborn in his refusal, and although our frayed tempers found release in the messy ruins of my sleeping mat, I felt more distant from him than ever by the time he left.

The following day, I found my thoughts shying into troubling places. Kin had said much of my father's selfishness, of my family's inability to rule fairly, and of Katashi's unconcern for the people he would call his own. I'd had strong arguments once, but fear is a corroding force and I was growing afraid of the Katashi I could not control.

I tried talking to him again that night, but discussion soon became argument, and when we ended up gasping together on the floor my fear only increased. I began to imagine all the awful things he could be planning and tried to convince myself it was all necessary, only to hear Kin's damning words. *As if the god Otakos ever cared whether they did the right thing.*

The next day we travelled only half the usual distance, because Katashi sent groups of soldiers out to burn the fields as we marched. He would not talk to me nor even look at me all day, and ill ease churned ever more sickeningly in my gut. *I have worked hard to ensure Kisia had the stability it needed to grow and thrive*, Kin had said, *but your cousin cares nothing for the people and thinks only of his own desires.*

Every day Katashi asked if I wanted to leave and every day I refused, caught between assuring myself his plans could not be that bad and the fear he would soon commit an atrocity I could never forgive. So when he did not come to see me that night, I did not send for him, not sure if I was more afraid he would convince me the burning had been necessary or that he would not.

The following morning, I woke to emptiness beside me, but it was Tili's presence quietly shuffling around the tent that was out of place. The sunlight too was brighter than it ought to have been, and still drowsy from a night of worries, I asked how late it was.

"The sun has been up some two hours, Your Grace," she said. "Breakfast is here. It may be starting to get cold, along with your washing water. You were so deeply asleep I didn't want to wake you."

"Are we not packing up the camp today?"

"No, Your Grace. Scouts came in the night. There was some enemy movement, and as there's a . . . blind pass? It was decided this morning that we would stay here another day."

Enemy movement meant another engagement. I closed my eyes, my thoughts darting from the Kisian soldiers left to die to the burning fields to the alliance with the pirate enclave, and I felt sick. "Has Katashi—? Have the soldiers already left?"

"No, Your Grace, I'm not sure why. Everyone seems to be just waiting around."

I let out a sigh and hauled myself up off my sleeping mat, though fatigue tried to hold me down. "Help me into my armour. I had better go and see."

The camp was oddly tense and quiet when I stepped out of my tent—Pikes and soldiers all gathered in groups and talking in low voices. I received the usual bows of acknowledgement from those who saw me pass, but though they were all dressed for battle, no one seemed to know what was going on.

I found Katashi, General Manshin, and Captain Chalpo standing together at the edge of the camp, staring out at the churned earth of what had once been a green meadow. There was no sign of anyone approaching, but the three of them were as intent on the horizon as they were on their discussion.

General Manshin turned first, a humourless smile spreading his thin lips. "Ah, Your Grace. You find us standing around to no purpose this morning, I'm afraid."

Katashi greeted me with a nod and nothing more, and I could not tell if he was merely maintaining the guise of disinterested respect or wished me elsewhere. "We were expecting to meet one of Kin's battalions in the field today," he said, returning his gaze to the horizon. "But the scouts now tell us they are marching this way with white flags."

"Surrendering?"

"So it would seem," General Manshin said. "It may be a very dishonourable ruse, of course, but we are ready if that is so."

I wished I could send both him and Chalpo away, sure there was more to the situation than Katashi was letting on, but there was nothing to do but walk away or join them. Failing to catch Katashi's eye, I ranged myself alongside General Manshin and stared out at the flat expanse. Such level ground would grow increasingly rare as we moved south, the land around Esvar the most mountainous in the empire.

I fidgeted with my sash while we waited, unable to be calm. If the others noticed they showed no sign of it, just as Katashi was seemingly unaware of my ongoing attempts to catch his eye. All too soon, white flags appeared on the horizon, followed by the dark mass of an approaching army. Pikes, imperial soldiers, and camp labourers began to gather behind us, some with their hands on their weapons, others merely craning their necks to better see the show. Katashi stood at his ease and watched them approach.

There had to be at least a thousand of them, a broad force that stretched the width of the plain upon which we camped. Most wore the uniform of Kin's imperial battalions, but a large portion were dressed in the common garb of town guards. There were even a few military messengers dotted about their ranks.

Leaving his soldiers at a little distance, their leader stepped forward holding a white flag high. Katashi could have walked out to meet him, but instead he stood patient as the man came to us.

It was a middle-aged man with bright, clever eyes, who halted before Katashi and let his white flag drop onto the churned earth at his feet. His sword followed with a thud. "Your Majesty," he said and bowed. "My name is Commander Ko and I have taken over command of this military district. The previous commander was not a friend of yours, but he was... persuaded to step aside."

The man gestured to one side of his force where a portion of the soldiers stood in chains.

"I see," Katashi said. "And the rest of you and your men want what, Commander?"

"To fight for you, Your Majesty, we live to serve the true imperial blood."

I held my breath, looking from the commander with his head bowed, to Katashi, to the general at his side. Seconds stretched in the still morning, until at last, Katashi nodded. "Very well, Commander. You and your men will take the oath, but first, bring forward the traitors."

Without hesitation, the commander turned. "Bring them," he called back to his men, and with a shuffling of many feet, a large chunk of his force started forward. Again, I was conscious of a desire to step closer to Katashi, fearing what he meant to do, but I could only stand and watch while Kin's men were brought forward.

It was perhaps a quarter of the army, a whole great mass of soldiers hustled together to face the emperor they had refused to serve. Katashi stared back at them, and I not the only one who held my breath.

"Kill them."

"What?" I cried, but the word was drowned beneath a tumultuous cheer as Katashi's soldiers thrust their weapons into the air. "Katashi, you can't mean to—"

"Now."

Had I been standing any closer, blood would have splattered

over me, for as soon as the order left Katashi's lips, Commander Ko slit the first prisoner's throat. Blood poured down his neck, and the man slumped onto his knees. Another joined him, straining at his chains to reach his throat as all around them the soldiers who had switched sides killed those who had not. Within minutes, they all lay dead, a pile of discarded bodies with their hands still chained, heaped before their new emperor. It took all I had not to empty my stomach upon the grass.

"Get rid of the bodies," Katashi said to General Manshin. "And I want each of these soldiers to come to my tent and give their oath in person. All of them, and any who doesn't goes the same way as their comrades."

"Yes, Your Majesty," General Manshin said, but Katashi was already striding away, and pushing through the closely packed spectators, I hurried after him, my pulse thrumming in my ears.

"Katashi—Your Majesty. Your Majesty!"

He looked over his shoulder, the crowd of his soldiers parting before him. "Do you really think this is the time?"

"Those men had surrendered," I hissed, hurrying to catch up so I could keep my voice low. "None of them had to die. You could have imprisoned them or set them to work or sold them back to their families. You could have—"

Katashi pushed his way into his tent and rounded on me with a snarl. "This, this is why we can't keep doing this. Yes, I could have done those things, but then I couldn't have been sure of the other soldiers' loyalty. Had they hesitated, I would have known I could not trust them and could not have them fight for me, but now through the deaths of a few, we have gained many, and that, Hana, is worth the sacrifice."

"Hardly your sacrifice."

"Men who sit on thrones may be able to live by such honourable ideals, but only after they have paid in blood to be there. You think

Kin got to sit on the Crimson Throne by sparing all the lives he could? No. The only way to survive is to be ruthless, that's the lesson the Usurper taught me before I was even old enough to understand it."

"There must be other ways, Katashi, ways that don't involve bloodshed!"

"You think Kin will give a damn about anything else?" he raged. "Do you think anything else will make him break? This is a man who has let the pirate enclave raid up and down the coast for years, pillaging villages because that trouble was far away and not harming his power. See how he likes it when those same pirates sail right up the Tzitzi River and burn Shimai to the ground. That is the only show of power that can make a man like him surrender."

"Is that what you plan to do?" I said, shock stealing strength from my voice.

"Yes, because I will do whatever it takes to win this."

He spat the last words in my face, his bright eyes wild, and I stepped back, trembling at his ferocity. A whole city. He was planning to let pirates sack and burn a whole city, no regret in his words, no remorse for the men already dead, just chill fury. He would watch the whole empire burn if that was what it took.

"Now you finally have your answer, my dear," he said, a sneer twisting his lips. "Plenty of time to wish you had not asked. Go on, get out. I have oaths to receive."

I ran. There might already have been soldiers outside waiting to take their oaths, but I saw no one for the tears that stung my eyes as I hurried the short distance to my own tent. Tili was still there, and as I burst in with a sob, she looked up, worry creasing her brow.

"What is it, Your Grace? What has happened?"

All Katashi's reasons chased his crimes to my tongue, but looking into Tili's worried face, I recalled her warnings and could not help but think of the heads mounted on spikes in the passage at

Koi and the blood on the executioner's block—all the things I had chosen not to see. All Kin's words I had chosen to ignore. Katashi was still my emperor, but I could not let him do this.

"Tili, fetch ink."

She brought the lap table and knelt, stirring the ink and mending my brush while I tried to steady shaking hands. I kept looking toward the tent entrance, expecting Katashi to appear as though drawn by the treason I contemplated.

"Find Wen for me," I said when Tili was done. "But make sure he is alone when he comes."

"Yes, Your Grace."

She went out, leaving me staring at the blank page, wondering what to write, my hands still shaking as I nibbled the tip of the brush. In the end, I managed nothing more than a few short sentences, carefully crafted for anonymity. I rolled up the paper and thrust it into Wen's hand the moment he walked in. "I need you to get this to Kin through one of the physicians tending his soldiers."

"Your Grace?"

"Please, Wen, I need you to do this for me. It's extremely important and no one can know. I can trust you not to betray me to Katashi, can't I?"

14. DARIUS

I left Kimiko sleeping. Curled up as she was, she looked no bigger than a cat, her hair fanning from her head like a magnificent aura. I dressed at the other end of the room and watched her breathe, the covers rising and falling with every reassuring sign of life. A lifetime ago, Avarice would have stood just so, watching me sleep, checking in as often as he could to be sure I was still alive. This room had been his and it had become my sanctuary, the home of a child long left to the ministration of an ever-dwindling number of servants.

As I tied my sash, my gaze shied to the panel behind which I'd long ago hidden my treasure box. It had contained the first Errant set I had learnt to play with, a favourite book, a silver cup, and my mother's pink sash. But keepsakes were sentimental, emotive. Weak. I had cast them into the fire the night my father died. It had cost me a pang to burn the book, but by the time my mother's sash slipped into the flames, I had thought myself free.

I tugged my sash tight and turned my back on the room. Out in the hallway, Endymion was fighting wakefulness with many a long sigh and rustle of covers. He had piled old blankets on top of himself as though it were the middle of winter, but now they lay strewn across the floor from an uneasy sleep. His chestnut hair stuck to his brow in a damp tangle, his Larothian features more apparent at rest. Avarice had called it an "arrogance of brow," and looking at Endymion, I could see why. He never looked proud when awake, but the natural resting state of his face owned something of Malice's arrogant look. No doubt Kimiko would say I had it too.

The set of his features changed while I watched, becoming more like the Endymion to whom I had grown accustomed. "You're awake," I said.

He opened his eyes. "Why are you staring at me?"

"Because you are such a handsome specimen of manliness."

"Is that supposed to be funny?"

"Do you see me laughing?"

Endymion propped himself up on an elbow. "You sneer a lot, but do you ever laugh?"

"Sometimes," I said. "When something is funny. I am no less a man than you, you know."

"I know."

I heard extra meaning in those words and wondered how much he could see of my inner fears. I had come here in the hope that continuing to fight for Kin whether he wanted me or not would return the burden of control to his shoulders, but the situation was fraught with too much fear and anxiety to just let it go. Losing too many battles to Katashi might lead to losing the whole war, and under those conditions, I could not relax, could not be still, could not just accept whatever would come.

And then there was Kimiko.

"Get up," I said, cutting that thought off where it began. "It's time to play."

"Play?"

"Errant, of course. How else do you expect to learn anything?"

"But I don't know how to play."

"Then it's time you learnt that too."

I continued along the passage, leaving Endymion to scramble up behind me, but it would take more than determination to understand what he wished to learn. I was not even sure I could make him truly understand with a few words what it had taken me years to recognise. That the root of Empathy was not compassion; it was fear.

Out in the courtyard, early morning sunlight was breaking through the thick covering of vines, the air heavy with a sickly-sweet scent of fallen petals. It was a smell to which I had grown accustomed but not one I had ever liked. I ought to pay someone to sweep the stones and trim the vines, to paint the gates and fix the kitchens and send up all the food Kimiko kept reminding me we needed, but... while each was a little thing, the whole was a level of care I could not bring myself to take.

"Where do we play?" Endymion asked, looking around, and for the first time, I envied his sheltered upbringing. He had never had to live here, unwanted and forgotten and unloved.

"You're standing on the board."

He looked down. Numerous Errant boards were carved into the stones, each with its own pot of obsidian pieces. Everything here had once been decorated in obsidian, mined from the pits that had brought money to the estate.

"We sit on the ground?" Endymion asked.

"That is a very Chiltaen objection."

He shook his head. "I was merely thinking about that robe you're wearing."

"This robe is already beyond salvation. Why is it everyone assumes I would never recover from the mere dirtying of my robe?"

"Perhaps because you always look so neat."

I had to smile. "I never used to be," I said. "Ask Avarice one day."

"The last time I asked Avarice about you, he told me that I talk too much."

"He used to like talking."

Endymion shrugged. "Time changes men, I suppose."

"No," I said, holding back a sigh and pointing to the pot of pieces. "Empathy changes men. Bring the pot."

He asked no more questions, just went to fetch the pot, half-carrying, half-dragging it across the moss-bisected stones while I settled myself on the ground. Cross-legged, the silk of my robe fanned out around me.

Endymion settled himself opposite. "Well?" I said, finding him staring. "Get the pieces out. You know how to set up the board, I assume."

"I recall being taught how, before Jian gave up on me."

"Your priest never gave up on you," I said.

The old clay screeched as Endymion slid off the lid and dug out a handful of smooth stone pieces. He scattered them across the board, returning to the pot again and again until he had them all.

"Don't you want to know if he's alive?" I asked when he made no further mention of his priest.

"I already know he is. I looked for him."

"Looked for him?"

"The same way I looked for you. I think it only works with people my Empathy has touched before. He's that way." He pointed in the vague direction of the capital. "And he's not in pain anymore."

I examined his features, looking for the young man I had first seen back in Shimai. He was there in the tousled brown hair, in the carelessness, in the set of his soulful brown eyes and the restlessness of his hands. But he held himself up now, straight, tall, his gaze direct, his lips slightly curled. He was becoming the god he wanted to beat, and he couldn't even see it happening.

"That," I said, trying to keep my voice steady despite the fear of such words, "is not something you should be able to do."

"I know." He looked up from his examination of the empty board. "That's why I'm here. I'm scared, Darius. The moment I relax and let my mind drift, it... really drifts. It's getting harder to focus."

I pointed at the pieces. "Then let's play."

"All right. Teach me."

"If I must teach you from the beginning, your education has been very poor."

"Who taught *you* to play? Our father?"

Bitterness. He thought he was the one who had missed out. "No," I said, taking up the pieces. "Avarice."

His surprise rang clear in a way his other emotions weren't, but he accepted the answer without question and gathered the pieces I had left behind. "I know there is one king, with a crown painted on the bottom," he said. "I know I can place it wherever I like and shouldn't let you know where. I know we're supposed to jump pieces and I know we're supposed to make it to the corner."

"The Gate," I corrected. "Yes. That is the general idea."

Seeking my king in the cluster of painted obsidian, I set it on the board, followed by the rest, one after the other. Endymion watched me, then did the same, the usual click of wood on wood replaced by scraping stone.

"Lead or follow?" I asked when he had finished.

"Which is better?"

"One is not better than the other. Errant is played the best of three rounds. The person who chooses to lead starts first in the first round and follows in the second."

"And what happens in the third round?"

"In the third, the pieces are placed at random."

"So I won't know where my king is?"

"No."

Endymion stared down at the board. "Lead," he said.

"As you wish."

"Why do I feel like I made the wrong choice?"

"Perhaps because I am looking at you with disdain," I said. "But is that because you made the wrong decision? Or because I want you to think you made the wrong decision?"

"Or because you're an ass?"

It was the sort of quick wit that made Kimiko's company so enjoyable, and I laughed without thinking, able only in its aftermath to fear such lack of control.

"I thought you didn't have a sense of humour," he said, even as I crushed the smile between hard lips.

"And I thought you wanted to learn."

"I want to learn how to control myself. I don't see what that has to do with Errant."

I sighed and pointed at his pieces. "No lesson worth learning is ever straightforward," I said. "Play."

"That sounds like nonsense."

"And that sounds like someone putting off making their first move because he doesn't want to mess it up. Play."

Endymion pinched a piece between thumb and forefinger. "To the corner?"

"The Gate, yes," I said. "Or you can win by turning my king."

"But I don't know which one it is."

"Perhaps if you watch the way I play, you might figure it out, yes?"

He gave me a strange look and moved the piece forward. I copied without pause, the world vanishing as I gave my mind to the game. Endymion stared at the board, but I could feel the weight of his Empathy against me, sticky like a humid summer day. It ranged around me, touching, searching, though he appeared unaware of it, his sole focus the carved board between us with its army of black glass.

"Do you know what empathy is, Endymion?" I asked, watching him pinch the top of another piece like a court lady lifting the lid on a teapot. "True empathy, not the sort you were born with, but the way other people experience it."

"Feeling other people's pain."

"Vicarious participation in another's emotion is the way our father put it. To imagine yourself in another's place. Whether that is painful or pleasurable is not the point."

"What is the point?"

"The point, dear brother," I said, "is that Empaths are not empathetic. We do not choose to participate in another person's emotions on compassionate grounds. In fact, compassion is the only thing that's making you want to control what you are now, control the invasion of another's privacy, control the pain you can so easily cause. Compassion is the opposite of our Empathy in many ways."

He pinned me with a gaze frightening in its intensity. "Is that why you wanted to control it? Because you didn't want to hurt people?"

"Is it not your reason?"

A frown flickered across his face. "I'm … not sure. I mean, yes, of course I don't want to hurt people. Brother Jian taught me all the tenets, and I don't want to harm anyone, but … he also believed my skills could be used for good, and … maybe he's right, I don't know, but it's *eating* me, Darius, and I can't stop it."

Repressing a shiver, I pointed at the board. "Play. We're going to start with a thought exercise. Tell me, did your priest ever teach you how to lie?"

"No." He turned a pair of my pieces though seemed to be paying little attention to the game.

"Did he ever teach you what it looks like when other people lie? Fidgeting, touching their nose and their lips, unable to make eye contact."

"No."

"Good, because that's only what bad liars look like. Do you trust me, Endymion?"

Again, he looked up from the game, and I forced myself to meet his gaze. "Yes," he said. "Otherwise I wouldn't be here."

"You believe I won't lie to you?"

Endymion didn't answer.

"Let's try this then," I said, jumping three of his pieces. He showed no interest when I turned them, unwittingly letting me know none were his king. "Ask me a question and then tell me if I lie."

"What is your name?"

"Darius Kirei Laroth. Who's the ass now? Ask me a question you don't already know the answer to."

He was slowly edging his king toward my Gate, shifting it with a nonchalance that was terrible to behold. Perhaps he hoped such carelessness would be infectious. "Where were you born?"

Behind me, I could feel the house like prey feels a stalking predator. "Beneath a bush," I said. "In the gardens beyond the house."

Those eyes scanned my face, but they would find nothing. I had learnt to control my expression.

His Empathy struck like a sharp gust of air, its ghostly hand crushing me in its grip. Snarling, I lifted my shield with the strength of desperation. "Not like that!"

The pressure dissipated, pulling away like a beast to lurk, reluctantly, beyond my range.

And he hadn't even touched me.

"Look at my face," I said, each breath coming a little too quick. "Look at my face and tell me if you think I am lying."

Endymion stared at me mildly, seemingly unaware of the leashed creature he held in his hands. "You're lying."

"Am I? Why do you say so?"

"Because even peasants aren't born beneath bushes."

"And that's what you're basing your decision on? The probability of my words being true?"

"What else?" He moved a piece, jumping three of mine without touching the stone board in between. At the end, he put the piece down, and turning only the middle man he had won, he flipped my king. Its white crown faced the cloudless sky. "I see with the eyes I was born with," he said. "I have no others."

I stared at the board. I had deliberately formed an appealing string for him to jump, close to the Gate and away from my king, but he had gone the other way. He had known. He had felt it, and I had not noticed the intrusion.

Again, I forced myself to meet that direct gaze.

The eyes he was born with. Malice had always called Normals blind, deaf, mute—like a pale brood of mice shut away in the dark. Without the Sight, the world was dulled, every sound, every smell, every colour, every taste.

I picked up my Errant pieces and turned them over and over in my hand like a nervous child.

"Did our father try to kill you?"

The question came from nowhere and I flinched. "Stay out of my head, Endymion."

"I'll take that as a yes, shall I?"

"You know nothing about it," I returned fiercely. "He showed you more kindness than he ever showed me. I was nothing more than proof of his sickness, something that needed to be eradicated. So yes, he did try to kill me, and he failed because he was weak. He couldn't do it himself, couldn't stick his sword into me and have done. No. No such quick death for his only legitimate son and heir. Why not let nature kill what it had created instead."

The words stopped spilling, but I was breathing fast, the memory so real that for an instant, rain lashed my face, obscuring Endymion's intent gaze. I wanted to push him away, to demand he stop staring at me, but that would only crack my armoured skin further still. All I had ever wanted was my father's love.

"Is that why you think about Malice so much?" he said. "Why you miss him? Your father never loved you but Malice did. Now Kimiko is beginning to, and you want it so much that it scares you. But you're tired of suffering too, and if there's even a small chance you could stop your Empathy from defining you, you would take it, and that frightens you even more."

His eyes had glazed as he spilled fears from my mind onto the stones, so stark and raw, each a blade in my skin. Endymion ought to have been horrified to hear it, but he seemed not to know his own words.

"Tell me, how many people are in this house, Endymion?" I said.

"Two."

"How many people in Esvar?"

"One thousand seven hundred and nine."

His eyes grew even less focussed, and I felt sick to the pit of my stomach. "And the Valley?"

"Twenty-two thousand eight hundred and seventy-seven."

It was a truth I could not verify, but with about a hundred and fifty villages farming the land, it seemed accurate enough.

"And Kisia?"

Eyes closed, Endymion grew still, his long fingers resting lightly upon his linen-clad knees. His frown deepened.

"They took my husband in the last war," he said in a scratchy whisper. "They won't take my son. Forty bushels? That's barely enough wheat for thirty. Wine, girl, not water, what stupid bitch gives a man water? That ship will never come back. The storms are coming."

He opened his eyes. "One million three hundred and twenty-one thousand four hundred and two."

I couldn't but stare it was so horrific and yet remarkable, his strength immense even for a Whisperer. Yet at Koi, he had been barely more powerful than Malice. Could so short a time really make so great a difference?

I held out my hand. "Touch me."

Endymion lifted his hand and we connected over the stone board. He did not have to force it. At first touch, our souls joined, and he began drawing me out, thoughts and memories sliding through my fingers. He had done the same at Koi, but I had given them to him then. Now his every breath sucked emotion, sucked life. And he wasn't even trying.

In the darkness, men screamed.

I pulled my hand away, fingers shaking like the wisteria as a breeze gusted through the court, picking up a flurry of petals. In mere weeks, his strength had doubled. Malice had been right. If he lost himself, there was no way I could control him on my own.

"He's coming," Endymion said.

"Malice?"

"Yes, he'll be here in a few days." He touched his palm to his chest. "Or maybe a little longer. It's hard to tell."

Reaching over the Errant board, I gripped his shoulders. "You said you broke his mark. How?"

"Fill it with hate. Hate is what hurts him most. Hate and abandonment." It sounded like a quotation, but though I did not recognise the words, I recognised the sentiments. The two things Malice had always feared above all others: being hated by those he loved and being abandoned. Someone else had come to know him well enough to see it, to see why his marks kept the Vices close and why they had to obey. He had never been able to see that obedience and love were not the same thing.

"Love," Endymion said abruptly, and I withdrew my hands. "Your marks are full of love because that's what you've always wanted. Love and control, and you're afraid it's not you she is falling in love with at all but just the mark inside her."

He looked over my shoulder. Kimiko was standing in the doorway, and I tried to tell myself it was the sight of her that sent my heart thumping, not Endymion's words.

I got to my feet, leaving the Errant pieces set for a game not yet played. "Keep out of my head, Endymion," I said. "I won't warn you again. When you come back to your senses, find me. I can't teach you anything when you're like this."

I could try to shock him out of it, with cold water or a jolt of emotion, but too full of my own fears, I turned toward the house.

"You don't need to believe Kisia needs no god, Darius," he said. The words halted my steps like a hand upon my shoulder, and I turned back. Endymion had not moved. He knelt upon the stones, vines rising behind him like a throne. "You are one, and you are already here."

———————————

My makeshift office on the portico had begun to feel like home, and I let out a sigh as I knelt before my desk. I had been too busy and distracted to keep it tidy, leaving no space for my tea tray amid the thick covering of papers, so I made space by using it to push other things off.

"That is not a very orderly way to clear your desk," Kimiko said as she dropped onto the pile of cushions she had brought out a few days ago, preferring to read while I worked than be inside by herself.

"My thoughts are not yet orderly enough for orderly desk clearing, for which you are entirely to blame, my lady."

"Oh, are we on formal terms again now?"

I met her laughing gaze. "I hardly feel that is possible when my back is so riddled with cuts."

"There's some blood on your lip too."

I touched where she had so recently bitten me, and my fingertip came away red. "Is that really necessary?" I said. "Being reminded of you every time I move already makes it hard enough to concentrate on *orderly desk clearing*."

Kimiko rose from the cushions and padded over in her bare feet. "Here, let me get it."

She bent and gently kissed the corner of my mouth, sucking clean the remaining blood. "Oh." She groaned as she straightened. "That was way more exhilarating than I was expecting. I should bite you that hard more often." She licked her lips as if hunting for any lingering trace of my blood, and my kindling desire died with a grimace.

"Sorry, my dear, I'm afraid that was just me you were feeling."

"What do you mean?"

I tapped my lip. "My blood. It can carry emotions and sensations that even those who aren't Empaths can feel. I was more than halfway to wanting to tear your robe off again, and you got that when you…"

I faltered beneath her intent stare. "Are you telling me that if I want to know what you're feeling, I can just drink your blood and find out first-hand?"

"It's really not that simple. And please don't. Have some tea instead." I held a bowl up to her, and she took it with a seemingly unconscious little bow of thanks.

"Fine," she said. "Tea it is, but I guess that explains why I like the taste of your blood so much, when…" A troubled look flickered across her face, but she shook it away. "Even without that added spice, you would taste better than this tea at all events. Have you ordered fresh leaves yet?"

"No."

"Food?"

"No."

"Fresh robes?"

I grimaced rather than repeat the negative.

Kimiko rolled her eyes. "Honestly, I don't understand you at all on this, Darius. I know you want fresh food and clothes and tea, but all you will send out for is information and spies. If your mind is too busy thinking of other things, then give me permission to go down into the town, or send Endy—Takehiko if you don't trust me."

"Not trust you? I told you who he really was, didn't I?"

Taking her tea with her, she settled back onto her cushions, managing not to break her gaze from mine. "Yes. I wanted to ask you about that, it's been bothering me."

"Then by all means, ask away, my dear," I said. "If I can answer you, I promise I will do so honestly."

She gave me an odd look, but it was the unsure little flutter in her heart that made mine thump hard. Her growing love was like a jolt of adrenaline, and I revelled in it despite the fear scratching at my thoughts. Hate it though I did, Endymion had been right. I feared it was nothing more than the mark I had left inside her staining her heart with false attachment.

"So," she said, setting down her tea bowl and splaying her hands on her knees. "He was not Emperor Lan's son, but he was still in the line of succession, wasn't he?"

"As far as I'm aware, yes. I believe he was acknowledged despite what seemed to be a general understanding that he was my father's bastard. That fact certainly makes him ineligible to take it, however."

"Yes, he's not the threat he might have been, though I imagine Kin would not like to have him floating around making trouble. Katashi certainly would not. Does he know?"

"His Majesty? No."

"You never told him?"

I had promised to answer honestly, and what a foolish promise it had been. "No," I said. "I didn't."

"Why?"

Why hadn't I? It had just seemed wise at the time not to trouble him with even more fears, but that was hardly a good reason. "I think...I think I didn't want to explain the dangers of having an Empath in a position of power." Again, the rawness of such honesty was like cutting my own skin and I wanted to look away.

"Like having one as the minister of the left?"

"Exactly like having one as the minister of the left."

For a moment, she mused on my answer, but any hope of escaping further questions was soon dashed. "Why didn't he tell us who he was? He travelled with us from Nivi Fen to Koi and never said a word."

"Probably for the same reason Hana never told you. Malice is very persuasive, and it's easy to believe your brother would kill anyone necessary on his way to revenge, even members of his own family."

She made no reply, perhaps remembering that he had sold her to Malice for a way into Koi. When she faded, ghostlike, for a moment, I was sure of it.

I'd come out here to attend to a number of small tasks, although for the most part I was just waiting on news from District Commander Yao. But I couldn't tell Kimiko about our plan to ambush Katashi at the northern pass, nor that Malice was on his way.

I ought to have known it wouldn't be long before he came in search of me. I could leave, could keep running, but what sort of a life was that? And then there was Endymion. If he failed, I would need Malice more than I had as a lost and lonely boy watching his world burn, and from there, what a frighteningly small step it would be to letting go entirely.

"You could leave here, you know," I said. "I could order you to leave so it doesn't hurt."

She scowled. "Bored of me?"

"Hardly, but I know you hate being stuck, and it's…not going to be safe here much longer."

Kimiko sat up straighter on her pile of cushions, her tea totally forgotten. "Because of the war?"

"No. Endymion. I think he's going to fail."

Her bright eyes roamed my face, her brow creased with worry. "You're teaching him how to control himself, aren't you? How to stop being an Empath."

"How simple you make everything sound, my dear," I said, and I could hear the sneer in my voice. "We were born with the marks and we will have them until the day we die." I drew back my sleeve. Three horizontal lines cut the inside of my wrist, crossed by a single diagonal.

Kimiko looked away, and though I knew it for a momentary instinct, that only made it hurt all the more.

I let my sleeve fall. "You should go."

"I'm sorry, but do you think this is easy for me?" She brandished the book she had been reading. "Do you think it's easy to give your heart to a man you know is capable of even more terrible things than ordinary men?"

"What happened to 'Empathy need not define you'? I warned you not to read the books, yes?"

She flinched. "Don't say that."

"Say what?"

"Don't say 'yes' like that; you sound just like him."

"I am just like him."

"Darius—"

"You should go." I stared down at the papers but did not see them, only the sneer with which Malice would mock me if he could see me now, could see how pathetically my heart ached.

With a rustle of cushions, she got to her feet. "I'm sorry, Darius, I am. It ought not define you, it doesn't, but just as you struggle to accept that, so must I learn to always trust it. To trust you."

"You should still go."

"Why?"

"I told you why. Endymion is going to fail."

"Then let him fail. What has that got to do with you?"

I looked up at her, the way she held herself and the great mass of her curls always making her look taller than she was. "I don't think you understand how powerful he has become, Kimiko. For now, he listens to me, he trusts me, but what will happen when he forgets everything his priest taught him?"

Despite the warmth, Kimiko shivered. "What will he do?"

"I don't know. I don't want to know. He killed one hundred and four men on the road to Rina by filling them with despair. He's capable of worse. I hoped I could teach him enough to combat the growth, but it's too late. I think he's beginning to realise his own strength, and nothing corrupts men faster than power."

She bent and gripped my chin, her fingers and thumb digging into my cheeks. "Why do you have to be so noble?" she said. "Why do you have to be such a good man?"

Holding her wrist, I prised my face from her grip. "You said earlier that I could do terrible things. Which am I? The monster or the paragon?"

"I don't know, but the monster would be easier to leave if that's what you really want me to do."

"I remember you saying something like that before. That you wished I were easier to hate."

"Or easier for my conscience to love."

I cringed. "A fine way to put it," I said. "I am not noble. I am the worst man you know, but still I cannot run and leave Kisia to its fate. Or Endymion."

Kimiko let out a long sigh and crouched beside me. "That was an awful thing for me to say. I'm sorry."

"You have already said that many times."

"Yes, and I think I will have to do so many more times. You see, I never planned on even liking you, Darius. Endymion scares me, and I hate Malice so much that I hope one day to repay him in kind for that scar of yours. Yes, I know it was him. What was it you said, that you got it the last time someone loved you? And if his heart is on the wrong side too, then I'll just have the joy of stabbing him twice."

How could I say I did not want her to? I could not defend his actions toward her nor even toward me, and yet had he appeared here and now, I would have held her back rather than let her kill him. An admission that even in the privacy of my own head sounded more like the foolish boy I'd once been than the man I was trying to become.

I glared down at the papers on my desk, and Kimiko kissed my cheek, the way she leant forward sending her curls cascading over my arm. "I'm truly sorry for what I said." Her breath tickled my cheek. "Do you know why I am reading the books?"

"For ammunition?"

"No, so I can accept you for everything you are and everything you are capable of, rather than holding on to some rosy view of you that can easily be shattered. No one is perfect, Darius, not you, not me, no one. Don't you think it's better that I understand you as you really are?"

Malice had been the first person to understand me, to understand the pain and the hurt and the anger, to understand the need for mastery and control that had seethed through my veins. He had understood and encouraged, inspired and adored, and hundreds if not thousands of people had suffered for it.

Her hand stroked my cheek when I did not answer. "What is the dark place your thoughts keep going to?"

Malice is coming. Words I could not say.

"It is still too dangerous for you to remain here," I said instead.

"Between Endymion and the war. Trouble is going to keep coming."

"We could just leave, you know. Together."

I turned to remind her of all the reasons I had to stay, but she pressed her finger to my lips. "Hush, let me have my little daydream." She threw her leg over mine and settled on my lap, wriggling close. "We could find some little cottage somewhere in a forest and stay there forever," she said, her body pressed against mine. "We could forget the rest of the world exists at all and just... stay there, arguing about fresh tea and fucking until we're so old one of us breaks their back."

"Does one of us have to break our back?" I said, happy to shift the conversation from its dangerous ground.

"Nothing can ever be perfect, so something bad has to happen." She rocked back and forth slowly as she spoke, rubbing her cheek against the stubble I'd not had time to shave that morning.

"This," I managed to say as she sped her rocking, eliciting the sort of groan from my lips that so many layers of fabric ought to have prohibited. "Is not a good place for this. Imagine my scribe's horror when he comes back from his errand."

"Think of it as highly educational. He's probably never touched a girl before. Or a boy." She slid her hand down between us. "Besides, I think we could make this very quick."

Someone cleared their throat, and I looked around her, expecting to find Endymion had emerged from his trance. Our regular messenger stood on the edge of the portico, a broad grin stretching his lips. "Not meaning to intrude," he said in the most intrusive way he could. "But there're some dispatches come for you special and they sounded important."

Not moving from my lap, Kimiko rested her head on my shoulder while, still grinning, the man dropped three scrolls beside my desk. "There you are, my lord, though I daresay they aren't half as important as—"

"Thank you," I interrupted. "I have no messages to send right now, so you may go."

"Going. Going," the man said, jumping down off the portico and still grinning. "I'll be off and maybe I'll not come at the same time tomorrow, eh?"

"That precaution won't be necessary," I said, feeling Kimiko shaking with mirth against me.

"Just as you say, my lord, just as you say." He walked away, whistling loudly, and unable to contain her amusement any longer, Kimiko snorted.

"What an amazing man he is," she said. "We must be sure to be at it again at this time tomorrow just to see what else he might say."

"No, you wretch, we are not going to do that." I reached for the closest scroll, a task made no easier by Kimiko's weight. "For all we know, he'll tell everyone down in the town, and next time we'll have an audience."

I cracked open the wax seal on the first scroll while Kimiko nibbled my ear. "That could be amusing," she said, but if she said any more, I didn't hear it.

Lord Otako's army spotted several miles north of the pass. A few thousand men larger than expected. The third and fourth western battalions have arrived on their way to join His Majesty at Orotana, and we will engage the enemy when they move this way.

District Commander Yao

It was dated yesterday. I grabbed the next scroll, but it was merely an update from Monomoro on yearly estate income from the farms in the west quarter, and I threw it aside. Kimiko had stilled on my lap and made no effort to stop me reaching for the last scroll.

Lord Laroth, Sixth Count of Esvar,

> *I, Loalin Ko, have hereby taken command of the district of Esvar in the name of His Imperial Majesty Emperor Katashi Otako, long may he reign. I am pleased to inform you that no battle took place in the northern pass. The only men who lost their lives were the hundreds who insisted upon loyalty to the Usurper Kin in the wake of a coup by true servants of the imperial throne. Many are we.*

> *District Commander Ko*

I closed my eyes. "When you were travelling around with your brother, did you spend much time in the Valley?"

"A bit." Kimiko said, no ardour left in the way she sat astride me. "But Katashi is good at making friends everywhere. He'll win, you know, even with *you* trying to stop him."

"Then I look forward to facing the executioner before long," I said and threw the scroll onto the desk.

"I won't let him do that. He owes me."

"Then I'll have reason to thank you for saving me from him—twice!"

Kimiko leant back and gave me a severe look. "Would it really be so bad were he emperor?"

"He just executed hundreds of soldiers," I said, jabbing a finger at the scroll. "That is not the action of an honourable man. If he wins this war, he will root out and destroy every last person who ever supported or fought for Kin and will no doubt oppress the south more than Kin has ever oppressed the north."

"Bullshit," Kimiko said. "When Kin killed my father, he slaughtered thousands of our supporters or exiled them, took lands and imposed taxes. This is not the way of one man; it is the way of any who want to take power. Fear and unyielding determination are as important as love and loyalty. You just picked a side and now won't sway. There may be much bloodshed before my brother sits on the throne, but he will rule fairly once he is there. Trust that I know him better than you do."

I have to believe Kisia needs no gods.

I took a deep breath. How easy it would be to fall into my old habits, how easy to make use of the Vices and shape the world the way I wanted it. But if I did, I would lose everything I had gained and have nothing but self-hatred to flavour my success—a success even Kin would not thank me for.

No, the answer was not to be a Vice again; it was to be a minister.

"Quick, hand me my brush," I said, reaching around her for a sheet of empty parchment. "I have to write a letter."

15. ENDYMION

Pale predawn light trickled into the courtyard, drawing dense vines from the night. With the sun came the birds, singing in a new day, heedless of the knot tightening in my stomach. I sat and stared at nothing as time flowed past. Perhaps if I sat still long enough, I would turn to stone.

The sound of footsteps came to me like a dream. The steady, unhurried click of sandals on floorboards.

"Hiding?" Darius asked.

"I want to learn," I said, too afraid to voice the other words in my head. *I'm afraid next time I won't come back at all.*

Linen shifted by my ear, and Darius sat on the step beside me, stretching sandalled feet toward the sunlight. He stared at the gate at the far end of the courtyard, his perfect profile slightly frowning. "Do you understand what you are?"

Slivers of the previous day came back to haunt me. He had been afraid. Of me. "I'm a monster," I said.

"The beast lives inside you as it lives inside every man. Yours just has access to greater power." He turned to look at me then. "Men are animals, Endymion, it is what allows soldiers to kill and torturers to maim. It is hatred, lust, power, justice, everything that turns your blood to fire. In this, you are no more special than any other. Despite his foolishness in taking you to Kokoro, your priest taught you well, he—"

"They shouldn't have hurt him."

"No?"

"No. He was innocent of any crime. He was a priest. An old man."

Darius's brows rose. "Innocent? I think hiding the heir to the Crimson Throne would be a crime in most people's eyes."

"He didn't know who I was. Only Father Kokoro knew. They ought to have tortured him instead."

"But he is the court priest."

"That makes it even more unfair."

"The whole world is unfair, Endymion. It is broken in every possible way. That's why we invented gods to see our justice done, because it is easier to say, *Don't worry, he'll go to the hells for killing that boy*, than to deal with a world in which the wicked get away with whatever they want and the good suffer for it."

He scowled at his hands, twitching the dark linen that covered his Empathic Mark. He looked different in linen, more natural, no longer the perfect doll of the Imperial Court. This Darius was a man, troubled in the way all men were.

"You don't believe in the gods?" I asked.

"Didn't you tell me yesterday that I am a god?"

Had I? I could remember the start of the Errant game but no more; somewhere in that first round, everything had faded and melded into whispers and ... nothingness. "I'm sorry," I said, unable to think of anything else to say. "I don't know why I said that."

"You said it because it was true. I might have learnt I ought not think of myself like that, but I always have and still do." He got to his feet, his linen robe stirring around his ankles. "They say power corrupts a man. What do you think being a god does to him?"

Darius walked away. "Come on," he threw back over his shoulder. "We're going into the back field today. I have something to show you."

Knives of sunlight sliced through the vine-laden portico as I jogged to catch up, falling into step beside him as he turned down a narrow path between the house and the outer wall. It ran the length of the main building only to spit us out in an overgrown pleasure garden. There, a dry canal wound through beds choked with fleeceflower, the bridge that spanned its width weathered to brittle grey sticks. Wisteria ruled here too, let run so wild its thick stems had crushed its wooden support like twigs in a man's hand.

Darius seemed to know the easiest route through the tangles, and once over the bridge, we found a path. At its end, a gate was set into the garden wall, and there Darius stopped and bowed, gesturing for me to step through before him.

What waited beyond was a field of lush green grass, stretching all the way to the brow of the hill, crowned by the distant shadow of the Kuro Mountains.

"Welcome to my grave," Darius said, joining me.

"Your grave?"

"This was where our father tried to kill me. There used to be a maze here, an enormous thing, or at least it seemed so to me as a boy. The townsfolk said people used to come from far afield to walk it, back when the house was welcoming. Of course by my time, it had become as overgrown as the rest of the garden, the original paths barely recognisable from weed."

I looked around the field again, this time seeing the scars. Here and there dark patches peeked through the grass, and the charred stumps of old growth protruded like knuckles from the ground.

"I was a very sickly child," he went on, looking out at the waving grass with ill-concealed loathing. "Empaths often are, I believe. Half a dozen times, the doctors prophesied my death from little more than a chill. So one night, in the middle of the worst storm of the season, our father dragged me into the centre of the maze and left me there in the dark."

It was cold. It would have been so easy to lie down and give up, but I wanted to live. I want to live.

"You survived."

"Obviously," Darius said. "And I came back and set it on fire. I stood right here and watched it burn. It was the closest I ever got to telling my father how much I hated him. Even when I watched him die, I could not say it."

"Why not?"

He gave me an odd look. "Because I couldn't talk. It was my Maturation. Despite everything he did to me, I was a late one."

The wind whipped past us, rustling the tips of the tall grass.

Darius's eyes narrowed. "You must have had one," he said. "A time when you couldn't speak. It felt like my voice had abandoned me."

"Yes," I said. "After we met in Shimai, but I didn't know it had a name. Malice never said."

My Empathy brought back whispers. *After Shimai? No wonder he was so weak. Brought up by a priest who was never cruel to him. And Malice knew. Still keeping secrets, Brother?*

"You were looked after too well," he said, breaking upon his own thoughts to speak. "Maybe that's why you're different. Your priest thought kindness would be the making of you, that if you were good, you would forget what else lurked inside you."

One. Two. One thousand seven hundred and eight.

He ought to be home.

I hope the war doesn't come this far. It didn't last time, all praise Qi.

Twenty-two thousand eight hundred and seventy-seven.

I dragged myself free to find Darius watching me. "Tell me how to control it. How to kill it."

Those amethyst eyes glittered almost angrily. "Your Empathy isn't alive, Endymion, it doesn't have a life of its own. It does what it's told. If you want to connect to someone, it connects, if you want to hurt someone, it hurts them, if you want to kill them, they die. It is as much a tool as your arm or your leg, but just because you own a hand doesn't mean you should slap someone."

I wanted to slap him, to stop him spilling wise quotes as though they would help. "Are you saying there's nothing I can do?"

"No, I'm telling you to stop blaming your Empathy. It doesn't have its own mind. It only does what it's told. It has no personality. It has no thoughts. That whisper you hear in your head isn't some dark creature that has taken over your soul, it's just you, just your thoughts magnified by fear or anger or lust. You are the only one you can blame. I had to learn that the hard way, had to learn that it was me, *me* I hated. I could never stop being an Empath, so I had to stop being myself. Stop letting things matter. Stop caring about the very things that I cared most about." *Control. Love.* "Do you have any idea how hard that is?"

I stared at him, the revelation so stunning I could not speak. But I did not hate myself, not the way he did, and transfixed, I said, "Then why did you do it?"

"Why?" Darius repeated. "What choice did I have? It was either live the crippled life of a Normal or go back to being the boy who had hunted helpless children for sport, just to see them run crying to their mothers. I gave them such fear, filling their heads with nightmares. Anger was fun too. All I had to do was infuse them and sit back to watch them rip each other to pieces over the last nut in the bowl."

Darius stepped closer, his gaze flicking from one of my eyes to the other. "I know that expression. I used to see it on my own face in the aftermath of a bad night. Malice never suffered from contrition, but I did. It was so easy for him. So easy to sleep at night. Trust me, if there had been a way to kill the Empathy, I would have found it."

My heart pounded with his anger. "If you could control it, then so can I," I said. "I killed one hundred and four men on the road to Rina. I drained them of their hope until they killed themselves. I don't want to do it again."

"Then tell me why you did it."

"Because Malice told me to."

"But you didn't have to. You weren't marked." Darius jabbed me in the chest. "Why did you do it?"

I shook my head. The field was spinning and I felt sick, bile pooling in my throat. "To protect Hope. And Avarice. And Ire."

"Ah, noble and selfless in fact. What about the guards in Shimai?"

I shook my head, not wanting to think about the fear that had filled me so completely there had been no space for other thoughts.

"Why did you kill them?"

"It was an accident. I was afraid."

"No," he said. "Try again. Why did you do it, Endymion?" He gripped my shoulders and shook me so hard my teeth snapped together. "What makes you angry? What drives you? You can't beat it if you don't know."

"They deserved it." The words came out of my lips without thought, a mouse's whisper with a meaning that cut deep.

"There, say it again."

"They deserved it."

"Louder."

"They deserved it!"

The words echoed over the field, the morning suddenly quiet. Sweat dripped down my cheek. Or it might have been tears, I couldn't tell, could only look into that beautiful face and wish it would not smile.

"Those men in Shimai should never have hurt Jian," I said, desperate to fill the silence. "Or me." I swallowed hard. "They treated me like a monster, a freak. They never gave a thought to how it would feel on the other side of the bars, to be afraid, to be taunted with such cruelty. No one understands. No one cares. No one knows how it feels. I never asked to be born this way!"

At least we schooled our anger. The whisper came unbidden from Darius's head. *We learnt to make it do what we wanted. So many journeys down the hill to Esvar in search of victims. Experimentation became practice, and practice became sport. But he is too strong, too fast, and it isn't going to stop.*

"Justice," he said. "You want justice. You want to right the wrongs of the world."

"Yes." The power thrilled through me. "And I can."

"No." Darius took my face between his hands. "You have to let it go, Endymion. You have to fight what makes you angry. You have to stop caring. Don't pretend you have no heart, don't have one at all. Your compassion will kill you."

"But—"

"No buts. We are at war, yes? So what? Let the children become orphans. Let the women be raped. Let the men die. Let the wrong people live and prosper. Do you understand?"

If you don't, you will kill them all.

One million three hundred and twenty thousand eight hundred and seventy.

I stared into those violet eyes.

Please, Endymion. You have to try.

One million three hundred and twenty thousand eight hundred and seventy.

One million three hundred and twenty thousand eight hundred and seventy-two. One million three hundred and twenty thousand eight hundred and sixty-eight. One million, three hundred and...

The stables were poorly lit, but Kaze was always happy to see me, a novelty that had not yet worn off. Darius had left me out in the field, yet I could remember walking back steeped in his thoughts, a mixture of worry about me and fear for himself, neither of which was comforting.

He was in the house now, Kimiko too, and though my stomach rumbled, I stayed sitting on the hay-strewn floor staring at dust motes. Not be myself. Not care. Let it all go. It sounded so simple in theory, but how had Darius managed to so completely shut himself off?

One choice at a time, he had said. *Beginning with the hardest.*

His had been leaving Malice, the only person who had ever shown him love. He hadn't said so, but he hadn't needed to. I wasn't sure what mine was.

I leant my head back against the wall of Kaze's stall. "What am I meant to do?" I said to him as he shuffled his hooves in the hay. "We could leave, but I'm not sure how that would help. I'd just be like this somewhere else. Perhaps this was why my father ended up trapped here. Did someone lock him up, do you think?"

I ought to ask Darius, but I wasn't sure I wanted to know the answer. Nor did I want to consider it an option. Surely the best way to stop worrying about injustice was to make the world just. I bit my lip, knowing the thought was wrong. "Maybe that's what Darius means about believing he's a god but knowing he shouldn't."

"Why do you talk to him?" Kimiko was standing in the doorway, her hands on her hips. I hadn't felt her coming, but as it could have been as much through inattention as choice, I gave myself no credit for it.

"I like talking to him."

"Because he doesn't reply?"

"He replies. At least, I can hear him."

She came in and began rummaging in the bag of feed. *Darius says I shouldn't be scared of him but I can't help it; I can feel the touch of his Empathy like a hand. Darius doesn't feel like that.*

Choice.

I pulled my Empathy away with an effort and held it back, hands clamped to fists and fingers whitening. Kimiko looked around as she poured feed into a bucket but said nothing. Could she feel the difference? Did she know? The desire to check if she had noticed almost let the reins slip from my hands, but I clenched my teeth and closed my eyes and wished I could close my ears so I could not even hear her moving around.

"You should come in and eat soon," she said when she strode back toward the door. I wondered if Darius had told her to say so and whether she knew how much he needed her, how much he thought of her, how much he could love her. It would be so easy to tell her; it might help, might make a difference. That was what Jian had always wanted me to do with my Sight, use it to help people and—

Her footsteps faded away across the courtyard. I counted ten long seconds, then let go my held breath. There had to be a better way than this.

Why won't he talk to me? Does he not like me? I gave him my favourite doll.

Gods save us if the rains are late again. Better they come now. Better a half harvest and an end to the fighting.

Oh, it hurts so much. Why does it hurt?

Kaze snorted. Before my eyes, dust motes danced lazily on.

Eventually, I gave in to the promptings of my stomach and wandered back to the house. It had been another warm summer day, but with evening came a sharp breeze that sent petals dancing across the courtyard. There were hundreds of them, twirling and skipping like children over the uneven stones.

One million three hundred and twenty-one thousand one hundred and four.

I took a deep breath and tried to focus on the petals and nothing more, tried not to even search for Darius or Kimiko in the great pile of a house.

Neither were in the back room and no rice had yet been cooked, so taking coals from the box, I knelt to heat the cooking stone. It had once been my job every evening to heat the stone and wash the rice while Jian prepared what little else we had to eat. Our dinners had always reflected our location, consisting of fish in port cities and goat curd in the mountains. Once, we had bought a catch of fish and dried them ourselves, rubbing in salt and stringing them from the side of the wagon.

Now I could barely remember the taste of food. Had I eaten the night before? Kimiko had offered me rice, but I could not recall consuming it. Jian had never let me go without, even sacrificing his own meals to see me fed. A growing boy needs more food than a drying-out old man, he had always said.

Sadness opened its maw in my stomach as I thought of him. He really had done his best to make me feel loved and cared for, to guide my steps despite knowing so little about what I was and what I needed, and all I had been able to think about was my family. All I'd wanted was to belong.

The stone was getting hot. I looked toward the open door, darkness thick beyond its rotting frame. "Darius?"

I had thought I felt him there and went to the door, peering into the dim passage. "Darius? Kimiko?"

My voice barely reached a few feet in front of me, its echo deadened by old air. Stepping back into the room, I took down one of the lanterns.

"Darius?"

Still nothing, so with the lantern held before me like a talisman, I crept through the lifeless house, committing each turn to memory. Right. Left. Right again. Moth-eaten fabrics and broken screens adorned the way, everything stinking of dust and moss like the waterlogged forests around Lin'ya.

Right. Left. Left again. I followed Darius like a vague scent on the air and he led me into an enormous room I had never seen before, its roof the broad canopy of a great tree. Against the moon-lit sky its leaves fluttered like a thousand bats, covering the floor in dancing shadows. Thick roots had cracked tiles in search of water, and discarded leaves made the old mosaic slippery, but I picked my way across the floor toward the base of a broad stairway edged in broken fretwork.

The first step creaked beneath my feet, its glittering obsidian inlay winking like stars. The bannister was rotten and my fingers sank into its soft, crumbling wood, but I carefully made my way up to the second floor beneath the tree's watchful gaze.

A pair of passages waited at the top, one dark, the other lit by a spill of golden light halfway along. It drew me on, mesmerised. Voices murmured through the open door, and perhaps I ought to have turned back, but the air was stained with such pain and sadness and heartbreak that I crept closer.

Two lanterns lit the room, sitting side by side on a low table. Their puckered paper covers had been painted pink and coloured the room with life, glinting off glass vases and pretty trinkets, all dusty and tarnished.

Darius had discarded his robe and sat on the edge of a divan, his bare skin glistening with the sweat of a summer night. Kimiko sat facing him, her arm concealing the line of her breast as she held him close, her cheek resting on his dark hair.

It was a fragile moment, like the thin shell of a painted egg, beautiful in its transience. Like all others, it would end, no world existing in which time stood still.

As if at that thought, the image came to life. Darius's shoulders shook with grief and Kimiko ran her hands through his hair, tugging gently at the strands while she sang. It was a sad song, full of roaring emotion, and catching a gasp, I stepped back into the darkness and leant against the wall.

Don't let them feel you. Don't let them feel you. Don't let them feel you.

I trembled at the effort and scolded myself for having come, but though I tried, I could not stop the wash of emotion that sloshed about my feet like an insistent tide.

Don't care. Don't care. Choose not to care.

I had poured hatred into Malice's mark, maybe I could pour indifference into myself. Not just indifference, but all my hopelessness and loneliness and fear, magnifying every smothering emotion in an attempt to numb my Empathy.

Pressing my hands to my cheeks, I forced it all back in on itself, and my knees crumpled. Agony sheared through me. But in its wake came a glorious moment of silence, perfect and clear, before the pain roared back and I fell onto my hands and knees and threw up on the floor.

16. HANA

Tili and I made our way through the town in the last of the evening light. I had almost insisted on going by myself for her safety, but it would have drawn more curious gazes to see a well-dressed noblewoman on her own than one accompanied by her maid.

It had taken days to set up this meeting, days during which Katashi had been marching his army hard and there had barely been time to set up camp and rest before we were moving again. Carts were left packed, some abandoned, and while the meals became more basic, such deprivations were nothing to Katashi's cold aloofness. He would not listen to me. He would not talk to me. He had made up his mind and there was nothing I could do.

Except this.

With the war so near, Orotana was gloomy, owning little of the cheer it ought to have now the sticky summer heat had given way to a cool night. Few people were out and about, yet mindful of the dangers of being recognised, I still kept my hood up all the way to the teahouse Wen had chosen—a decent house, clean and pleasant but not large, not the sort of place that would ever expect a visit from an emperor. If he came.

"My lady." The landlord bustled up as I entered, and possessing no hint of recognition he bowed to a randomly selected depth somewhere between an artisanal master and a scholar. "Welcome. Welcome. If you are after a private room—"

"Yes." I shoved my fear down into my sandals and drew myself up. "I am expecting...a companion."

"Oh...Oh! Yes, of course, my lady, yes." The man winked, and I hoped the light was too dim for him to see my cheeks heat. "You booked the room. I have of course set aside my very best. With your permission, I will show you to it?" He glanced at Tili as he spoke, asking a silent question.

"Yes, please do," I said, hating how dirty he made me feel. "My maid will await me here, somewhere she may go...unseen, if we may."

He winked again, and I wanted to rip his eyelid off. Instead I forced a smile and nodded farewell to Tili, before following the man along a lantern-lit passage lined with screen doors. He led me to one on its own at the very end—all the better for the romantic tryst he seemed to think he was aiding.

"I hope this is acceptable, my lady," he said. "Shall I have refreshments sent in now or would you like to wait for your guest?"

"Now would be good. Not just tea but also wine, and some food—whatever you have will be fine, I am not picky."

In fact, my appetite had long since abandoned me, but I would appear at my ease if it killed me.

Once the landlord departed, I chose a place directly across from the door and knelt to wait. Food soon came, and while a serving girl set out the dishes, I listened for new arrivals. Every footstep made my heart leap into my throat, and every prolonged silence made me fear he wasn't coming at all.

The time for the assignation came and went with a flurry of gongs tolling the hour. Still there was no sign of him. How long ought I wait before giving up? And what would I do next if I had to?

The street door creaked open and footsteps cut through the

murmured talk in the main room. It could have been just more patrons, yet something in the weight of the steps made me freeze in place. Two people—no, three. Boots, not sandals, not milling around either, rather the firm, economical steps of men with weapons who did not doubt their welcome—steps that were coming along the passage. All of a sudden, I wished there was another way out of the room and hunted every corner before I pulled myself together.

I picked up a cold tea bowl with shaking hands, determined to look natural and in command as the door slid.

General Ryoji walked in, his hand on his sword hilt. His gaze took in the room at a glance before coming to rest on me. "Lady Hana."

"I think you'll find this is Her Grace of Koi now, General," Kin said, a rustle of movement producing him from the passage behind his guard. He slid shoulder first into the room and stood with his arms folded, scowling down at me. "Is that not right, Your Grace?"

"Indeed it is, Your Majesty, though might I suggest we close the door before exchanging further pleasantries."

I had forgotten how fierce Kin's scowl could be, but he nodded to General Ryoji. "Wait outside, general," he said. "Ensure our conversation goes undisturbed."

"But, Your Majesty—"

"Yes, there is every chance Her Grace is planning to finish the task of assassinating me, but—"

"Assassinating you? I—" I stopped. I had tried to do exactly that the night Katashi had taken Koi, acting on the all-consuming rage Malice had gifted with his blood.

Both men were staring at me, and through the open door, distant figures moved around in the main room at the end of the hall.

I drew myself up. "I can assure you I have not come here to do any such thing."

Silently, Kin nodded again to General Ryoji, and with a bow first to me and then to his emperor, the man stepped out and finally closed the door. Despite how confident he had seemed of his safety, Kin stepped no closer. His look of disgust dropped my heart into my feet.

"You owe me an explanation for that night, I feel," he said. "Before I take the risk of sitting down."

I ought to have expected the question, but understanding Malice as I did and knowing he was to blame, I had been able to move on. Kin had not. "It was not... deliberately done."

"Not deliberately done? I am quite sure you deliberately came at me with a blade."

"No, I did not. It is complicated to explain, however, so by all the gods, do sit down instead of glaring at me from such an awful height?"

For a moment, it looked as if he would refuse, but he soon shrugged off his cloak, the sudden burst of crimson silk seeming to brighten the room. In almost every way, it was the same robe I had so often seen Katashi wear and for the first time I wondered whether Katashi had been wearing the imperial robes Kin had left behind. He'd have hated that, but not so much that he wouldn't have worn them and made them his own. He'd enjoyed watching me slowly peel them off him, wearing that sleepy half smile he saved for when we were alone.

Don't think about Katashi. Don't think about Katashi.

Spreading his robe as I had done, Kin knelt opposite, and but for the robe, it couldn't have been a more different emperor I faced. I had forgotten in the joy of Katashi's ease and charm how stiff and formal Kin could be.

"Well, is that better?" Kin said, meeting my gaze across the table. "Will you now consent to tell me in what way I am mistaken about the happenings at Koi?"

"Do you remember what I had on my hands?"

The notch on his brow cut so deep I ought to have seen bone. "Blood."

"Yes, but not my blood." I spread my hands as though their current clean state was evidence of this. "Malice has a way of sending messages that involves small containers of blood." That notch cut even deeper and I sighed. "You have no reason to believe any of this. I understand it must sound like nonsense to anyone who hasn't seen the things the Vices can do."

"At no point did I say I did not believe you."

"That great gouge between your brows is saying it quite loudly on your behalf."

With a self-conscious start, he touched his forehead, only to drop his hand with an even darker glare. "I was not aware that my eyebrows knew how to talk. Do continue or we may never get to the reason why you are here."

"There isn't much more to the story, really. He sent a message with one of his Vices, and I touched it, only..." I sighed again. "It was stupid really. He'd never sent me...emotions in blood before, only words, so it didn't occur to me that there could be any danger."

The dreaded brow notch was back. "Surely if Malice wanted me dead, he had any number of Vices with any number of opportunities. Why pin his hopes on you when he could be sure you would not make it past my guards?"

"Oh, he didn't want you dead at all, he just wanted Darius to have to do something drastic to save you. Which he did, if you weren't aware. And then he stood before Katashi and refused to take the oath, pronouncing you the true emperor in front of the whole northern court."

"And?"

"What do you mean, 'and'?"

"Is he dead?"

There was such coldness in the words that I stared at him a long time without answering, so long that he lifted his chin in challenge. His jaw was set hard and there was a ferocity in his eyes, but...

"Well? Is he?"

"You care."

"Damn it, Hana, of course I care! He is—was—just tell me!"

I shook my head. "He escaped before he could be executed, but it was kept quiet, as you can imagine. Although where he is now, I don't know and rather thought you might."

He laughed a short and unamused little laugh. "Maybe it really is him then."

"Maybe what is?"

"There is a man making a great noise down in Esvar claiming to be my minister of the left. I...didn't dare hope in case it was merely a Vice trick."

"Malice does like his tricks, but I'm not sure what he would gain by impersonating Darius. Either way, you can be sure neither is allied with Katashi anymore."

Aware of how informally I spoke of them all, I forced myself to meet his questioning gaze and say no more. After a few moments, Kin looked down at the food. "You seem to have ordered yourself quite the spread, Your Grace. Might I enquire if I am expected to pay for this grand entertainment or will you be doing so yourself?"

"I can't say I have given it much thought. Are you trying to be provoking in payback for what happened in Koi?"

"No, my lady, I was hoping to have some conversation before we got to the point of this meeting, since I'm quite sure once we broach the topic, it will be all argument from there."

I couldn't but smile despite the seriousness of my mission. "Somehow I feel this is based less on a premonition and more on past experience, Your Majesty."

"Why yes, how strange that you have noticed that too, Your

Grace. Our conversations always seem to start out so well and devolve rapidly. No doubt you will say that is my fault for being… what were your words? Imperial and overbearing?"

"You are certainly quite capable of that, but I would rather have said our arguments stemmed from too much honesty."

"Or too little ability to compromise."

Unable to face the intensity of his stare, I looked into my tea bowl. "Yes, we're both stubborn, but perhaps I listened more than you thought I did. The longer this war goes on the more I consider what you said about duty. About my father. That he believed being an emperor was about rights, not responsibilities. What did he do that made you say that?"

"The answer would be a dull catalogue of decisions designed to benefit the Otako family and its closest supporters rather than the empire and its people. I understand he was well taught in such practice by his own father—your ancestors stopped caring about anything but what they could wring from the empire a long time ago."

My cheeks reddened at the contempt in his voice. There was still time to get up and leave, still time to change my mind, but I could not forget the wild hatred in Katashi's eyes. Vengeance was all that mattered to him.

"I have some information for you," I said. "No details, no specifics, just a piece of advice you would be wise to heed."

"I make my own decisions, but I will hear you out."

"Do you have ships?"

His scowl was eclipsed by a genuine look of surprise, and he leant back from the table. "I am certain you cannot harm me with knowledge you surely already possess. And yet I am still hesitant to answer."

"Perhaps if I answer first. I have no ships."

"Assuming you have inherited the full rights and property of the last duke of Koi, you do in fact own a fair number of merchant ships. You do not own warships, but that is understandable given how far Koi is from the sea. I would not be very well equipped, however, if I did not."

"Then use them and blockade the mouth of the Tzitzi before it is too late."

Kin stared at me across the table. "Why."

"I said I would give you no details, whatever my sense of duty."

"As I am well aware you have been marching with your cousin's army, you cannot expect me not to make obvious connections. If Katashi is planning to raid—"

"No details," I said. "And I will not hear my cousin disparaged for the sort of choices you have made yourself, Your Majesty."

Kin's jaw clenched hard. "Your meaning, Your Grace?"

I sighed. "You and Katashi are the same. Both of you would hate to know it and would never admit it, but your love for your empire and your family is superseded by only one thing—hatred of each other. What wouldn't you do, what wouldn't you give, to see him crushed and destroyed? Not just beaten in a slow, draining war, but truly broken, his very image and legacy devastated beyond recall? He feels the same way about you. I, on the other hand, am still sane enough to see there are some paths one should never walk, regardless of their destination."

"Such as attacking Shimai, perhaps."

"Perhaps, or considering getting Chiltae involved in this war to crush Katashi."

He met my gaze as I spoke, barely a change in his expression. "Something you have reason to think I have considered?"

"Why wouldn't you have considered it? It was the first thing I thought of when I heard you were pressuring Katashi's allies. You must have known he could not leverage more northern support by restoring lands taken in the treaty without incurring the wrath of Chiltae. How short a step from there to considering incurring their wrath on his behalf? But that might soon become your war too, and it is hardly the act of a man who believes in an emperor's responsibilities over an emperor's rights."

Silence hung while Kin's jaw worked, until at last he clasped his hands upon the table before him. "You would make quite a formidable opponent, Your Grace, but I must admit I'm at a loss to understand you."

I lifted my chin. "Oh?"

"You ride with your cousin's army, clearly showing that you have chosen a side in this war, and yet you take great risk to be here tonight, breaking faith with him in a way I do not imagine he will easily forgive."

A stab of panic flared at his words as I imagined, not for the first time, just how furious Katashi would be if he found out. I swallowed it down and tried to appear calm and unconcerned.

"This," he went on, "is a sacrifice you are willing to make for Kisia, for the greater good of her people, yet still you choose not to do the one thing that could more surely shorten this war than anything else. When it comes to marriage, your sense of duty has no power over you."

"Is it not enough that I ride with my cousin's army?" I said, slowly spinning my tea bowl. I wished, foolishly, that support of Katashi did not mean outright rejection of Kin. I had come to respect him too much.

"No, it is not enough," Kin said. "You are no treasonous general. General Manshin makes a point by choosing to fight for Katashi, you make a point by choosing not to marry him—forgive me if I am mistaken in that assumption, of course," he added stiffly. "But I feel quite sure I would be one of the first made aware of such a change in circumstances."

I swallowed hard. "You are correct. I have...refused to marry him."

"That added to the fact that he has named you duke of Koi speaks merely to the fact that you are ambitious for your own sake, nothing more. By your own admission, you know there is no chance of mediation here. I detest your cousin as he detests me, and neither of us would spare any power we possessed to destroy the other—that, I'm afraid, cannot be changed. And as evenly matched foes, this could be a very painful and very drawn out war that neither of us is willing to concede, not least of all because to do so would mean instant and most likely excruciating and humiliating death.

"But…" He rested his chin on his palm and regarded me across the table with something almost like an apologetic smile. "As Emperor Lan's daughter, you carry all the weight of ancient legitimacy. By marrying one of us, you swing the balance, and many who have so far sat this fight out will side with you and the emperor you choose. That would mean a faster end to a war that might otherwise kill thousands and drag Kisia back to the dark days it suffered after your father's death. I know you have your reasons not to marry, but I hope your reasons bring you enough joy to make up for the misery they inflict on others." He leant forward. "You have a power, Hana, that you are choosing not to use."

I wished I could be angry. Wished I could hate him for his words. But too much truth stood at the centre of so enraging a speech. I went on turning my tea bowl slowly, staring into its golden depths. "You make it sound as though you would rather I chose Katashi than that I made no choice at all."

"No."

With a rustle of that stiff imperial silk, Kin rose and came around the table, owning for an instant a hint of Katashi's predatory grace. "Hana," he said, kneeling on the matting beside me. "I swore to myself that I would not ask you again, that even Kisia was not worth such a blow to my pride, but how can I ask you to give up something important to you for your people without doing so myself?" He bowed, touching his forehead to the floor by my knee. "Lady Hana Otako, would you do me the great honour of sitting beside me as my empress, equal under law, and..." He looked up. "Much beloved of your emperor?"

I ought to have seen it coming. Perhaps I had, but now little in the way of thought was making it through the fearful pounding of my heart. Equal under law. It was exactly what I had told him I wanted. He had listened, not only to that but to everything else I had said and was looking at me now, if not with the same heat that always burned in Katashi's eyes, with enough intensity to make my stomach flutter. I could say yes, could make what felt so much like the right choice for Kisia despite my family pride, but the consequences of that single word made me feel so sick I could not speak.

"If you are frightened of your cousin's reaction, I promise you would be protected," Kin said, rising from his bow. "The only thing I cannot promise is that I will be merciful."

How could I agree to something that could so completely destroy Katashi? And yet as little as I wanted to say yes, did I want to say no? "I...am not...have not..." I swallowed hard, hating how suddenly childish and foolish I felt for having no definite answer. "Will you...will you please allow me a little time to consider your words, Your Majesty? I feel that, given the circumstances, it would be unwise for me to make any decision without giving due thought to all that has been said tonight."

A frown flickered across his face, but he nodded. "I respect that you are in a very difficult position."

I agreed, but he made no move to depart. Remaining at my side, he fixed me with his intent stare. "I meant what I said when I..." He drew a deep breath. "When I said you would be most beloved of your emperor. I have thought about you often and missed our... conversations."

"Arguments, you mean."

Kin snorted a laugh. "I have missed our arguments then and... often wished..." He leant closer, slowly enough that I could have backed away, excused myself, or escaped, but curiosity kept me planted. He did not brush my lips with his in the teasing way Katashi did, did not run his hands up my leg or devour me with his gaze. Kin was far more direct, but when he pressed a firm kiss to my lips it elicited no shiver of joy. None of the madness Katashi's very presence could imbue came over me, and though the kiss was not unpleasant, I was glad when he pulled away.

"My apologies, Your Grace," he said, a little thickly. "I ought not to have done that."

"What is the purpose of being an emperor if you cannot occasionally do whatever it is you wish?" I replied lightly, preparing to rise. "I will send my maid to you with a reply in a day or so, Your Majesty. Please let your guards know to expect her, else she may be too frightened to come."

"You may assure her that whatever answer she brings, she will be in no danger."

"Thank you." I bowed. "As good a moment to part as any, I feel."

He finally moved then, rising from his place, though it was a few moments' hesitation before he returned my bow. "Indeed, Your Grace. I will bid you goodnight."

"Goodnight, Your Majesty."

He swept toward the door, and I was glad I would soon be alone with the tumult of my thoughts. The meeting had gone as well as I could have hoped and yet I felt exhausted and bruised.

The door slid open revealing General Ryoji blocking the passage. Quiet words passed between the two men, then with a nod, the general stepped back. For a brief moment, I caught his gaze over Kin's shoulder and was shocked by his grim expression. He seemed hesitant to depart and I began to fear I may have been in more danger than I had thought.

Whether or not Kin had considered taking me prisoner, the two men were soon gone, replaced by Tili, who came in to ensure I was all right. Still kneeling at the table, I parted my lips to spill all that had happened upon her, but none of it would come out. How could I give voice to so much confusion? Duty made Kin the wisest choice, he the most established, the most stable, the most difficult to root out and destroy, and yet... How could I put into words that no matter how much I respected him, I could not love him, that I doubted he could ever make me feel the way Katashi did. It sounded so selfish to say that was important to me, but the truth was that though I might have been able to marry Kin for the sake of Kisia, I could not while his goal was the complete destruction of the man I loved.

"Lady Hana?" Tili said, kneeling where Kin had so recently sat beside me. "Are you all right?"

"No. I feel like an animal being tracked and I cannot even blame my hunter," I said, feeling a little better to have some of the words out of me. "What wouldn't I do to save my own life? That's what it boils down to, isn't it? Whoever loses the war dies."

Whether or not she fully understood my meaning, Tili said, "His Majesty let Lord Otako go when he was young, my lady. You might be able to persuade him to be merciful again."

Kin had said he would not be, but even had I been able to change his mind, I could no more condemn Katashi to return to the broken pieces of his old life than I could see him die. The truth was he ought never have been exiled at all. His father had committed treason, but that treason had died on the executioner's block and ought to have left him emperor. No doubt Kin would say Katashi had been too young, or that public sentiment had turned against the family, or that in the aftermath of the war, it was best that the empire was led by an older, sturdy hand. But no man takes up the mantle of emperor through blood if he does not want to lead.

Never before had I wished I could rub the Otako off me, that I could scrape away all power and responsibility the name granted and be just Hana. I did not want to decide Kisia's future when it meant condemning a good man to death.

"I am tired," I said. "We should head back before we are missed."

"As you wish, Your Grace."

Before I could rise, heavy footsteps came along the passage and I tensed, listening, sure for a heart-stopping moment that Emperor Kin had changed his mind and sent soldiers back for me, his desperation outweighing all sense of honour. But when the door slid open so hard one of the paper panes snapped, it was not General Ryoji on the threshold but Shin.

"Where is he?" he demanded, stalking in with the landlord hovering behind him.

"Such behaviour is scandalous in a house of this repute," the man said. "I asked you to wait, and—"

"Allow me to apologise for the commotion," I said. "This man is a servant of mine and if you would but leave us, I am sure he will soon come to his senses."

He looked shocked at being so dismissed but did grumblingly depart, shouting to all the interested onlookers in the passage to quit gawking.

Shin had not stopped seething by the time the door closed. "You," he growled, jabbing a finger at me, "are a traitor."

"I? How can—"

"Let me spare you the trouble of devising one of your eloquent speeches for me. That you felt the need to do this behind my back tells me all I need to know."

I was sure it had been the right thing to do, yet his words stung, and I leapt up to meet him glare for glare. "Am I required to pass my every decision beneath your gaze for review?"

"You're supposed to not commit treason! What did the Usurper

244 • *Devin Madson*

buy you with, huh? What did he promise you? Pretty jewels and nice horses? An army of soldiers to satisfy your needs?"

I slapped him, the sting on my palm as satisfying as the shocked wince that passed across his face. "How dare you. If I had wanted such things, I would have married Kin the first time he asked, would have—"

He gripped my wrists, twisting enough that I gasped. "And if you had, I would have slit his throat and strung him up to drip-dry—"

"Let go!"

"—which is what I ought to have done while I had the chance and what I am going to do now."

His fingers dug so painfully into my arms I was sure my bones would crack, and trying to pull free only made it worse. I kicked his ankle, once, twice, a third time as hard as I could, wriggling to escape his loosening hold, but he hissed and hauled me back, shaking me so hard my short curls tumbled into my eyes.

As abruptly he let me go, wailing like I had struck him. Landing heavily on the matting, he scrabbled away across the floor, only to hit the wall and stop, throwing his arms over his head and burying his face into his knees.

"Shin?"

He was sucking in fast gasps of air like a man who couldn't breathe.

"Shin?" I took a slow step closer. "Are you all right?"

He didn't look up, didn't speak. He trembled from head to foot and seemed not to hear me at all. Not even when I knelt before him. "Shin?" I said. "It's Hana, can you hear me? Are you in pain?"

I touched his arm, and he flinched but did not pull away. "Shin?"

"I can't. I can't," he rasped, shaking his head. "No. It has to stop, it has to end. He has to end."

"Shin, what are you talking about?"

He lifted his head, but though he looked at me, he didn't seem to see me at all. "I'm sorry," he said. "I'm so sorry. I shouldn't have done it. I shouldn't have . . . shouldn't have . . ."

"You're scaring me, Shin." I glanced around at Tili, but she shook her head, her eyes wide with fear. "Shin?" I tried shaking him, then I slapped his arm, unsure of how else to get him to snap out of the nightmare into which he had fallen. "Shin! Are you hurt? Ought I to send for a physician? Shin!"

He gripped my shoulders. "Hana."

"Yes, yes, it's me, are you all right?"

"No." He got to his feet as suddenly as he had fallen, lifting me with him as though I weighed nothing. "But I will be soon. Girl," he snapped at Tili. "Go fetch your horses. We're leaving. Now."

"Put me down!" I hissed. "Or I will shout for the landlord and have him call the guards on you. I am not going anywhere unless I choose to and definitely not until you explain what just—"

"Go on!" he snarled at Tili. "Or are you a traitor too?"

"Shin, this is ridiculous. Put me down now or I will shout for help."

He grunted and dropped me on the floor, and for a stunned moment I could not move. Until his arm slid around my throat. Panic seized me then and my feet scrabbled for purchase on the smooth floor, finding nothing. He tightened his hold and I gripped his arm, trying to prise it loose, trying to croak out a plea, but his muscle bulged and I could not breathe.

"It's time this was over," he said. "Truly over. But I'll deal with your treason first."

Darkness swarmed in, rising like a black tide. I lifted my head, trying to stay afloat, but the water kept rising, rising until there was no light, no thought, nothing but the darkness as I sank beneath the waves.

17. DARIUS

Endymion hunched over the cracked ceramic basin and retched. A trickle of rusty bile dribbled from his lip, the last of it hanging there by a string of saliva. Pushing his hair back with trembling fingers, he spat, a deep breath shuddering out of his lungs.

"Darius—"

He retched again. I took the thin linen towel from my shoulder and dipped one end into the water bucket. The fabric darkened as it sucked in moisture and crinkled as I squeezed it out again. "Here," I said, holding it so it hung within Endymion's sight. "You'll feel better."

"Really?"

"Probably not, but it won't hurt."

He sat back, letting out a groan and taking the towel. In the doorway, Kimiko shifted her feet. "Is he just sick, or is it...?" She left the question unfinished as I shook my head and got to my feet.

"I'll fetch you water," I said to Endymion, the boy replying with a retch as I left the room. Kimiko followed.

"Well?" she said when we had put enough distance between us and Endymion that he ought not hear us. "What's wrong with him?"

"I'm not entirely sure," I said. "It feels like Void, but—"

"Void?"

I closed my eyes and wished myself already on the other side of this conversation, but there was no getting around it.

"That pain you felt when I refused to leave the castle with you." It seemed a lifetime ago now, the memory of her fist hitting my face and waking in a haze of borabark one I would not soon forget. "We called it Void because it was like... anti-Empathy. Empathy turned in on itself. It's hard to explain because we never really understood how it worked, only that it did."

"Are you saying he's attacking... himself?"

"I think so."

"And that will work?"

"Hopeful for his sake or mine, my dear?"

Kimiko folded her arms. "That isn't fair. I am at least trying; you are the one who is struggling to accept who you are and who you can be."

"Always brandishing honesty like a whip."

"You would find a way to ignore the truth if I was any more subtle."

I gave a dramatic hiss as though she'd struck me again, and she laughed, but it did not turn her from her insistent line of questioning. "What happens if a Vice keeps disobeying? Despite the pain?"

"They die."

"You've seen that happen."

"Yes." He'd been young, stubborn, and filled with the sort of assurance in the gods there was no arguing with. "And before you ask, yes, I honestly think if I tried what he's doing, I would die too. I forced myself to be a different person to close myself off from the draw of my power. He is attacking himself."

She reached her hand out involuntarily, brushing my sleeve. "Then you had better promise me you're not going to try it, Darius."

"You think me so willing to meet the gods?"

"You were going to let my brother execute you."

"And you were going to let the Void kill you for disobeying."

Her grip closed on my arm. "We both had something to die for."

"Do we have something to live for now?" I thought of my mark in her skin and the only other person who'd ever carried one, their devotion to me unswerving. With every passing day, my fear grew, beginning to consume me.

As though sensing the dark turn of my thoughts, Kimiko tilted her head and tightened her hold on my arm. "What is it?"

Endymion had poured hate and abandonment into the mark Malice had made and broken its hold on him. It might not work if done from the outside, might cause her pain and wipe away all her love for me at a stroke and yet... Every day the decision to do the right thing. Beyond everything I had tried to teach Endymion, it all boiled down to *choice*.

"I may be able to remove the mark I put on you." She parted her lips, but I hurried on before she could speak. "I think it might work if I do what Endymion is attempting to do to himself—fill the mark with... things it hates."

"What do you mean things it hates? Is it alive?"

"It's me, a piece of me. Yes."

Kimiko lifted her hand to her heart. "And you what? Kill it?"

"In a... soul destruction sense, yes, I suppose that's essentially what I would be doing. Hitting it with all the things that make it weak so it shrivels away."

Her mouth twisted into a look of horror as back in the other room, Endymion splattered more bile into the bowl.

"It's only a theory," I said when she made no answer. "I've never tried it before. It might not work, and even if it does, it might hurt. A lot. Or it might not. I really can't be sure. I don't—"

She slid her hand down my arm to nestle her fingers amongst mine, and I could not bring myself to look at our joined hands or to tell her how much this could change if it worked. The words *you might not love me anymore* remained dammed behind my lips as much from pride as fear.

"I understand." She squeezed my hand. "But I would like you to try. I am very tough, you know."

The simple pride with which she spoke only made it harder to force a smile and tell myself this was the right thing to do. Choose to be good. It had been hard when the habits of selfishness ran so deep.

"Do you want to try it now?" I said, letting go of her hand before I could not.

"As long as he'll be all right for a bit without us." She looked over my shoulder, back along the passage to where Endymion still sat hunched over his sick bowl, groaning.

"I'm sure he can go on vomiting in our absence, but..."

"If I feel the urge to throw up, I promise to aim away from your feet. Should I lie down, do you think?"

She moved to the divan without waiting for an answer, the same divan upon which I had so often curled as a child. I could not look at it without thinking of the first person I had marked and how much suffering it had caused. Oh, to have been born without a conscience like Malice, how much easier life would have been.

Kimiko lay down, so much like someone awaiting a physician that I grimaced. Perhaps understanding, as she so often seemed to, she said, "It's all right, I know you don't want to hurt me."

"No."

I wanted to say more, but the words were trapped beneath a lump in my throat and would not come out. Fear urged me to walk away, constricting my chest and burning through my skin, but that was not the choice of a good man. For once the right thing to do was to use my Empathy.

Before I could think better of my decision, I gripped her hand exactly as I had the night I overlaid Malice's mark. Kimiko didn't flinch, and licking my dry lips, I let out every emotion that made me weak, everything I had ever used my Empathy to fight against. The father who had never loved me. The illness that had made me frail. The lack of control I'd had over every moment of my life. Weak, unloved, forgotten. Just like I could be again if this worked.

Kimiko had closed her eyes, but as all that darkness slid through my fingers, she opened them with a gasp and gripped my wrist, digging in her fingernails. But whatever their pain, the cuts in my skin were nothing to the pity in her eyes as she felt everything I fed her, everything I had feared, everything I had yearned for and been driven to best.

Gritting her teeth, she looked away, and unable to feel how much it pained her, I could only trust she would stop me if it got too much.

I had wondered if I would feel it, if Malice had felt Endymion destroy the piece of his soul, but there was no pain, only scratching doubts as I kept my hand upon hers. Sweat beaded her brow and she writhed at my touch, but just when I thought I could do it no longer I caught the flicker of her soul, like a voice at the very edge of my hearing. All but buried beneath the noise, it was a faint cry full of pain and fatigue and love, and all of it was draining, fading, dying.

I ripped my hand away. Kimiko gasped, her eyelids fluttered, but there seemed to be no mark, no hurt, no pain. Just the lingering traces of my emotions and memories floating around like ash from a raging fire.

Clenching my hands tightly, I stepped back and watched her sink into a deep sleep. She looked peaceful, and it was all I could do not to wake her. That it had worked on some level I could tell, but I would have to wait to learn my fate, to find out if there had been anything real behind her growing affection for me.

Nothing good had ever come from my curse, but rather than let doubt rage, I went to check on Endymion. He was still slumped over his sick bowl. "Water," he rasped, holding out a hand.

I unhooked the scoop from the side of the water bucket and I drew half a cup. He took it, his shaking fingers sending water slopping onto the floor and down his robe. Only the final dregs made it to his mouth.

The scoop clattered on the ground as he lunged for the bowl, bringing the water back up.

"Did this ever happen to you?" he asked when his stomach stopped convulsing.

"No." I sat on the floor beside him. Moss was growing through cracks in the floor, and the room had the same musty smell as the rest of the house. I set my head against a rotten door frame. "No. I never tried to do what you're doing. I think it would kill me if I did."

"But you survived the storm." He spat into the bowl. "It's working, Darius, I can feel everything...shrinking in."

"It was just a storm. I was only sickly until Maturation."

Everything had changed that night. Power had flooded through me, and I had thought myself invincible. The maze had burned, and there amid the smoke had stood Malice, awkward and unsure, despite the fine robe he had found for the occasion. There, the first and last time he had spoken his real name.

Endymion sat back on his heels, wiping his mouth with his filthy sleeve. "When did Malice have his Maturation?"

"That isn't my story to tell," I said.

"He won't tell me."

"Then you must accept that you will never know the answer."

His narrowed eyes scanned my face with the same ferocity his Empathy had once scanned my thoughts. "Why do you keep his secrets?"

"Because I do."

"Because you love him."

I sighed. "You know, if I wanted to spend the night with my thoughts, I could do so without your help."

"He's still coming, Darius. You should leave before he gets here. We all should."

"No. I already told you I will not run."

His Empathy came at me like reaching fingers, its first gentle touch growing stronger as he hunted. I swatted the air. "It's amazing how heavy-handed you are."

The change was instantaneous, and Endymion gripped the foul-smelling bowl. Nothing came up, not even bile, yet still he retched. His body would not stop fighting, not stop trying to rid itself of the plague, the Void, that inhabited his skin.

There was nothing I could do to help. It would either work or it wouldn't, and while it was too early to be sure, I had my doubts.

"What will happen when Malice comes?" he asked, sitting up again and continuing the conversation as though it had never been interrupted.

"I don't know yet," I replied, thoughts sliding back along the passage to where Kimiko lay unmarked. That I had succeeded at something I'd long thought impossible strengthened my resolve to stay, yet I couldn't but flinch at the memory of his blade sliding between my ribs the last time I'd tried to leave him.

Eventually, Endymion subsided into a stertorous sleep with his cheek mashed against his arm, and leaving him to rest, I went back to Kimiko. She lay dozing as I had left her, and feeling like a nurse with two patients, I settled down at her side and watched her sleep, until at last, I too fell into a doze beside the divan.

———————

I woke to someone's hand on my hair and sat up to find her watching me. "How peaceful you look when you're sleeping," she said, letting her hand fall back at her side.

"Even with my cheek all smushed and—" I pinched a hair from the tip of my tongue. "And furs in my mouth."

"Yes, because you didn't know either of those things so you weren't scowling."

Pulling another hair off my lip, I said, "Really? Is that so? And how are you feeling this . . . morning?" And it was indeed morning. Faint dawn light eked in around the shutters.

"Fine."

"No . . . different?"

She frowned, and with a brief burst of her deep sadness, she passed her hand through the wall. "No? I still have that, I see. Is that normal? Ought I to feel different?"

"I don't know. I've never unmarked anyone before." I had been so sure I could feel the love and life and soul draining out of her as I killed the mark, yet she was smiling at me as though nothing had changed, and I allowed myself a moment of hope. Hope that I really was capable of being a good man even with the Sight.

"We should hire a cook," I said. "And fix the kitchens. I'm hungry and sick of rice and salted fish."

"Some fruit came yesterday."

"Did it? We still need a cook."

Kimiko's frown deepened. "I've been saying that every day since we arrived. Are you all right, Darius?"

"Never better, my dear. I think I'll send for Monomoro today, and—"

A distant shout echoed through the house. My heart jolted with the fear it could be Malice, but turning my ear toward the door, I caught the gruff syllables of my full name. Not Malice—at least not yet.

"Hold that thought," I said. "That sounds like our messenger. I'll be back in a moment."

I strode out along the passage, glancing in at Endymion as I passed his room. He was still asleep, curled around his sick bowl, and hoping he would rest a while yet, I went in search of the voice. The repeated shouts led me not to the portico like I had thought but toward the main doors. An imperial messenger stood in the decrepit hall, wearing exactly the uniform in which I had hidden Shin. I froze. I knew most of Kin's military messengers by sight, but not this one, yet there was no mistaking the lines marked out on his sash. I had dared not hope Kin would reply.

"Lord Darius Laroth?"

"That's me," I said. "You have a message for me?"

The man pulled a scroll from his satchel and held it out. "I'm to await a reply. A yes or no will suffice."

My fingers shook as I broke the imperial seal and unrolled the short scroll.

D,

> *I have received yours and accept your offer to meet. We are camped in lee of the spur south-east of the village of Airima, and I will expect you in the early hours so no one sees you coming or going. Destroy this message immediately and do not fail me, old friend.*

K

I did not even have to think for an answer. He wanted me back. I had proved myself loyal. I could take him the crown and be officially the minister of the left, and never again would Malice have any hold over me.

"Yes."

"You have memorised the contents?"

"Yes."

The man drew flint and tinder from his satchel and, lighting the tinder with an expert flick, set its flame to the scroll. I pinched the corner and watched as fire ate Kin's message, but though it consumed his words, it could not consume their meaning.

I dropped the last scrap on the floor before the flames reached my fingers and stomped it out. The messenger bowed. "Your Excellency," he said and was gone.

Kimiko was still lying on the divan when I returned, her welcoming smile adding to the joy humming through me. It was a joy I was sure I did not deserve, but I would take it with both hands and run before the gods realised their mistake.

"I'm afraid Monomoro and the kitchens will have to wait until tomorrow, or the next day. I have been summoned by His Majesty."

She froze in the act of reaching her hand to my cheek. "Summoned?"

"He is camped near Airima, which isn't far from here. I must go meet him tonight and take the crown. He wants me to be his minister again."

"That's wonderful!" she said, and perhaps I ought to have heard the brittle note in her tone, ought to have caught the flash of fear there and gone, but she was up in a flurry of furs and making for the hot stone. "Let me make some tea while you sit and plan."

"There is not all that much to plan," I said. "But I ought to gather my papers."

Once again, I crept out past the still-dozing Endymion, this time all the way to the portico. My scribe had not yet arrived, and making a mental note to tell Kimiko or Endymion to send him home when he did, I gathered up all the maps and papers I might need. By the time I returned, Kimiko had water boiling and was just pouring it into the pot. The rising steam was cut off abruptly as she dropped the lid on.

I sat on the divan and rolled the papers up, making an easy bundle to carry on horseback.

"That's a lot to take with you."

"Katashi moves around a lot," I said, setting the bundle aside. "He thinks he's very clever, but I know where he is."

I took the proffered tea bowl from her hands and, blowing off some of the steam, set it to my lips. It was hot, but that was all that could be said for it. I really ought to get fresh tea sent up. Another sip made me shudder. "We really need new tea."

"I think I let it brew rather too long," she said, taking a gulp of her own. "It's very bitter. I'm afraid I make a poor housekeeper."

"It's a good thing I don't want you to be my housekeeper then."

She must have caught the weight of meaning in my tone, for her eyes widened. "Would you have me leave instead?" she said, a mixture of aching hope and heart-thumping anxiety bleeding beneath the door of her heart.

"No." I hadn't meant to speak of it, not yet, couldn't be sure it was even safe, yet the warmth of the tea and the room and the scent of her all over me were making my head fuzzy. I swallowed a mouthful of the vile tea just to wet my lips. "I want to try to build a real life here. A normal life. Fix the house up. Be a good landlord. Give... parties. Is that something normal people do?"

Kimiko gave a watery chuckle. "Don't get ahead of yourself. Just drink up your tea."

I took a mouthful, and it sent another shudder through me, so bitterly had it steeped. "No, you're right," I said, my heart hammering so hard I could feel my pulse in my throat. "That's not even what I wanted to say, what I wanted to say was—"

"Don't."

I blinked at her. The room seemed to be spinning, but all I could see were the tears in her eyes. "Why?"

"Because I'm afraid of my answer."

"You don't..." I felt drunk and sweat prickled my skin. "You don't want to marry me?"

Kimiko cupped her hands around mine, both of us holding my tea bowl. "Drink up," she said, and too hazy to resist, I let her tip the last of the tea into my mouth. I couldn't even taste it. Couldn't feel it. Tears ran down her cheeks, but everything was getting dark and bleary and I could not focus on them. "Darius," she said, tilting her head to look right into my eyes. "I think I would like that. A lot. And if you ever forgive me for this, then maybe..." She wiped one cheek with the back of her hand, and I tried to wipe the other, to ask what I had to forgive her for, but I couldn't speak. Couldn't move.

"I'm sorry," she said as the tea bowl slipped from my lifeless hands and smashed upon the floor. "I can't let you destroy my brother, not after everything we have been through, not after what Kin made our lives. Don't worry, it's just the end of the borabark Malice gave me. You'll sleep and then you'll be fine. I'm sorry."

Malice. He was coming. Would be here soon. I tried to tell her, but my lips would not move, not even to voice the fear that rang shrill in my head.

She pressed her lips to mine, but I could not kiss her back, could not scream though fresh panic went on filling my thoughts. I tried to beg her not to do this, tried to beg her to listen, but I could only stare at her tear-filled eyes and think of Malice finding me asleep and Kin walking into a trap I had not meant to lay for him.

Sleep crept upon me like thousands of ants crawling up my skin. I tried to fight it back, to swat at the darkness, but soon all I could feel was the gentle touch of her lips. Then nothing at all.

18. ENDYMION

Kimiko shook me awake and I immediately lurched for the bowl, dry-retching into it until the spasms died down.

"Still not feeling well, I see," she said. "Can you ride?"

"Like this?" I said, my voice cracked and dry and sounding as terrible as I felt. Like I'd lain on a track and let carts roll over me all night.

"Yes. We have to leave."

"Why?" *Keep it turned in, don't look, don't look,* I chanted to myself and retched again.

"Because Katashi's army is almost here and we can't stay. Darius had word this morning and rode off to meet with Emperor Kin. Lucky me, I'm entrusted with getting you away safely."

I didn't need my Empathy to catch the sound of annoyance in her voice.

"I might be able to ride Kaze," I said, hating to once more find myself the object of her dislike. "At least, I could hold on and he could follow you, or..."

"We'll make it work. Here." She held out a cup of water. "Drink this and see if you feel a little better. Then I'll help you out to the stables."

"We're going now?"

"Yes, now. There's no time to waste."

Kimiko sat gnawing her lip while I alternately sipped the water and retched, every part of my body taking its turn to tremble. Apart from asking me once if I was cold, she said nothing, just clutched a bag of supplies and watched the door. When I had downed as much of the water as I could, I gripped the rotting windowsill and hauled myself onto shaky feet.

I might have fallen had Kimiko not ducked beneath my arm to take my weight. "I'm sorry, I'll be better on Kaze."

"It's fine," she said and, with her arm around my waist, guided my steps out through the door that seemed intent on spinning.

The house was quiet, owning none of the soft sounds that had begun to inhabit it of late, no rustling papers or footsteps or humming messengers, just silent, dead air. The urge to stretch my Sight out was strong, but I swallowed it down and curled an arm around my stomach.

Without faltering, Kimiko helped me out the door and across the courtyard, where piles of old leaves and petals had been swept away from the discoloured Errant boards. Darius had started making small changes to the house, and I could only hope it would survive the war so he could finish the job. Perhaps when the war was over, he would let me live here as I ought to have done, but however pleasant that thought, it was followed by a far grimmer pursuer. *Like you are going to make it out of this alive. This is killing you. Feel it killing you.*

My foot caught the lifted edge of a paving stone, and but for Kimiko's arm, I would have fallen and struggled to get back up, so weak I felt, every limb little more than the trembling branch of an undernourished sapling.

Somehow, we made it to the stables without incident, and there was Kaze. He bent his head to me, but I felt no glow of pleasure at my arrival, not even when I put my hand to his neck. A stab of loneliness pierced my heart.

"Are you all right?" Kimiko said as I wiped my eyes on my sleeve. "I've already saddled up and checked everything over. Do you need me to help you up?"

I shook my head, but she did so anyway, helping my foot find the stirrup as though I'd been at the wine. The effort of hauling myself the rest of the way left the stable spinning, and I retched some of the water she'd given me onto the straw. It didn't make anything spin less, and I lay down upon Kaze's neck, unable to feel the care and concern he would surely have exuded.

By the time the world stopped seesawing around me, we were through the gates. There Kimiko halted and looked back toward the house, its derelict façade peering mournfully over the old wall.

"I had forgotten what fresh air smelt like," she said, forcing a smile as she set her horse walking. Kaze followed, and wishing we could already stop so I could lie down, I clung on, hating every step.

Instead of following the road, Kimiko turned south off the carriageway, brushing through a tight knot of trees. Kaze tossed his head as leaves flicked him in the nose, his complaints silent where once they would have been vociferous. "Calm, my friend," I said, trying to shakily push the branches aside. "We'll be out soon."

But the thicket stretched on, seemingly without end. We stopped once to rest, but it did my aching limbs no service, and all too soon we were moving again.

By the time we reached the edge of the woods, noon had come and gone. Kimiko's shortcut had brought us to a plateau where wavering heat rose from the black stones. Below us, a spur jutted from the mountainside, and jagged rocks dropped away on either side. "All right?" she asked, stopping to look back at me. "If you need me to, I can lead the horses while you lie over the saddle."

"That sounds even more uncomfortable," I croaked. "How much farther are we going?"

"Not much, I think."

"You think? Where are we meeting Darius?"

"He said there was a village down this way and he'd meet us there. We can rest here and then keep going."

I dozed a while on the grass but still felt no better when the time came to mount again and move on. In this stop-start fashion, we slowly traversed the wild terrain until the sun began to set, sliding ever closer to the distant bulk of the Kuro Mountains.

"Are you sure we'll make it before dark?" I said when Kimiko halted at the edge of another rocky spur. "Why don't we stop here for the night, where there's cover?"

"No. We keep moving."

"And if one of our horses sprains its ankle stepping into a rabbit hole? We have less than an hour left of daylight, if that."

"Its ankle?" She turned a quizzical look over her shoulder. "Don't you know anything about horses?"

"Not much. But I know they can hurt themselves."

"It'll be fine. The rest of the way looks easy."

I looked blearily at the track down the mountainside, through sharp black rocks and nests of thin grass tangled like hair. "After this bit, you mean."

"Yes, after this bit. Hold on, all right? You'd probably break something if you toppled off and went rolling down there."

With our backs to the setting sun, we began the descent, cutting diagonally down the slope. Kimiko's eyes darted everywhere and she gripped her reins tight, crushing the leather in whitening fingers. Wherever we were going, I just wanted to get there, just wanted to lie down and never move again.

Despite her assurance, night soon fell upon us, and as darkness gathered, the urge to use my Empathy strengthened. Without it the night was full of nothing but unexpected sounds that sped my heart to a fearful frenzy.

Kimiko stopped. "I think we have company," she said, her eyes darting at shadows.

"What? Who?" I hissed.

"Shhh!"

Fear that it would consume me was all that kept my Sight from ranging over the world, seeing as I had always seen. I hated having no warning, hated being unable to hear or feel the intent of those who might be coming for us. It took everything I had to keep turning my Empathy in.

The world spun, and unable to hold on to Kaze any longer, I tumbled onto the hard ground.

"Endymion!" Stones crunched as she landed beside me. "Are you all right?"

"Fine," I croaked, a hand to my aching head.

You'll get used to it, I told myself. It's the way everyone else sees the world.

But you aren't like everyone else. You're a god.

More footsteps sounded, then a new voice brought lantern light that glared into my face. "Who are you?" it growled. "And what are you doing out here?"

"My name is Lady Kimiko Otako and I am here to see my brother."

I looked up as she spoke, shock momentarily stopping the world from spinning. She met my gaze, no apology in her expression, only a mutinous setting of her jaw.

"Lady Kimiko Otako?" the newcomer said.

"Yes."

I hadn't questioned her. I hadn't even thought to doubt or mistrust because she carried Darius's mark, because she loved him, because it had sounded so true. Because for once, it had been nice to trust without the assurance of my Sight.

"And who is this?"

Looking at me again, she said, "A gift."

I closed my eyes, too sore and sick and tired to do more than let out a breathless laugh at how easily I had been played. The war *had* come to us. Katashi's army had been right nearby, but she'd never intended to run.

Strong hands lifted me, a shoulder jammed into my gut, and the sickening swirl of the world continued while I bumped along against someone's back. Too fatigued to care, I let myself be carried, Kimiko's feet all I could see of her now.

"Where's Darius?" I managed, the only question that seemed important anymore.

"I left him behind," she said, no break in her stride as she kept up with my carrier.

"At the house?"

"Yes. I gave him some bark that puts you into a deep sleep. He probably hasn't even woken yet, or if he has, he's feeling as poorly as you are."

I thought of Darius waking alone in the house to find himself abandoned, just like the boy our father had once dragged into a maze and left to die.

Firelight flickered and a gentle susurrus of voices and soft steps rose around us.

"I had no choice," Kimiko said, though I had not challenged her. "He would have taken the crown back to Kin and led Katashi into a trap. I may be angry he sold me to Malice, but Katashi is my brother. I could not let him be destroyed for the Usurper."

"But you'll let Darius be destroyed by Malice?"

Her silence was an itchy, uncomfortable thing, and for the first time I was glad I could feel it no closer.

"Darius didn't tell you Malice was on his way? I warned Darius he was coming. He…" It took such effort to keep talking when all I wanted to do was sleep. "He said he would stay. Face him. Not… run."

She stopped, but the man carrying me walked on without pause. "Oh gods." It was a small, plaintive moan, barely audible over the chatter of the army camp, yet I heard as much horror and agony and remorse in it as I could ever have felt with my Empathy.

"What have you got there?" called a voice ahead.

"Lady Kimiko Otako and a gift," returned my carrier. "Is His Majesty in?"

"Katashi!" Kimiko dashed past in a cloud of curls and pushed through the tent flap. My carrier followed, red fabric brushing over me as we passed from darkness into bright lantern light. Before my eyes could adjust, I was dropped onto a square of matting so fresh it still smelt of the sun, its reeds like spun gold. Overhead, spoke a familiar voice.

"Did Malice send you? What does he want?"

"No. No, I'm free. But—"

A sharp slap of skin and Katashi gave a grunt of pain, his hand flying to his cheek.

"I deserved that," he said.

"You deserve worse," she said as she slid her arms around him and was crushed in an embrace. "You owe me and I need your help. I need you to send some of your men to Darius's house at Esvar to find him and bring him here safely."

Katashi stepped back, holding her at arm's length to search her face. "Laroth? Why?"

"He's the one who let me go, Katashi. I cannot let Malice take him back."

"Malice? Kimiko, you go too fast for me," Katashi said. "And why do you have Endymion with you? He looks half-dead."

"I will explain it all in a moment, but first, please do this for me? You owe me, Brother, you know you do."

"I do, but if you're free of them, I'd rather not get mixed up in anything the Vices are doing. The pair of them have almost cost me everything."

She reached up to grip his cheeks between her hands, forcing him to stoop as she hissed in his face. "I am not asking you to get mixed up in anything, Katashi, I am asking you to save the man I love from Malice."

Unable to feel anything from them, I could not understand the moment of silence that hung, could not fathom the stillness, the little grimace on Katashi's face or the quick squeeze of Kimiko's fingers into fists as she let him go. There was just emptiness and nothing, then he nodded. "Fine. I'll send men for him. Lots, in case he's not alone."

"Oh gods, tell them to hurry, Katashi. And tell them not to harm him."

Scowling, Katashi left the tent and muffled words sounded outside. We were alone, but Kimiko did not look at me. She went on clenching and loosening her fists and, when she caught me watching, began to pace.

A few minutes later, Katashi returned. He swept me in his frustrated gaze. "Men are on their way. Now I hope one of you intends to tell me what the fuck is going on."

"I will tell you about Darius later," Kimiko said. "First, I have some fine gifts for you." She unslung the bag she had been carrying since Esvar from her shoulder and held it out to him. "Here. You can have it back."

Katashi took it. His fingers worked loose the ties and from inside rose the spikes of the Hian Crown. "I thought it might have been you who stole it."

"Yes, but only because I had to. Now I'm bringing it back. Along with the information that Dari—Lord Laroth has organised to meet with Emperor Kin in the early hours of the morning to tell him the location of your army. Darius was out in his calculations, however, and thinks you are still a few days from here, but either way, he told me where Kin is and it's close. Really close."

"Close enough to attack tonight before he realises his mistake?"

"Yes, but if you really want to make him hurt, send Endymion to the meeting in Darius's place first."

Katashi had been checking the crown over as they spoke, but he stopped at that and glanced up. Despite the kindness he had once shown me, there was no friendliness in his eyes now. "Why am I sending someone to meet the Usurper when I can just attack him?"

"Because Kin won't know what to do when faced with Takehiko Otako."

Katashi stared down at me, his eyes a pair of hard sapphires set beneath heavy brows. "Takehiko? *You're* Takehiko Otako?"

I could find no strength to answer and closed my eyes, as though to block out the rage that was surely coming. It was enough confirmation for Katashi. He crouched in front of me, silk shifting with every movement of his body. "You lied to me."

"Yes."

"And I thought we were friends."

I shut my eyelids tighter as though I could keep from hearing the note of hurt in his voice, but it was still there and it was everything I had ever wanted it to be. Friends. If only I hadn't been something he hated. Hadn't owned a name he feared.

"Lord Takehiko Otako," Katashi said, rising to stride across the floor from the dry reeds to the carpet and back. "Lord Takehiko Otako, heir to the Crimson Throne."

"I don't want it."

"No?" He spun back to face me. "Do you think it matters what you want?"

"I'm not Emperor Lan's son."

He laughed, but the feeling of mirth that had once played its joy through my body was absent, making his laugh sound cruel and strange. "I know that," he said. "Everyone knows that. But you were officially acknowledged, so it doesn't matter that you were a freakish bastard squeezed from between your mother's legs, you're still the rightful heir. I've seen the papers." Katashi spat. "And here you are, back from the dead. Do you expect to be welcomed into the family?"

Stung, I went to rise, only to feel the weight of a hand upon my shoulder. "Don't even think about moving," my carrier said. "Stay on your knees."

"Or you'll kill me?" I said, turning to see the tail of a black sash. "I'm already dead."

"You soon could be." Katashi lifted Hacho from her holster in one smooth movement. The arrow was in his hand, an instant all it took to nock and draw, Hacho's body pulled into a grin. "I could put this arrow through the back of your head in a heartbeat and save myself a lot of trouble. Tell me why I shouldn't?"

"You idiot, Katashi," Kimiko snapped. "You shouldn't because you should send him to meet Kin. Give him an imperial robe and parade him in so Kin cannot just get rid of him."

Katashi relaxed his bow arm but did not turn the arrow aside. It was pointed at my right eye, and staring at that barbed point, I began to wonder what it would feel like to die.

Slowly Katashi's lips broke into a smile. "The honourable Emperor Kin," he said. "Once master of the Imperial Guard. He took the oath. Yes, and not just any oath." He barked a laugh. "General Kin, sworn protector of Emperor Lan and all of his children. He is honour-bound not only to keep you safe but to uphold your claim to the throne. And if he doesn't . . . everyone will know.

"I think it's time I gave the Usurper a present." He drew Hacho's string taut and shifted his aim. The arrow was all I could see, the world containing nothing but this sharp metal point, darkened with black ink.

"Katashi!"

The barbed tip pierced my skin, throwing me off balance. Again the tent spun but I was on the floor now, breath hissing in and out through my clenched teeth.

"What a mess," Katashi said over my rapid breaths. "If you hadn't moved, it would have just gone clean through your arm and stuck well."

"Katashi, you didn't have to do that!" Kimiko snapped. "He needs to be alive to meet Kin, not dead."

"Yes, but this way, everyone will know who sent him."

Standing over me, Katashi was looking the wound over critically. I could not look at it, but my fingers found a mangled lump of flesh wet with blood, sharp barbs sticking through what was left of my skin. Sick, I tried to rise only to fall back shaking.

"Leave the arrow in him," Katashi said, speaking to the man who had carried me in. "Bring me ink. I'll write Kin a message to go with so wonderful a gift."

"Yes, Your Majesty."

"That was totally unnecessary," Kimiko said.

"Perhaps." Katashi knelt before me. "But I feel much better."

He touched the arrow. It bounced gently, tearing a strangled cry from my throat. "We conquer. You bleed," Katashi said, stroking the Otako motto branded upon the shaft. "This is nothing personal, you know. But I have a war to win."

Footsteps returned. An ink stone was placed on the floor beside me, and Katashi brushed the hair from my forehead. The ink was cold. I tried to focus on the shapes he formed, to read his words, but all I could think about was the hot blood dripping down my arm.

When he had finished, he dropped the brush back onto the stone. "Take him to Kin," he said, nodding to his guards. "Let's see how honourable the Usurper really is."

19. DARIUS

For the second time in my life, I woke with a mouth so dry it might have been filled with dust. It took a moment to recall why, but knowing didn't make it any better.

No horse this time at least, no swaying motion or bright, searing sunlight. She had laid me out on the divan, a show of kindness that left a bitter aftertaste. Gods only knew how long I had been out, but though fears for Kin poured in, I couldn't bring myself to move. Beneath the crushing fatigue, nothing seemed to matter very much.

After staring at the shadowy ceiling for a while, I managed enough energy to turn my head. The scent of Kimiko was all over the pillow, and I closed my eyes, only to find her in the darkness behind my eyelids, speaking her apologies over the top of my silent screams.

Kin was walking into a trap. I ought to move, ought to do something, to fight, not just lie there, but every limb felt heavy and it was hard to focus, hard to even think what I ought to do. She could have a whole day's start on me and had probably taken the horse and—

"Endymion?" I forced the croaky word out and licked my dry lips with my dry tongue. "Endymion?"

No answer came, not even an echo. Had I owned his strength,

I might have been able to range my Sight over the house and know where he was, but my far lesser skills brought me nothing but silence. And a certainty born from knowing her that Kimiko would not have left him behind. Not when he could be so useful.

Whatever his parentage, he was still Takehiko Otako.

Eventually, I managed to roll onto my side and caught sight of the cup of water she'd left beside the divan. Had I been less thirsty, I would have exorcised some fury by knocking it over, but my mouth was too dry for rage. I heaved myself up onto an elbow and drank it all in one gulp before flopping back, exhausted.

She would be taking Endymion and the crown and knowledge of Kin's whereabouts to Katashi, and there was nothing I could do.

I groaned and went back to staring at the ceiling, exactly as my young self had once lain just here and stared at that very patch of peeling paint, wishing for the strength to change the world. Wishing my father would come to see me. Would talk to me. Smile at me.

So deeply did I fall into memory that I would not have been surprised by the sound of Avarice's footsteps or his old songs echoing along the passage, but when footsteps sounded, they were not his.

Still lying upon the divan, I turned my head to the door, and there stood the scribe I had hired from town, a couple of scrolls in his hands. "Your Excellency, I'm sorry to disturb your rest, but—"

"But bad news doesn't wait," I croaked. "Bring them in."

"Oh, it's not these, Excellency, it's..."

More footsteps, and emerging from the shadowed hallway, he stood, a silent figure at the edge of the light. He wore simple linen, his dark hair, dark brows, and deep-set eyes giving him the look of a creature born from the night. "Good evening, Brother," he said and bowed, mockingly low.

The scribe hovered, and for a mad moment, I considered telling him to throw Malice out or begging him to run for help, but with a weak smile and a wave of my hand, I dismissed him. The young man hurried away, leaving me to face Malice across the room. For a time, we just stared at each other, but when I made no move to speak or rise from my pillows, his mocking smile soured to a frown. "You're unwell? I must admit that is not very sporting of you, yes? I did not come all this way to feel sorry for you."

The last thing I wanted to do was explain how he came to find me so, but just as Kimiko commanded honesty from my lips, so too would Malice, except he would take it by force if it was not offered.

"Not sick. Borabark."

One of Malice's brows rose. "Adversity?"

"By Kimiko," I corrected. "Yes. She is no longer yours to name."

"Ah, so I guessed. Where has she gone?"

"I don't know."

"You don't know? You stole one of my strongest Vices and have just let her... wander off? Excuse me if I am enraged, yes?"

"You'll forgive me," I said. "You love me too much."

Malice had been leaning against the doorframe and running the tip of his ponytail through his fingers, but he paused at that. "How well modesty becomes you, Darius."

"And how well walking across Kisia like a peasant becomes you, Malice. I take it the full cortege of Vices and your brightly coloured wagon would have been rather too conspicuous in lands controlled by Katashi."

He flashed me a humourless smile. "Indeed, and that's something else I have to find it in my heart to forgive you for. I do not take kindly to having to chase you like some unwilling woman. I sent Vices to save your life after you so foolishly threw it away to make your honourable stand, and this is how you repay me? I am getting rather sick of your ingratitude, yes?"

I laughed, the sound still dry and throaty from the borabark.

"Shall I thank you for the knife wound too? And for getting me dismissed from one of the most powerful positions in the empire? Admit at least that you came chasing Endymion as much as me and I could accept some of your annoyance as warranted."

"Some of my annoyance as warranted," he repeated, seeming to muse on the words. "That boy broke my mark, Darius. No one has ever done that before nor even come close. He is dangerous, yes? But I'm sure you recall me warning you of that, recall me telling you how important it was that we take care of this together."

"I know he's dangerous. That boy, as you call him, followed me across Kisia, sniffing like a dog. One connection, and I had given him enough to seek me out from any distance."

His suspicion smothered me like a heavy blanket. "And why did he come to you?"

"To learn control, what else? I made the world believe I was not an Empath for five years, or had you forgotten?"

"Forgotten? How could I when you left me alone for those five years?"

"Hardly alone."

"Without you, I am always alone."

That small room felt suddenly smaller, and with slow steps, he came across the floor. "You and I were made for one another, Darius, each the only one who can ever fully understand the other. Can fully love the other."

He sat upon the edge of the divan, his scent infiltrating the lingering presence of Kimiko's. I struggled to rise to my elbows and failed.

"My poor Darius," he said, running his hand down my cheek. "Don't tell me. Dear Kimiko abandoned you like this so she could take Endymion to Katashi."

The amount he had guessed without looking in my head shocked me enough that it must have shown on my face. "It is not so difficult to work out," he laughed. "Did he tell her the truth or did you?"

"I did."

This time he ran the back of his hand down my cheek. "Ah, my poor trusting little brother. How prettily she must have duped you."

The memory of her lifting the tea bowl to my lips flashed into my mind, only to be thrust away, as much for the pain it gave as the fear Malice might see it. "Indeed," I said. "And as you find me feeling quite sorry enough for myself already, do excuse me from entertaining you with a quarrel."

He smiled down at me, one of his genuine smiles, his eyes half-lidded with lazy affection. "Oh no, my dear, I will wait until you are feeling rather better for that. It's no fun otherwise, yes?"

He got up on the words and began to move about the room, first filling my empty cup from the water bucket, then lighting the coals beneath the hot stone and washing some rice. They were tasks I had once lain just so and watched Avarice perform day in and day out, and despite the fact it was Malice moving with ease about the room, it was oddly comforting. His forbearing mood was unlikely to last, but while I lay in a fog of fatigue, I couldn't but be grateful.

At some point while he worked, I must have dozed off, for the next thing I knew, he was running his hands through my hair. I opened bleary eyes to the sight of that same affectionate smile, while behind him, steam rose from bowls on the table. "You will feel better able to quarrel with me when you have eaten, yes?"

The extra sleep had done me good, leaving me with enough energy to reach the table without help. Once settled there, we ate in silence while darkness closed over the house. Malice lit the lanterns, filled my water and my plate, all watchful solicitude. How easy it had been in the pursuit of hatred to forget all the kindness he had ever shown me. Would Kimiko so soon forget my every attempt to be a good man?

"What a mopey bore you are, yes?" Malice said as he watched me eat. "What is troubling you, sweet love? Shall I fix the world for you?"

Fix the world. I could use the power I had been born with, use the power we were capable of together, could harness everything the Vices were and ever could be to make everything right again. The urge was there, calling to me with the fervour of desperation and the ever-yearning remembrance of how *good* it felt to be powerful. To be in control.

"No," I said before I could voice the *yes* that ever hovered on my tongue. "I will find a way to fix it myself when I feel less like I've been put through a wine press. Why did you come?"

"You know why. What have I ever wanted but my brother back?"

"An empire?"

Tea bowl in hand, he gave me a meaningful look over its rim. "When was that *my* ambition?" He set the bowl down slowly, the deliberate click of it upon the table hollowing my gut with anticipation. "I've only ever wanted what was best for you. To make you happy."

"Did it never occur to you that I was happy serving Kin?"

His brows lowered and his gaze searched my face. "No, you weren't," he said with a slowly spreading smile. "Content to be a miserable martyr, but not happy. You thought that was your due, yes? That you deserved no love and satisfaction in life, that you ought only to serve."

Content to be a miserable martyr. The truth of those words struck me with such force I just stared at him across the table. I had hated having to control my every thought and emotion and expression and had pushed everyone away except for the man whose position meant he could have no true friends.

Malice picked up his tea again. "I want my brother back, yes?"

"Even against my will?"

He sighed, closing his eyes in a moment of pain. "You're breaking my heart, Darius, yes? Where are you hiding my Mastery?"

"He's gone."

"You're lying. With Hana's pretty face upon the throne, you were going to rule the empire from the shadows, the power—"

"Enough."

Malice's fine eyebrows rose. "Denial, Darius?"

"I did not stay to talk about me. It's Endymion we need to do something about."

"Very well, and after that?"

I held his gaze. "We go our separate ways."

"To slowly grow old? To wander the world telling the story of our glorious battle? You intrigue me. What do you propose I do when we ... part ways? Again."

"Whatever you like."

"Whatever I like. Almost you have me convinced, Brother. I sacrifice my time and skill to protecting Kisia and all its fine peasants from Endymion's wrath and, I assume, fight to end the civil war, letting Kin keep his blood-soaked throne, only to leave the battlefield with nothing. Shall I disband the Vices too? Shall I send them back to the families who cared so much for them that they sold them to me?"

"That's up to you. Those are my terms."

He pushed his empty tea bowl to the centre of the table, lantern light dancing on its finely painted surface. "You are expensive, my dear," he drawled. "I do not like your terms, yes? Do you hate me so much that you would bargain a future without me?"

The lie stood on my tongue and made itself fat, paralysing speech. I forced it out. "Yes," I said, the word tasting wrong.

Throwing out his arm, Malice swept the bowls from the table. They flew from its edge and smashed, thin shards of porcelain scattering to every corner of the room as he lunged forward, gripping my arm. "Something has changed," he said, eyes roaming my face. "You're using your Sight, but you're still not my Darius."

He pulled me forward, the edge of the table digging into my stomach. My pulse thrummed in my ears as his fingers crept toward my hand, every moment he wasn't touching my skin like a hellish eternity. Slowly, he peeled back my sleeve. There, my birthmark. There, my skin. But he did not touch me. His hand hovered, teasing, the urge to make the connection myself almost overwhelming.

At last, he clasped his fingers around my wrist, opening the path between us. It was well travelled, a little overgrown perhaps, a little strange from so many years apart, but beneath the new growth beat the old, so natural, so true. I could not hide, not from him. He held the keys to every door.

But now there was Kimiko. Her taste, her smell, her curls against my cheek. Her love and her anger and her stubborn insistence on drawing from me every truth. Her betrayal was there too, like a great scorched scar across my soul, but it was not that which made Malice drop my hand with a hiss, real shock twisting his proud features. "You've let her mark you as much as you marked her."

I slid back off the table, straightening my robe as I stood, even so simple a movement an effort after the borabark. "She's gone now. Leave it be."

"Leave it be?" Malice rose and came around the table with a predator's soft steps. The door was behind him, but I repressed the urge to run. "Leave it be?" he repeated as he stepped close, the smell of him unchanged by so many years. "You are mine, Darius." He leant forward to breathe the words into my ear. "I will not share you, yes?"

He gripped my hair, dragging back my head. "You think she will be hard for me to find? Perhaps my Vices would also enjoy getting to have their way with Otako's spirited little sister."

I thrust my palm into his chin, pushing back his head. "She'd kill them first," I said as his grip tightened in my hair. "She'd slit them from groin to throat for even thinking about it."

His wet tongue darted across my fingertips and I slammed his head back so hard his teeth snapped together. Hair ripped from my scalp as he fell back. "You think they couldn't hold her down?" he said, grinning. "They—"

"Like you held me down?"

Anger flared across his face. "That was different."

"No, it was exactly the same!" I thrust him from me, and he hit the edge of the table and fell heavily, his head slamming back. His ribbon snapped, sending little shards of bone scattering across the worn tabletop. And while he lay stunned, I snatched the pot off the cooking stone. It was heavy, its base made of iron. I swung. Malice rolled and the pot hit the table, splitting down the middle, spilling cold rice like an army of maggots.

Malice pushed to his feet, panting, his hair falling around him like a veil. His eyes gleamed. "So angry, Darius," he said. "Did dear Kimiko tell you that you deserved better? That you weren't the monster you've always been?" He picked up the book she had been reading from the divan. "Did you let her read the horrors committed by others so you wouldn't have to tell her about yours?"

I was breathing fast, pressed lips keeping back words I could not trust.

The book slammed down upon the table and Malice stalked closer. "Did you tell her the truth, Darius? Did you tell her that you made the first Vice? Did you tell her that it was you who pushed to perfect the process with experimentation? That it was you who stole people from their homes and ordered their bodies buried in the back field when you were done? Did you tell your dear Kimiko how much blood was on the hands you touched her with? No?" He was smiling again now. "Perhaps you should do that the next time your fingers are so far up her cunt you can't see them. Tell her you made the Vices. Tell her you made *me*."

A monster would be easier to hate. A monster would be easier to leave.

Malice shook his hair back from his eyes like a mane. "It sounds like fun, yes? Maybe I'll do it myself. Do you think she'd like that? The little whore has a taste for Empaths, perhaps."

Too easily could I imagine her moaning at his touch instead of mine, digging her claws into his shoulders, tugging on his hair and biting his lip. He knew how to be charming when it suited him, knew how to touch people in ways they would never forget. In ways they would never want to forget.

"I'm right, aren't I?" he said. "How loud did she scream for you, Darius? How loud will she scream for me?"

My pulse pounded like a war drum and I lunged, wanting nothing more than to choke the words from his throat. He ducked and came up grinning.

"Too angry, Darius, too angry." He gripped a fistful of fabric at my throat and pulled me in. His skull slammed into my brow bone sending white lightning across my eyes. The room spun and I staggered back, blood dripping down my face.

"Did you tell sweet Kimiko about our father?" he said, the words ghosting past my ear. "Did you tell her about your mother? Did you tell her that every time she begged for it, she was begging for the chance to die?"

His sharp fingernails cut my cheek, shredding the skin like a handful of knives. Hot blood bloomed.

"Do you think she'll still love you with your pretty face all cut up?" he crooned, his hand on my other cheek. "Such a fool you are, Darius. Did you really think someone else would love you, truly love you, knowing everything I do?" He chuckled. "No, you're too clever for that. That's why you never told her the whole truth."

"Vatassa matas!"

Malice laughed. "How I missed you, yes? Resorting to Avarice's Levanti when you are enraged."

"Shivats to your truth."

"The truth is she betrayed you. She hates what you are and what you fight for. But we are *gods*, Darius."

"No, she loves me."

"Love," he spat. "You've forgotten what the word means. Do you remember the day our father told you he loved you?"

The words were an ethereal jab that robbed me of breath. *I love you, Darius, you are my son and I love you. Remember that, promise me you will remember that.*

That night, my father had dragged me out through the garden. The storm had lashed at my face, and I had kicked and scratched and screamed, trying to make him let go. My Empathy had been immature, and he had brushed it aside like the reaching tendrils of the overgrown garden, bearing me inexorably toward the dark hedge looming from the night.

"I swore I would never let anyone break your heart again," Malice said. "Do you remember for how many days you didn't speak?"

"Two hundred and thirty-nine." I barely needed to think; the words said themselves.

"And what was it I said to you the night before you broke your silence?"

Blood was dripping down my neck. It was on my hand and my sleeve, and running down my arm, determined to cover me with its pain. A drop of blood hit the floor, full of my anger, my guilt, my hurt. The floor would not feel it. But Malice...

"I will not let you hurt her," I said.

"And how do you plan to stop me? Going to kill me, Darius?"

"I ought to have done so a long time ago!"

Peeling my hand from my cheek, I flicked the blood at him. He flinched, and in that moment of shock, I stepped in, slamming my blood-smeared hand into his face. His nose flattened beneath my palm, a single eye left to peer between my fingers. Malice's whole body stiffened, that eye mad with my pain, his mouth gasping for more air than the room contained. Holding him pinned, I gripped his neck and squeezed, loving the feel of his hard throat beneath my hand.

And there I held him, an inch from death, unable to kill him, unable to let him go. Between my bloody fingers, his eye crinkled with laughter.

What did I say to you the night before you broke your silence? he asked, pushing his Empathy into my hand.

Footsteps thundered through the house, some part of me aware enough to hear them, though nothing mattered beyond this man I knew better than I could ever know another. "You said, 'I would die for you. I will never let you lose your way.'"

The steps grew louder. Closer. Voices shouted. But still I stared into that single eye.

I meant it. I am yours, Mastery.

A lantern appeared beside me, its bright light causing Malice to squint. Voices filled the air. Someone gripped my shoulder and yanked me away, my hand leaving a bloody print across Malice's face.

"Lord Darius Laroth and Whoreson Laroth," spoke a voice, filling the room with such authority, such a feeling of importance. "You are under arrest on the orders of Emperor Katashi Otako, True Emperor of—"

I turned, catching the man around the throat with my bloodied hand. He had none of Malice's barriers, none of Malice's strength, and where Malice's eye had laughed, this man's screamed. I poured my hatred into him, my contempt for his pitiful sense of power all because an emperor had given him a command. Beneath my grip, his heartbeat quickened, rising to such a tempo it could not long sustain him. He clawed my arm, every breath a choke. I had the power. He would live if I let go. He would die if I held on. The room, the stage, belonged to me.

His eyes rolled back, showing their whites. The clawing stopped. And my soul sang as his useless body crumpled at my feet.

The men packed into the doorway stared at their fallen leader in horror as Malice came to my side. There were at least a dozen soldiers. More outside. Katashi knew what he was dealing with.

A man wearing a black and silver sash pushed his way to the front of the frozen group, his lips turned in a sneer. "We were warned you two were freaks," he said. "But the way I see it, men all bleed the same, so you'd best come without a fight."

Malice snarled, the sound bestial.

"I'll take that as a no." The man lifted his bow, an arrow already nocked. Aiming for Malice, he drew and released with whip-crack speed, and Malice staggered back, an arrow through his leg. Hissing pain, he lunged, but I grabbed him, locking my hands around his chest. "Stop," I said. "Let them take us or they'll kill you."

He tried to throw me off, to twist out of my grip, too caught by fury to think clearly. "Stop," I said again. "I don't want you to die."

Malice stopped, his chest straining within my hold. Against my cheek, his tangled hair smelt so much like the past from which I had run, too weak to accept the truth.

Bunched together, Katashi's soldiers watched us, unsure. I glared at them over Malice's shoulder. "What are you waiting for?" I said. "Tie us up if you're going to."

They approached warily, weapons ready. I watched them come. Malice watched them come, our thoughts undoubtedly the same. There were too many. Even gods weren't invincible.

Malice growled as they bound his hands, but he did not fight. He watched as they bound me, watched me suppress every instinct that urged me to attack, and when they had finished, he bowed, an appreciative smile on his face.

"Mastery," he said, his lips taut, his face growing pale. Blood was flowing fast from the wound in his leg.

"Malice."

A soldier shunted me toward the door. "I don't think Katashi wants us dead yet," I said, addressing the man with the silver line through his sash. "You had best bind my brother's wound."

The man grunted and jerked his head back at the corpse on the floor. "*Emperor* Katashi gives me orders, not you, freak. Are you going to help my captain if I help him?"

"He's dead," I said.

"So are you when we get back to camp, so let him bleed, I say. Get them out of here."

20. HANA

It took all day to reach Katashi's camp, a journey made all the more difficult because Shin would not let me ride. I had pleaded with him, explained to him, shouted at him, begged and cajoled, all to no avail. And hitting him had just made him bind my hands with his black sash.

Tili had been no help. In truth, there was nothing she could do even had she been a match for Shin. Where could I have run to? Back to Kin? To a marriage for the good of Kisia?

Between Shin's stoic refusal to talk and Tili's quiet monosyllables, I had plenty of time to imagine such a future on the ride back to camp. Kin always respectful, always controlled and moderate, even his smiles measured rather than expressive. Perhaps like Katashi, he would be a different man in private, when he did not need to consider the appearance of his position, but perhaps not. There had been no heat in his kiss, no passion, no honesty. Had I never met Katashi, I might have been satisfied with Kin's stiff, formal attentions, but I had met Katashi. Loved Katashi. And for all my professions of duty, it was to him my thoughts returned. Yet the closer we got to his camp the more fear leached into my mind, tainting every thought of him with reminders of what he had done. What I had done.

It was dark by the time we found Katashi's camp—a distant

gathering of lights tucked into a hollow between two hills. They had travelled two days since I'd left, but despite what fears Katashi must have harboured about my purpose, he had not changed his plans. I could not decide whether his choice to camp where I could find him was a demonstration of his trust or his stubborn determination to show no fear.

"You can still turn around," I said as Shin started down the steep hill, tall stalks of grass brushing at our feet. "You can still choose not to take me back like this."

"So you can run back to the Usurper?" He spat. "He is not the man you think him."

"Perhaps not, but he has more sense of duty than you ever could."

Behind me, Shin growled like a bristling dog. "A man does not climb to the Crimson Throne over the bodies of thousands because of duty. He does it for power. No. This is where you belong."

"And if Katashi condemns me? Did you ever consider that he might execute me, Shin?"

"If that's what he wants to do."

The indifference in his tone stung. Ever since that ill-fated trip into the palace, he had been my guardian, my protector, and closing my eyes upon frustrated tears, I said, "Why did you stay with me, Shin? Why did you stay with me in Mei'lian? Why did you stay all the way to Koi? Why look after me at all if you care so little for my life?"

He seemed to chew upon words, but every time he took a breath as though to answer, none came out. With nothing but an annoyed grunt, he guided our horse down the steep slope, turning every now and then to be sure Tili followed.

Camp noise slowly washed over us as we descended, and at the bottom of the hill, Shin whistled and called his name to the men on sentry duty. They came, bringing a lantern to lift into our faces, a proud look all I could muster in spite of the sash binding my wrists.

With nods and bows, they let us pass, and I kept my head up high despite the fear clenching its hand upon my heart. Between rows of tents and around clustered groups of soldiers we wound, but they were not resting or eating or playing at dice, rather preparing to fight.

"What are they getting ready for?" I said as Shin continued toward the central tents.

"An ambush, maybe," he rumbled. "Or perhaps there's fear of an attack in the night."

"Then wouldn't it be safer if you—"

"No."

Katashi's tent was growing large in my vision, its tall pennons snapping in the wind. A glow of golden light spilled from the tent opening, and a guard stood in its pool, his hand straying to his sword hilt as we approached.

Shin reined in, our sweating mount backing as though in exception to the guard's fluttering sash. "His Majesty in?"

"He's in," the guard replied. "But he's got a visitor."

"Tell him I'm here with *Her Grace.*"

"As you say, Captain." The guard gave a little shrug and turned to poke his head through the tent opening.

With my back to his chest, I could not see Shin's face. "What are you going to tell him?"

"Whatever he asks."

I twisted my neck around harder and caught a glimpse of his stern expression over my shoulder. "Will you let me explain?"

His look owned no kindness, but he nodded. "He already suspects the what, but you can try to spin a nice palatable why."

Before I could ask what Katashi already knew, the guard re-emerged from the tent. "Go on in, he's waiting for you."

The words made my heart thump hard against my breastbone. Behind me, Shin slid from the saddle, only to stand ready to help me dismount. He hadn't untied my hands, and the guard was staring at them now, and rather than make more of a scene, I let Shin lift me down. My stomach dropped as he set me on the ground, as much from the sound of Katashi's voice as the sudden movement.

"After you, Your Grace," Shin said, and it took all the courage I possessed to hold my head up high and walk inside, wondering if this was how it felt to meet one's executioner.

Katashi's tent was large, but there was no hiding from him or the anger hanging so palpable upon the air. He was sitting in the middle of the floor with Hacho laid across his lap. She was unstrung, her limbs curving back like the legs of an enormous insect. I might have shied from so indecent a sight even without the scowl Katashi bent upon his work, but his fury made me flinch.

"Good evening, Cousin," spoke a voice, but it was not his.

Someone stood in the shadows beyond the lantern light, a diminutive figure with a wild fountain of dark curls and bright, intelligent eyes.

"Are you...?"

The woman tilted her head. "You have other cousins?" She looked over my shoulder. "It's good to see you, Shin. It's been a while."

"Too long, my little sparrow," he said, emotion in his gruff voice I hadn't thought to hear.

With such a resemblance, the woman could only be Katashi's sister Kimiko, a suspicion Shin confirmed when he crushed her into a fatherly hug. Never had I seen Shin touch anyone except to kill them and for a moment I stood more transfixed by this show of devotion than by Katashi's anger.

It didn't last long. Katashi's smouldering glare could have burned through steel as he said, "Where did you find her, Shin?"

"Orotana," he said, letting Kimiko go. "Meeting with Kin like you thought."

Katashi went on waxing Hacho as if Shin hadn't spoken, but the look of reproach Kimiko flashed my way chilled the space enough for the both of them.

"I think," she said, looking down at her brother, "that we are much in the way and ought to depart, Shin. I was looking forward to meeting you, Hana, but it seems this is not a very opportune moment."

She bent to plant a kiss upon Katashi's head. "Strength, Brother."

With a last intent stare my way, Shin allowed himself to be carried out in her wake, leaving Katashi and I alone. All the air seemed to vanish with them.

"Do explain to me why I should not execute you for treason," Katashi said, still not looking up.

"I can't."

His hand paused part way along Hacho's length. "Do I not deserve an explanation?"

"Yes, but...no matter how I explain it, my actions are still treason."

"For which you ought to be executed."

"Better that than knowing I could save thousands of innocent lives with a few words yet choosing to do nothing."

Gently, he set Hacho from him and pressed his fingers to his forehead in a moment of pain. "And what," he said to the floor, "were your 'few words'?"

"I told him to blockade the mouth of the Tzitzi," I said, hating the breathlessness in my words and the trembling of my voice. "That was all. No details. No plan. Nothing more."

"That's all?" he said, his laugh devoid of all joy as he finally looked up at me. "That's all? As though that were not enough. As though that information alone did not put everything I have worked for in jeopardy."

He got to his feet, the slow uncurl of a waking predator. "You embarrass me, Cousin," he said. "You betray me. You risk having yourself caught and bargained back to me or worse. And yet you can still stand there proudly." He took a step closer, seeming to tower over me more than ever before. "I told you why I had to kill the men who surrendered," he went on, fury throbbing in his voice. "I told you why I had to attack Shimai. I have given you every reason you have demanded and every opportunity to walk away, and this is what I get in return."

"I could not let you do it," I said, forcing myself to look up into his face. "I could not let you kill so many innocent people and you would not listen to me."

"Had you threatened me with this I might have."

"No, no you wouldn't have, Katashi. You would have berated me and stalked out. You would have set Shin to follow me everywhere. You would have had me escorted back to Koi in chains if that was what it took to keep me quiet. Anything rather than consider that death was not the only way to take an empire."

Hissing a breath between bared teeth, he advanced another step closer, and it was all I could do to hold my ground. "The entire history of the empire is built on blood, Hana."

"But it doesn't have to be."

He ran his hands through his messy hair and blew out a breath in frustration. "We have had this conversation before. How can you not see how precarious my position is? All it takes is one tiny thing to go wrong and it will be over. And there will be no going back, because I will be dead."

"So you would burn a city? You would kill innocents? Women? Children?"

"I would do *anything*!"

"Listen to yourself! This is not a war against Chiltae, Katashi, where a leader must do anything and everything they can to protect their people. Kisia was prosperous. At peace. In no danger at all. What difference does it make to the common people who their emperor is? Whatever else you can say of him, Kin has taken care of the empire. It didn't need saving."

"Are you saying I should have just shrugged and walked away, after he killed my father and ruined our family, ruined my life?"

"No, but you cannot pretend that these people, your Pikes, your soldiers, your enemies—the people of Shimai—are dying in service of the empire. They are not. They are dying for you."

He's scowl grew uglier in the lantern light. "As they died for Kin when he—"

"No, do not tell me that Kin has shed as much blood or list what atrocities he has ordered. We are Otakos, Katashi. We are better than that. Better than him. We are the founding gods of the empire, protectors of its people, and if we cannot do that, cannot be that, then we deserve no throne."

"And he does?" he cried, throwing out his arm in the vague direction of Mei'lian.

"No, but he has it, and to much of the empire, we are nothing but a rampaging conquest destroying lives and land. Right now you are the last of the Otakos. Is that how you would have us remembered? As barbarians?"

He closed his eyes, pain in the lines of his face, and I knew then that he was listening, that I had finally found the words I needed to make him understand.

I stepped forward, my bound hands outstretched. "I believe in our family's right to the throne," I said. "I believe in you, in us, in everything Kisia could be under Otako rule, but with the right advisors, the right strategy, we would not need to resort to bloody, ruthless plans that will more surely set our people against us than win us an empire. We need to be smart, Katashi, not barbaric. Between us, you and I, we can win this the right way."

He opened his eyes but there was no kindness in his gaze. "You say 'us' a lot for someone I ought to execute," he said quietly.

"I am not sorry I did what I did, and I won't lie and say that I am. But I am sorry I could not find the words to make you listen sooner, and that I refused to do the one thing that could help you most, that might have made all of this unnecessary."

It might gall me that my greatest power lay in marriage, but I could not deny Kin had been right. Following Katashi's army was not enough to sway those hesitant to pick sides. As the only daughter and last surviving child of Emperor Lan Otako, I had to vote with my name, my body, my future.

With my hands still bound, I knelt at his feet and set my forehead to the floor. "Your Imperial Majesty, it would be a great honour if you would accept my hand in marriage."

Katashi's fingers closed around my arms, hard enough that I winced. "Hana..." He pulled me up to face him, his gaze scouring my face. "Do you mean that?"

"I don't think this is a good time to be joking, do you?"

And yet he scowled, not seeming to believe me.

"How can I expect you to do all this," I said, "and yet withhold from your cause the power I have to sway Kisia's people?"

"How very romantic you make that sound."

He still looked grim and I could tell he hadn't forgiven me, might never do so as long as he lived, but that didn't mean all was lost. There was no space between us left to close, so I rested my bound hands on his chest, unable to tell if the rapid pulse I felt was his or my own as I looked up into his face. No smile, no peeping dimple, nothing but the harsh lines of his anger. "I love you, Katashi," I said, pressing my palms flat against him. "I love you and I want to fight this war with you, at your side as your empress. I don't expect you to forgive me for what I did, but I would tie my fate to yours and win or lose this together."

My dispassionate sense of duty might argue that marriage to Kin was best for the empire, and it would be right, but in Katashi's presence, it was impossible to be dispassionate, impossible to forget the hurts of our family, or how alive he made me feel. As though together there was nothing we could not achieve.

After a long silence, he took hold of my forearms, pressing them hard against him. "I ought to refuse you. I ought to strip you of your title and throw you in a cell. I ought to never again listen to a word you say. But though the gods may strike me down for such madness, I don't want to do any of those things. I am very far from forgiving you, but all I want to do is hold you close and never let you go. I want you to be my wife, Hana; I want to fight this fight together. Tell me I will not regret it. Tell me that one day our son will sit on the throne when I am gone."

"You will not regret it," I said, the words threatening to stick in my throat. "We can do this together, all of it, even making sure there is an empire for our children to inherit."

Slowly, he bent his head to mine, and I stretched up into his kiss, soft at first, then owning all the ferocity of our first embrace. Yet there were no teasing kisses on my neck or my brow, no gentle trace of his hands down my spine. Gripping my face, he pushed me back as he devoured me, until we were once more upon the floor like in that meeting room at Koi.

When he pulled away to work my sash loose, I held out my bound hands. A few seconds were all it would have taken to untie me, but instead he gripped the silk knot and lifted my arms over my head, pinning them to the floor. A thrill shivered through me and I spread my legs, every part of me yearning for his touch as he tore at the knot in his own sash. It fell free, and before I could do more than twist to see what he was doing, he wrapped it around my already bound hands and tied me to the tent pole. I tugged instinctively but the knots would not give, and I was shocked to find how much I liked it.

Katashi had kept his robes on, but the sliver of his naked body

I could see through the open silk panels only deepened my need for him. I wanted to touch him, to caress him and for an instant wished my hands free, though the moment he spread my robe and gripped my hips, all thought vanished.

With the desperate need of lovers long parted, there was no teasing, no playful words or loving assurances, everything a ferocious blur from the moment he first thrust into me to my final cry of pleasure—a pleasure made all the more thrilling by how hard I could pull at the sash and not get free.

No words at all from the moment I had given him my promise to the moment he collapsed on top of me, and yet so much had changed. The air had felt so charged with tension, the moment so fraught with hurt and anger, but in the aftermath of our passion, there was nothing but the tumultuous rhythm of our hearts beating against one another.

"I hope I didn't hurt you," he murmured once he had caught his breath.

"Oh no. No, not at all. That was quite something."

He lifted his head enough to grin at me. "I thought you were enjoying it. We'll have to try it again another time."

"Or perhaps I can tie you up next time."

A half shrug and that lopsided smile was back, warming my heart. "Why not?"

"I'll maybe tie the sash a little looser though."

With a little groan, he slid out of me to untie the knot Shin had kept tightening every time I wriggled it loose. What a long time ago that seemed, though it had only been that morning.

Rubbing my aching wrists, I said, "You haven't actually answered me, you know."

"You're right," he said, and with his robes hanging open around him, he bowed his forehead to the floor. "I would be honoured indeed to be your husband, Your Grace," he said, and looking up, he met my gaze with laughter in his eyes. "I am very conscious of the distinction you are bestowing on me."

"You might well be, given how many times I have refused. Mama Orde would be truly horrified."

"One day I hope to meet this good woman," he said, rising to his feet and looking down at me. "I will tell her how stubborn and impulsive and determined her daughter is, and how much I love her."

I pushed myself up on my elbows. "I think she would like that. And agree with you on all points."

Outside, the guard cleared his throat. "Your Majesty?"

Katashi gathered his robe around himself. "What is it?"

"One of the soldiers has brought a message from Esvar, Your Majesty. They picked up both Lord Laroth and the head Vice. They should be here within the hour."

"Good. You had better go let Lady Kimiko know."

"Yes, Your Majesty."

Katashi sighed, and bending down, he kissed my hand front and back. And in response to my silent question, said, "For Kimiko. I'll explain later, it's all... quite the story. But if they're on their way, we need to dress."

Rather than retie his robes, he shed both into a heap on the floor and picked up his armour from beside Hacho. I had forgotten to ask why all his soldiers were prepared for battle at so late an hour, but watching him pull on his under-tunic, a sense of ill ease crept over me. "Armour? I noticed all the men were dressed for battle, but why?"

"Because Kin is camped a bare few miles south of here and won't be expecting us in the middle of the night." He took up his leather tunic and shook it out. "He won't know what hit him. Don't look so worried; Manshin will be leading the attack, not me." A small flicker of relief flared, but not enough to dispel the sudden but inexplicable fear that had engulfed me. "I won't join them until after I see this done."

"See what done?"

He paused in the middle of tying his breeches, a scowl darkening his face. "Your guardians. If Darius is as reformed as Kimiko says, then he can go free, but it's time we did away with Malice for good."

21. DARIUS

Katashi's army ought to have been days away, making its way down through the serpentine passes of the northern Valley. And it ought to have been smaller. As we approached and more and more lights emerged from the hollow in which he'd camped, I let out a curse on a long, drawn-out exhale.

Malice had his eyes closed, but his lips twitched in appreciation.

"I seem to have calculated the distance very poorly," I said.

"Or calculated Katashi Otako very poorly," he replied, still not opening his eyes. "You are used to the ways and speed with which Kin moves about his empire, yes?"

"If I was any good at my job, it ought not make a difference."

He chuckled and opened bleary, bloodshot eyes to look upon me with familiar affection, until the jolting of the cart made the arrow in his leg bounce. He hissed and closed his eyes again.

The driver slowed as the track steepened, the curve of the hill seeming to suck us down into the hollow below like an errant ship into a whirlpool. It would have been hard enough to navigate in daylight, but with nothing but the running lanterns to light the track ahead, it would have had even Avarice swearing.

"How's Avarice?" I said, as much to keep Malice's mind off the pain as because I wanted to know. I had told myself for five years that it didn't matter, that he was part of an old life I had left behind, but he was the only person who had never let me down.

"Ah, beginning to feel sentimental, my dear?" Malice said, tightening his arms over his chest and tensing at every bump of the cart. "He is himself, as ever. Misses you and does not say so. Takes every new Vice in dislike. None of them know how to tend their horses properly, yes?"

The memory of his scolds made my heart ache for the past. "Does he still threaten them with beheading?"

"Every time. They don't find it comforting when I say he'll make sure they're dead first."

From the other side of the cart, one of Katashi's soldiers glared at me as I snorted. He looked as if he wanted to say something but just received my smile with an even darker scowl and turned away. When I looked back down at Malice, it was to find him steadily regarding me. "I've missed you, yes?" he said.

"I've tried not to."

He smiled, but there was more pain in it than amusement as the driver took a sharp turn down the side of the slope. The cart tipped so steeply I slid and, with my hands bound, could not stop myself hitting the soldier beside me. He growled and pushed me away.

As we drew into the camp, voices began to rise above the rumbling cart wheels. It was late and few soldiers were visible in the dim rows between tents, but some of Katashi's labourers stopped to stare as we drove past the outer sentries, and by the time the cart slowed, we had quite an audience.

The guards who had sat in the cart with us leapt out before it had even stopped.

"I don't think they like us very much," I said, making no effort to move.

Malice had kept his eyes closed and looked pale in the torchlight.

"You killed one of them with your hand. I might find that extremely arousing, but I am special, yes?"

"Well," came a voice as a figure approached through the shadows. "Look who's back."

"Ah, Shin," I said. "Did you miss me so very much?"

The man stopped at the end of the cart, his arms folded and a hateful glare twisting his scarred features. "Hardly."

Malice chuckled, but Shin made no acknowledgement of his presence. Instead, he turned and looked around at the gathered audience. "What are you all staring at?" he called. "Piss off and do something more useful than stare at our freaks."

With muttered grumbles, the labourers slowly dispersed until only Shin was left. "The Emperor wants to see you," he said.

"He's not *my* emperor."

Shin's scowl deepened. "I don't trust you even as far as I can throw you, Laroth. What are you planning?"

"If I was planning something, it would be very foolish to tell you so, don't you think?"

He leant close. "I have been with Master Katashi since his father died," he hissed in my face. "I have seen him weather more pain than any boy should have to suffer, especially one whose future ought to have been laid out clear before him. Now that he has a chance to reclaim that future, I cannot and will not let you ruin him. Nor help your Usurper to do so."

So easily could I see Avarice in the fierce protective spirit facing me that all thought of a sneer died on my lips. "Kin was merciful to him once. He could be again."

Shin laughed, not an amused sound rather one that chilled my blood with its cruel edge. "And I thought you were so clever, Laroth. But it seems even you aren't immune from clinging to beliefs that make life easier."

"And what beliefs are those?"

He leant close again. "That Kin spared him. Did he tell you it was to retain the loyalty of the northerners, perhaps, or that he wanted to end the civil war rather than draw it out longer?" He leant closer still until all I could see was that lidless eye filled with fury. "It was me who got Katashi out of that prison, and if I hadn't, he would have gone to the executioner, same as his father. It didn't matter to Kin that the boy was innocent, that his life had been torn apart, but then it wouldn't to a man so dishonourable he could go back on every oath he ever made."

My pulse thrummed in my ears and I could not look away, as mesmerised by his gaze as by the horror of his words. And relentless, Shin sneered and kept going.

"You think your Kin is so honourable," he said. "Why don't you ask him who paid me to murder the Otakos. Why don't you ask him which hell he'll go to for betraying the very people he swore to protect. It was Kin who hired me to kill the emperor. To kill his heir. His children. And even the empress Kin himself claimed to love. I may have held the knife, but their blood is on *his* hands."

I could not breathe. My lungs seemed not to work, my voice broken. Cold horror flooded through me as everything Kin had ever said took on new meaning, and I could not disbelieve what was so easy to accept. That hard, implacable hatred and determination. The stillness in his Errant play like a lioness watching from the grass, waiting, waiting, owning no mercy.

Beside me, Malice started to laugh, at first a chuckle but soon rising to a manic sound. "Oh my poor Darius," he laughed. "My poor, poor Darius. You chose the wrong god."

I heard him, but it was Shin I stared at. "You serve them in penance."

"Yes," he said.

"You stayed with Hana to make sure no harm would come to her because she was the child you couldn't kill."

His jaw hardened. "Yes. While you were trying to feed her to the very man who'd destroyed her family."

The bitter words pierced my flesh, and I closed my eyes in a moment of grief I could not hide. "Do they know?"

"That I did it?" His lip curled and he pointed at his scars. "Grace Tianto knew. Go ahead and threaten that you'll tell them all, I don't care. It ends tonight. This is goodbye, Laroth. By morning, your precious emperor will be dead."

He twitched a humourless smile and strode away. Hot and cold warred for possession of my skin as I stared at where he had stood and fought the urge to call him back, to ask all the questions pooling in my mouth. To ask more would be to end all doubt, and I held on to that doubt like it was a raft in a choppy sea. Shin was a thug. A killer and an honourless man. He had every reason to lie. Except that he didn't.

Kin, the commander of the imperial guard, had killed them. Not with his own hand, but only a naive man could say that made any difference. He would have hired another assassin if Shin had refused, and that made it Kin's crime. Hana and Endymion were only alive today because of Shin. Had he killed the others first? Had he made his way from emperor to empress, then down the corridor from room to room, his conscience twinging as the children grew younger, until he was looking into the faces of a trusting three-year-old boy and his baby sister, squalling in her crib?

Kin had blamed it on Grace Tianto so he could take the throne. He had dug fake graves for Takehiko and Hana so no one would know they lived. He had mourned the very woman he had ordered killed—the woman whose death had driven my father mad.

Malice had not ceased laughing, but as though he was following the trend of my thoughts, his laughter rose to a breathless wheeze, tears running down his cheeks. "Poor, poor Darius," he repeated again. "Even when you're trying to do good, you're a monster."

I had to believe the empire needed no gods.

I tried to focus on the thought, but to the tune of Malice's mirth, my world was collapsing around me. This man I had served. Had respected. Had called friend. All that talk of rebuilding the empire after the civil war, when the whole thing had been caused by the ambition of a common soldier.

Clenching my bound hands to tight fists, I roared at the night. But the guttural cry seemed only to solidify my fury, and I sucked deep breaths and let them go while my mind darted from memory to memory, moment to moment, scouring five years of loyalty to an honourless man who had demanded honesty only to feed me lies. I had told him everything. Had trusted him. Believed in him. Had seen my reclamation in his service, my rebirth in his friendship. But it had all been a lie.

I barely heard the soldier who came to fetch us, though he must have spoken; barely felt my feet move, though I must have walked; barely heard Malice hiss, though his pain continued unbroken. There was just the darkness of the camp, then a brightly lit tent, and I was blinking to bring the figures present into focus. Katashi. Hana. Kimiko. Guards. It was like being dragged before a court of judgement, even Kimiko's gaze appalled as I was thrown at her feet. This woman who had forced borabark down my throat and left me to fail.

My anger flared hot. "Why, good evening," I said, eyes only for her as I struggled upright with hands still bound. "How displeased you look to see me, my dear. What is it that's not up to your standards? Is it all the blood? Do you not like the cuts on my face? Or were you hoping I'd be dead?"

Her cheeks reddened, and part of my mind tried to shout that she had only acted to protect her brother, had needed to only because of Kin's crimes, but I was so full of anger and hurt and betrayal that it felt good to throw it in her face, to see her quail beneath my rage.

"What happened to them?" Hana asked. She and Katashi sat side by side, he in his armour while she wore a fine robe, a proper robe, unlike the ones she had donned in Kin's court.

"We found them like this, Your Grace," spoke a soldier behind us. "If we'd left them at it, I think they might have killed each other without our intervention. But we stuck the arrow in that one after Lord Laroth killed the captain."

Kimiko paled at these words, and I curled my lip at the reproach in her eyes. The disappointment. "Didn't you want me to be more of a monster so I would be easier to leave? Behold me." I bowed in her direction. "With my compliments on your fine trick, my lady."

"Darius..."

"I heard your apologies the first time," I spat. "And pray you make no further attempt to make me feel like a fool."

I had not meant to speak so, had not meant to let the hurt rule my tongue, but it spilled out of me like blackened bile and I could not stop.

"Your professions and your sentiments were all very pretty, how-ever, so pray don't waste your talents on me when you could have such a brilliant career upon the stage."

You and I were made for one another, Darius, Malice had said. *Did you really think someone else would love you, truly love you, knowing everything as I do? Did you tell her the truth?*

"Well," Katashi said, speaking for the first time. "If ever I have seen a man spurned. You have made quite the conquest, Kimiko."

Even as he spoke, it was her I glared at, the hurt words of a child boiling up, only to be held back behind gritted teeth.

I needed you to believe in me.

I needed you to trust me.

I needed you to love me.

Words I could not say.

"Lord Laroth," Katashi went on when no one answered. "My sister has begged your life be spared, and I am willing to grant her wish—"

"So forbearingly kind of her," I sneered. "Truly, I shall be forever in her debt."

"—willing to grant her wish," Katashi repeated. "Should you take this final chance you are being offered and kneel before me as your emperor."

I got to my feet, anger all that fuelled the effort. "Gods serve no emperor. It is you who should bow before me."

"No, Darius, don't do this," Kimiko whispered. Behind me, Malice, still slumped on the floor, began his mad laugh once more. "I am sorry for what I did. It had nothing to do with you and everything to do with protecting my family." She got to her feet, her hair settling around her like a mesmerising cloak. "I am here for you, but you have to listen to me. Don't do this." A step closer. "Please." Another step, and she was almost near enough for me to reach out and touch, but there she stopped and, in a quiet voice for me alone, said, "I love you, Darius."

I looked down at the space between us, the distance the length of my arm and a little more to be safe. Safe. "But you don't trust me."

I had thought my heart could suffer no more wounds, that Shin had dealt the final blow, but those long seconds in which she kept her distance tore the last shards from my body. "You may as well have wielded the knife yourself," I hissed, thumping my scarred chest with my bound hands. And over her head, I glared at Katashi. "I will swear no allegiance to you or anyone, Otako."

Katashi nodded and stood up. "Then I hereby—"

"Darius, don't!" Kimiko closed the gap, stepping close enough that I could smell her hair, and gripping my bound hands, she tore at the knots. "I trust you, I—"

"Kimiko!" Katashi grabbed her arm and yanked her back, but not before my bindings were loose enough that I could shake them free. "Don't be a fool! By the gods, he was dangerous enough with his hands tied. Guards!"

Soldiers crowded into the tent opening, most of those who had come to Esvar for us recognisable on the threshold.

"By order of your emperor, kill these men at once!"

Outcry rose on shrill lips, but whether it was Hana or Kimiko who protested, I couldn't tell, all attention on the first advancing soldier. He had been on the cart with us, and drawing his sword, he swung, forcing me to leap back, hitting the tent's central pole. The whole canopy shook. "I've been waiting to stick you, freak," he said, his face contorted. "Now stop dancing around and stand still."

He lunged. Instinct took over: stepping, twisting, hunting skin. A slash came close and I ducked, hands to the floor. His bare feet scuffed in reed sandals.

Skin.

My hand closed around his toes. The man tried to pull away, yanking his foot back with a shocked cry as I forced the connection.

His knife hit the matting as his scream tore the air. Kicking madly, he caught me in the chest, slamming me back against the pole again. But although the connection broke, the scream went on. Gripping his head between his hands, he ran, shoving comrades out of the way as he turned in tight circles, his legs working without reference to his broken mind. Soldiers had been gathering in the tent, but they halted at the opening now, faces filled with horror.

But there was something beautiful about the broken man, about the disconnection, the freedom of a body no longer slave to its mind.

From outside, one man shouldered his way forward. Drawing his sword, he caught the mad soldier's arm, and thrust the blade through his stomach and up into his heart. The screaming stopped. The man tried to breathe, tried to swallow, the mindless body determined to keep living though blood leaked from its skin. But the merciful soldier clutched the dying man close, waiting for him to still before letting the body fall.

In the frozen moment of horror that followed, I helped Malice to his feet, his hand lingering in mine. That was where it belonged, and when he let go, I could still feel him, his palm imprinted upon my skin.

"What are you waiting for?" Katashi shouted at the men in the doorway, and the note of fear in his voice was delicious to hear. "Kill them!"

"Do you want to die?" I asked, looking at each man in turn. "Do you want to lose your minds to a lifetime of agony?"

"You don't scare us," Katashi said. "I will give the Laroth fortune to the man who brings me both their heads."

The merciful soldier swung first, forcing us back, the bloody tip of his sword sweeping past my face.

"You'll have to do better than that," I said.

"Oh, I'm just playing with you. How big is this fortune?"

"Big enough, but you'll never touch it."

Malice growled. "We'll take you all to the hells with us."

The merciful one laughed as others joined him, their eyes gleaming with the same avarice. One stepped toward Malice, spinning a dagger. He licked dry lips, the veneer of his bravado thin.

Malice gripped my hand, and for a single heart-stopping moment, his Empathy sucked emotion through my fingers. It was nothing to the strength with which Endymion had so nearly ended my life, but he formed it into a weapon with much more ease. Aiming cleanly, he discharged it in a single burst, knocking men back. But we were too weak, too tired, and they were up again in a moment.

Death approached on dozens of dirty reed-clad feet.

I lashed out at the first soldier to step close, gripping his wrist just long enough to elicit a cry of anguish from his lips. The joy of it made my breath come fast, and I lunged for another, a sharp connect sending the man reeling back only to be replaced by another.

I could no longer see Malice, no longer sense him or anyone. Even Kimiko was fading from my Sight as fatigue took its toll. I was sinking, the stink of blood and sweat and leather and oil all I could smell, like I was drowning in a soup of soldiers. The world became a blur. I reached for more skin, narrowly missing death as steel scraped my arm, my face, my fingers, every cut fuelling me with greater pain.

Another man appeared through the press, sleeveless armour leaving an expanse of bare flesh. My fingers flew for him, thin, pale, closing around damp skin.

I didn't see the blade until it sliced into my wrist, sinking into flesh. Into bone. The connection I'd been making died as the knife cut clean through. And Kimiko screamed. A scream that rose in pitch, seemingly without end. Katashi knelt before her, shaking her shoulders and speaking her name, but she went on screaming, her small hands ripping the hair from her head.

Grasping my arm, I found a slick stump, hot with blood. But there was no pain. Whether by some lingering threads of my mark or some other means, she was taking it all, drawing it all from me as easily as my blood leaked onto the floor.

Writhing, Kimiko's nails cut into her own skin. Katashi gripped her wrists, fighting to hold her. "What are you doing to her?" he demanded, glaring up at Malice. "Stop this, you monsters!"

Monsters. A monster would be easier to leave.

Dead men obscured the floor. The soldiers hung back now, wary, watching their emperor rise to his feet. But as Katashi approached, Malice stepped before me—there between me and the rest of the world, where he had always promised he would stand.

"Get out of my way." Katashi shoved through the press of his men. Soldiers stumbled, thrust aside as he advanced toward Malice. "You too, Spider."

"You'll have to move me yourself, yes?"

"I'll kill you soon, I promise. But he dies now." Katashi pointed at me. "Hiding behind your brother, Laroth? Afraid of me?"

"Step aside, Malice," I said, holding my injured arm against my chest. Despite what Kimiko was taking, pain was beginning to leach into my awareness, making every moment a struggle to stand, to breathe.

"Darius—"

"Do it!"

Dragging his injured leg, Malice stepped aside, his expression ugly beneath the crackle of dried blood. Behind him, Katashi's soldiers gathered, their eyes alight, their weapons ready.

I cradled my arm, my sleeve sodden to the elbow.

Katashi stepped forward. "If she dies, I will cut your body into a thousand pieces so the gods never find you."

"Good."

"Good?"

"What else would you like me to say?" I spread my good arm. "It's not like it's going to happen."

A twitch of his lip gave him away, and I stepped as he lunged, lifting my hand to catch his fist. His knuckles slammed into my left palm, and I let connection flow, but there was no skin, no warmth, just the dark leather of an archer's glove.

His other hand grabbed my arm, his look of triumph gleeful.

"Do you think I'm an idiot?" he said, the words a sneer. "What now, Empath? Can't touch me now."

Gritting my teeth, I punched my stump into his arm. Pain was all I knew. The tent spun, and Katashi tightened his grip, his eyes laughing like the flames of the furthest hell as he drew his dagger. He was too skilled a fighter to trick, and my body was too riddled with fatigue to fight. All I had was Empathy.

I needed skin.

Using his grip, I pulled him toward me and leaned in. Our lips met. And in the space of a breath, I forged the connection with a kiss.

We monsters need no gods.
We monsters are gods.

22. ENDYMION

The ink tightened my skin as it dried, its presence as weighty as the Traitor's Mark on my cheek. At least for now a sack hid their messages from the world. Katashi might want to parade me before Kin, but he would not risk me finding my way back to his camp with his enemy in tow.

The horse carrying me through the night felt like Kaze, but I could not be sure, could not touch him or hear him or see him. A voice spoke nearby. Someone laughed. Every breath filled the sack with hot, damp air, and every step made the arrow in my arm wobble, tearing the skin little by little.

Calm.

The horse lurched into a ditch, and the arrow bounced, cutting a barb free of my skin. I retched and tried to vomit down so as to miss the sack, but although I heard some hit the ground, it was all over me, stinking and foul.

Calm.

My companions laughed. "Fine thing for a prince," one jeered. "Oh right, he's just a bastard."

The arrow slowly worked its way free. I could feel it twisting and loosening with every step, cutting threads of flesh.

Another jolt and I retched again, the sour smell of bile sticking to me.

More voices emerged from the night. I couldn't make out what they were saying, but we slowed our pace. A whispered conversation hissed past me like a breath of wind. No numbers, no thoughts on my tongue. There were men out there, and a whole empire full of souls whose minds were a touch away, and yet here I sat, blind.

Normal.

Calm.

I could have hurt Katashi.

"Calm," I muttered to myself. "You don't want to kill anyone."

"Shut up," someone hissed.

"All right, so maybe you do." I continued whispering to myself. "But how long until you're just like Malice. Or worse."

"Someone shut him up. Kin will have scouts out."

"I don't care," I returned. "You're taking me to him anyway, aren't you? Hey, scouts!" I shouted through the darkness of my sick-stained sack. "Lovely evening, don't you think?"

Someone punched my right arm, the jolt causing the arrow in my left to tear free. I hissed out the pain and almost retched again.

"His arrow fell out," one of my escorts whispered.

"Then put it back in."

"Hey! Wait. No!" I twisted in the saddle, causing the horse to back.

"I don't have a bow with me."

"So? Just jam it back in."

The sound of hoofbeats drew closer. "What are you fools shouting about?" a new voice said.

"The bastard shouted. And his arrow has fallen out. Frit says I've got to put it back in."

"Did your mothers bang your heads against the wall when you were born?" the newcomer asked. "Stick the arrow through his sash and bring him along. They're camped exactly where His Majesty said, just waiting for Laroth."

Someone landed on the road. Fingers tugged at my sash, and an arrow slid through it, its form unyielding.

We were nearing Kin's camp, but without my Sight, I had to listen for little sounds to know when we arrived. A whisper came first. Then a distant whinny. The rustle of shifting fabric. A clink. The snap of a banner in the wind.

Kaze halted, his hooves crunching on stones. "You go the rest of the way on your own," one of my companions said and lifted the sack from my head.

Hundreds of eyes stared at me from the gloom, looking from my face to the arrow to the wound in my arm, and a hiss of whispers filled the night. Someone set Kaze walking, and under the eyes of so many, I was carried into Kin's camp, ink running into my eyes.

Rather than look at my audience, I stared at Kaze's ears and tried to calm the rapid beating of my heart. But though he must have sensed my fear, he walked on, allowing someone to grip his reins and lead us toward the central tents. Whispers followed us all the way.

My new escort halted outside the grandest tent, where light spilled free in welcome. Word must already have run ahead, because the two soldiers standing outside asked no questions. One stepped forward and gripped my elbow. "Throw your leg over."

To refuse to dismount would only look ridiculous, so I wriggled out of the saddle with his aid. My aching knees buckled as my feet found firm ground, but I was pulled forward before I could right myself. Stepping blindly, I tripped, sandal scuffing onto reeds as I fell into the presence of Emperor Kin.

Light stabbed into my eyes and I blinked. I had only ever seen Kisia's emperor close up once before and now here he was kneeling before me, frowning—the sort of frown that digs deep lines upon even the most handsome face. A frown cut from the cares of an empire.

His dark eyes focused on the ink staining my forehead, and his frown deepened.

"What did he write on me?" I said, before I could think better of asking so bold a question of an emperor.

Emperor Kin moistened his lips and glanced up at his men. "You may leave us. No, wait. Fetch warm water and a fresh robe."

"Yes, Your Majesty."

The men left, the tent silk sighing as it fell closed behind them.

"It says, 'Bastard Prince. Pretty Takehiko,'" Kin said. "Hold out your hands."

I proffered my bound hands. Kin had to grip my bloodstained fingers to keep them steady while he slid a knife between my wrists. Its cold caress ghosted across my skin, and the rope fell away, leaving angry red grazes.

My injured arm throbbed, but Kin did not let go. Pulling back my sleeve, he turned my wrist until my birthmark stared up at him.

"I saw this mark when you were born," he said. "Lord Nyraek Laroth had it. Darius has it. Everyone knew you were not an Otako."

He released my hand, and I lowered it slowly, bringing it to rest upon my knee. I wasn't sure what to say, unable to divine his intentions from his face as I once could from his heart.

"How did you get the branding?"

"Darius," I said. "I was arrested for witchcraft in Shimai and he came to see me. He told them I was just a traitor and ordered them to brand and exile me."

A little smile flickered upon those thin lips. "Thought I would kill you, did he? How full of secrets he continues to be. Where is he?"

"At his house, or on his way, I'm not sure. He meant to be here. He had the crown for you, but Kimiko drugged him with something and stole it back for Katashi, and . . . and so I am here instead."

His scowl grew more ferocious as I spoke, and I faltered, recalling before whom I knelt. This was the soldier emperor of Kisia.

Despite his frown, all he said was "Katashi's sister? How full the world is of fish these days."

A man backed in through the tent flap carrying a wide bowl draped with linen cloths. With a bow to his emperor, he set it down on the matting, placed a neatly folded robe beside it before exiting again without a word.

Kin nodded toward the bowl. "Clean yourself up. The ink might stain, but I think the vomit and blood can be dispensed with. Is it your blood?"

I slid the arrow from my sash with a shaky hand and held it out. Kin took it, his gaze travelling from the bloodstained tip to the wound in my arm. "Captain Rosh," he called, turning the arrow slowly in his fingers.

A man's head appeared through the tent entrance. "Yes, Your Majesty?"

"Send for Master Kenji. Tell him to bring his box."

"Yes, Your Majesty."

I took up the cloth and dunked it into the warm water. Wringing it out, I scrubbed the ink from my forehead, then dragged it down my cheek, letting its heat melt the aches from my skin. Long after it cooled, I held it there, like a child with a favourite doll.

"It would seem you have angered the great Katashi Otako," Kin said, placing the arrow upon his lap table. It was strewn with maps and papers, a brush drying upon his ink stone.

"You could say that," I agreed, swapping the cloth to the other cheek, then running it down my neck. All I wanted to do was lie down and sleep and never wake.

"No doubt he does not like that your claim to the throne is greater than his." Kin spoke quietly, his eyes never leaving my face.

"And has sent you to me because your claim is also greater than mine."

"And because you swore an oath to protect me and uphold my name."

For the first time, he looked down at his hands rather than at me, and I yearned to feel what he felt and hear what he thought, and my head spun as I forced myself not to look, not to yield.

"I did," he said. "Might I ask where you have been all these years, Takehiko?"

"Travelling. The orphan ward of a priest. I—"

Emperor Kin held up his hand as the tent flap shifted once again and a middle-aged man walked in, a lacquered box hanging at his side. He bowed, light wisps of hair like soft down dancing on his head. "You sent for me, Your Majesty?"

"Yes, Master Kenji, my guest requires your attention."

Guest. Emperor Kin's expression told me nothing.

Master Kenji came forward with his box, its painted blossoms shining beneath clear lacquer. "He looks awfully ill, Your Majesty," he said, kneeling before me and peering into my face. "Shaking. Feverish. His eyes are dilated and he's very undernourished. You look to be suffering a great deal, child. What can I do for you?"

I pointed to my arm. He smiled a sad little smile. "Ah, well I guess that is the thing that might kill you fastest, but when I am done with that, I will have to do a full examination. Can't have you dying on His Majesty, can we?"

There was cheeriness in his tone, but it was so forced that I wished I had a mirror so I could see what he saw.

"Just tend the wound for now, Kenji," Emperor Kin said. "The rest can wait until morning."

"As you say, Your Majesty. Let me see this arm of yours." The

314 • *Devin Madson*

physician spoke in the gentle way one might address a child. I turned, every movement painful, and kneeling at my side, he peeled away the torn sleeve. "This does not look pretty," he said, his gaze lingering on the Traitor's Mark. "Might I ask what happened?"

"He fell foul of an Otako," Kin said, indicating the arrow on the table.

Master Kenji gave a little snort. "A gift from the Great Fish, eh? I have been seeing more of these wounds than I like. He uses barbed arrows, and they are not good for the flesh."

"Clearly," Kin said.

Attempting no further conversation, Master Kenji helped me to remove my soiled robe. He did so with the practicality of a man to whom there was no shame, making no mention of the smell nor appearing to even notice it. Once the robe had been disposed of by the simple expedient of throwing it outside the tent, Master Kenji opened his box. Neatly organised glass vials and silken pouches filled much of the space, the rest taken up by a collection of strange metal tools I did not want to think about.

Taking the cloth, Master Kenji began to clean the wound. I gritted my teeth, holding my other arm across my naked torso, the watchful eyes of the Usurper unblinking.

"You have a second branding on your arm," Kin said after a time. "Can a man be a traitor twice over?"

Master Kenji, who had pinched a dry piece of linen between his teeth, let it drop to say, "It might have escaped your notice, Your Majesty, but the boy has one on the back of his head here too."

Eyebrows rose. "Three times a traitor. You were branded in Shimai, I think you said."

"Yes." I felt Kenji's eyes on me and added, "Your Majesty."

"Only a few weeks ago, by the look of the scarring."

Again, Master Kenji glanced up from his work. "If you wish my professional opinion, Your Majesty, I would say they were not administered by a trained man. These wounds are deeper and angrier than we commonly see. This scabbing too–"

"Three brands administered by angry men," Kin interrupted. "In Shimai a few weeks ago." His gaze slipped to my left wrist, to where the origin of the Traitor's Mark had been born upon my skin. He knew. He knew what I had done.

Master Kenji went on with his work while Kin and I sat in silence, staring at each other.

Little fragments of memory dribbled in like dreams. My mother in her furs. Her sad smile and the touch of her hand. And General Kin. Stark. Silent. Ever-present. Every single guard in the palace loyal to him.

Those dark eyes stared back.

Perhaps feeling some awkwardness, Master Kenji paused in the act of grinding herbs and glanced at his emperor. Kin did not meet his gaze, but whatever the physician saw in that face made him work with greater speed. Hardly aware of the pain now, I let Master Kenji apply a cold poultice, pressing it into the wound with skilled fingers.

"It is not as bad as it first appeared," he said, taking a length of linen from his box and lifting my arm. "Assuming you are staying with us, I will check it again in the morning. Keep the bandage on for at least a week. Take it off for a few hours every afternoon to let it dry in the sun. Sunlight is very good for wounds, though not, of course, as good as avoiding them in the first place."

He finished tying the bandage and looked again toward his emperor. No words passed between them, but Master Kenji quickly packed his things back into the box without their former neatness, and when he had finished, he bowed himself out, murmuring, "Good night, Your Majesty."

Kin made no reply, just glanced down at the folded robe. "You may dress now," he said and waited in silence while I did so.

When I had finished, I sat back on my heels in imitation of his own restful state. But even without my Sight, there was nothing restful about the mind that moved beyond those dark eyes. Trouble leached from the deep furrows of his brow, a whisper at the edge of hearing. Katashi had sent me to force Emperor Kin's hand, to force him to make a decision everyone would speak of.

"I wish you would tell me a story, Takehiko," the emperor said, shifting his weight as though his foot had gone to sleep. "I wish you would tell me how you come to be here and what you plan to do now that you are."

"I don't want your throne." The room spun sickeningly as I kept forcing my Sight in, and I propped myself up with shaking arms.

"Even if it is your throne? There are papers—"

"I've seen them."

His brows lifted. "Have you indeed? So you are not the latest Otako assassin sent to end my life?"

"No."

In the silence that followed, I caught the sound of voices outside. "Your Majesty?" The same guard as before stepped in through the open slit.

"Yes? What is it, Captain?"

"There is a man here to see you, and a woman," the captain said. "The man says he is Lady Hana Otako's guard, and the woman is her maid. They bring a message."

Kin's expression told me nothing, and I clenched my fists tighter still. Relief? Anger? Fear?

"Tell them to wait," Kin said. "I'll hear what they have to say when I am finished here."

"Yes, Your Majesty."

The man retreated. "It seems I am to be inundated with Otakos tonight," Kin said, turning back to me. "Your sister."

"Half-sister," I corrected. "But she doesn't know who I am."

Emperor Kin sighed, seeming suddenly older. "What am I to do with you?" he said. "You're a Laroth, and yet your great cousin is right. I took an oath to protect you, as your father's blood, an oath I am honour-bound to uphold."

"But I am not his blood."

"What do you want? You say you do not want my throne, but why then did Katashi put an arrow through you? Why, in fact, are you here at all?"

Why was I? All I had ever wanted was to know who I was, to know where I belonged, to know the mother I dreamed of every night in the hope of finding my family. I had wanted truth and Father Kokoro had condemned me for it. Jian had been tortured for it, and I had been broken and was still breaking, every suppression of my Empathy bringing me closer to death as every use of it had brought me closer to madness.

"I . . . I don't know," I said, my thoughts tangling together. "I just want what is right. I want the gods to judge every man for what they are and what they have done."

Justice.

"And what is right? Sometimes the difference between right and wrong is merely a matter of opinion, entirely dependent upon whose side you are on."

The silken tent flap rustled again. "Majesty?"

Kin closed his eyes, seeming to draw strength. "Yes, Captain?"

The captain's eyes darted from his emperor to me and back again. "Sorry, Your Majesty. It's this man with the message from Lady Hana Otako. He says it's urgent."

Kin rose from his place, the folds of his simple robe settling about his feet. Only the crimson colour gave away his position; for the rest, he might have been anyone.

"I will see this messenger now, and we will talk again when this business is concluded."

He strode out, slapping the silk out of the way. Every part of me ached and I just wanted to sleep, but curiosity took me to the tent opening in his wake. There I sat and leant my head on one of the outer poles, while Emperor Kin stepped onto the dark grass. He didn't seem to notice me, but both his guards gave me strange looks, their eyes focussing upon the cheek where my brand stood proud.

The open space before Kin's tent was dotted with watching soldiers, mere spectators in the darkness. Two shrouded lanterns filled the circle with shadows, while in its centre, Kin's two guests stood alone. They bowed low, respectfully, but the taste of something else hung on the air.

No, don't listen. Don't feel. Don't taste. I clenched my fists and turned it in upon itself, cutting death a little nearer.

The woman's face was red and swollen from tears, her hands shaking. All eyes were upon her, the man just one of Katashi's soldiers, a Pike by the look of his clothing.

"Your name is Tili," Emperor Kin said, speaking to the woman. "You are Lady Hana Otako's maid."

"Yes, Your Majesty." The woman bowed again.

"You were once in my service and I will trust your word. You look distressed. Has something happened to Lady Hana?"

The woman shook her head. "No, Your Majesty." She glanced at her companion and added, "When we left her, she was in good health."

"You bring a message then?"

"Yes, Your Majesty. One I feel would be... best imparted in... in private. Your Majesty."

While she stammered her words, my gaze slipped to the Pike beside her. He stood with perfect predatory stillness, his wiry arms hanging at his sides, taut and ready. No one had eyes for him, yet from his broken face, a familiar man stared back.

Old memories reared, slipping into my mind as though they had never left. A man standing over me. This man. Blood splattered his torso and stained his hands, like a dye maker who had dipped too deep into his vat. But the face had been younger, unscarred, nothing like the terrifying mask the years had given him. Blood had dripped onto the floor. Hana had cried, the call of a helpless baby breaking the silence. And all the man did was stare.

"You," I said, and unable to hold it, my Empathy rushed out. Emotions clogged each breath: tension, fear, anger, heartache; and this man with the lidless eye flicked his gaze my way.

Patience. You've waited sixteen years. A dead tiger strikes too soon.

The words hung in my head, and I could not unhear them, could not stop the feeling that I was leaking from a thousand holes.

His soul flared, the whispers scrabbling over one another to be heard. *Sixteen years. I couldn't do it. But his blood will be sweet. I'll take her his head. I'll tell her the story. Even if she hates me for it, she has to hear it now.*

Every eye was upon me.

"I've seen you before," I said as the memory faded into the warm night air. "You were there."

The scarred man's fingers quivered. Shock. Fear. And I knew all of a sudden we were in that moment together—man and child, with the smell of blood thickening between us.

He pulled a knife and lunged toward Kin, but I was not ready to see either man die yet. I needed the truth.

Justice.

My blast hit the Pike mid-air, and shocked into a tangle of loose limbs, he plunged into Kin, knocking both men to the ground. Like predators at a kill, Kin's guards leapt upon him. For a moment, the world became a mess of shapes and moving figures in the shadows, a scuffle of limbs and grunts as fatigue blurred my vision and the scarred man was yanked to his feet.

Kin held out his hand for a lantern, his fingers beckoning impatiently. One was offered, and he snatched at the handle, ripping off the shroud and swinging the bright light into his assailant's face. The man did not fight, just calmly gave Kin back glare for glare, two of the emperor's guards holding him pinioned.

The emperor moved the lantern closer still.

"Shin Metai," he said. "Time has not been kind to you."

The man spat. "Nor you, Usurper."

"You were right to say you know this man," Kin said, turning to me as he lifted his voice for all to hear. "His name is Lord Shin Metai. Make sure you all get a good look at him, because there won't be anything left of him come sunrise. This is the man who killed Emperor Lan. This is the man who murdered Empress Li and butchered all her sons." He lowered the lantern. "You have escaped justice too long. Tonight you die."

A whistle cut across his words, a high whine on the edge of hearing. Lord Metai smiled, his expression demonic in the half-light. "No. Tonight *you* die."

Hana's maid screamed. She covered her head with her hands, her cry rising like the call of a harbinger owl. I looked up. The night sky was dotted with dozens of pale flecks, like raining stars. Someone shouted, the call taken up by others until it ran through the camp like fire, rousing men from their tents.

And then the arrows fell.

23. HANA

The world seemed to end in the moment Darius's lips met Katashi's, time halting with the beat of my heart. Everyone held their breath. Wide eyes watched from fearful faces, every guard's advance halted mid-step, weapons quivering. In a touch, he ought to have been dead, could have been, but I knew Empaths were capable of so much more.

I threw myself toward them, all motion and fury and desperation. "No! Darius, don't do this, please!"

Malice caught me. "Hush, little lamb, hush." He laughed by my ear. "He won't be hurt, yes?"

"Let me go! Stop them!"

The words came hoarse from my lips, but no one seemed to hear me. Katashi's soldiers weren't just shocked, they were caught in the perfect silence of incomprehension, confusion sticking them to the floor like glue. I could feel it scratching at my mind, trying to grip me as it gripped them, but I thrust it aside, knowing it for what it was—Darius was stronger than I had known, stronger than I had ever thought possible.

I tried to duck free of Malice, but he only tightened his hold. "It'll be over soon, yes?"

"No! Katashi! Fight it, please, don't let them do this, don't let him make you one of them."

Tears poured down my cheeks, and for a moment, Katashi seemed to look right at me, to see me through the haze. And it was *my* Katashi, all warmth and love and laughter, and for the merest second, I thought he would fight, that maybe, just maybe, I would be enough. But then his scowl grew heavy, and it was too late. They had made a new Vice.

Darius stepped back. The confusion with which he had held everyone began to drain, but I had eyes for no one but Katashi. He had not moved, not even blinked. But the close air in the tent grew hot. He flexed his fingers. Rolled his shoulders. Passed his gaze over everyone, even me, and seemed to see nothing. And then he roared—not the shout of a man but the furious, guttural rage of an animal. Fire licked from his fingers, from his palms, from his whole being, rising to set the tent aflame. It seared overhead as Malice threw me onto the matting, his weight pinning me while tiny pieces of charred cloth rained around us. Screams rent the air. Running steps thundering. Across the other side of the tent, Kimiko lay silent where she had dropped, and I tried to wriggle free of Malice to reach her.

An ember fell upon the reeds and started to smoulder, followed by another, and I kicked until Malice loosened his hold enough for me to crawl toward Kimiko across the blood-soaked reeds. Gripping her hand, I dragged her toward the tent wall, dodging stomping sandals. "Kimiko." I shook her fiercely, tears all but blinding me, though whether they were from grief or smoke now I couldn't tell. "Kimiko?" Her scalp was speckled with blood from patches of missing hair. "We have to get out of here. Please wake up."

"It hurts," she moaned softly, curled upon herself like a sick child.

"I know it does," I said, coughing a lungful of smoke. "But this whole floor is about to be on fire, we have to get out of here!"

"Through the wall," she whispered. "Just walk through the wall.

I'll do the rest." She gripped my hand, and having no time to question her, no time to think, I dragged her forward.

I shivered, hairs rising along my arms and down my legs, as we passed through the silk and into the night. Smoke poured toward the sky, and the small portion of Katashi's army that had been waiting on him was milling around, shouting.

"You're safe here," I said, dragging her away from the edge of the tent to where a group of Pikes stood clustered, their black sashes made orange in the firelight. "Here, look after Lady Kimiko," I shouted at them. "Stay with her. I have to go back in."

One called after me as I sped back toward the tent, but I was already shouting. "Katashi? Katashi!"

Soldiers were stumbling out, singed and coughing, smoke pouring with them. Darius and Malice had escaped and lay together on the grass, injured and barely moving, no one daring to get too close. And through the remnants of the tent's opening, Katashi strode out.

Almost I could believe he was still my Katashi, so much the same did he look. The fire had not touched him, not burned his skin or his hair, not even scorched his clothing, but it lived in his bright eyes now like the fire was in his soul and could not be extinguished. He had been marked, changed, but while Ire and Apostasy and Conceit and all the others called on their power when they needed it, Katashi's seemed to seethe beneath his skin, present at every step he took.

Darius had been too strong.

"Katashi!" I called to him, not daring to move closer. "Katashi? Can you hear me?"

He stalked over, the swirl of his crimson surcoat like flames around his feet. I fought the urge to step back as he came to me, a dark scowl upon his face.

"Hana," he said, his voice unchanged, and yet the very sound of it sent fresh tears spilling down my cheeks.

"Katashi." I reached up to touch his face and he did not stop me, but his scowl did not lift and the flames still blazed in his eyes. Heat radiated from his skin and almost I pulled away as I might from a hot brazier. "Katashi, is it still you? Are you still here with me?"

The question seemed to cool him, yet smoke still rose from the tent behind him like a billowing crown.

He gripped my hand, his hot. "Always," he said. "I love you, Hana. Together, you and I can take back what is ours, can have revenge on those who took our lives from us, our empire from us. I will kill every last man who fights for the Usurper. I will beat his armies back again and again, and when I am done, I will burn him alive, his screams the last thing I will ever need to hear."

Heat flared in his hand as he spoke. It seared my skin, but I could not pull away. Tears kept flowing, this hole in my heart knowing no end. "No, just walk away with me now. Please."

His grip on my hand tightened. "I...can't." He struggled with the words as though his lips did not wish to speak them. "I must... obey."

I knew too well how Vices worked to miss the tensing of his jaw as pain flared through him. They had to obey. Had to remain close. In the beginning, I had swallowed all Malice's lies about it being just a precaution, but none of them had wanted to be marked; none of them had ever wanted to be turned into monsters.

"No," I said. "I will not let this be."

Darius and Malice had not moved from their prone positions on the grass, one with a sluggish wound in his leg, the other cradling his severed wrist. Pulling free of Katashi, I strode toward them.

"Your blade." I held out my hand to the closest soldier, his face lit with fear and firelight.

Fumbling, he handed me his dagger, not his sword—the act of a man who knew what I was going to do.

Darius did not appear to be conscious, for which I was thankful

as I bore down upon him, intent on slitting his throat. It mattered
not what he had once been to me, all he had once done—he had
to die.

"No." Katashi's hand closed around my wrist like a scalding
iron. "I cannot let you do that."

I looked up into his face, such fire in his eyes, while on the
ground beside Darius, Malice wheezed. "No Vice can allow their
master to be destroyed," he said. "No Vice can stray. No Vice can
go against their orders, but it wouldn't change anything even if you
could do it, little lamb. Even if Darius unmarked him, he will be
changed forever, yes?"

"At least he would be free!" I wrenched from Katashi's grip
and lunged at Darius, but arms closed around my waist and I was
hauled back, kicking as I left the ground. I dropped the dagger as
Katashi crushed me like a coiling snake, the rumbling crackle of
flame sounding on his every breath. I tried to loosen his grip, tried
to squirm free, but his hold only tightened, searing my skin. At the
stink of my singeing hair, I squeezed my eyes shut, a sob bubbling
from my lips.

His grip loosened, and twisting to see him, I found a look of
such horror and shame and anguish contorting his face. "Oh gods,
Hana, you have to go," he said, dropping me as though I had been
hot. I landed in a tumbled, winded heap at his feet, wincing that
a body could own so many aches and a heart so many hurts. "You
have to get out of here, before I am compelled to do something I
cannot stop."

He backed away, looking at his hands and then around at the
watching soldiers, all loyal Pikes who had remained to ride into
battle with their captain. "Wen, take her away from me! Get her
out of here now!"

I wanted to refuse, wanted to go to him, to promise him that
everything would be all right and we would get through this

together, but every word would have been a lie. There was no coming back from this, no changing it, and tears streamed down my face as the blurring figure of Wen appeared at my side.

"Come, my lady," he said, holding out a hand to help me up. "Let's go."

"Katashi…"

He backed away from me, his face full of fear, and I spun on my old guardians and kicked Darius in the shoulder as hard as I could. "I hate you!" I screamed. "I hate you, you monstrous, evil—"

Fire flared behind me, and I staggered, all fury swallowed by a frightened sob.

"Take her away now!" Katashi roared. "Leave, Hana! Go! Please!" He had folded his arms tight, pressing his flaming hands to his own skin, and though he did not burn, pain pulled his face tight and I knew I had lost.

"Come, my lady, let's go." Wen gripped my arm, tugging me away. "Come on."

"You can't let her go," Malice snarled, half rising from the grass. "You can't let her run to the Usurper."

"Go, Hana! Now!"

I had lost. Kisia had lost. And if I did not leave before Darius woke, I would never escape at all.

"Go!" Hot tears poured down Katashi's face, and choked with grief, I let Wen pull me away amid Malice's shouts. The last thing I saw was Katashi falling to his knees and howling at the night sky, turning the grass beneath him to ash.

Wen ran for horses, leaving me to gather a barely conscious Kimiko from where I had left her. In a sleepy murmur she asked where Darius and Katashi were and I could not answer, could only quiet her grief with lies as I could not quiet my own.

We can have revenge on those who took our lives from us, our empire from us. I will kill every last man who fights for the Usurper. I will beat his armies back again and again, and when I am done, I will burn him alive.

Vengeance. Commanded by Darius's hand. A force all too capable of destroying an empire. Kin had to be warned before it was too late.

"I have to get to Kin," I said as Wen hurried back with horses. "Where is Shin? And Tili?"

"Shin already went to Kin's camp, my lady, just after the fre— after Lord Laroth was brought in. He took Tili with him."

Because with the maid whose message I had told Kin to expect, Shin could get close enough to kill. "You mean to tell me that Kisia could have lost both its emperors in one night?"

Wen didn't answer, but he didn't need to.

"We have to stop him. I only hope we aren't too late. Help me get Kimiko up before me."

"Are you—?"

"Yes, I'm sure," I snapped. "I'm lighter, just hurry."

Pikes had begun to gather at a distance, but though I expected them to stop us, expected tongues of flame to rend the sky, all was watchful silence. Even the burning tent had died to a smoulder.

It was difficult to ride with Kimiko semi-conscious before me, but once we were ready, I urged my horse out of the camp, forcing myself not to look back, not to hope, not to mourn, just to ride.

Once we were free of the camp, I sped to a trot, lips clamped upon grief. Wen followed, and knowing the way better than I did, he soon pulled ahead into a canter as the worn track rounded the tip of the spur. He rode bow in hand, an arrow pinched between two fingers, his gaze turning to look back as often as he scanned the path ahead. I had to trust him, too preoccupied with Kimiko to be wary of pursuit.

An age seemed to pass with Kimiko's hair bobbing before my nose and her weight pressing back against me, but it could not have been more than an hour before our cantering mounts brought us to a narrowing track, rising up the densely choked hills that spread from the spur. A trail of bruised petals followed us onto the scree, clumps of crushed peonies evidence that others had come this way. At the top of the rise, a thick patch of trees stood apart from the forest, their tall trunks sidling up beside a crossroad. There, a body lay sprawled across the stones. A horse had been gutted, glistening entrails spewing from the carcass to taint the air with their stink.

Wen slowed, and I looked down as my horse shied around the corpse. The man was wearing black—not the black of a Vice or a Pike, but the plain black of a scout. One of Kin's men.

"Smoke." Wen pointed at the night sky. Smoke was rising above the trees, the black plumes tinged silver.

"We have to hurry."

"Are you all right? Lady Kimiko—?"

"Lady Kimiko is fine. Move."

He asked no more questions but picked up his pace, his horse's hooves scattering stones as he turned down the hill. I could smell it now, the acrid stench of a burning camp, and feared we were too late.

The trees thinned as we climbed to the top of the ridge and the Valley opened up before us. And there on the other side of the slope was Kin's camp, a stretch of bamboo palisade burning bright. More fires dotted the Valley floor, turning the mass of soldiers at the bottom of the slope into shadows.

Wen turned his horse, its hooves dancing. Smoke crowded around us. "There's no way you'll get in there," Wen said. "That hill is covered in soldiers."

"Then we go down this way where the fighting is thinnest. It looks like Kin's men are holding the ground before the gate."

"They'll kill us if we ride down there and I wouldn't blame them."

"Which 'they'? Them? Or us?"

"Either. Both!"

I held out my hand. "Do you have something white?"

Wen gaped at me. "You want to cry peace? They'll think it's a trick."

"Stay here if you're afraid."

"Afraid? What if they fill you with arrows?"

"Then they fill me with arrows!" I snapped. "I will not wait here and do nothing."

He laughed ruefully. "I think you will either make a very formidable empress or a very dead one." With these words, he opened the leather satchel he always carried and pulled out some scraps of linen. "This is the best I have, not quite white, but we'll be lucky if they see them at all."

"It will have to do," I said, taking one from his outstretched hand. "Wait. 'We'?"

"Emperor Katashi told me to look after you, and by the gods, that's what I'm going to do, even if I hate it."

The beginnings of my smile faded at mention of Katashi, but there was no going back now. I reminded myself that he was lost to Darius's madness, that he could not be reclaimed, that I had to do what was right for Kisia, and started down the slope. "Come on," I said, as my horse's hooves slid on the loose stones. "Come on."

All along the ridge, Katashi's soldiers were still emerging from the trees. Shouts and screams rent the air as, metal on metal, the sounds of battle raged. With one hand gripping the reins, I lifted the scrap of linen high above my head. Wen did the same, the wind tugging at our only defence as we rode down the hill.

An arrow whisked by and I gasped, snatching back my arm. Wen sped his pace, riding for the gate as fast as he dared, straight to where Kin's men held the ground.

He pulled ahead. A soldier pointed. Others looked up, and

gritting my teeth, I thrust the linen scrap up as high as I could. Arrows were nocked, bows pulled taut, and my heart hammered in my ears.

"Identify yourselves!"

Wen glanced back at me. It was my answer that would save us.

I tried to swallow, my mouth dry. "I am Lady Hana Otako and I would speak to your emperor," I called back, waving my aching arm.

The soldiers held their arrows. Whispers passed. The injured and dead were being dragged in from the main battle, and if I showed an ounce of fear, Wen and I would join them.

"Lady Hana Otako?"

"Kill me if you doubt it!"

A hissed argument took place as Wen began to slow, my mount following his lead. I kept my arm lifted, fingernails cutting into white linen.

"Stand down!" A man in a crimson surcoat gave the order, and every bow was lowered. "Move out. Move out. I'll deal with this." Arms akimbo, the man stood watching us approach, glaring at Wen. "Well, well, Lady Hana," he said. "My name is General Rini, and might I say what an unexpected honour this is at an... unexpected time."

"No pleasantries, General," I said. "I have to see His Majesty and I have to see him now."

"My lady..." The general trailed off. A messenger was pushing through the gathered soldiers, bloodied and limping. "What is it, man?"

"General, they've breached the north wall!"

"Captain, hold the ground. Men of the Fourth, with me! I'm sorry, my lady." He was gone on the words, his soldiers charging off in their general's wake.

"We need to find Kin," I said to Wen as I tried to adjust my grip on my reins without Kimiko falling from the saddle. "His tent is as good a place to start as any."

"If he's still alive." On the words, Wen dug in his heels and his horse leapt forward. Kimiko's awkward weight made it difficult to follow his lead, so skilfully did he wind his way around collapsed tents and knots of soldiers. Noise bombarded my ears. Men were shouting. Screaming. Horses charged past. Arrow boys darted around us, carrying loads of linen and water, arrows and armour, memorised messages muttered on their lips.

A man rode past, shouting above the uproar. "Barricade the gate! Barricade the gate!"

At last, a crimson tent appeared through the smoke. I saw Endymion first, hovering alone at the edge of a clearing, and for a moment our eyes met, his expression hard to decipher. Then I saw Kin. Even dressed in plain red linen, Kin was the centre of his world, this man snapping out orders amid the chaos. Crimson surcoats flew as he dispersed his men, each one dashing away through a forest of standing arrows.

"Look after Kimiko," I said to Wen as I slid from my horse in a daze, heart racing.

Half a dozen steps took me into the clearing and I stopped. Shin was there, caught between two guards. They had his arms bent back ruthlessly, but he was no subdued beast. Seeing me, his eyes narrowed, his lips parting to show a hint of teeth.

"Lady Hana." Kin stepped toward me, only to halt as Wen joined me, standing like the guard Katashi had commanded him to be.

"Careful, Majesty!" One of Shin's guards stepped forward, that instant all the Pike needed. In the space of a breath, Shin ripped free of his other captor, jabbing fingers into his throat before drawing the guard's sword and sticking it through his gut.

Leaving the man to fall, Shin strode across the grass, the bloodstained sword gleaming in the moonlight. "This ends here,

Usurper," he growled, advancing on Kin. Kin was unarmed, but he stood his ground, one hand raised to keep his guards back.

"Do something!" I hissed at Wen, his weapon held slack.

He shook his head. "That isn't my decision to make."

"Then I'll make it!" I slammed my knuckles into his elbow. Wen gasped as the sword dropped from his grip and I caught it on its way down, already moving before he could do more than cry a warning. Dashing the short distance to where Kin stood, I threw myself before him, catching Shin's first strike on the side of Wen's sword. The metallic rasp screeched in my ear, the force of the swing throwing me back. I slammed into Kin and fell, rolling as I hit the ground. Scrambling up, I found Shin on me again, teeth bared as he swung with more force than finesse. I ducked, his blade ripping through the air with a shriek.

"Are you going to kill me, Shin?" I asked breathlessly, backing away.

He lunged, vibration jarring my hands as his sword slammed into mine. "I will kill anyone who protects him," he growled, only to leap back as Kin aimed a thrust at his side.

I ceased to exist as they turned on one another. Shin struck first, a speedy jab, forcing Kin to dodge. Words of warning leapt to my tongue, but I bit them back as Kin faced his opponent with the vigour of a younger man, each of an age and skill that they might have been comrades in a different time, a different place.

"Shin!" I cried. "Katashi is lost! Kin is the only hope Kisia has left!"

He seemed not to hear, just charged at Kin with greater force, catching him with his shoulder and knocking him off balance. I darted forward, but Kin kept his footing and threw out his hand in warning. "Stay back, Hana, it isn't your fight."

"The hell it isn't!"

I made to charge in, but Wen gripped my wrist and yanked me back. "You can't interfere, my lady," he said. "This is his fight now.

Too many people are watching. They won't respect a leader who cannot fight his own battles."

Hopelessly, I stared around at the spectators, every man wide-eyed and hungry. I wanted to shake them, to scream into their faces. These were Kin's men, yet they would stand by while he fought to the death, held as much by their thirst as their honour.

I pulled out of Wen's grip but did not move. Kin might sooner forgive me for the attempt on his life than were I to step in and save him now. But Shin was quick. He slashed and jabbed, moving with such skill that my grip tightened on the sword I was not allowed to use. Their blades met and parted, the sharp zing of steel a melody to the beat of their shuffling feet. There was beauty in the way they moved, but each wanted nothing more than to end the other.

Please gods make them stop.

My prayers went unheeded. Kin's men cheered their emperor on, chanting and stomping their feet as the bloodlust flowed. They jeered too as Shin dodged and ducked. He was always moving, dancing in and out, curved sword slicing at air. Kin was patient, stepping, blocking, backing away, his own blade hovering still.

The cries for blood grew deafening. His soldiers had failed to protect him, and now they chanted for death.

Kin's blade sliced an arc as Shin stepped in. The Pike ducked, but the tip only missed him by a breath. I gasped, and as Shin leapt back, his gaze flicked my way. It was just for a moment, but there was such anger in those eyes that I flinched.

"Please stop!" I shouted though he had already withdrawn his attention. "They marked Katashi, Shin!"

A terrible rasping sound shivered through the night as sword ground upon sword, and with his opponent's blade caught, Kin gripped the front of Shin's tunic. I saw his lips move, saw the words begin to spill forth, but they were lost to the heavens as Kin dropped his blade and thrust a dagger into the stunned Pike's stomach.

"No!"

Wen caught me around the waist. "Be quiet!" he hissed. "It is done."

Blood leaked from Shin's mouth, staining his lips. Like two lovers, emperor and rebel looked into each other's eyes, but there was no understanding, no acceptance. Shin spat, spraying a mouthful of blood over Kin's face. "You will always be a Usurper," he snarled.

Kin ripped his dagger out. Blood gushed onto the grass, and Shin staggered a step before collapsing to his knees amid cheers. In his last lifeless moment, I met that lidless gaze and read only bitterness. He had carried his hatred to the end.

He hit the grass face first and still the soldiers cheered. Their respect for their leader had been renewed, but all I could do was stare at the lifeless form of Shin and hate that it had come to this. I had already lost so much.

"Sound the retreat."

Wen dragged his gaze from Shin's body. "What?"

"You know how to do it," I said. "Sound the Pike retreat. Go and tell General Manshin that Katashi isn't coming."

"But—"

"If you do nothing else for me, you will do this. Listen to me, Wen. You saw what they did to Katashi, what he has become. I do not expect you to change your allegiance as I must, but at least grant Kin the chance to survive until tomorrow in case he is the only emperor Kisia has left."

I whispered the last words, a lump in my throat. Nearby, Kin was already shouting orders, the crowd of soldiers thinning fast.

"Please, Wen," I added when he didn't answer. "Do not let any more men die for nothing. Call the retreat. Let Katashi's soldiers regroup behind their leader if they still wish to follow him, but please, give Kisia a chance. Give me a chance."

He let out a long breath and nodded. "If that is your final order, I will go, my lady," he said at last, holding out his hand for his sword.

I handed it back with a bow. "Thank you."

"You don't need to thank me," he said. "I did see what happened and I . . . cannot unsee it. I will do what ought to be done, though if we both continue to follow that path, the next time we meet, we'll both be dead."

A rueful smile turned my lips. "You may well be right," I said. "But at least we have a beacon to guide us through the murk." His own rueful smile joined mine, but there was no more time for reminiscence or thanks. "Be safe, Wen. Kisia needs more good men like you."

He pursed his lips and nodded, a little smile but no more words. Taking his horse's reins, he mounted, the remainders of Kin's men throwing him dark looks. But their emperor gave no order, and they made no move to stop him disappearing into the chaos, my last sight of him a glimpse of the satchel he always carried at his side. It contained all the tools of the healer's craft, and he would need every one of them tonight.

With Wen gone, I stood alone in an unfriendly camp, the eyes of every soldier flicking my way. Kin did not look at me. Showing no sign that I existed, he gave orders and cleaned his sword, and when a guard brought him a damp cloth, he cleaned the blood off his face, erasing Shin's last existence from his skin.

Endymion had not moved since I arrived, and when our eyes met, I turned away, hating the pity in his gaze. "Endymion," I said, a quiver in my voice. "Take Lady Kimiko somewhere safe. She should be looked after, not left to lie upon the grass."

He did not argue, did not speak at all, just bent to gather Kimiko in his arms. Bones jutted from his skeletal wrists as he slid one thin arm beneath her legs, the other disappearing into her curls.

Endymion departed, but although I stood alone, Kin still did not look my way. "Your Majesty," I said, gathering my courage and starting toward him. "I—"

"While we fought, you said..." Kin interrupted, halting me in my tracks. "You said Katashi had been marked, do you mean—?"

"He is a Vice, yes. Darius. You must get out of here. I will explain later—cannot now—" I let out a shuddering breath and covered my eyes, and from the darkness, Katashi smiled. We had been going to retake our empire together. "I have sent Wen to call a retreat, but by morning, they could be back. And with Katashi and Darius and Malice. You know what the Vices are capable of. You have to leave here tonight."

"And do you come with us?"

What were my choices? I could not go back. The future I'd had with Katashi no longer existed, and any hope of a future for the empire hung upon this man.

When I didn't answer, he closed the remaining space between us. "If all is as you say, then Kisia needs you, Hana."

I was sure he said it to force my hand, and yet there was truth in every word. If Darius was as set on seeing Kisia burn as Katashi was on burning it, then it would take everything Kin had and more to stop them. Including me.

"I...owe you an answer, Your Majesty," I said and knelt at his feet just as I had knelt at Katashi's in another life. I was glad of the protocol of bowing my face to the ground for the moment it granted me to compose myself, though inside I was screaming. "I, Lady Hana Otako, accept your honourable and gracious proposal."

I rose to my feet to find his intent gaze on me. "Hana," he said. "For both myself and my empire, I thank you."

His words thickened in his mouth and he stepped closer. A bloody gash glared through a rip in his sleeve, and his hair tumbled loose from his topknot, but whatever their similarities, he was not my Katashi. Never could be.

Just like back at the teahouse in Orotana, he pressed his lips to mine, and it was all I could do to stop tears spilling down my cheeks, all I could do not to draw back. I let the kiss linger, hoping his closeness and his warmth might spark something in my heart. But all I could think about was the hot grip of Katashi's hand as he told me to run, his eyes so full of a fear he could not voice, a fear of what he had become.

Our lips parted, but Kin did not move. I could taste him, smell him, feel him there, yet I could not meet his gaze. At last, he stepped back, beckoning to one of his guards. Orders were given. A horse for Lady Hana. General Jikuko was to be found. I heard it all, but it slurred as it entered my head, such mundane considerations as getting away from this camp hardly important anymore beneath the weight of my grief. And to make it all the worse, two steps away, Shin lay on the blood-soaked grass.

While Kin was busy about his orders, I knelt beside my one-time protector. Someone had rolled him over so he stared up at the night sky, and though I closed one of his eyes, I could not close them both. One eyelid had been removed before I knew him, leaving tiny scars across his brow. They were nothing to the one that travelled the length of his face, so pronounced that I had never before noticed his high cheekbones or the straight set of a fine nose. I had never asked about his past, never even asked how he had come by the scar that dominated his face. All I had done was wonder who had been able to best Shin. And now he lay silent, never to speak again, his words lost with him.

I touched his cheek. In the distance, the Pike retreat call rang through the night. "You fool," I said. "Why did you have to leave me too?"

"Hana. We have to go."

Kin was behind me. I could feel him there, could see the hem of his robe in the corner of my vision.

"A moment to say goodbye, if you please," I said. "Whatever he has done, I cannot forget that he risked everything for me."

I glanced up to see Kin's face set in its harsh lines, but he nodded and forced a smile, perhaps realising, perhaps not, that it was Katashi I cried for. For the life he ought to have had. For the life we almost had together. He would hate what I had just done. All I could hope was that maybe one day he would understand it. Understand I had done it for Kisia.

24. ENDYMION

Kimiko did not move. She lay upon the sleeping mat like one dead, her hands neatly folded. Even the loudest sounds were powerless to rouse her.

A constant stream of footsteps and hoofbeats passed outside, the sound of scouts coming and going, of boys running messages and soldiers burying lost comrades.

I shifted my weight for the hundredth time, trying to find a comfortable way to sit in this tiny, airless tent. It wasn't tall enough to stand in, and the floor owned barely enough space for Kimiko, but Kin was travelling back east with only a small complement of soldiers, leaving only so many tents to go around.

A group of soldiers passed with loud voices and heavy steps, rustling the tent fabric. Light reached across Kimiko's still form. Six men immediately outside, another two dozen across the row—

I shook my head. No. Now was not the time to get caught in the numbers, or in the souls that called out to me. *Concentrate, Endymion*, I snapped. *Don't lose yourself yet.*

I let out a long breath and touched Kimiko's brow. She was warm, too warm. Sweat beaded along her hairline, dampening those unruly curls. They were singed and bloodied, and I brushed them back with my hand. Still she did not move.

Footsteps stopped outside. A man cleared his throat, the sound loud and deliberate. I rose, my hair catching on the underside of the tent as I shuffled, bent double, to the tent flap. Outside, I squinted into the face of one of Kin's guards, his soul filled with disquiet.

"Yes?" I said, hoping my own did not show. "Can I help you?"

The man stared at the branding on my cheek. "His Majesty requests your presence."

Behind him, the sun was setting, turning the sky blood red. "You may tell him that I will be there presently."

"I am to take you to him now."

"Do you plan to drag me there by force? I am needed here."

The soldier stared at me, his gaze once again slipping to my branding. "Ten minutes," he said. "His Majesty will not wait longer."

He turned on his heel and strode away. I had hoped to have more time.

Back inside the tent, Kimiko still had not moved. I stared down at her from the entrance, letting the flap fall closed behind me. My wounded arm ached. The bandage was tight and uncomfortable, and it was her fault it had happened, but I could not hate her for it. Not while I could feel her hurt so keenly.

"Well, this had better work," I muttered, crouching down beside her and setting my hand to her forehead. "Come on, Kimiko, wake up."

The piece of Darius I'd carried since Koi was never hard to find. Closing my eyes, I let it swell, this living shard of him, this collection of memories and words and thoughts like whispers in the dark. Like breathing prayers over a corpse, I let it out, threading it through her flesh.

Kimiko's eyes snapped open and she sucked fast breaths, her gaze darting around the dim space. She shrank back at sight of me. "You. Where am I?"

"Kin's camp," I said, giving her space as she sat up. My arm throbbed. "But you're safe here. Hana is here."

"Where's Darius?"

"I don't know."

Kimiko pulled the blanket around herself. "What do you mean you don't know?" she said. "You followed him all the way from Koi, you must know."

"Yes, but I didn't know where he was, just in which direction I had to walk to find him. I need you to tell me what happened. I can't... I can't help him if I don't know."

She eyed me warily, dark shadows beneath her eyes. "Am I a fool, Endymion?" she said, letting out a long breath. "Is he a good man?"

"I think he knows how to be," I said.

"That isn't the same, is it?"

"I don't know. Empathy is complicated."

She let out a little snort—half laugh, half sob—and said no more.

"Kimiko," I began, listening for the returning guards, feeling the souls pass, one, four, eighteen—

"What?"

"What what?"

"You were going to ask me something, but you closed your eyes and said nothing."

It's not fair. It's not justice.

I blinked a few times, trying to focus, to resist the urgings of my Empathy. "I'm running out of time," I said. "Tell me what happened to Darius."

"I don't know. Katashi's men brought him in with Malice and he was different. I expected he would be angry with me for what I did, but not like that, not so full of fury and hate and... and hurt. I tried to talk to him, but he didn't even seem to hear me, and when Katashi ordered them both killed..." She trailed off. "I don't know what happened after that really. He'd taken his mark off me, but I felt such pain, Endymion, such pain when they cut off his hand, like it was my hand, and I don't know why."

Tears ran onto Kimiko's cheeks and she brushed them away. "That's all I know. You'll have to ask Hana the rest."

"He marked Katashi. She told me."

Kimiko closed her eyes and let out a shuddering breath. "Oh gods."

Gods. We were the gods.

"This is my fault, isn't it?"

Four men outside. I could feel their purpose and I froze, kneeling upon the linen. "They're coming," I said, lowering my voice. "Whatever happens to me, remember you have nothing to fear from Kin."

"Why? What's going on?"

Outside, footsteps halted once again, and through the slit in the tent, I glimpsed four pairs of sandals: three reed, one wood with the edge of a family crest branded into the sole.

"His Majesty will see you now."

Kimiko parted her lips, but I pressed a finger to my own and shook my head. "Stay here," I whispered, making noise as I stood so they would know I was coming. "I won't be back."

Again, she looked as if she would speak, but I shook my head and turned away, ducking out into the dregs of the evening.

Four of Kin's soldiers waited, each man wearing a crimson sash adorned with the Ts'ai dragon. They all stared at my cheek and looked me up and down like I was the dirt beneath their feet, though they must all have known my name. Just like the guards who had branded me in Shimai.

Justice.

"We will take you to His Majesty," said the man who had come for me earlier, satisfaction oozing off him. "I suppose you are ready now, are you?"

I had never been good with the subtleties of tone, but this one was undoubtedly mocking. "Yes," I said, managing a smile of which even Malice would have been proud. "I am ready. Lead the way."

They did so, two ahead and two behind, through the busy mess of the small camp. Everywhere, men went about their business, saddling horses and loading carts with everything from tents to provisions, while overhead, crimson flags hung heavy from their poles. The noise made conversation impossible. Soldiers shouted to each other, talking, laughing, while boys scurried underfoot with armloads of crimson silk and dozens of dangling lanterns. The presence of so many people was a weight upon my mind, tugging my thoughts this way and that as my Sight connected me to every soul, but to them, I was nothing but a passing shadow: a plain man in a plain robe, owning no name, no purpose.

Emperor Kin's tent stood proud in the centre of the camp. The long-tailed dragon of his family covered every side, dozens of mouths open to speak, to warn me, the whole construction alluding to the man I would find inside. My escort motioned me in, and I felt like a ghost, slinking into the presence of an emperor.

Kin was writing, kneeling at a long, low desk, and but for the paper, it might have been a kiri wood zither upon which he plucked the strings of the empire. Dressed in armour, he wore a crimson surcoat almost as an afterthought, an unnecessary reminder that this stern man held the reins of history.

Light flickered across his parchment, and he looked up as the tent flap fell closed behind me, shutting out the camp. We were alone, the lantern-lit space thick with the smell of fresh parchment and melted wax.

"You've kept me waiting," Kin said, a little crease between his brows. It was a sign of anxiety, but I didn't need to see it to know how he felt.

When I said nothing, he favoured me with a perfunctory smile.

"You have been sitting with Lady Kimiko, I understand. Might I enquire how she is?"

"She will live," I said. "But she needs rest."

"I will ensure she is well looked after."

Emperor Kin let the parchment scroll roll up and, pushing it aside, set his elbows on the desk. "Your sister—your half-sister—has done me the honour of accepting my offer of marriage. As you are not recognised as the head of her family and I am at war with Katashi Otako, I have dispensed with the usual custom of contracting."

"An emperor may do as he wishes," I said, still standing in the middle of the matting floor, the top of the tent some way above my head. "Although nevertheless, you have my blessing."

"Fortunate for me that I am an emperor," he said, ignoring this. "Hana would not have taken well to being sold as a piece of property." He stood and came to stand before me. We were of a height, Kin perhaps a little taller and certainly stronger, his shoulders owning the true set of a soldier. He was older too, the lines between his brows permanently etched.

With a constricted smile, he put his left hand upon my shoulder. "You are welcome to stay, Takehiko," he said, "but—"

The sudden intent was like a pinprick in the world of whispers. He moved quickly, the point of the dagger touching my side as I gripped his throat with my bare hand, skin on skin. "No," I said, looking into those dark eyes. "Empaths are never welcome."

For what seemed like a long time, he said nothing, the point of the knife not shifting. And while he did not move, I forced nothing through, not even connection. I did not need it anymore.

A smile flashed across Kin's face. "You're quick," he said.

"I can read you."

"And what do you see upon my pages?"

The whispers came to me, insistent, forcing their way into my head.

Justice.

"Katashi was wrong about you," I said, feeling the pulse throb in his neck. "I don't think he knows what I do. He cannot see what I see."

"No?"

"No, but you love Hana. That is no lie."

There, a twisted little smile. "No, that is no lie."

"And she respects you, but she won't understand. I can see your every thought and feeling and memory as though it were my own. I understand you, but she never will."

"If you understand me so well, then you know why I have a knife in my hand."

"I do, but I know you are aware of my ability. I am stronger than either Malice or Darius, and what I could do to your mind could be done in an instant if you plunge that knife into my gut. You might, of course, retain just enough sanity to retaliate, however, so perhaps we are better off making a deal rather than a mess."

The knife did not budge. "And what do you propose, Lord Otako?"

"That you let me leave. Your secret will be safe and no one will have to clean us up."

"And where do you go?"

"To Darius."

"I would be better off gutting you where you stand," he said. "I know what you two did that night in Koi. Together, you are more dangerous than apart. Together, you can take my throne."

"Yes," I admitted. "But I already told you that I am no rebel. If I wanted you dead, I could have killed you a hundred times by now and so could he. I don't want the Crimson Throne. I might have been born Takehiko Otako, but I'm a Laroth. I'm a god."

Emperor Kin's lips pressed into a thin line. Outside, soldiers continued with their work, the noise unceasing. "A god?"

Justice.

"There are four guards standing in front of your tent and six behind. One hundred and twenty men in your camp here. Three thousand eight hundred and ninety-one back near Esvar. Twenty-six scouts and travellers in the Neck. Thirty thousand nine hundred and sixty-four people in the Valley. One million three hundred and eighteen thousand and five souls in your empire. And I know your secret. I am a god and I do what is right. At this very moment, what is right is saving my brother from himself if I can and killing him if I cannot."

He no longer held the knife with such certainty, those dark eyes leaping around my face. "And what then?"

"Then I will kill Malice. And myself."

"And I am to believe that? If I let you walk out of here, I will regret it."

"If you don't, you will not live to regret anything."

His frustration burned like a fire between us. "Your brother betrayed me. Tell me why I should trust you to do what you say rather than join him."

"Because I don't lie. And because I am the only one who will never hate you for killing my mother. It might have been Shin Metai's hand, but they were your orders, Your Majesty. A single order and a palace full of Otakos lay dead."

"Except for you."

"Except for me. And Hana. But it was Nyraek Laroth who made sure of that, not you."

Kin took a step back, withdrawing the knife. I let my hand fall from his neck. "You loved my mother," I said. "And that was the hardest of all."

"We all make hard choices." The words were clipped, harsh.

"Don't tell Hana."

"No," he said, sliding the knife back into a leather slip beneath his surcoat. "Better to live with my guilt than inflict that pain upon her."

"Then, Your Majesty, I think we are in accord. I, Takehiko Otako, hereby renounce my claim to the Crimson Throne in favour of Emperor Kin Ts'ai, first of his name. Darius once told me you were the only man who could rule Kisia, and I hope he was right. Goodbye, Your Majesty." I bowed deeply and strode toward the tent opening.

He did not stop me.

As I stepped into the last of the evening light, the smell of reed matting and incense gave way to the frantic scents of a dying summer. From their places, Kin's guards watched me, awaiting an order that never came.

Thunder sounded in the distance. The storms were coming. They would hit Kisia hard, but this year, the swollen rivers would run red with blood.

One million three hundred and seventeen thousand nine hundred and fifty-six souls in the empire, and if Katashi marched on as Vengeance personified, that number would keep falling.

Yet for now, the only number that mattered was two.

Two brothers.

Two gods.

But Justice comes to everyone, even gods.

Acknowledgements

Unlike for the other two books in this trilogy, it appears that I never wrote acknowledgements for this one when it was originally published. This is a shame, since I had a lot of fun editing the other ones for everyone's amusement and will now have to do this the traditionally boring way.

This book is very different to its originally published version, and though plenty of thanks for that can go to my wonderful and ever-patient editor at Orbit, Nivia Evans, I think she got rather more changes than she bargained for. And for letting me so drastically alter the contents of this book without batting an eyelash, I must thank her a second time. Her faith in my ability to take it apart and put it back together again in a way that was both still true to the whole story and would make it a far better book never wavered. Or at least if it did, she never let me know it.

Thanks must also go to Emily Byron, my editor at Orbit UK; my brilliant copy editor who stops me looking very silly, Maya Frank-Levine; and Amanda J. Spedding, the first editor to ever get her hands on this book so many years ago that I feel old now. Double thank you for also being a truly remarkable friend, ever-present and compassionate no matter what; you're a gem, Mandy. (She's going to hate that, so I'll leave it in to see if she reads this far.)

Moving on, a massive thank you to Gregory Titus for the

beautiful cover art that adorns these editions, and to Lisa Marie Pompilio for her always so stunning design work. And of course a big thank you to Ellen Wright and Angela Man, publicity duo extraordinaire. In fact to everyone who works behind the scenes at Orbit, making this such a wonderful company to be with, thank you.

To quickly finish off, I must add the usual suspects, the people without whom I would struggle to do this job, or remember to eat when on deadline, or shower, or...talk to humans. Firstly my supportive parents, who took me to the library at a young age and let me get away with sneaking out of bed to read in the middle of the night. Secondly my partner, Chris, for uncomplainingly picking up all the slack I drop (and while rewriting this book it was A LOT of slack) when hard up against deadlines. You are a treasure, a rare, utterly kind human, and I couldn't imagine life without you, so thank you. Thirdly all the members of my Discord families—you all know who you are. Whether it's celebrating or commiserating or just making crass jokes about penises, you are always there for me, always present, and I love you.

extras

www.orbitbooks.net

about the author

Devin Madson is an Aurealis Award–winning fantasy author from Australia. After some sucky teenage years, she gave up reality and is now a dual-wielding rogue who works through every tiny side-quest and always ends up too over-powered for the final boss. Anything but Zen, Devin subsists on tea and chocolate and so much fried zucchini she ought to have turned into one by now. Her fantasy novels come in all shades of grey and are populated with characters of questionable morals and a liking for witty banter.

Find out more about Devin Madson and other Orbit authors by registering for the free monthly newsletter at www.orbitbooks.net.

if you enjoyed
THE GODS OF VICE
look out for

THE GRAVE AT STORM'S END
The Vengeance Trilogy: Book Three
by
Devin Madson

Vengeance has come.

Katashi Otako walks with the Vices, burning everything in his path. Now the spirit of Vengeance, he will stop at nothing to destroy Emperor Kin and take the Crimson Throne.

The empire is facing its greatest threat, and with Darius controlling Katashi from the shadows, Emperor Kin finds his every move pre-empted. Out of options, Kin and Hana must marry in secret to secure the support they need, but the ceremony takes seven days, and seven days can change the world.

As the flames of vengeance engulf Kisia, Hana will have to fight for the right to defend her empire. A ruler must do what is necessary, but no choice is easy when the enemy is the man she once loved and the guardian she once trusted.

When gods fight, empires fall.

1. HANA

In darkness we waited. Silent. Tense. A group of imperial guards on the east bank of the Nuord River, watching for the flash of a lantern.

It was a starless night, and under layers of leather and mail, I carried my weight in sweat. Especially beneath my helmet where my hair stuck sodden to my head, but how else could one hide blonde curls? *No one can know*, Kin had said. *You're just another soldier.*

Beside me, General Ryoji shifted his weight. He was little but an outline in the darkness, yet the blended scent of leather and sweat and cedar oil was impossible to mistake. There were traces of Katashi in that smell, and I wavered between wanting to move away and draw closer, fighting with my own instincts. My own memories.

The general shifted again, letting out a short huff of air. We had been waiting too long.

On my other side, a whisper warmed my ear. "Are you all right, my lady?"

Tili's voice trembled. General Ryoji had cautioned against her involvement as he had cautioned against the entire mission, but tradition dictated the presence of another woman, so another woman there would be. Kin would risk no mistake.

I nodded. "You?"

Despite the darkness, I was sure she nodded back, but when I felt for her hand, I found it tightly clenched and shaking. I squeezed it and wondered how much more strongly an Empath could feel her fear.

For weeks, there had been nothing but bad news. First, we had lost Risian. Then Lotan. News no longer arrived from the north, and heavy losses stalked the heels of every victory like a plague we could not shake. We held Kogahaera, but only thanks to the Nuord River, its roar even now cutting the silence of an oppressive night.

"We need to move," Kin said in a low rumble.

"There's been no signal, Majesty," General Ryoji returned.

"If they're dead, they can't signal."

"If they're dead, we should turn back."

General Ryoji seemed to hold his breath, statue-still as he waited for a reply to such brazen honesty.

"It's too late for that," Kin said. "We go to Kuroshima without them."

The general bowed, and again I wondered what Malice or Darius might read in his rigidity that I could not. More than fear? More than the ill ease of a man ordered to act against his better judgement?

"Ji. Tanner," Ryoji said, speaking over my shoulder. "Stay with…her."

"General," I began. "I am armed and quite capable—"

"Yes, my lady, but they have their orders."

Ji and Tanner filled the space he left behind. They were often with me, but though I knew their names and their faces, I trusted neither the way I had come to trust Ryoji—the ever-present sentinel who had saved me from the pit a lifetime ago, whose loyalty to Kin seemed to know no bounds.

We started to move, and Tili remained pressed to my side as we climbed the gentle curve of the bridge. At the peak, my sandal caught an uneven stone, but the press of soldiers was so close I could not fall, could only jog on as we descended into enemy territory—Otako territory. For years I had carried the name with pride, but tonight I would give it up to become Kin's wife—Kin's empress.

I had always dreamed of sitting on my father's throne, always dreamed of ruling. Tonight that dream would come true, but it was a very different wedding to the one I had planned when I had asked Katashi to marry me. Fate had allowed me mere hours of such a joy—a joy so great the world had seemed to break beneath the strain of it.

Perhaps hearing my trembling breath, Tili pressed closer, but although she hampered my movement, I could not push her away. Her presence was the only comfort left.

We slowed as we gained the far bank. Ahead, light flickered through the dense shield of soldiers as it might through trees, glinting off buckles and patches of leather worn shiny with use.

"Spread out."

Drawing weapons, they fanned out.

"No, not you, my lady," General Ryoji said, once more appearing beside me.

"How can we maintain the ruse if I do not do my job?" I said.

"This is not your job, my lady, but keeping you safe is mine."

Again a hint of Katashi's scent—some oil perhaps, or just a cruel trick of memory—and though Ryoji could not have seen my expression in the darkness, I turned my face away. Ahead with his own escort, Emperor Kin led the way toward Kuro-shima village.

It lay about a mile from the river, a gathering of small houses in the lee of the mountain. At this hour, they were shadowed and silent, the only light a lantern at the base of the climb that led to Kisia's oldest shrine. There, two men in priest's white were waiting beneath an arbour of becalmed leaves.

Leaving me with Ji and Tanner, General Ryoji hurried to join Kin, his hand as close to his sword as could be considered polite in the company of priests. I made to join them, but Tanner blocked my way with his arm. There was tension in every line of his body and his eyes darted, watching the soldiers move about the silent village. Without lanterns, the distant buildings melded into the trees. Dark. Lifeless.

Tili huddled closer still, as though I were a fire by which she could warm herself. Seconds dragged by, until at last General Ryoji made a sign, and Tanner lowered his arm. "My lady," he said and bowed.

Tili and I joined them at the base of the mountain. Other soldiers gathered.

"What's going on?" I hissed at General Ryoji. "What of our scouts?"

He glanced at the two priests. "It seems they never arrived."

"But they were experienced soldiers."

"Yes, my lady," he said.

"They can't have just gone missing."

The general pulled at his bottom lip for a troubled instant. "No, my lady."

"It's quiet. Is the village empty?"

"All but, like we expected. The war is too close. Even at the base of the old mountain, no one is safe."

"We are not alone here, General, the risk—"

"The risk of being attacked while retreating is just as high, my lady," General Ryoji said, and I wondered if they were Kin's words. "With none of the benefits of success. We go up."

He moved on with a nod not a bow, maintaining the pretence

that I was a mere soldier. I liked the informality, taking what small joys I could in being treated, for once, like just another man.

A flotilla of paper lanterns spread light through the group, and I took one, thinking of another time I had gathered in the dark with a group of men in imperial uniforms.

No, don't think about Katashi.

I edged toward Kin. "It worries me that the scouts have not been seen," I whispered. "We should leave."

"No, we proceed as planned, a group on each branch of the stairs just as tradition dictates."

"Are you sure it's wise?"

He grimaced at me. "I am sure that anyone who wanted us dead could have killed us by now. Take what comfort from that as you will."

"Very little!"

"We have no choice. We have to do this right or risk losing all legitimacy."

He was right, but I hated it. Hated the silence and the darkness, the still press of the air and the nervous looks of the soldiers. Hated to have found myself here at all.

No, don't think about Katashi.

General Ryoji ordered half the men to remain behind and split the other half into two groups, one to accompany His Majesty up the right branch of the stairs, the other up the left branch with me, braving all one thousand four hundred and forty-four steps to the Kuroshima Shrine.

The forest into which we climbed was thick and dark, our winking lanterns the only stars, our steps and huffing breaths the only sounds. One thousand four hundred and forty-four stairs, one for every day the goddess Lunyia had waited for her husband. She, the goddess of loyalty and fortune, to whom all Kisians prayed upon their marriage. I counted them to give me something to think about other than what awaited me at the top.

At 210, General Ryoji stopped a few steps ahead. "Lim."

"General?"

I turned, swinging my lantern so fast the flame drew dangerously close to the paper. Behind me, the guard identified as Lim touched a hand to his sword.

"Run back down," the general said. "Tell Rashil to send for reinforcements."

"But General, there's no sign of enemy movement, and His Majesty said we could not risk—"

"Send for reinforcements. There was nothing before the skirmish at Cherry Wood either," Ryoji said. "Or when they hit us south of Risian. If the bastards want to play games with us, then this is the place they'll choose. Send for reinforcements."

"Yes, General."

Fast footsteps faded away down the steps, and I turned back to see the general's features screwed into a scowl.

"You would think by your expression that you *want* to be attacked, General," I said.

His eyes darted to my face and a rueful smile dawned. "Not exactly want, my lady, but I don't like uncertainty."

"Surely even if they know we're here, they don't know we are doing this. We were careful."

The guards behind me stood silent to listen, and I winced at how desperately hopeful I sounded.

"Yes, my lady," the general agreed. "But Lord Laroth has a habit of knowing things he ought not. I cannot say I liked the man, but only a fool would not respect his skill and take it into consideration."

Darius and I had argued often, but never had I thought to find him truly my enemy. Even after what he had done, and the passage of weeks in which I had called him so, it still felt wrong.

A grimace crossed General Ryoji's face. "Apologies, my lady, I did not—"

"You expressed no thought I have not had myself, General," I said. "And if you're right, we had better keep moving."

The whole procession lurched on, climbing faster now as though our enemy were right behind us. I tried not to think about the burning in my thighs or the fate that awaited me at the top of the mountain, and instead stared all but unseeing at the novice leading the way. His white robe eddied, ghostlike, about his feet. White robe, white sash, and plain reed sandals. It was an impractical colour for all but those who spent their lives in pursuit of piety.

I had stopped counting the stairs, but my legs ached enough that we must surely have passed 1,444 and missed the shrine entirely. Absently, I wondered where the path would lead us, it seeming to own no end, when at last the novice turned his head to say, "We are almost there, my lady."

I made no answer. My whole body ached. One thousand four hundred and forty-four steps from the village to the shrine had left me cursing my robe, my armour, my helmet, and the heavy soldier's sandals that were like a weight upon each foot.

My stomach dropped as the last step vanished beneath me.

"Welcome to Kuroshima Shrine, my lady," the novice said, halting beneath an arch of tangled branches hung with wild flowers. Beside me, General Ryoji's steps crunched to a halt upon the path, light spilling onto his feet. Inside, Kin would be waiting. I had asked him to marry me, but he was not the man I had wanted to rule alongside.

Don't think about Katashi.

Kuroshima Shrine was famous throughout Kisia, so I had expected it to be grand and imposing, not a cosy bird's hollow.

There was no gleaming woodwork or fine art, no thick beams or broad sweeping roofs, just a simple curved wall of interlocking iron branches rising to form a low, rounded ceiling hung with paper lanterns.

Kin stood in the opposite archway, watching a priest approach across the slate floor. Every fourth tile was painted a jarring red, and whether by accident or design, the man avoided them.

"Your Majesty, it is an honour to welcome you to Kuro-shima," he said, bowing very low before his emperor.

"Thank you, Father," Kin returned, gesturing for the man to rise. "I have long wished to witness so great a part of our empire's history, and what better occasion than upon the event of my marriage."

The priest wore serenity like a blanket and bowed again. "Indeed, Your Majesty. We are honoured beyond words."

Although Kin smiled, he did not speak again, leaving the priest to glance around in search of the bride. His gaze hung for a moment upon Tili, a slight frown between his brows at so curvaceous a soldier.

I pulled off my helmet. Sweat-dampened curls fell loose upon my brow, and the old priest stared, sucking in a breath before sinking into another low bow. "Lady Hana Otako, our shrine is humbled indeed."

"You are too kind, Father," I said, and with every eye on me, I hunted for something more to say. Darius, Mama Orde, and all my tutors had sought to instil in me the sort of grace and learning that would allow the uttering of pretty speeches, but until now I had only been representing myself. Now my words would reflect not only upon Emperor Kin but upon the whole of Kisia. I cleared my suddenly dry throat. "In truth, I feel there is little that could humble so old and so beautiful a shrine," I said, the courtly words not even sounding like my own. "We are transient, but it endures. Is there somewhere I can make myself presentable, Father?"

The man's eyes bulged, and he glanced at our novice guide. A silent heartbeat passed before he said, "Of course, my lady, follow me."

Once again avoiding the red slates, he led me toward the opposite archway, my armour clinking with every step. I caught Kin's eye as we passed, but though his lips smiled, his eyes did not. His attention, like General Ryoji's, was elsewhere.

The priest led the way to a small pavilion off the main path. It had a simple reed floor and walls lined with spare robes, white sashes, prayer chains, and pouches of fresh incense. Its smell filled every breath with the taste of sandalwood.

Tili followed me inside. Frowning, the father was moved to speak, but I stopped him. "My maid, Father," I said. "We could not be too careful."

Tili removed her helmet and bowed to the old priest. "Father."

His disapproval did not shift, but with a sharp nod, he left, ignoring Ji and Tanner as they took up silent vigil outside the door. There was urgency despite the calm night, and before the door closed, my sword belt and weapons hit the floor. Whatever other conventions I had persuaded Kin to set aside, I could not kneel before the Shrine Stone armed.

"Help me out of this," I said, tugging at the soldier's knot that held my crimson sash. It went first, followed by the leather tunic and its linen under-robe, gauntlets and breeches—every trapping of the common soldier had been made to size, but once more, tradition dictated I could not take my oath in it. Tili unrolled the ceremonial robe she had carried tied in a bundle, and though its beautiful silk was creased, being dishevelled was a small price to pay. No one watching our progress from the camp at Kogahaera would have reason to suspect Lady Hana made one of the party. They might recognise Emperor Kin, but what could be more natural than an Emperor making a pilgrimage to Kuroshima in a time of war?

I ran my fingers through my hair, and Tili helped me into my robe. We did not speak. There was little to say, and we had not been good at small talk of late.

A knock fell upon the door. "My lady?"

I had no mirror to be sure I was ready, but there was no time to do more. "Enter," I said, running my hands down my creased robe.

The door slid to reveal the novice who had been our guide. "I'm sorry, my lady, but Father Hoto is anxious to begin."

The young man stared directly at me as he spoke, not effacing his gaze as etiquette required.

My pulse quickened. "He sent you?"

"Yes, my lady, he is anxious to begin the ceremony." Still he did not drop his gaze, and I hunted his face for some clue of what he was trying to tell me. No fear that I could see, no meaningful glance at my sword.

"Then I will of course come at once," I said, and only then did he step aside to let me pass.

Back outside, the air was humid, the night quiet. I tried to make eye contact with Ji and Tanner as I passed, but neither was used to looking at me. All I could do was stride toward the main hollow, counting the steps behind me. Tanner. Ji. The novice. Tili at my side. No surprises, yet I was fretful with only stiff silk at my hip.

Light spilled from the main hollow of the shrine, and I strode through the narrow arch only to halt on the threshold, my heart thudding against my breastbone.

Conceit stood at the altar, a knife pressed to Father Hoto's throat. Behind him stood a dozen soldiers in Pike black, hooded and anonymous, while Kin's soldiers faced them across the red slate floor, hands tense upon their sword hilts.

"Why, Lady Hana, you have kept us waiting," Conceit said, his pretty features and malicious smile a memory from another life. "How kind of you to finally join us."

A grunt sounded behind me and Ji crumpled, his blood spraying over my feet. The novice pressed a bloodied knife to Tanner's neck. "Don't move," he quavered, his white robe splattered with blood. "Don't move or I'll have to kill him too."

He trembled, but the blade remained steady against Tanner's throat.

"She's thinking about moving," Conceit said, holding every gaze. Kin's soldiers hovered out of range like wary cats. "As you can see, your companions have not been welcoming, my lady. And to think I only came to give you this gift."

He gestured to the altar. There lay a black sash where a white one ought to be. "It's a more appropriate colour, don't you think?"

No one moved. No one spoke. All eyes were on this man. "No? You don't get it?" he said, when no one answered. "The sash of a whore instead of an innocent bride?"

"I'll slit your slanderous accusations from your throat," General Ryoji said.

The man clicked his tongue. "My, my, General Ryoji, how venomous you are toward your guests. But—" He nodded at Father Hoto. "You need him, don't you? He's the only one here qualified to perform a marriage ceremony."

Conceit laughed suddenly and removed his knife from the priest's throat. Father Hoto collapsed upon the stones, curled up like a child.

"Father Hoto." The intruder knelt at the altar. "Would you do the honours?" He didn't wait for a response but pursed his lips piously. "I, Conceit," he said, mimicking a ceremony, "most trusted of the Vice Master, pray the gods never saddle me with such a whore for a wife. I would not wish my children to be born of such loose loins, smeared by the seed of so many men as they claw their way into this world."

"Shut him up," Kin ordered. "Now."

Conceit seemed not to hear. "In the eyes of the gods," he said, "I offer the Imperial Whore this black sash—"

An arrow leapt for the unguarded Vice and hit him full in the chest. But there was no satisfying crack of bone. No gush of blood. The arrow clattered uselessly off the wall as Conceit disappeared.

From across the altar, a new Conceit laughed. "I, Lady Hana Otako, the Imperial Whore," the second Conceit continued in a high-pitched voice. "Cannot wait seven days to have my robe torn off. Take me now, commoner, give me your enormous—"

The second Conceit rolled as another arrow came at him.

"Ha! Now we're playing." He leapt to his feet. "You would kill a woman making her prayers?" He clicked his tongue reprovingly, and behind him, the small group of hooded Pikes drew their swords.

"Hold your ground," Kin growled at his men.

"Is this how you treat every guest bearing wedding gifts?" Conceit asked as he drew the deadly sickle Malice gave to every Vice in his service. The man's smile turned predatory.

"No," Kin said. "This is how I treat foul-mouthed traitors. Cut him down!"

As one body, the imperial guards advanced. I had left my weapons with my armour, but I snatched up Ji's sword and ran in on anger-fuelled steps.

"My lady, stay back!"

I shouldered the concerned guard out of the way. "Don't you dare tell me I have no right to defend my own name!"

Dark figures swarmed. Someone shouted. Another screamed. I dodged a clumsy swing and charged on, looking for Conceit. He, a flash of blond amid the chaos. Curls of incense smoke framed his tragically beautiful face.

"Why, Lady Hana," he said, arching high brows over dead eyes. "Or should I call you Captain Regent?"

"Shut your mouth or I'll shut it for you," I growled, jabbing at his gut.

Conceit danced out of the way, laughing. "I didn't mean what I said, you know. I'd have you no matter how many men had loosened you up first."

Anger took control and I thrust wildly. A lighter sword might have touched him, but I hadn't the strength to send this heavy lump of steel through his chest.

"Dressing like a man doesn't suit you," he said. "And that sword makes you clumsy. Perhaps your beloved Kin doesn't wish you well-armed. Here, have mine."

He threw his sword up and caught it by the blade. All confidence, he held it out to me. "Call it a wedding gift."

I swung at his outstretched arm, prepared to hit bone. But it was Conceit. Of course there was no resistance, no real flesh, and I fell off balance as the blade passed through him. He did not retaliate, just stood there with a hurt expression and one arm missing. "My lady, I was only being kind."

I thrust my sword into his gut. I knew there would be nothing, that I was only fuelling my anger, but rage had me in its grasp. Conceit's laughing face disappeared, yet my blade found flesh. Black sash. Black short robe. A Pike, his shocked cry like the wail of a bird.

The Pike dropped his sword, his slim hands fluttering in panic as he plucked at my sleeve. Beneath the hood his shadowed features looked youthful.

"I…I…" He gulped for breath, like a drowning man. Then a high-pitched moan and a gesture of despair that was all too feminine.

A woman. Dressed in black.

"Shit!" I looked into the dying whore's face. "I'm so sorry! I—"

Blood oozed down her chin and bubbled in her mouth as she tried to speak and only managed to spit crimson.

"I'm so sorry." I yanked the sword free and she fell to her knees. "Stop!" I shouted. "Stop! Don't kill them, they aren't Pikes!"

No one seemed to hear me, so I ran at the closest woman and threw myself between her and the imperial guard seeking to run her through. "Stop! Put down your weapons!"

"My lady!" The guard lunged, gripping my robe and yanking me forward as a blade touched my side. I overbalanced as he let me go, leaving the room spinning as pained grunts and fleshy sounds sickened my stomach.

"They aren't—" Bodies littered the floor. Most wore black, only a few crimson sashes there to break the monotony. Conceit was nowhere to be seen, but his flair for the dramatic had left behind a massacre. Only one robed and hooded woman still stood. I started toward her as someone grabbed my arm.

"What in the name of the gods do you think you're doing?" Kin demanded as he pulled me around. "How many times have I told you not to do anything foolish?"

"Foolish?" I snapped, already turning back toward the woman. "As foolish as striking down enemies who—?"

It was already too late. The last false Pike had been skewered upon the end of an imperial sword, and it was all I could do not to be sick as she slid to the floor dead. "That was unnecessary," I hissed, spinning back. "They weren't Pikes and you knew it."

"But they attacked us and did not stop even when their leader was gone. What else would you have had me do?"

A dozen things, but I could find voice for none of them. It would change nothing even if I could.

Into the silence, Kin said, "In seven days, you will be my wife, and I will not let you run unprotected into battle."

"Then as you are to be my husband, I will not let *you* run unprotected into battle either. Shall we dig out an Errant board and sit back while others fight for us?"

He gave a disgusted snort. "An emperor should always lead his men."

Kin held out his hand for the sword. My grip on it tightened. "I am the daughter of an emperor," I said in a soft growl, the words only for him. "I told you I would not sit idle and become a pretty doll for your ministers to leer at. I could have kept the title Katashi gave me, but instead I am here. You gave me your word and I expect you to honour it, *Your Majesty*."

I threw the sword at his feet, the clang of metal on stone loud in the silent space. Kin did not flinch. "I told you not to throw Katashi in my face," he said, speaking just as quietly. "There are enough whispers about you and him to fill the Valley. I don't need more."

My heart pounded against my ribs, and the shrine full of dead whores and soldiers faded to nothing but Katashi's warm body beside mine and the soft fall of his hair upon my shoulder as he held me tight.

"I want you Hana," he had breathed against my neck. *"I want this. May I make love to you? I won't without your permission."*

"I need you safe, Hana, not dead," Kin said, neatening the fall of his bloodstained robe. "The whole purpose of this night is to show the people who they should fight for, not for you to prove your bravery."

He walked away on the words, already gesturing to General Ryoji. "Keep guard in case that Vice comes back," he said. The general nodded and moved away, leaving Kin to contemplate the mess. "Father Hoto!"

The dishevelled and trembling priest peered over the top of the altar. "Y-your Majesty?"

"How long were they waiting for us?"

"S-since this morning, Your Majesty. They k-killed my novices and said that if I did not p-play my part, they w-would kill you and Lady Hana too." The man straightened, folding his hands together to hide their shaking. "I am sorry, Your Majesty, I am wholly at your mercy."

"I have no need of a dead priest," Kin said. "Do your job and you may consider yourself forgiven for your part in tonight's farce."

"My job?"

"I came here to be married, Father Hoto, and married I will be."

Enter the monthly

Orbit sweepstakes at

www.orbitloot.com

With a different prize every month,
from advance copies of books by
your favourite authors to exclusive
merchandise packs,
**we think you'll find something
you love.**